Born in Bangkok, Thailand, a former art student and a resident of Leeds, UK, David McGowen never aspired to be a writer, but it was his only effective medium of letting out his ideas.

Autistic, writing has helped him through multiple hardships in the past.

His first novel, *Carnian Street*, was written during the COVID-19 lockdowns and is the first in an upcoming series of novels and short stories, all of which are set in the same universe.

For Grandad

David McGowen

CARNIAN STREET

AUSTIN MACAULEY PUBLISHERS

LONDON • CAMBRIDGE • NEW YORK • SHARJAH

A CIP catalogue record for this title is available from the British Library.

ISBN 9781398474031 (Paperback)
ISBN 9781398474048 (ePub e-book)

www.austinmacauley.com

First Published 2023
Austin Macauley Publishers Ltd®
1 Canada Square
Canary Wharf
London
E14 5AA

I would like to thank all the staff that worked or are working at my regular for providing me with the most welcoming environment that allowed me to acquire inspiration for my book. Cottingley Court transitional housing unit for providing me with safe housing during my hardest year. My family and friends most especially, because this book would have not been possible without their support. And of course, I must thank Austin Macauley Publishers for their courtesy and efforts in the reviewing and production of my book.

I was going for a "David Attenborough meets David Lynch" sort of drama!

Table of Contents

Prologue

It was a warm, bright English summer day (one could dare to say) with minimal cloud cover. That type of day tended to draw out every character conceivable. One of them was a plump, old male ginger tabby cat walking along the footpath of a street with a cobblestone road, rows of houses on either side of the road and a church black as granite occupying a space left of the street. There was commotion, which had the tabby pause and turn its head right in the direction of the kerfuffle. The cat ran along the pavement and was faced with a sea of people, more than he had ever seen in his existence.

A leader of a land within a land, with a name that sounded like a sort of dessert, had permitted an influx of disorder among its populace. The participants of which kept hollering the same mantra, which consisted of three words. Anarchy, destruction was their integral purpose, and it was transparent in such a vintage, cultural setting vulnerable to the stains of alleged progress.

The mob were all young, of breeding age, and there was nothing attractive or sure about them. They waved signs and banners, most of them had the three letters of their mantra or words of scorn, behind them cars, property and garden ornaments were shattered. Most of the crowd were wearing masks that concealed their mouths and noses. Whether male or female was hard to identify, and they were of different colours, but not down to ethnicity; some had their faces painted in a rainbow assortment of colours, trying to look tribal like warriors, of which they were not. They were chanting irritably loud, inferring that individuals with darker pigment were priority above those having the same pigment of which they had.

To the tabby cat they were loud, otherwise they would be considered hilarious, if it wasn't for the damage they were causing on the street. One masked member smashed an old grey hatchback with a crowbar, while a young woman that looked like a man with short, dyed bright blonde hair, glasses and loose, baggy jeans was boiling with insanity, crying and shouting, the cause of the outburst unclear, though it had her jumping about like a toddler and kicking the doors of a car. The graveyard of the church was littered with streams of toilet paper thrown on headstones, some tarnished with colourful graffiti of three lettered words, profanity and other obscenities that couldn't be accepted as art with a normal mentality. Then again, anything as low and sickly as stools being defecated onto the floor could be perceived as such these days.

On the cobblestoned street, an elderly man with a moustache remonstrated this puerile act of destruction from the gates of his home without having to raise his voice. There were plenty of agitated hand gestures and waving of arms from fellow neighbours, aimed the way of the church graveyard, where some of these masked members sat or leaned on the tombstones while filming themselves on their phones. One individual was urinating on a tombstone. This obviously wasn't well received and was pointed out by the old man, who was pushed to the floor by one of the masked, three-letter mob, who shouted at him, pointing fingers down at him. His followers consummated the act of violence with noises similar to a monkey's and continued their three lettered chants. The tabby cat blinked. This was war, and there didn't appear to be any repercussions for this mob. But there were some things that shouldn't be disagreed upon. As of now, there were *limitations* to what could be challenged.

That same masked hooligan who had pushed the elderly man to the floor was violently shoved down to the floor himself by an unseen assailant. He remonstrated with abuse and his face was obscured by a foot dressed in a smart, polished black shoe swinging its way at high speed. Further down the street, ignorant to the occurrence, a male member of the masked mob approached the wall of a house that had an English flag displayed on the upper left window, which had a foot wide hole in it, and began spray painting it with pink lettering, the only words he managed to spray were: **B-L-A-**

And he didn't spot whomever was coming his way, unobstructed through where he wished to further vandalise, he was struck through the diaphragm and sent falling and tumbling back down the concrete steps as though a car had somehow come through the wall.

The vandal's fall was noticed across the street, the perpetrator dead in sight spotted by a small teenage boy with spiky hair and a black scarf wrapped around his mouth approached, his motivation surged full of testosterone instead of logic. He shouted abuse, as though it was effective as ammunition with the perpetual three-word chant still going in the backdrop. Ignoring him and beckoning down on the floored vandal with a blank expression was a tall, imposing man, complexion pale as concrete, slick black, three quarter parted hair on the right, styled in a severe but perfectly melded undercut, dressed in a black, three piece suit with a silky, crimson red tie with a black, tribal print of a tiger against a black dress shirt.

More volatile words were spewed from the obnoxious vandal that shuffled away from the approaching figure with the tiger tie. But his words failed to stop tiger tie from raising his foot, which came down swiftly, crushing the skull of the masked mob member like a melon under a heavy-duty press. The daisies on the patch of untarnished lawn to the left were witness to the bloodied, pulverised remnants of the mob member's face.

This delusion of absolutist control over a way of life was being challenged, the proposed *immunity* was compromised when the mob saw the fall of their comrade. The one with the tiger tie stepped onto the cobblestone street, the masked mob hesitant but determined to do something about him. A can was thrown at his head by the hyped up teen with spiky hair, he didn't flinch or blink as it bounced off. One mob member, who was armed with a golf club ran his way for retribution, expecting to achieve it as easy as bending a knee in submission. He was knocked back by a forward kick to the chest from the one with the tiger tie, whom swiftly and elegantly chased it up by rushing his way and kicked him in the stomach, causing blood to burst from around his mask onto the road. The mob screamed and this tall male member with cropped orange hair, a white T-shirt and black skater shorts and an unsightly pot belly fled the scene, his abdomen flopping about as he went.

More mob members charged at the one with the tiger tie, while others pelted him with missiles ranging from cans, bottles and stones. He ignored them and dealt traumatic blows to whomever came up to his face. It didn't matter what their physical stature or gender, which was almost irrelevant given the near homogenous crowd, all were incapacitated by the one with the tiger tie through single blows to the face, from knuckles, back of fist and elbow.

The bulk of the masked mob had seen that. They screamed whatever it was they thought should be their way of the world, then next they were searching for the one with the tiger tie, their wide, spooked, startled eyes stood out against their masks. The one with the tiger tie reappeared behind one of the members that was wearing a bushy, bright rainbow coloured wig, clutched in his right hand was a *wakizashi*, a short, slightly curved sword which a samurai would carry accompanied with his katana, though this version had an obsidian black blade a foot long, the handle while decorated in masterfully folded red linen had no guard on it.

This exotic blade-wielder slashed at the hamstrings of rainbow wig in a left to right motion, the blood spillage was more aesthetic than their graffiti and incoherent statements. Rainbow wig screamed and fell face first on the cobblestone road, his nose broken from the fall, he remained on the floor and cried out drawing attention from the mob that rushed to his aid, their focus suspiciously absent from the one with the tiger tie, whom reappeared seconds later, but at the other end of the crowd metres away, his black bladed wakizashi wasn't in sight. The mob member that had broken the car window with a crowbar spotted him, and thought his tool would make him a superior challenger. He ran towards the unarmed figure with the tiger tie, weapon gripped with both hands and swinging with the intention of only just breaking a few ribs to make a statement.

But he didn't expect tiger tie's reflexes to be so adept as the tool was caught, yanked out of the mob member's grasp, the force of which resulted in bloodied grazes to his palms, which he risked inspecting while the crowbar was tossed aside to the right and clattered to the cobblestone. A masterful foot sweep to the legs floored him, the impact while painful did not render him unconscious, though the follow up elbow from tiger tie to his forehead did. The ginger tabby cat witness remained sat and watched the mob begin to scatter in fear. The one with the tiger tie reappeared in the direction of the fleeing crowd, his sudden appearance causing several members to recoil and/or fall in fear and disperse in the opposite way.

The hot-headed teen with the spiky hair was present on this side of the street and unwisely didn't take the path of the crowd. Seeing tiger tie he spread his arms confrontationally, shouted abuse, reached down and threw pieces of broken glass from the vandalism of the cobblestone street at him. Words or missiles did not impede passage as he continued towards him, the hot head still continuing to hurl profanity and glass his way, demanding a fight he believed would end in his victory. That was proven traumatically false as tiger tie stepped forward with extended fingertips on his right hand, violently driving that arm forward, plunging it through the mask of his lippy adversary as though it was insubstantial as water.

The undesirable adolescent froze suddenly as tiger tie coiled his fingers around the bend of his jaw, his left palm planted firmly on his forehead, before the right arm viciously retracted, along with the mandible, the gratuitous spew of red that followed the tabby cat couldn't see in its vision, though could hear the horrified response of whomever had witnessed the assault, the jaw being flung unintentionally in the direction of the tabby, which ran towards it. The cat paused to inspect the separated mandible, the frontal teeth were either missing or bent, still attached to the gums. The cat licked curiously at the jaw, until being frightened off by the racket on the street. It dashed away and hid underneath a car, where it watched the figure with the tiger tie quickly *sink* below the ground like an elevator.

Without any potential threats coming its way, the tabby walked along the pavement until the cobblestone street terminated into modern tarmac, the area still tarnished shamelessly with graffiti and vandalism. The cat made a left turn and stopped at the foot of a large tree mere feet from a red bus stop pole, the trunk of the tree of which was pinned with flyers with them three key words from the mob. Yards across the road from the resting tabby were another cluster of masked protestors, that seemed blissfully ignorant to the events on the cobblestone street.

And walking in the direction of the site along the pavement was a young woman. Outwardly, she appeared to be in her early/mid-twenties, tall, attractive with a finely sculpted figure bordering on the athletic side, her nose curved, eyes blue and wide, her hair long and sun ray blonde, tied back perfectly into a medium height ponytail, makeup kept to a minimal with her eyelashes black, lips and face appeared polished like precious metal. Her outfit was sophisticated yet simple; a thin black turtleneck sweater, form-fitting white jeans, glossy black riding boots. She didn't have any visible jewellery on her, yet she was the embodiment of feminine perfection.

From appearance alone, it appeared superficially that she was not associated with this three-letter mob. Those members, still unaware of the violence being inflicted on their own kind, surrounded her like a pack of wild dogs. One of the obligatorily unattractive female members pointed their finger at her accusingly in a jabbing motion, while other members of the mob laughed with exaggerated gestures. The unmasked blonde woman didn't react. A stone was thrown at her, which bounced off her flat stomach then bounced about the cobblestone road several times.

The childish mob dared to laugh, pranced about and spewed insults but ceased to do so any further as their bodies were all simultaneously enveloped in flames, the source of ignition unknown. They were living, screaming torches, the flames of smoking flesh trailing as they ran away from the blonde woman, flailing and spinning in confusion, the cause as much of a paradox behind their anarchy, those repetitive three letter mantras ceased for the sake of survival. They fell to the floor and perished and none of their kind attempted to help them. The young blonde woman didn't react to the carnage around her. She didn't even breathe.

"The sun will shine, on good or evil without compromise." Quoted this speaker, the voice masculine, metallic and distorted and resonating from above. The perfect blonde woman turned her head right, where the figure with the tiger tie appeared out from the air in what appeared to be a black cloud of dust with an inward rolling motion to it similar to the cleansing mechanisms of a drive-in car wash.

~

An agent of existence persists in immeasurable variety during its stretch of existence, in any spot.

– Jean K

Chapter 1

On the third planet from the star of one solar system, there lay just a singular cluster of land, *Pangaea*; the rest was the *Panthalassa*, a single ocean covering two-thirds of the planet's surface. This supercontinent was for all parts dry and arid expanses of reddish earth, with its sun beaming down harshly from a cloudless sky. But beneath the crust was an insurmountable abundance of activity; flows of molten rock thousands of miles deep safely sealed beneath, lubricating a break up of this seemingly impervious cluster, the land was moving even if it did appear totally still. Unnoticed, unobservable in a lifetime, but highly impactful as it allowed passage for water inland, lines of blue bleeding inward over the millennia and the impact of lakes, rivers and estuaries sprouting green paradises along their borders.

One spot of land located on the central northern equatorial line of the Pangaean supercontinent was one of the more fertile regions of the planet. The tallest objects aside from hills, rises, dunes and mountains were the trees, evergreen *coniferae* with their thin, bristly leaves and cones, which harboured their seeds. Growing below them were shrub, fern, cycad with their ragged wooden trunks and long fleshy growths of divided green leaves and *equisetopsia*, bright green with segmented stems and bristly leaves mapped the ground forming undergrowth.

Among the tall/dominant plant life stood other tall plants: *lycopsids*. They were as tall as trees, if not more prevalently taller, and far sleeker with their limbs and forks located at the very top. These were not actually related to trees but a more primitive brand of plant, they bore spores, their method of reproduction like the ferns of which they were in fact related to…a product of convergent evolution. The lycopsids though were a peripheral species to the wooden conifers, once they had reached up for the skies in the masses and had turned the land green the world over.

Shade was provided from the brutal sun, and beneath the distinctive shadow of a cycad leaf, rested a *hulavitah*, a small burrower just short of a foot long, four limbs sprawled outward with five long, clawed fingers, a long tail and a body covered with pronounced, sharp overlapping scales desert beige in colour with grey spots outlined thinly with black. The hulavitah's skull was triangular with golden yellow eyes large with brown slit pupils, encircled by a thin black patch which was bordered by smears of grey/green, a pair of short, backward pointing spikes stood out on the back of its head plus three smaller spikes lining the side of the crown all the way down to the cheek.

Hulavitah was a reptile, a procolophonid. On land, reptiles were the second most common animal after spineless arthropods, and specifically adapted to a hot environment. The hulavitah tilted its head to the left a few short degrees and blinked as company came skittering into view at the foot of the cycad. It was a male *jesspodopterus*. He too was a reptile, but nowhere near as rudimentary as his spiky crowned neighbour. He was an archosaur, a ruling reptile. In spite of this prestigious title jesspodopterus was inconspicuously small, if not tiny; only 9 inches long and standing at a height of 5 inches he was a sleek and slender animal, weighing in at a mere 100 grams. His head was proportionately large with large yellow eyes with black, circular pupils, a tapered, triangular snout grey in colour with a white keratinous covering at the front, the nostrils located at the tip, a bold black patch encircled both eyes and elongated into a triangular patch on the middle of the snout.

The jesspodopterus was scaled, though these were much smaller, denser, were hexagonal in shape, tender-looking and brown in colour with a vivid grey/green tint, dappled with a thick, black spotted patterning. Mingling evenly with his scales was a pelt made up of thin, grey/white fibres, a short crest of them stood behind his head, and they were longest on the underside of his arms, which were short and held off the ground, folded and tucked against his body, hands ended in five short clawed fingers, the palms facing inwards, the fifth finger was almost twice as long as the others.

His body was angled horizontally, he stood on long and stick-skinny triple jointed legs that were positioned below his hips and didn't bend outward like hulavitah's. He stood on four toes with a fifth on the interior of his feet that pointed backwards, there was a flap of skin behind the hind limbs that connected the tail, which was long and slim and ended in a tip of fur that was near diamond-shaped. The jesspodopterus moved on his hind limbs, using both simultaneously which granted him a swift hopping form of locomotion that allowed him to cover a lot of ground for his size. In this world, it was the first time animals would stand up on and use full function of just two legs.

The movements of the jesspodopterus were more frequented than most reptiles; he had fewer pauses and a fluidity. He was not a cold-blooded creature. The jesspodopterus came to a stop and raised his head, where he spotted a source of food. Insects were safe in the air. *Anisoptera*, dragonflies with their four proportionately large wings, the hind pair broader than the front and an elongated abdomen extending out behind them, large, unflinching compound eyes constantly scanned the air and detected prey.

Dragonflies had an ultra-high success rate of seizing prey from the air through their speed and deft, aerodynamic precision which made them the apex predators of the air, as they had been for over a hundred million years. This success was so profound that even they were not safe from each other. There were larger dragonflies flying about, fiery red ones with an iridescent yellow patterning on their thorax, their wings buzzing louder, swarms of them were like proxies to the racket of annual storms that brought refreshing water to the dryer areas of the planet. The big red ones hunted their smaller brethren by coming at them from below and seizing them with their frontal limbs. But the big red ones were a good-sized meal for the larger jesspodopterus, if he could catch them.

The jesspodopterus hopped after the insects, leaving the hulavitah to scatter, his speed accelerating with each hop. He came to a stop, tail raised and stood below the swarm now evading him. He intercepted their evasive tactics and hopped to the side. This agility he could also execute backwards. Then he leapt up on the spot with his mouth opened, flaunting a jaw filled with tiny sharp teeth as well as a pair of canines at the frontal centre of both jaws. Quick bites sheared his catch into smaller pieces, allowing him to swallow it back, which involved him jerking his head back repeatedly. He lowered himself to the ground, his claws made contact with the soil, his eyes rolled upward and blinked.

Then he quickly raised his head, a small pouch at his throat bulged as he produced a shrill of alarm. The ground yielded plenty of dangers. From around the base of a tree appeared another archosaur: a female *freysaurasuchus*, something the jesspodopterus would do good to stay clear of.

Two metres long, with a sleek and lean body covered in predominately brown, square-shaped scales, with intricate grey, yellow/brown and black markings that resembled foliage and a back covered in a double row of overlapping armoured plates. She walked on four slender limbs high above the ground, the hind limbs were longer than the forelimbs, the tall neural spines of her long tail made her hip region appear arched and accentuated the curvature of the tail. Deep amber eyes with small round pupils were set high on a low skull with a long, triangular snout a dark brown spotted band patterning wrapped around both jaws, a pair of short, scaly ridges stood above the mid snout, the opening in the skull was covered with leathery patches of flesh bright yellow in colour, the scales highlighted in black.

The freysaurasuchus opened her jaws baring large, curved, sharp teeth located only in the front half of both jaws, the upper jaw had fewer teeth. She was hyper carnivorous, and the flesh and bone of a jesspodopterus would satisfy her hunger for a short while. In the face of such a predator, there was no chance of fight for the minor skipping reptile. But when it came to the option of flight, there was a chance. The jesspodopterus darted towards the bushes, found an entrance gap, ducked and skipped far in for the maximum concealment the foliage could provide. He spun around in a hop and crouched, peering up and remaining completely still as he watched as the freysaurasuchus walk by, her elegant tail swaying steadily behind her.

~

Stationed safely on a branch of one of the trees high above the predator was another reptile, another oddity a *virgatyke*. Twenty centimetres long, tall neural spines gave it a hunched back, four limbs gripped the branch below it, five digits on each, the claw on the index finger was enlarged and hook-shaped, its tail was long, tall and flat, comprising more than half its body length, the end bore a claw, which was coiled around the branch. The virgatyke had a small head, with large eyes, the snout comprised of a light brown beak, it almost resembled the jesspodopterus despite not being remotely related, the body was leafy green and was heavily mottled with every other colour and imperfection a leaf could take during its existence with specks of decayed browns, sickly yellows, dying maroon as well as a horizontal row of squashed black square spots that ran along the upper flanks. Short, white keratinous spines ran along the back, and a pouch covered in spiky pink scales blushed faintly with red hung below its throat.

The virgatyke was a drepanosaur, a freshly evolved group of arboreal reptiles, adapted to living life in the trees. It moved slowly, but meticulously one limb at a time, its tail loosened with each step, bright yellow eyes with bold round pupils flickering and head adjusting in the direction of potential prey, which were the dragonflies. The virgatyke froze, its tail end squeezing the branch where it remained perfectly still, its intricate coloration allowed him to melt into the background foliage. A dragonfly flew over in the reptile's direction and began to hover around the branch in all directions, investigating. Then it flew a foot in front of the virgatyke, wings buzzing. It wouldn't seem this slow, static reptile could even attempt to prey upon creatures with such rapid reflexes.

Any doubt was scored wrong as the virgatyke lunged forward, its beaked mouth open and an even row of tiny sharp teeth and a short, heavily moistened pink tongue exposed.

The reptile snatched the insect from the air by the thorax, inside its beaked mouth, escape was not possible. It was a swift, but perilous move; the success of the motion caused the branch to shake wildly, the virgatyke's prehensile tail and a clawed hand holding it place, saving it from falling to the ground below. It consumed its catch while the branch continued to sway. The sun set, and with the dimming light the scorched earth beyond the greenery turned a deeper red as the shadows of dusk advanced.

~

Morning. Bubbles appeared on the surface of a marsh located in a shallow creek from a resident submerging itself after taking in a breath of air, swamp matter drifting downward in the process. It was a *fensalirpalus*. Six feet long, body bulky and cylindrical, the murky yellow flesh loose with mottled brown spots, the tail was short and flat and bore a fleshy finned crest above and below it. Its large, bulbous half-moon-shaped head was a third of its body size with a triangular, smooth fronted snout, halfway down the skull were gelatinous-looking eyes, positioned high with oval-shaped black pupils and golden eyeballs. Fensalirpalus was an amphibian, a temnospondyli member.

Once upon an era these vertebrates had grown to colossal sizes, thriving in heavily forested and swampy regions the world over and breathing in a dense atmosphere rich in oxygen. But a reduction in oxygen due to climate change through the ever-changing landmass had shortened down mass gigantism in amphibians and arthropods altogether. Nonetheless, a handful of giants remained the world over, thriving in the more lush areas. But in this global arid era they were facing competition from the reptiles.

The periscopic eyes of the fensalirpalus surfaced. The marsh it dwelled in lay among a labyrinth of waterways that steamed thickly with humidity, the slopes of the creek were ridden with greenery, fungus was plentiful and above was an overlapping canopy with bright rays of light prying in leaving elongated shadows of whatever shaped foliage they struck. The collective popping croaks of other residential amphibians and songs of insects created a unique ambience within the creek.

And the female freysaurasuchus had found her way into the creek, away from the exposed dry open, her camouflage highly effective in this setting as she melted into the background while making her way towards the water for a drink, unaware of the formidably sized amphibian below water. As the freysaurasuchus drank she dunked her lower jaw into the water, tilted her head back, then raised her neck up. After her second gulp, she paused upon spotting the fensalirpalus. Their eyes met, and neither creature flinched. A challenge would have greater consequences for the soft-skinned amphibian as the tougher skinned archosaur was adapted for the dry land, moisture contained within her scales. The two opposing vertebrates continued to look at each other.

~

Not too far up the creek the rises became shallower, and were bright green, below them in a clearing was another archosaur, a male *bakebonrursus*. He was a three-metre long quadruped weighing in at 400 kilograms, body covered with thick, squared scales each coloured a cloudy brown with tiny darker brown spots, his underside grey/white with a bulky, distended abdomen. His entire back was lined with rows of flat horizontal plates of earthy red/brown armour, the tail long and heavy held off ground bore outgrowths of jagged scales along the sides and thick black bands. The head of bakebonrursus was short and low with beady black eyes and a snout ending in a short, fleshy proboscis with a downward slanted end, the nostrils located at the front. This appendage was a *trunk*, an odd trait for a reptile—this wasn't an adaptation for a carnivore. He was herbivorous. The pinkish appendage had a ribbed detailing on the top and its prehensile movements aided as the bakebonrursus foraged and extracted plant material which he shredded crudely with his oval-shaped teeth before swallowing.

This herbivore, well protected from lean predators like freysaurasuchus had found its way into the secluded creek through a tight, fungus-ridden path around the western side, and concealed from other foragers that would otherwise compete the herbivore was free to gorge. But the rises on this part of the creek were at their lowest. And he was being watched from above the hill, directly behind him. Appearing at the top of the ditch was a female *cuthbrodsuchus*, a rausuchian, a family of archosaurs that had evolved into the land's top predators. Also three metres long, but weighing nearly 100 kilograms less she moved on all fours, the forelimbs were sleeker while the hind limbs were thickly muscled, each limb had five toes, three of which were strongly clawed, the outer ankles though bore a backward pointing spur.

Unlike the bakebonrursus, her abdomen didn't bulge so much and was compacted, while the head was large and rectangular, flat snout to crown with a leathery appearance, ridged eyebrows stood above golden eyes with broad dark brown pupils with visible red veins encircling them. Her dense jaws bore long, sharp, curving teeth, her lips had a downward, concave curving motion to them giving her an unsettling expression while a muscular neck provided power to her jaws. Her body was black with a rather bright yellow/orange underside, the ridges of her eyebrows had a dotted patterning of white. She too was armoured but with rows of variously shaped and sized bony scutes instead of plates along a leathery back, while small triangular scales lined the top of her long, muscular tail held off ground.

An ambush predator cuthbrodsuchus preferred not to hunt out in the open like other predators due to her size. She moved along the edge of the rise, the drop of which wasn't perilously steep but long, allowing her to advance downwards. She lowered her head, discerning and calculating the motions of her prey so she could find a blind spot. If brought down, the bakebonrursus would provide her with sustenance for weeks. The cuthbrodsuchus positioned herself, she remained still with her head and neck unflinchingly locked at a lowered angle then descended, her footsteps were near silent, masked by the organic ambience. Though she wasn't aware that there was an easier way down... She stopped upon seeing the herbivore turn his head. No sounds or movements indicating alarm she continued down.

Her right forelimb struck a cluster of fungus and released several rocks contained within the soil, which consequently crumbled downhill. The bakebonrursus stopped and looked about while chomping down on a mouthful of plant matter, his tail began swinging about rapidly, but the cuthbrodsuchus continued on.

Then the bakebonrursus turned his head to the left, tail curving in the opposite direction, which his body followed in a quick stepping motion, facing the source of alarm directly. Having lost the advantage of ambush the cuthbrodsuchus charged. For the carnivore going uphill was a strain. But going down was a different matter. She lowered her body down, then pushed herself upward then charged downhill, not on all fours, but on her hind legs.

The predatory archosaur towered over two metres in height and her speed accelerated, though her nimbleness was challenged by the incline and risked toppling over, more rocks and other disturbed plant matter rolling down.

As her feet touched flat ground she staggered momentarily on her back legs, even while she continued to run towards the herbivore with the intention of attacking his skull, her thrashing tail smashing into the foliage at her side. The bakebonrursus moved to the side, head safely away from the cuthbrodsuchus that was in strike range, her jaws opening wider with each step, sharp teeth exposed with thin strings of salvia connecting both jaws. She bit down, the grip was brief as her mouth slipped off having clamped down on the armoured back, teeth scraping through bone, keratin and shedding only droplets of blood and strafed tissues.

The cuthbrodsuchus made a sound, an airy amplified rasp with her throat throbbing on both sides before rearing up again and savagely slamming her forelimbs down on the herbivore's back as her frontal body weight forced her back down, the armour challenging the predator's power. She began to rake at it with her claws but she was shoved away by the herbivore and the giant archosaur landed back on all fours, causing a splash against a shallow pool as she landed. The bakebonrursus automatically lowered himself to the ground in a crouched posture, tail thrashing and his flanks expanding. He opened his mouth, proboscis curving upward and grunted, the noise had a bleating character to it. The cuthbrodsuchus opened her jaws without unleashing any sound then made a lunge for the bakebonrursus which side stepped to the right and swung his tail at her, striking her left shoulder and causing her to jerk to the side, though it appeared to have deflected there was a cutting motion to the impact. The jagged scales on the tail of the bakebonrursus had heightened the damage of the blow and had left broken chips of armoured scutes and some minute spillage of blood out of grazed flesh. The cuthbrodsuchus rasped and stood her ground, mouth opening, enticed by the smell of blood.

~

Observing them was a *ratatorskr*, a two feet long burrowing creature and a paragon staple of oddity in this age. A rhynchosaur, it was a distant cousin of the archosaurs with a superficially basal reptilian body plan, though stockier with a short tail, and short, robust claws, body a reddish brown with black, spotted rings on the back and an underbelly mottled heavily with a mouldy yellowy white colour. The ratatorskr had a large bulbous head, beady dark eyes and a simple beak made up of a tightly packed pair of enlarged incisor teeth and deep set jaws that allowed it a powerful bite—it practically thrived off the toughest of plant matter, which was plentiful in this creek. Once widespread, the rhynchosaurs were now an endangered species, their cloistered lifestyle giving them an edge in this highly competitive world.

The two duelling mega archosaurs were in its way, and there wasn't much room to navigate. Yet the ratatorskr scurried forward, braving the pounding legs of the two, not knowing which beast was deadlier, the only distinction was rotted plant matter and decayed meat, which collided and fused together to create an anomalous odour. The one with sharp teeth was pushed into a cycad, which split several of its stems apart and sent the foliage flying. The ratatorskr made it through the gauntlet. But a dragonfly nestled on one of the broken off cycad stems feet away from the conflict took flight, seeing the rhynchosaur as a potential threat and flew around the duelling pair of titans. The cuthbrodsuchus quickly stepped back as the bakebonrursus shoved her in the direction of the insect, another push forced the carnivore left, where she swung her head the dragonfly's way, flesh-ripping jaws closing unintentionally and missed. The dragonfly flew past the predator and flew above the canopy, away from anything that could pluck it from the sky. The outcome of the battle metres below on ground unclear as it headed towards water.

~

Further away, moving along the banks of a shallow estuary was a 12 feet long *gudifosaurus*. A tanystropheid, it was another cousin of the archosaurs, this stellar preposterous reptile had an elongated neck seven feet long, which was over half of its total body length, behind a small, flat head with its eyes placed high, the body broad and fairly bulky and covered in small scales, dark grey with bronze brown spots that mingled with broad, slanted black stripes and smaller spots on the underside, the reptile's short, fat tapered tail bore black striped bands. The dragonfly that had left the archosaur battle at the creek hovered by the gudifosaurus as it headed for the water to feed on all four limbs, which bore long, clawed toes with slight webbing and longer toes on the hind limbs.

A semi aquatic predator, with a preference for soft-bodied, mouth-sized prey, the gudifosaurus moved slow but smoothly into the brackish shallows, its body's bulk had some buoyancy to it, as a result its feet never straying too far from the bed of the stream and long neck sustained by the water, which it curved and swept side to side. The gudifosaurus opened its mouth, which contained long and sharp, forward facing teeth concentrated at the front of the jaw. Foliage from further inland and small prey moved along the current, the latter scattering at the sight of the long necked reptile, bright rays of light glittering on the water's surface reflected against its black eyes. The dragonfly continued onwards, mile by mile the tree lines were replaced with incalculable blue horizon as it headed towards the coast.

~

As with land there was an adaptive radiation going on in the sea, which had hugely benefited reptiles more than any other species, phenomenal considering 17 million years ago *almost* all of the life on the planet had been annihilated by the spontaneous upsurge in volcanic activity to the north east of Pangaea, that had slowly superheated and suffocated the globe for over 10 million years. At the turn of the new era of life, there were plenty of ecological niches to be filled in, and evolution had exploded in its diversity. One such example was *cyamodus*, a visitor from further east navigating its way along the corals in the shallows. Of all the oddities prevalent it might just be the oddest; its flat and wide, sternly triangular skull ended in a short, wide brown beak, eyes an amber brown with vertical oval pupils. The flat body of cyamodus was protected by an armoured shell-like carapace over two feet wide, plus a separate one that protected the hip, spiked scales lined the sides and widely spaced rows covered both carapaces, a similar arrangement applied to its long flat tail, its short limbs with webbed, clawed toes sprawled out against the seabed, the body algae brown/green all over.

The cyamodus was a benign creature, and being a member of the placodontia family the reptile didn't possess an abundance of sharp teeth but sparse, albeit large, solid flat dentaries circular in shape, useful for crushing food of a hard nature; like shellfish which were as abundant as the marine vegetation. The reptile sifted for said hard-bodied prey through the seabed, creating brown clouds of sediment, and upon snatching them crushed their carapaces with its rock hard teeth, the clouds concealing the action but the sounds prevalent. Over four feet long, its heavily armoured body plan didn't allow cyamodus any swift method of propulsion, and trying to swim upwards exerted too much energy. But being so well protected and capable of inflicting a traumatic bite as well as occupying the shallower parts of the sea, the cyamodus didn't need to move fast.

Floating yards below the surface above it were *ammonites*. The ammonites had circular, coiled and roughly segmented shells, their slim tendrils flailed about acquiring tiny prey with the current. These cephalopods had been around for over 150 million years, and their lifestyles remained unchanged while life evolved and flourished around them. Everywhere on the seabed and shore had an expired ammonite, after their expiration their shells sank and settled on the seabed, where they accumulated, layer by layer in the millions, like the plankton.

Not too far out, the water's surface foamed white in scattered pockets that amounted in the hundreds. These were from *thoracopterids*, they were foot long bony fish, with light silvery blue scales that outwardly didn't appear too special. Say for the fact that they weren't swimming, but gliding. Their extra-long pinkish pectoral fins were beating almost like insect wings while their partly elongated tail fins beat against the water's surface, leaving broadened zigzags. Flying fish! The collective pelagic racket created a very unique ambience above surface, an act of which was used to escape predation. This noise would not be heard again until such an event occurred, which would not be too long in these seas. The fish plunged back into the water, and nearly two hundred metres behind their initial flight path, a *cymbospondylus* lingered just below the surface in easy reach of oxygen.

She was an ichthyosaur, a rapidly flourishing and diversifying family of marine reptiles fully adapted to life in the seas. Nine metres long, her skull bore a long, tapered snout, jaws armed with small, sharp teeth, large, bulging eyes with circle pupils, and behind that was a long, cylindrical body with smooth, pebbly textured skin. In place of hands and feet were fleshy oval-shaped flippers, her long tail half her body length kept her afloat, the last third of it slanted downwards while the top bore a fleshy, triangular crest, taking on a crude imitation of a fish's tail fluke.

The cymbospondylus was coloured a dark murky brown, transitioning into a near black shade with small, watery white spots along the back and oval-shaped white patches on her mid snout, which crudely resembled the outline of fish. Though aquatic, her body was in fact in a transitional shape with traits of a terrestrial ancestry visible, such as the bendiness to her body, the flexibility to the fluke of her tail and the bones that made up her flippers were in fact still fingers and toes. While an ocean dwelling apex predator, specialised in hunting near the surface, this female had ventured into the shallows for tender reasons; she was giving birth.

Fully aquatic, cymbospondylus and her kind did not lay eggs but were ovoviviparous, in that she produced and incubated eggs within her body, the young would sustain themselves off the yolk of the eggs until they had reached the correct stage of maturity for birth. The first cymbospondylus pup appeared, demonstrating this process of reproduction, its tail wiggled out from the mother's cloacae with clouds of blood rolling out, oxygen being supplied to them from within their mother to avoid them drowning. The first newborn was discharged, its body fully formed, a micro-sized version of its mother but with disproportionately larger eyes. It made no interaction with the mother, and just swam instinctually towards the surface.

The mother dispensed a second progeny, and attracted by the blood from her labour several *hybodus* came swimming her way from several angles. These were a unique kind of *selachimorphids*—a highly diverse family of cartilaginous fish. Better known as sharks, which had been around for over 200 million years, and long before the first life on land, hybodus had survived the mass extinction event and were faring well globally. Short of two metres long and bulky with a snub snout, body coloured a very light brown with a white underbelly the hybodus were very typical, but their bite was to be avoided. The males bore short horns on the side of their heads and spikes on the fronts of their dorsal fins. These particular specimens were a regional species known as *hybodus thewlis*.

The mother cymbospondylus had dispensed two offspring already, which were out of sight. The surrounding coral would provide them with refuge. Should they make it at all... The mother dispelled a third, after which she thrashed her tail and breached the surface for air. There, she did not catch sight of that pup being seized by a hybodus, the variedly shaped but razor sharp teeth and jaw power instantly crushing the baby and the violent thrashing tearing it into pieces, ending its life of only a few seconds. The mother cymbospondylus submerged herself and dispensed four more lives carrying her genetic material into the sea. As far as her eyes could see they had made it to safety. But it was her last litter that was becoming a concern; it seemed to be stuck within her birth canal, and as the mother tried to eject it she released more blood and thrashed around in a rapidly creeping panic. The sharks came in closer. One came too close, but a thrash of her tail nearly missing contact repelled it indirectly. The mother cymbospondylus lowered her head, her eyes shimmering with the pelagic light catching the reflection of a shark swimming her way. This apex predator had never been so vulnerable…

~

On the scorched white sand shores, a gathering of seven *ryaanburd* had picked up the scent of the marine predator's labour and congregated expectantly, some of them wading ankle deep into the shallows, only to jump back as they got splashed by the waves. Only a metre long, these particularly distinct archosaurs had short, rectangular skulls, fairly large, squinty blue eyes that reflected the sunlight in twinkling star white, scaly lips covering small and sharp, backward curving teeth and a curvature to their moderately long necks which held their heads high off the ground. The ryaanburd were fully terrestrial and stood on their hind legs balanced by their long tails, their hands, free from the floor, were too short to engage in any quadrupedal activity and bore five fingers, four of which bore short, curved claws, their legs were slender and visibly muscular around the calf and thigh region, three clawed toes laid out on the sand with a tiny fourth digit on the inner ankle aiming backwards. The ryaanburds' bodies were covered in small, hexagonal scales a sandy yellow with black, spotted markings dense around the dorsal, a bone white throat pouch, dark brown scaly filaments covered their upper bodies as well as a vertical, triangular crest arrangement of them at the end of their tails.

There was a very flagrant gender dimorphism among the species: the males bore a crest of black quills behind their heads and had a deeper coloration, a blushed vein red patterning at the throat and brown rings at the end of their tails, while the markings of the females were sparser. To multiple degrees the ryaanburds resembled jesspodopterus. This was no coincidence as both archosaurs are in fact siblings, branches in the highly evolved clade *avemetatarsalia*, and unlike other archosaurs both species were warm-blooded and hollow boned, the latter of which allowed them a lighter body, ideal for swift movement and a more active lifestyle.

These predators were highly efficient, metabolically and with their diet; a selective appetite was a potential killer in itself in this unforgiving world. Yet they were still essentially fodder in the wake of heavier, larger toothed predators like freysaurasuchus and cuthbrodsuchus. The horizon before the ryaanburd onshore was…seemingly infinite. As was the Panthalassa, *which wasn't theirs to explore, let alone conquer.* The quick, corrective head movements of the ryaanburd conveyed only a single-minded curiosity concerning the countless variety of carrion the sea would cough up. Despite their size, the continuously unfolding genetics of these animals had a grand future ahead of them. The fairly recent mass extinction, as a matter of fact, might just be the greatest opportunity in geological history.

The low, chortling rasp produced by this one female ryaanburd, that had her head ducked low to the sand, didn't suggest any such proposition, merely an agitated emotion as she hadn't eaten sufficiently for the past two days.

Back in the water the female cymbospondylus opened her mouth and lifted her head up, then with multiple exertive beats of her bendy tail the front half of her body cleared the water, her large eyes appeared as erratically shimmering gold disks as they reflected the sun. The momentum unwittingly rolled her onto her right side and caused a splash creating an underwater cloud of white. The impact also resulted in her stubborn, final offspring wriggling free, concealed from the sharks by the bubbles, the discharged blood mixing and creating a bloom of pink which drew the sharks in and elicited an aimless frenzy, distracting them as the pup darted for the corals. Unhindered and without concern, the mother cymbospondylus swam away heading back out to the gloom of the deeper ocean, leaving a rapidly fading trail of blood behind her.

For the ryaanburds, there would be no giant carcass swept ashore any time soon. Though they did not fret over it they still loitered.

~

Back on land and approaching dusk, the male jesspodopterus was hopping about freely in the slowly red tinting open, dragonflies scattering two hops before striking range. He stopped upon spotting a different creature to his left lying under the shade of a cycad, a foot long, and fairly plump. Instinctual curiosity got the better of the jesspodopterus. He came hopping its way.

The creature reacted and ran out from the shade, exposing itself. The jesspodopterus saw it in glimpses. It moved like a reptile on all fours. Not uncommon. Had a short, thin tail. Not uncommon. And a large head. Again, not uncommon. But that was where the resemblance ended; the creature's snout bore a fleshy, moist tip and didn't have scales, but naked flesh covered completely with soft, fluffy evolutions of it that rendered it completely foreign. Uncommon. And even while moving at speed, the archosaur could detect a peculiar, *musky* odour from it. But the peculiar creature was more than fast enough to evade the jesspodopterus, as it was able to crawl down into a nearby orifice in the scorched earth. These things lived underground.

Before the Great Dying, the ancestral cousins of these anomalous creatures had become the dominant life on the planet. But in the new world order these survivors were degraded to a peripheral species. The jesspodopterus investigated the creature's opening of retreat. His limbs weren't equipped for digging out prey, and neither was his snout. But that didn't stop him from trying; he probed his head down into the hole, while trying to configure and adapt his limbs for such a use. But in the end too much wasted time left him exposed out in the open. The fading light had maximised the cover of shadows in undergrowth yards away to the right, where the female freysaurasuchus spotted the same hopping archosaur she had failed to target yesterday. And was already making a run for him on all fours. While the jesspodopterus was alerted to the freysaurasuchus in good time and had turned and began to flee from her, there wasn't enough space between him and the predator to out run her.

He skipped towards the base of a conifer tree, which he would run face first into.

Had he not leapt up anyway, hands and feet facing the bark, his tail bending backwards but not too stiffly. It turned out he was anatomically equipped with another ability: an arboreal adaptation. The jesspodopterus spread his arms out and gripped the tree's surface with his clawed forelimbs, which provided aid for climbing, his elongated fifth fingers stretched outwards and his springy hind limb locomotion allowed him to ascend the tree in a hopping motion, though he still had the reptilian side to side bending motion to his backbone. The freysaurasuchus below looked up at her evasive prey then reared up gaining a metre in height, the claws of her forelimbs making contact with the trunk which she leaned against, while remaining static.

The jesspodopterus scaled the conifer's trunk onto a branch nearly 30 feet up, where he began to move along it on all fours, as though he was a quadruped. The freysaurasuchus turned around and began moving away. The jesspodopterus turned his head left, facing the red tinted skyline and reared up on his hind limbs. There was a swarm of insects before him, out of his reach, which appeared like a black cloud under the fading light. He made his way towards the edge of the branch, which was hardly bending at all under his light weight as he advanced in the direction of a neighbouring tree a couple of yards away, while the freysaurasuchus left the scene below, turning her head expectantly left to right. On the end of his branch, which was bending down under his forgiving weight, the jesspodopterus reared up and spread his short arms out as far as he could. If only he could glide… Flight would be convenient. But he was capable of neither.

The jesspodopterus took a leap of confidence, in spite of the fatal drop below him, not that it would result in an instant death but a crippled limb, leading to a slower one from a multitude of factors. The jaws of predation would be ideal. Airborne he revealed a flap of skin an inch across on both flanks, covered partly in pelt, extending from his elbows to knees, his legs split and spread out revealing another flap, the one connecting the legs and tail. The jesspodopterus managed to land against and grip the trunk of the opposite tree and nimbly climb up onto a branch to the left, folded his arms and looked up, where he spotted an object in the multi-coloured sky. This one object wasn't falling from the sky, as had been for the past four billion years in the form of rocks carrying foreign parcels, contributing to the fabric of the planet's biosphere as it was at present. This object though was completely static.

Chapter 2

Date: November 20th 2009. It hadn't been a good summer this year; Mum had caught that swine flu going about which had left her bed ridden for a couple of days, and Emily had had to play the role of nurse. Hopefully nowt like that would be going about again. A Capricorn, Emily's nineteenth birthday was a week's past, and she didn't do too well remembering dates, they were nowt; trivial with the exception of birthdays, appointments to keep and paydays for college EMA. As for today, all she knew were that it was a Friday night at the Stanley Parker's pub up in Barnothcroft, which was just over a mile away from Hoperwood Beck. And it was one of the roughest parts of Thewlington.

Looks wise, the pub wasn't the best, it had this U shape to it, an ancient carpet ridden with grey coin-sized pieces of chewing gum, there were two pool tables, a pair of fruit machines and a punch bag machine (thankfully weren't in use right now by the lads), and a jukebox playing *breathless* by The Corrs. Emily was stood at the bar, a bottle of rosé and change handed to her by Karl the barman. He was a big bloke with a pot belly, wore a white dress shirt, wire-rimmed glasses and had this goofy expression to him made worse by his spiky ginger hair.

"Cheers, Karl." Emily thanked, collecting her change, flaunting her star sign symbol, tattooed into her upper right wrist. She was as attractive as lasses could get, had faded freckles that didn't require too much foundation to cover up, her skin carefully tanned, her jaw close to square-shaped, nose slim with a button tip, her eyes were wide and a sapphire blue, mascara and eyeliner gave her eyes a cat-like appearance. She wore a gold crucifix pendant around her neck, her ears held a single plain gold stud in each lobe and two rings in her upper left ear and one on her right, she had a silver stud in her right nostril—all the lasses her age had one—and a silver ring in the left side of her mouth she had had done at Garbot Arndale in town where all them alternative kids hung out.

Her straight brown hair was cut symmetrically into a short angled bob, the hair on the left side tucked behind her ear and with a sweeping fringe on the right. Emily had thought about getting herself a bowl cut fringe but didn't think it would work, unless she wanted to look like one of them flappers from the 1920s; her hair weren't long enough for that. She thought she had a pretty decent figure; hourglass-shaped with C cup size breasts, pleasingly wide thighs, and tonight complimented her figure wearing a short, black shrug cardigan over a short plain white, sleeveless body-con dress with a medium height neck line and white five-inch platform heels with straps around the ankles. Apart from being the fittest lass in the pub Emily looked very normal. She had never felt the need or pressure to change any part of her face—the idea of plastic surgery was just like no-no!

Emily returned to her seat, managing not to get knocked over by two charging kids, who shouldn't even be in the pub at this time. Sat across to the left was her youthful-looking mother, Debbie. She was an attractive individual herself, her jaw was triangular, had a clef in the centre, her nose straighter than her daughter's, eyes broader and irises a lighter blue, set below permanent eyebrows, her skin less fine with a blemished, pasty texture that required plenty of foundation, and her eye makeup was applied thicker. Her hair was long, rigorously straightened and dyed black, though it used to be dyed blonde and would have up to three different colours of highlights.

Mum wore a short quiff on her crown held in place by a clip, wore three gold, hooped earrings in each lobe, a gold dimple piercing on her left cheek, a black choker on her neck, a lime green sweater hollowed out at the shoulders, with a low-cut neckline that showed off most of her breasts, the one size surpassing her daughter's, was due to implants put in earlier this year. Mum appeared to have slimmer, longer legs than her daughter, but that was due to the illusion from her height of 5'11", she wore white jeans over them with black leather gladiator style stiletto heels, her toenails were painted white.

Mum was smiling constantly, looking at her emails and texts on her phone, which she gripped with inch long white painted fingernails, she had a ring on almost every finger and could be seen flipping her phone around taking selfies. Emily didn't take selfies where there were people about, although that didn't mean she passed the chance daily; she took at least twenty or so in her own space. Emily put down the wine and assembled her cash change while Mum screwed open the bottle and gave her below half-full glass a top up.

"I'm thinkin' of dying me hair, again," Emily said pinching a piece of her hair to the left side of her head. She spoke with a thick East Thewlie accent, the working class sort and a friendlier-sounding version of the rougher, unintelligent chavy version which was prevalent in the pub. Mum sighed without opening her mouth, reached out with her right hand and caressed her daughter's face with it.

"You should be on X Factor!" She sulked, admiring her looks.

"You could get us a mansion with servants so I han't got to work all the bloody time!"

Emily wished. She had won every contest at school for singing and being the fittest lass in class; and had even gone into town for a beauty contest, where she had come in second place.

Fame she was capable of achieving through effort, it were paparazzi that bothered her, she hated them cunts following you around and all that, getting all lippy and doing everything they could to provoke you. Emily had her attention diverted to summat more important; the girl of them two children that had run past her seconds ago started moaning.

"I wanna go home...!"

It was 11:42 PM—obviously they would cry out to get the attention of their trollopy-looking mother, who was pissed and mucking about on the phone, while their father, a real stuck-up-looking bloke dressed in a dark blue nylon tracksuit with his bottoms tucked into his socks were on the slot machine, swearing every time he got nowt back from it.

"I wanna go home, Mummy!" The daughter begged and jumped about, spilling tears from her eyes.

"I'm not gonna give yah another bloody warning yous! So shut your bloody mouth or I'll put you in a bloomin' cage!" The mother warned her child. Emily had had enough of it! So she got out of her seat and stepped in...

"What's up?" Debbie enquired and didn't get an answer. The abusive stranger mother whom Emily approached was going through her oversized handbag, oblivious to the drama, all the crap she kept in it heard racketing while her child's begging increased in volume and went ignored.

"Oi?" Emily called out without drawing attention. The mother cussed summat without enunciating and continued going through her bag.

"Ear you!" Emily retorted, the mother looked up and faced her, she had a wrinkly pockmarked face, her long hair was dyed black but had an inch of grey showing at the roots, a stud in her left nostril and her expression was thick as pig shite.

"How'd yous expect her to learn owt when you're not paying her any attention?"

In response to the criticism the mother's eyes widened, her jaw dropping revealing yellowed teeth and two missing incisors—*yeah, I'm talking to you!* Emily thought.

"You what!" The mother stupidly exclaimed. You had to put up with it at least once every day here in Britain. Emily had practised over the years, trying *not* to say it; you didn't sound normal, you sounded thick! And people like this lived off the taxpayer's pennies, it were bloody disgusting!

"What…?" The mother said her words were like a follow-up punch with the other arm. In the corner of her eye, Emily noticed the father, who was looking their way, smiling and shaking his head, amused and probably thinking summat like: *women, you don't need 'em!*

"What…?" the mother repeated.

"C'mon then yah bitch!" She urged her on. This hammering sound could be heard.

"Fuckin' hell, mate!" Some bloke could be heard mumbling. The source of excitement: Mum trotting over clumsily with half the blokes on this side of the bar looking at her bum.

"Ears? Don't yous be talkin' to me baby like that, yah fuckin' slag cunt!" She screamed, her voice sharp and piercing and not from the alcohol. She towered over her daughter and her source of bother.

"Ergh, you're a right fuckin' bitch you!" The neglectful mother called back with her tongue halfway out her mouth.

Karl was looking over the bar, while the father resumed his business on the slot machine.

"Alright! Yous lot better be off!" Karl called out smiling.

"Eh?" Debbie stalled and looked the barman's way.

"Do I have to fuck off now, Karl?" She protested.

"No Deb's, you're alright!" Karl assured her, keeping his smile.

"Fuck sake!" The mother cursed then fumbled through her handbag. "Alright, we gotta go!" She called out to her partner.

"You what?" He called out.

"We gotta go—we're being kicked out cuz of that bitch!" The mother had the balls to say, while the father poorly concealed a smirk.

"Ergh, you watch your language!" Emily automatically said back, ready to deck her but got no response.

"Oh so I've fuckin' gotta…?" The puzzled-looking father blurted with this dazed look while turning about on the spot like he was a swivel chair.

"Fuck sake…!" He mumbled and looked dead at Emily, like he was planning on doing summat about her, but did nowt.

"Elizabeth! Kieran!" The mother shouted for her offspring, smirking faces began looking her way while Emily mouthed several of the worst insults she could think of. The bad mother walked past Emily, a coat over one arm and shot her a poisonous glare.

"Ear? I'll fuckin' have yah!" The bitch said with this greasiness to her voice.

"Oh fuck off!" Emily boldly said back.

"OI?" Karl shouted out, put his hands on the counter and leaned forward a few inches while shaking his head with this toothy smile.

"Go on now, please will yah!" He politely ordered, not addressing Emily from the looks of things. The mother stormed off to collect her shit, while the children looked pleased, hopping about, the parents gave Karl lip as they passed by. The barman's smile began to drop.

"Ear? I'm not tellin' you again! Off! The lot of you!"

They left, with Emily's gaze slowly following them. Children never appeared so happy!

"Fuckin' slag cunt!" The mother muttered not quietly enough as she opened the door for her family, Debbie's mouth opening and permanent eyebrows lowered.

"Look out for your boyfriends—this tart, she'll shag any bloke!" She added, addressing the entire pub. There was a harsh ring of truth in it not worth speaking out.

"Ear? Fuck off!" Debbie screamed and walked forward like she was ready to bite a chunk out of her adversary's far less attractive face.

"Come on then!" She urged her on.

"Oh no, not in here, Deb's!" Karl's lightly spoken intervention was enough to stop her from getting an assault charge. And kindly enough the bad mother gave Emily the finger.

"Oh no! You fuckin' don't do that shite!" Debbie cursed in response while Emily scoffed and went back to her seat, where she nervously took a drink thinking of how to tame the stares of patrons with this catfight.

"Alright Nick?" Matt, a regular fella called out to her.

"Yeah…" Emily sighed and nodded, the frowns in the room from the drama comfortably being drawn to commotion outside from the abusive mother.

"Fuckin' laughing at me! No fuckin' respect!" Could be heard.

Debbie returned to her seat all tensed up, redness from heavily taken offence in her face dying down. She fell into her seat, her back smacked against the wall and she didn't care.

"That fuckin' trollop! Wish I'd fuckin' smacked her in her fuckin' big gob!" She cursed, grunted loud and angrily then furiously snatched up her wine and drank deep.

"Fuck me!" Remarked some unseen bloke on the other side of the bar.

"Calm down, Mum!" Emily insisted and gently coiled her fingers around her mother's wrist.

"Fuckin' hell!" A unanimous wave of them two words swept through the pub, Karl was seen frowning with this look on his face like he was thinking: *I love me job!*

Mum quickly calmed down, she sunk mellowed then looked at Emily and produced a grin on the right side of her face, her eyes fluttering.

"You alright me baby?"

Mum showed off her teeth, they weren't perfect, were yellowed partly with one of her incisors out of line. Emily nodded then took another sip of wine, more worried about the children of that ejected bitch than herself. Mum sighed loudly, went into her bag and trotted off out of her seat.

"I'm off for a fag!" She said like it was the cure for anything. Emily swallowed back wine and grunted, aware that her mother was hoping to catch the trollop and have a go at her. While Emily did smoke, she didn't feel the need for a cig at the moment, she sat back and played about with her phone.

The pub's music track changed, it was Justin Timberlake's *like I love you* and no conflict was heard outside, so them lot that had been kicked out must live locally. When Mum returned, she pushed her thigh into her daughter's and put her arm over her, looking at her with the utmost affectionate and caressing her face, which had blokes in the pub chuckling. Embarrassing as it could be at times

Emily had been fine with it since birth; better to be showered with it constantly than have none whatsoever.

"Go to New York someday…! Be on one of them fashion shows, catwalks!" Debbie started with more wishful, motivating words as common as every hug.

"I wanna go all over the place." Emily corrected and noticed her mother's eyes roll towards one of the blokes, a young fella with big shoulders and dark hair in a severe crew cut slouched over the other end of the bar waiting to get served. She held up her right arm and waved her ringed fingers at him, very slowly. *Go get him then!* Emily thought, all too well acquainted with her mother's charms.

~

Saturday morning. Emily stirred and rolled over with her blue eyes flying open and dilating. She wasn't hung over badly. The time was 10:09. The walls of her bedroom were white with sheered black curtains with white blinds beyond, the blankets of her double-sized bed were black and the pillows bubble-gum pink, and with Juicy Couture motif—she wished! Emily still kept all the soft toys and teddy bears from her childhood, had a bookshelf lined with all kinds of books, popular and that the deep thinkers preferred. *Harry Potter*, *Lord of the Rings* were among them, and as for *Game of Thrones*…when were they gonna do like a film adaptation or summat? Her mates chose popular celebrity figures, although Emily had a couple of recent Alicia Keyes, Cheryl Cole and JLS posters on her wall.

Feeling warm and confident enough to get out of bed Emily did a couple of yoga stretches of her legs, slowly lifting them both up a perfect 90 degrees then lowered them a few inches from touching the bed, feeling strain in her thighs and abdomen. She had taken it up a couple of months ago, although she could really do with her pink yoga mattress, which was lying on the floor to her left, and there was a sit-up bar she had fixed to her bedroom door. Emily slipped on her fluffy Ugg slippers, put on her velvety grey bathrobe and went to the bathroom, looked in the mirror and noticed her eyes bloodshot from fatigue. *Hydrate those eyes, young lady, if they're red!* Her grandmother used to tell her when she was a child. Emily removed her robe, revealing a flat stomach with a silver belly bar and a long and curving, black tribal tattoo on her lower left side then brushed her teeth, which had always been perfect most fortunately, then pulled her hair back into a short ponytail without combing it and fastened it with a bobble.

The bathroom was small, but Mum had done plenty to make the place look like luxury; the floor had sparkling black tiles installed, there was a fluffy hot pink floor mat, a constant fruity perfumed scent, some unlit scented candles were set on the window which had a slowly rotating council air condition fan, the loo had this fancy pink cushion seat with red and white floral patterning. Mum had had a proper shower installed next to the bath sometime last year, and the shower curtain was sweet and seductive; coloured gold with a sequined leopard spot pattern along with greys and pink, it also had a bit of an Arab belly dancer outfit look to it. Emily wasn't having a wash yet, nor was she feeling peckish, she had plenty of energy in her. She put on a hooded grey/black tracksuit with red stripes, and from her shoe rack she had a pair of red and black trainers which matched nicely.

Emily tucked her crucifix safely under her top, plugged in her earphones to her iPod strapped to her right arm, track playing was Lene Marlin's *sitting down here*, and exited the house, number 56 which, like every house on the street had a front lawn slanted downwards with a waist high wall instead of a fence. Carnian Street had a cobblestone road instead of a tarmac one, which Mum always avoided given her preference for high heels! You wouldn't have even thought Thewlington had such historical roads—it were summat you'd seen in them villages on the outskirts of town you went to on school trips. Apparently the place were all ancient; a class back in the primary school had taken them out on a tour around Emily's whole neighbourhood and said that it had been around since the Viking age or summat. Carnian Street had a church, St David's Catholic was across the road from home and black as charcoal from age and had a cross spire, where Emily and Mum regularly attended. Mum's car a white Suzuki hatchback was parked just three rows to the right, she didn't do a lot of driving as Hoperwood Beck—the local shopping centre was nearby and usually saved the need to go into town.

Since the age of twelve Emily had been highly conscious of her physical appearance and health, and had gone on daily jogs, and took every opportunity she had to work out. After shutting the wooden gate behind her, she bounced about, looked around to make sure there were no blokes or dodgy characters on the street then did a few squats, warming herself up then jogged off to the east. It was cold but the sun shined with less than half cloud cover. There were kids playing football on the road who hollered rude things she couldn't hear as the chorus of her current song, Take That's *patience* was loud enough to conceal it. Here in the outer and inner suburban settings so many people of every age were out of shape; obesity was totally normal and anorexia wasn't uncommon with the lasses. People couldn't be bothered burning off calories or eating healthy; it was one extreme or the other.

It didn't matter how thick or thin you were though, there was no change in the vulgar behaviour of certain people, demonstrated by this obese middle-aged woman that stepped out onto the pathway accompanied by what had to be her daughter, who was twice as wide with a square-shaped head and glasses.

"Love yah bum!" She heard the mother over her music after having to run around them, followed by giggles from the daughter.

"Run bitch, run!" The daughter included with her laughter shamelessly intensifying as though no one would dare stop her, as well as maybe slap her?

A mile out and Emily was breaking sweat which had stuck her trackies to her skin, the setting became more rural, farms were within walking distance, there was more traffic on the road. Attitudes changed; the people she passed by were nothing short of friendly, though she did get plenty of beeps, not traffic related. She reached the halfway part of her jog she marked as this beck with a wildlife plaque placed by the council, in front of a pathway which a senior couple acknowledged her as they exited. As the clouds moved aside a glare of sunlight struck Emily, who interlocked her fingers, raised them to the sky, stretched then returned to her run crossing over the road. Her face had been grazed by the wind by the time she came into Barnothcroft, and she was jogging by the Stanley Parker's, where drama had taken place last night, the place dead and the car park empty. Part of Emily expected her to somehow bump into that cow and finish what she had started.

She crossed the road on her left and continued down into an outer suburb district called Sancrott, which had plenty of Brookside streets and some woods which you didn't usually see around Thewlington. From there, it was just a five-minute run into Hoperwood Beck. Upon arriving back at the front gate of her home she panted gently, leaned back and stretched from various angles before slouching and leaning with her left hand against the limestone wall, tempted to look for things embedded in the rock, tiny featureless dots for fossils, once living things God knew how many millions of years ago existed, which were nowt to be excited about. Emily heard a door opening, it was her house's front door and out came that fella Mum were waving at last night, his hair was a bit of a mess and he had a smirk on his face that widened upon spotting Emily. And she hadn't even got his name!

"Alright?" He said.

"Yeah…!" Emily sighed then stood up straight.

"Going for a run?" The guest remarked. Emily nodded.

"No lass goes for a run here!" He laughed as he opened the gate.

"How old are you?" He asked.

"Nineteen." Emily answered without pressure.

"Fuckin' hell!" Last night's guest exclaimed then looked in the direction of the house. Emily knew what he was implying. Mum's youthful looks were no surprise; like the majority of lasses in this part of town she had given birth to her when she was a teenager—seventeen to be exact.

"Got a *yummy mummy* there, you!" The guest said as though it were meant to flatter.

"Tah…!" An exacerbated Emily tried not to laugh as the bloke left the residence of last night's pleasure.

Emily wanted to get herself gym membership, the nearest being at Hoperwood Beck; Mum went there. But there were too many blokes there, which was off putting. And Mum had gotten to know a few fellas from there so that were another thing to be concerned about. Emily removed her bobble and shook out her bob, she got inside and showered, had a breakfast of oatmeal porridge sweetened with maple syrup, which she really loved, and there were a few strawberries left in the fridge as she had had strawberry flavoured pancakes for breakfast all weekend. She chucked them all in then ate sat in front of the telly, wondering if there would be owt good to watch on the telly later on aside from X Factor.

~

Monday morning. Emily woke up to her alarm clock, the tune: Alexandra Burke's *bad boys*. Though her head was clear she still hadn't been spared an agitated awakening. She checked her phone, it was 7:00 and she decided to shut her eyes and lay back. But what seemed like a harmless snooze she regretted after she awoke and discovered she had less than an hour before the bus into town came! And it was cold this morning—really bloody cold! English weather was just crap! Emily was still tiered, she should have gone to bed earlier last night but had decided to watch that *Breaking Bad* which had only just come out. She staggered into the bathroom for her morning shower, cursing. Yesterday she had dyed her hair this fun purplish red, and she loved it taking every opportunity to look at her reflection. Wash, brush teeth then back to her bedroom to throw on a couple of under layers for the weather, blow dry hair, combed it then straightened, rushed but still presentable. Makeup chore: a thorough application of foundation over long faded childhood freckles, thinly applied black eyeliner then mascara, which took more than half an hour.

She dressed into her college course uniform: a white, short-sleeved beautician's top with matching bottoms, and instead of putting on an overcoat she chose a dark blue hooded Juicy tracksuit top she had bought from a charity store at Hoperwood Beck just down the road, unfortunately they didn't have the bottoms that would have completed it. And she was looking forward to starting a collection, once she had the money—she had a job interview for a cocktail bar in town soon. Emily fetched her black designer handbag she had got from the same charity store in Hoperwood then went downstairs. Mum was asleep, so there would be no fry up or owt waiting for her. There was no bread in the kitchen, but there were plenty of baked beans… And in any case there was no time for breakie!

Emily slipped on a pair of white flats that matched her uniform then left the house, draped the hood of her Juicy over her head. It was her first year at college, after having done six form and had passed secretively as a bright student, summat that was scorned upon in this part of town. Emily was adventurous, liked to read and watch documentaries, had a "temerity" to her…that was a good word she hoped she could use, in the right company. Currently though she was out of work; her previous job at the pub by the Chinese takeout at Hoperwood Beck had shut down, too rough was the word. But it were thanks to some dickhead who had set fire to the place. Fortunately Emily hadn't been there that night. At present, she was doing a beauty course, her plan was to get a job at a salon in Leeds, make money then worry about getting her driver's license and getting into uni later. Right now she wasn't sure what she really wanted to do with her life.

On her way to the bus stop, Emily paid a visit to the local shop and got herself a pack of prawn cocktail crisps and a 10 pack of cigs without being asked for ID. It was 8:48 and Emily was stood at the bus stop beneath this massive sycamore tree, it was like a landmark or summat, what few of them distinctive broadly, triangular tipped leaves remained had browned and withered ready for winter next month, allowing view of the tiny, singing birds perched on the branches. Emily would gladly run to college each morning, except she would be all sweaty; and there were no showers, except for the sports department, and there were just lads there, immature, foul-mouthed lads with too much testosterone and not enough manners! She prodded her mouth ring about with her tongue while listening to Cheryl Cole's *fight for this love*, she like any other lass, just had to listen to over and over. The 175 bus arrived and Emily showed the ridiculously moody driver her bus pass who had the courtesy to snap out of his miserable trance and give her a smile then went upstairs, she always went for the very back.

Usually there was no one sitting in the back around this time. This time there were. Sitting to the left was this fella, who looked about Emily's age. He was very distinctive—he stood out from everyone, but not in some dramatic way though; he weren't a geek, his dark eyes were free of spectacles and he weren't like deformed or anything like that. He was intense-looking like a passport photo, clean shaven and dressed suave like he was a *gangster* with a lovely blue shirt, a purple tie with silky red details and a black leather jacket, this very dark brown—almost black hair combed back slickly from his forehead old fashion style. And he was actually quite fit, white as bread but he'd look better with a tan. As well as a smile…

He looked like he was Spanish, Italian, maybe even Chinese—half? Emily didn't know from just looks alone and weren't the one to judge. Gangster looked up expectantly at her as she approached, looked as though he were pleased with what he saw. The seat next to the far right of him was dirty, some inconsiderate dickhead had left a mess; it weren't piss or sick all over the seat but roll-up tobacco. It wasn't grievously filthy or owt but Emily's freshly washed white bottoms would get stained easily. And she didn't want that on her bum. Emily moved away and sat in the seat in front of it, then looked back and noticed the suave stranger looking at her. She smiled and the stranger reciprocated. And he blinked a fair lot. Emily couldn't resist another look at him. He looked back at her. Emily smiled. The stranger grinned back.

~

Thewlington was like an ugly sibling of its neighbour Leeds, 15 miles to the east. And a boring sibling at that.

There was Bradford to the west, Harrogate north and Wakefield south, where everyone went for fun, and eventually opportunities later in life. As anyone entered Thewlie City Centre they were met with this World War I memorial, and a flowerbed that was dead for the coming winter and the Chamberlain police station to the left. The 175 had stopped on Furnivall Road, it was a main road in the town centre that connected all the high streets. Emily crossed the road to the right and walked up the steep main road, made another right and cut through Longford Centre, one of the big shopping centres in town, all the Christmas decor about and them seasonal ear worm of singles playing that just drove you mad while shopping!

Emily exited, crossed the road and entered a second shopping centre, the Isherwood Centre, which had an ASDA, and from one of the plenty of coffee shops in the centre she bought herself a latte with plenty of sugar, which she sipped on the way, passing by the Keighley Heels Wetherspoons across from Isherwood's back entrance then made a right turn, passed by the city's post office then by the connecting Copeland Tower Block, which was maybe the tallest non-residential building in the city, perhaps because it was located on one of the higher parts of the city. It didn't seem right as it was just on the fringe of Copeland Grange up road, which had these four identical towers of flats that looked like they were made in the sixties. And it was a reputed rough area.

She went through the quadruple block of flats then down a steep hill along a narrow path, crossed the hectic road and this shite-looking rough-looking pub called the Falcon Inn. It had been a half-mile or so from the bus stop when she came into Dilke-Sutton Road, a main road cutting through Oldmill Brig. The district was unforgivably dilapidated; like summat from another century. Unfortunately it happened to be where Dylan Beckett College was, and the design of the building was just awful—like someone couldn't be bothered thinking through with it; a cross between a church and a warehouse, the metal frames and stone just didn't work. And it was just so depressing to look at.

Emily had herself a cig then went up the concrete steps before the college entrance then took out her student ID from her bag which had a picture she loved to hate (not enough makeup and her hair dyed a faded pink with her roots showing unflatteringly) and wore it around her neck; so many students were stopped at the door by security for failing to visibly present their ID's, most of them cussed and solved the problem after dipping their hands into their pocket or handbags, while some quarrelled pointlessly. Emily went straight to class, which was on the first floor, removed her ID from around her neck and used the clip to pin it to her uniform top's pocket. She saw plenty of heads from male students turn her way followed by wolf whistles and whispers of a sexual nature.

Class was well lit and sterile-looking, the floor covered in spotless white tiles almost like a surgeon's, with rows of cream white makeup desks and matching seats, with a makeup mirror in front of each. Pinned up cutouts of models from fashion magazines crowded the corkboard-lined frames, varying with each desk, or not so much according to each user's taste. *Stimuli* the class tutor had called it from the first day. The classroom windows were large and dark tinted and there was an off limits balcony, both providing a look out to a miserable sight of the fields at the back of the college and outdated inner city buildings surrounding it. The classroom didn't smell as clean as it appeared; there was a faint, but very obvious sweaty/fart smell about, the cause unknown, and it had been there since the start of term. No one was going to open a window in this weather, and to combat it there were bursts of aerosolised perfume and other deodorants going off, at least every one of the white clad beautician students had perfume in their handbags!

"Alright Nick?" Emily was greeted on arrival. She had been christened Emily Cerina Nicole at the church across from her. Yeah, it was odd having three first names but she really liked her *nick* name. Pun intended! A look back at the classroom door was met by wide eyes and partial smiles from the heads of three male students peering into the glass, which prompted a swift middle finger to them by several lasses in class.

"OI? Fuck off! Privacy, yah bastard!" Called out Beth Huxley, a hot-headed freckled, perfectly proportioned lass with blonde hair lazily tied back from her face in a low ponytail, who loved to rave on about her "perfect jaw line". The lads were always trying to get a peek inside this room! And half the lasses here were attractive, or had the potential to be more than they were. There was a sorority thingy here with beauty and the aspiration to achieve more of what they already possessed being the most commonly talked about matter. Like with any sorority this class had its fittest lasses, and Emily was among the...*elite* you could say. This elite consisted of Jasmine Cartney, who was quarter caste, her skin a fine gold brown and she had a precise hour glass figure, her bum length hair was straightened, the hair comprising her crown, fringe included was dyed a golden blonde while the rest of her hair was an autumn red/brown which stood out against her uniform.

Isabelle Woodhouse had big brown eyes, a straight nose, long brown hair as straight as woven silk with very slim blonde highlights pulled back very firmly into a high, bushy ponytail. She had a lean, athletic build—she went to the gym and did plenty of cardio.

"…Saturday my boss had me up in Harrogate…" Isabelle betrayed her Aussie accent while talking to Maise Keavan, a brunette midget with dyed blonde hair, a bloated tummy who wore far too much foundation and was never once seen without her fake eyelashes. Isabelle's accent grabbed plenty of attention wherever she went, and she had a thing for wearing long boots whatever the weather and had a part time job at a pub in Leeds. Probably she was the most popular lass there and made male customers stay for a couple more!

Sat on her own and focused on painting her nails was the last member of the elite, Alice Solnhofen (however you spelt that!) she was half-German and half-Geordie—a bit of an odd combination! She had a door wedge-shaped nose, but from the front it appeared slim, her brown eyes were intense-looking, which she expertly highlighted with red eye shadow. Though she had blemishes on her face her skin was finely tanned, and she always wore her dark brown hair in a severely tight sock bun right on top of her head, which Emily thought was a bit extreme. Alice was a brilliant classmate—a good listener, didn't act so confused with the way people spoke around here and understood jokes, was spot on and updated with fashion; a fan of jeans, leggings and Uggs. But as of the near three months Emily had been in college, she hadn't had the chance to ask Alice out for a drink on a night, like she had with nearly everyone in class. She seemed to be a bit of a private lass and didn't seem the sort that would want to associate with Emily's company.

The elite lasses, while they got along as though they were mates, always had something of envy to share with one another, whenever they had the chance; Jasmine's hair, Isabelle's legs, Alice's bum, Emily for her…tits—well, she got a bit of everything! So far there hadn't been any bullying or piss-taking in class, not that Emily was aware of behind her back anyway.

The classroom door opened and in came the tutor Denise Hartley. She was a fairly tall woman in her mid-fifties but looked like she were in her early-forties, with a sharp, pear-shaped figure, long centre parted hair dyed jet black, a refined sun bed tan, had had plenty of work done on her face; wrinkles filled in and Botox injections on her lips, otherwise she wasn't a bad looking lady. She had these half inch long airbrushed fingernails and big breasts, she of course wouldn't reveal were due to implants or age, and was wearing a black uniform to compliment her hair, which also made her skin appear paler. Everyone in class got along with her.

"Our Abby been bothering you?" Denise asked Emily.

"No!" She denied. Abigail was a Facebook pal, and just so happened to be Denise's daughter. The class tutor had a Durham accent, and a bit of a posh one; she lived up in Blackly Thorpe, which was a fancy and peaceful part of town up in North West Thewlie.

When class began drawers and bottles were opened, the collective stench of so many different beauty products accumulated into an overpowering varnish-like smell; every second someone could be heard sniffing.

Music was allowed to be played, and everyone put on summat different on their phone, which created a notorious collision of tracks that created a garbled atmosphere. But there was a dominant track at every part of the room, the most apparent was a club remix of Dizzee Rascal's *flex*.

Class today was working on hair from wigs placed on faceless mannequin heads in front of everyone. The task was to cut it and give the mannequin's hair a simple bowl cut fringe without mucking it up—a little preparation for an actual job at the salon should anyone still wish to pursue one! Dying hair would be next week's task, which half the class were looking forward to. Emily was confident enough with the barber's scissors, her hand more than steady as she snipped off the synthetic hairs of the mannequin's wigs. There were squirms of dissatisfaction and discreet cussing heard in the background; someone was going to throw in the towel soon, and everyone was betting on it whether they admitted it or not.

"Got an appointment Saturday morning at the hair dresser's in town," said Isabelle, who looked as suave as a pianist at an opera with the task, "I'm gonna be putting a red streak in my hair."

You had to love that accent! She was met with praise and plenty of compliments. Where would she wear the red though? Emily had yet to comment on that. Then there was some proper comedy started by Zoe Burton in the centre of the classroom. She had long normal coloured brown hair with a centre parting, pouty lips, a nice face with an olive complexion but thick limbs (not necessarily making her one of the elite) and she lived in Badmington Moor, which was another shite hole!

"There were this old homeless fella come up to me in town, he had shit on his hand!" Zoe said with a strong, husky voice, disgust spread among all who could hear her claim; the commotion others which were quick to ask about.

"Were it *actual* shit?" She was asked by Jasmine sat three rows to her left who had this really concerned look on her face.

"Dunno—it bloody looked like it!" Zoe exclaimed. Emily chuckled without engaging.

"He says: *I'll do you a magic trick if you give us a quid!* And I'm like: "Go on then!" Then he puts this card thingy in his hand and he's all," Zoe mimed the movements of said beggar, raising her right hand, opening and closing it, fiddling about with it before raising her left hand and opening it.

"Then the cards in the other hand! *I don't get it...!*" She hollered and pretended to shudder with some lame sounding laughter from her company following. It sounded like a bit of a shit trick! Bad joke! While Zoe began to banter on about the odd incident further Emily left to visit the ladies room on her own, where the state of hygiene was dreadful; only two of the six lasses that left had washed their bleedin' hands! Emily kept silent, she wasn't gonna accept *anything* they offered her. She didn't have a joke for it, but them laboratories that studied viruses and had them infection categories level one to five would sound brill. *Filthy bitch level four!* Unwashed hands, doing your hair, then someone else's! Why end there? Why not do that before sorting out people's teeth at the dentist or surgery?

~

Back at home Emily was keeping herself busy playing boxing on the Nintendo Wii, which had been a present for her sixteenth birthday from a partner of Mum's that had only lasted a fortnight. And she was very grateful for that. That remote was just healthier instead of being sat down on your arse! And she was a fan of cute, child-friendly games instead of action games with shamelessly graphic blood and gore. The living room was tidy but quite cluttered, pink sheets and cushions covered the giant black leather sofa, a black coffee table topped with stacks of magazines, and a fancy and squeaky clean black glass ashtray, though Mum and Emily very rarely smoked indoors.

Under the coffee table was a fluffy rug, the carpets were orangey beige and needed to be replaced with summat more updated, the room had two sets of tall cabinet shelves which held not books but various ornaments collected from charity shops and souvenirs from towns here and abroad over the years, as well as some unopened bottles of champagne and a photo printer for the digital camera. There were numerous luxury fittings which included a massive, perfectly round mirror, a wooden dressing screen with African characters to it, decorative vases filled with artificial flowers, not the kind you'd pick up at a bargain shop but expensive ones ordered online, or given to her by fellas, and there was a triple rack of dumbbells in the corner right of the 40 inch plasma screen and a rolled up exercise mat.

Mum entered the room yawning loudly, she was wearing a brand new bikini, dark purple with silver and red rhinestone patterning, a pink robe draped over her trailing behind her. Good thing Emily had shut the living room curtains! Phone held up high in hand and the camera lenses aimed her way Mum was taking photos of herself, turning and posing with each step. Emily didn't want to know what she posted on the net, but she was certain she informed others of how proud she was of her boobs! Her caesarean scar from Emily's delivery had a tattoo above it, encircling her pierced tummy button that had been done for free by one of her ex's, who happened to be a tattooist. Not a very good one though, Emily dared not say. Mum had a large and much better done tattoo on her lower back, which she liked to show off while wearing crop tops with tight low waist jeans.

"You comin' out with us?" she asked with Emily pausing the game. Monday just wasn't the time to go out on a night.

~

Mum had insisted on coming out tonight; there was an event on at the Stanley Parker's, though she hadn't made clear what. Emily was upstairs just finishing up on her makeup which had taken over an hour, she wore her hair parted with a waterfall braid on each side, a pink top with white jeans and these crazy golden boots, that shined when light struck them. They guzzled down a couple of glasses of wine bought from the local off license, then Mum called the taxi.

"Fifty six Carnian Street!" She said out loud.

Mum wore her hair unstyled and straightened, let the bangs of her fringe fall down her forehead and was dressed rather formally: she wore a thin black turtleneck sweater, these silvery trousers and was wearing black leather boots with dagger-sharp fronts and stiletto heels. She looked like one of them teacher's all the lads dreamed of shagging.

Mum wore a fluffy gold top coat like she was a celebrity while Emily wore a black overcoat.

In the taxi, the pair were rocking side to side while singing the Spice Girls *I'll be there*, the driver didn't mind he wore a constant smile, his head delicately and joyfully bobbing with every word sung. Mum had been a proper Spice Girls fan back in the 90's. Mel C had been Emily's favourite.

"The fuck's wrong with us?" Mum called out to a male pedestrian.

"We've a bloody drink prob!" She added.

The pedestrian didn't respond.

"Fuckin' hell! He don't like me!" Mum complained then leaned into Emily.

"Show your tits me love!" She urged tugging at her top.

"Ergh, no!" Emily protested, her eyes automatically drawn towards the driver's mirror to see his reaction. Embarrassingly enough he was smiling, though his gaze respectfully flicked away upon Emily noticing, and she didn't react to it.

They arrived at the Stanley Parker's, *sexy chick* last month's craze playing with Emily lip-synching as much as she was shuddering. She needed some hot weather! Upon entering the pub heads of men, and the soon-to-be who legally shouldn't even be in the pub after seven, turned in the direction of the mother and daughter pair. It was busy but it wasn't too packed, and the right side of the bar, where the pool tables were, were cleared away with speakers, drums and other musical equipment cluttering the space with college-aged bands members sorting stuff out. Who was playing Emily didn't know but she was gonna ask. She went off to the bar while Mum went off to find a seat to the left of the pub, she didn't have to wait long for Karl to serve her.

"Alright Nick!" He greeted her.

"Who's playing?" Emily asked looking around for some advertisement pinned up on the wall or so.

"Thewaite Apostels. They're from Leeds," Karl answered—*you what…?*

Emily wasn't quite sure what she had heard.

"Han't heard of 'em!"

"Rosé?" Karl asked, Emily nodded.

After the barman turned around kneeling to the cooler, Emily looked around searching for other people she recognised. There was this fella stood at the far end of the bar, Emily didn't know his name but he came in quite regularly. And he was a cunt! He was middle-aged, obese, wore a shirt, these rectangular glasses had dark, very tightly curled hair in a ridiculous hair cut like a Lego block and always drank a pint of *Flibbigans*, which was the most popular bitter among working class blokes in Thewlington, cheap but shite for taste. But that wasn't why he was a cunt though; it was the way he looked at everyone in a very dodgy way and didn't try to hide the frowns as though they were like trespassers in his own private place. He didn't seem aware that he might just have them specks of his broken from having his face smashed in. Summat like that would make the night of most lads here!

After paying by card, Emily took the wine and glasses to where Mum sat, and after taking her seat these two lasses walked past. They both had dyed blonde hair pulled back too tight from their faces in high buns and overweight with potbellies (likely pregnant!) and chunky legs. But what was hilarious was that both had these big, bulging arses that looked like them dresses women wore during the Victorian ages! Emily concealed a smirk as she screwed open the wine and poured herself a glass.

Taio Cruz's *like a star* was playing, and Mum had invited this fella and his misses to sit down with them, and they were a decent bunch. They were talking about this supposedly brilliant computer graphic film coming out real soon about blue alien men, and that everyone seemed to want to see it, so that was summat to look forward to. From there on, between Mum going on about stuff Emily was just tuned into the pub banter, the lads and blokes of which dominated: there was a, "*fuckin*'" here, a "*cunt*" there, a "*he's from fuckin' Demain Gardens*", here and a "*he's come up from fuckin' Holbeck*" and a, "*his brother's just come out from fuckin' Armley!*"

You know what? It could almost be a song! Most of the lads in the pub appeared like clones…even if they didn't appear physically identical. Mentally they were. And Emily couldn't see anyone she fancied. An hour or so later and people were suddenly moving around to the other side of the bar, where there was practically nowhere for anyone to sit, never mind the Nicoles, most people were stood up anyway. Then the pubs lights dimmed down, the commotion paused then more came about, dark blue lights flooded the bar. On the band's space, this slim fella wearing a graphic T-shirt stepped forward, a microphone in hand.

"Good evening everybody! Thank you for coming!" He announced. Amplified strums of guitar strings followed as did unintelligible grumbles of arousal from the pub's patrons. Very few could be heard saying friendly replies.

"We're Thewaite Apostels," the lead singer called out on the microphone. *Wait Apostles* it sounded like, maybe due to the absence of the T. And the Leeds accent was more pleasant sounding than the Thewlie accent. The boom of the drums and its cymbals cascaded and drowned out the noise of the crowd who had plenty of disses to chuck the band's way.

"We're very happy to have come down to Thewlington and play for you guys!"

You were supposed to say it with just the E at first then lose the T after the G, so you made an "ewe" sound.

"*IT'S SHITE!*" Someone called out and was immediately fobbed off with a growling strum from Thewaite Apostels' guitarist as if to silence it.

"We *love* it though!" The lead singer protested and the bassist began plucking strings.

~

Monday morning, *November 30th—25 days til Crimbo!* Emily thought not too keenly and was up earlier having gone to bed early last night. She showered, blow-dried and straightened her hair, then put on her makeup, a chore this time took an hour and a half in all on account of more time. Emily was thinking of doing an outfit of the day vlog for YouTube—seemed worthy enough; a beauty guru in the making. Lacking freckles made applying foundation easier, and today she put on some light grey/blue eye shadow which reflected the dull November sky, then black eyeliner and mascara and a gentle application of lip-gloss. Mum hadn't pulled last night, so Emily need not worry about bumping into male company sneaking out while she lay snoozing. Downstairs in the hallway were plenty of framed photos of her and her mother, relatives and mates, which was an artwork in itself. Among the hundreds of photos was just one of her biological father, Adam his name was, holding Emily as a baby.

Daddy Adam was dark, Asian-looking with short black hair and brown eyes, he *were Italian* Mum had said. At first glance, you wouldn't think Emily was mixed race. And having Italian origin was summat to be proud of when telling others! But despite the mixed heritage Emily, born out of wedlock always thought of herself as being proper Yorkshire and couldn't get any more proper! She had no memories of her father, didn't know what he did for work or any other stuff about him—had just seen pictures. Word was that he had run off before she could learn to walk, and whether his doing or Mum's Emily didn't know. Mum rarely spoke of him, as though he were taboo—*men for yah!* She would cynically remark. Emily never questioned them.

An only child, she had had a pretty good upbringing she didn't dare trade being fostered by a millionaire couple. Her mother was priceless, despite what others might think. And she reminded herself of that, never daring to forget. From birth, Emily had always had a close relationship with her mother and despite her boozing, playgirl lifestyle she had never had a fall out, aside from the odd quarrel over a small matter, which were rarer than sightings of Bigfoot, that cooled down quicker than a cup of tea on a freezing cold day. Mum had told Emily that she *were crying the moment you were born.* A photo showed just that; Mum leaking tears of joy holding a baby Emily fresh out the womb, arms raised flailing about. Though she wasn't crying. Mum had said Emily hadn't cried until a couple minutes afterwards, and in that same picture Mum's hair was its natural brown colour and shorter—shoulder length. That was nineteen years ago.

One photo depicted Emily as a five year old on a summer's day up in Lake District, her eyes big and blue, freckled face too young for makeup, light brown hair with a cinnamon shade to it in a short, parted bob, she had had cut when she was just three year old, since fifteen she had let it grow a bit longer and had decided on having a fringe and had kept it that way ever since. In the photo, Emily was wearing a *Teletubbies* T-shirt and had an ice cream in hand. Bless herself! She would love to go back in time and give her child self a big hug! Emily had been a good girl all her years growing up, no detention or owt, no shoplifting, no bullying—no trouble with coppers. Though she had been to parties where she had gotten pissed, smoked, shagged underage…and had puffed the odd joint… That wasn't bad…?

How Mum had met Dad Emily didn't know, and she had only been as far as Majorca. Growing up without a dad or any siblings wasn't actually that bad, when you had such a caring mother. And there was the bonus of not having domestic quarrels like so many of her mates had, which was summat to worry about the next morning. Mum couldn't speak anything other than English, and it was the Thewlie dialect and all. And you couldn't quite call that *proper* English! Emily though had been pretty good at foreign languages at school; her French (the only language taught) was best in class and good enough still to this day, and she had picked up a couple of Polish and Latvian phrases, though she struggled to remember more than two at a time. Her knack was decent enough that she could actually study abroad, be adventurous, try new foods, exciting cultures and maybe meet some fit, charismatic bloke. It was a way out of this shite place…

The kitchen had red tiled walls, the electric cooker had an extractor fan above, there was an island in the centre with a stack of diet/cooking magazines and a simple spice rack which added a bit of decor and just one stool to sit at. Mum wasn't much of a cook, but when she wanted to do a proper meal she could really do it. But it was English food only! Emily though liked to try all kinds. On the kitchen wall opposite the fridge was a corkboard and pinned up on it were hundreds of printed off pictures of Emily and her mother, often together from various bars and nightclubs, all of which had a web address at the bottom. It was like a trophy collection. Emily could use a proper fry-up but couldn't be half asked, so she made herself a cup of posh Darjeeling tea with milk, which she drank with both hands like a child and had a simple but hearty breakfast of beans on buttered toast with a drizzle of Tabasco.

Just as she finished breakie Mum could be heard coming down the stairs. She walked into the kitchen in her lingerie and she had forgotten to shut the bloody curtains in the living room, as well as the kitchen blinds! Emily quickly stepped in.

"Mum…!" She complained nervously and closed the blinds.

"There's blokes on this street!"

"Oh sorry me love! I woulda cooked you a fry-up!" Mum said panicking not from her exposure.

"I'm alright!" Emily said while Mum turned around and headed back upstairs.

Emily took out her compact mirror and sorted out her hair, pinching a strand from her bangs and removing a previously unseen speck of dandruff from it. Mum returned shortly and apologetically handed her a fiver, she didn't actually require.

"I don't want you to starve!" Mum said then gave her a hug. Proper motherly love would never break.

Even when she was thirteen, instead of throwing tantrums at the world Emily were still baking fairy cakes with her grandmother and watching Disney films while her mates went in search of a shag, unprotected…and they had children to show for it. Abstaining from youthful recklessness didn't mean she was like queer or owt. No! She was just more sensible, and she didn't wanna be labelled by other people—didn't wanna worry about the burden of having children right now. Emily went back upstairs to fetch her black handbag and blue Juicy hoodie then left the house, bought some more cigs and waited for the 175 underneath that sycamore tree with four seniors chatting between themselves who happened to be her neighbours. The nine o'clock bus arrived without delay and Emily went upstairs.

Chapter 3

That smart gangster fella was sat at the back. Emily walked his way as the bus drove on, the seat opposite him on the left wasn't dirty this time, so she sat across from him. Gangster was still dressed the same in them bubble gum colours! He was wearing black trousers, smart black leather shoes with laces, and a belt, it was snakeskin like a cowboy's and it had one of them buckles with a brass snake on it! No lad in this neighbourhood wore a belt, never mind slicked their hair back, even if they were going for a job interview. Gangster looked her way with this cinematic look to him. And he wasn't so easy on the eyes. He said summat Emily didn't hear, so she removed her earphones.

"You what sorry?"

"You go to Dylan Beckett?" Gangster asked Emily then aimed a finger at her chest.

"I was real curious I see you girls wear those white uniforms." He was complimenting her outfit. No one ever had.

"They're nice! Angelic white!" He said.

"Aw tah! Yeah, I go to Beckett!" Emily said and the fella made this grunt, which sounded like he didn't care.

"I wondered what course you did." He said in this weird yet unique voice, like them serious characters in Japanese cartoons with them weird plots, that didn't make much sense and always involving extreme violence. And he was a bit spooky…his eyebrows were a bit too thick—they needed shaving and were shaped a bit like Christmas holly. And his lower canines were quite sharp, almost like he had filed them to look part animal, and his accent was pretty confusing…It wasn't local, and it didn't sound *too* English.

"I'm on a beauty course." Emily answered.

"Says a lot." Gangster said while blinking as though he was constantly nervous or summat.

"What you doin' at Beckett then?" Emily asked.

"Art course." Gangster said. Emily chuckled.

"You dress a bit *smart* for that—I'd have thought you were in business!" She said. Gangster pouted his lower lip forward, he had quite a lot of expression like some movie star. And he was still looking at her.

"What?" Emily complained without sounding irritated or obnoxious, and not drawing any attention her way.

"Just admiring your appearance," he said somewhat nervously.

"You're easy on the eyes…!" He added and made a fidgeting gesture with his right hand.

"Tah!" Emily said, quickly adding, "I like your clothes!"

She looked away and plugged herself into her music before she could hear a response. She couldn't resist smiling though.

~

Gangster got off after Emily on lower Furnivall Road, he didn't look back at her like other blokes would. Emily watched Gangster walk up the street with a black laptop bag strapped to his back, about as fast as someone jogged, and was quite heavy-footed, with a bit of a hunch. Emily grinned with flattery then ran her fingers through her bob. It was somewhat blasphemy here to call a lass "beautiful" or owt similar like that. The front of Longford Centre had a bunch of pigeons on the ground, hooting and not giving a care in the world as they fed on what people couldn't be asked chucking away in a litterbin. Emily was walking forward.

And less than halfway towards the entrance a flying pigeon swooped by, nearly missing a collision with her face. Emily froze, her heart skipping a beat and almost shouted out. She looked about the place, no one appeared to have noticed, silently ridiculing her. A single feather from the near missed bird though was shed, it was spinning and plummeting vertically instead of swaying. For Emily, it was too late to take out her phone and film it.

She walked on while the feather remained on the floor, didn't see the many people that unintentionally walked over it, each step dirtying and undermining it. Emily stopped in at that same coffee shop at the Isherwood Centre she had last time, and with Mum's fiver bought herself a large latte to go, part of the routine at least three times a week—whenever she could afford it. She walked the half mile to college, and instead of taking the rest of her coffee with her into the cafeteria, where everyone was all rowdy and thick as pig shite. Emily found a quiet spot that was literally just around the corner from the college building, there was a bit of grass about and a tree with no leaves. She lit a fag, then looked around. There should be more greenery in this city—more trees, parks and some places that showed exotic plants, summat to look at other than spend time messing about on the phone all the time. Emily stubbed out her cig then made her way to class.

~

Pangaea had begun to break up, like the neurological concept of interest, devotion and attachments in living things. A sudden, abnormal periodic frequency of monsoon rainfall over 60 million years ago had resulted in greenery sprouting the world over, albeit modestly in some of the inland regions, but nonetheless it had brought an end to the long global drought. A new seaway, the *Tethys* had formed, cutting Pangaea into two parts: Laurasia in the north and Gondwana in the south. Gondwana remained an indiscernibly broken cluster for the most part while Laurasia remained totally, indefinably broken. In equatorial Laurasia, one section of earth remained submerged, with the exception of islands upon islands peaking up against the expanses of blue shallow Tethys water glistening under the sun. One coastal area of this region was transitioning into land, an ongoing process where the lowest spots on the planet were on the path of becoming the tallest. Very slowly.

Emerging from the depths of the ocean in the direction of this area was a *temnodontosaurus*, a large, definitively sleek member of the ichthyosaur family over 10 metres long. The reptile's trunk was compacted yet lean and brandished an erect and sharply triangular mid dorsal fin and a crescent tail fin that it nearly resembled a shark, though it retained its four flippers, the hind pair shorter than the pectoral ones. Its metre long snout was slender and the bone reinforcing it was dense, teeth were sharp and cone-shaped, the sea reptile's scrolling light amber and black eyes three quarters of a foot wide, of which were the largest eyes of the animal kingdom allowed it to see in the lowest of light as well as the deep of ocean. The temnodontosaurus was jet black in colour with a lighter, greyish underside and soft black spots mapped along its body. It was an open ocean apex hunter, able to move at high speed and dive into deep water in search of food, its size and speed partners in evolutionary magnificence.

Light shimmered increasingly against its flesh as it ascended to the surface, where masses of ammonites lingered, then propelled themselves out of the predator's way. As with anything alive, the temnodontosaurus navigated through the invisible, intangible barriers and hazards that were reality whether that be the water, land, air and all other areas life couldn't access. It took a breath of air, and below it the shadow of another temnodontosaurus could be seen to its right before disappearing into the gloom. After taking in a lung full of oxygen, the temnodontosaurus submerged, its shadow cast underneath the sun on the seabed, invertebrate bottom feeders burying themselves in the sand for cover while a group of *belemnites* darted past the ichthyosaur. These cephalopods resembled squid, possessed a long mantel, swam using a pair of triangular fins, but there was a crucial difference: the end of their mantle ended not in a tip but an elongated point, and they had an inner shell, instead of an external one like the ammonites and other cephalopods. The belemnites had ten arms, which were evenly sized, and they lacked the elongated pair of tentacles their familiar squid counterparts possessed.

Above the water's surface was a frenzy of reptiles that had taken to the sky, the first order of vertebrates to do so. *Pterosaurs*, reptiles that had evolved wings. *Meranningdactylus* was a regional species, they had small heads with short, pointed bills and long, interlocking teeth that projected forward, which were longer at the front and shorter at the back. A pelt of fur covered their short bodies, which made them appear bulkier, their arms were slender and bore three clawed fingers, the bones of their fourth fingers were extremely elongated and resulted in a wingspan of five feet, the wings made of a fleshy, translucent membrane with a broadened tip that stretched from wing tip to above the knees. The legs were spread out horizontally in flight, the feet pointing back, flaps of flesh connecting the legs at the ankle, long, thin tails ending in a symmetrical broad crest extended out stiffly, independently of the joint hind limb membrane. The meranningdactylus were the lightest brown colour, with bold white underbellies, their heads were coloured a light yellow all the way down to the middle of their upper necks and their brown beaks bore a dense mess of tiny black spots arranged in slanted stripe-like bands.

The wings of the meranningdactylus had a bold black patterning along the outer rims, the membranes glowed pink as they flew under the sun's rays, their big black and yellow/grey eyes peering below the water intent on snatching the fish below. The ancestral cousins of these winged reptiles had once dwelled in trees, now in this age their descendants had evolved some rather convenient adaptations. The meranningdactylus folded their wings before they dived, then plunged into the water, the surface mapped with bubbling ripples and impact splashes. Submerged they raised their wings to slow their descent, then used their feet to propel themselves despite the supposed restriction imposed by the membrane that connected their legs, their wings and tails provided steering in unison. For creatures of the air, they were shockingly fast and efficient in the water, leaving white trails of bubbles behind them as they seized fish through swift, surprise lunges with precision. After snaring prey, the meranningdactylus swam back up to the surface with their catch, where they floated and consumed it swallowing it down whole, their throats bulging as it passed down their oesophagus. Some of them dived for another catch while others surfaced, some took flight, the pterosaurs wing beats were kept to a minimum until they reached a sufficient height where they could glide.

Under the bright light dimorphism between the sexes of meranningdactylus was highlighted: the males brandished beaks that had a redder tint to them and bolder yellow heads, dark patches around their eyes and more vibrant patterns on their wings. Those submerged and swimming scattered for the surface upon spotting something appearing from the gloom, while those floating took flight simultaneously, their squawking calls of panic spreading regionally in unison as the shadow of a seaborne predator, a seven metre long male *rhomaleosaurus* blacked out the translucent blue of the water below.

Rhomaleosaurus was a pliosaur, and a coastal contender of temnodontosaurus. This strong, marine reptile was large bodied, had a long neck a third of his body length bulging with muscle, connected to a flat skull with a triangular snout with a faint upward curvature, clouded black eyes positioned high, white patches on the mid snout, a pair of nostrils halfway down the upper snout releasing bubbles, the jaws yielding exposed long and solid interlocking teeth. The rhomaleosaurus moved through the water with four large flippers in a forward rolling motion, and a short, muscled tail ending in a simple vertically positioned fluke. The predator's body was appropriately counter coloured with a light grey underbelly and a storm cloud grey on the upper body, the back and all four flippers mottled with thin black spots arranged so that they resembled waves.

Nearby, dead in the rhomaleosaurus's sight was a hybodus. This genus of shark had been around for nearly 90 million years now, and a new species patrolled these altered waters, *hybodus lomax*, their upper body counter shading a silvery grey with faint brown spots, and they were larger than previous species by almost a foot. But they cleared a path and swam away from this reptilian predator, which opened its jaws and began steering its course towards this one shark to its right, which was a smaller sub adult. Guided by an enhanced sense of smell the rhomaleosaurus dipped his head and descended while the hybodus of interest swam on towards the surface, intent on snatching one of the meranningdactylus on a dive. Beneath the shark the rhomaleosaurus appeared almost invisible. That's when he attacked by beating his flippers forward in an upward motion, his speed accelerating with dual purpose intended: to seize the prey or stun it for a second go. The rhomaleosaurus seized the young shark with the first bite, jaws enveloped the middle of the body, teeth penetrating into its abdomen and the shark forced up, where it was ejected from the sea, the sun and reflection of meranningdactylus in its black eyes.

The reptile's bite was so powerful that it practically bisected the shark; the cartilaginous spine exposed and the carcass bending backwards with shredded, bloodied tissue and organs falling out, and raining and splattering against the surface creating a spot of red highly visible from a pterosaur's POV tens of metres above. The rhomaleosaurus swallowed down the acquired chunk then went back in for another bite, the shark's head in this case, which it crushed to a bloody pulp with some of the shark's teeth exploding out from the decimated skull, where they began to fall to the seabed amongst the flurry of gore. The pliosaur took the shark's corpse back up to the surface where it thrashed it about, the violent smacks against the water caused the shark carcass to loosen and break apart. While swallowing down the pulverised shark head in his mouth, the rhomaleosaurus submerged and tilted 45 degrees to the right, his flippers churning the clouds of shark blood and creating a cloudy pink spiral then slowly chased the sinking body parts of his kill.

~

Away from the carnage the temnodontosaurus had entered the shallows, into a small, brightly lit lagoon, far away from the matrix of the open ocean, and hopefully away from the radar of a rhomaleosaurus. It was a unique place that had been vast, geologically at some point, with no biological memory of such a formation in existence…but maybe fragmentary still hints of it embedded in exposed sedimentary rock formations on the seabed, which could not communicate nor could it be read. The most visible examples were fossils of older species of ammonites and an even amount of these ribbed exoskeletons with curving flat heads of *trilobites*, far distant relatives of arthropods that had once flourished on the seabed, which had become extinct through the Great Dying over 70 million years ago. Nestled among this stone grave was a whirl-shaped fossil, almost like ammonite shell, but these weren't connected calcified segments though but the most preposterous dentary arrangement of a shark relative, one that no longer swam in the present waters.

Swimming above the whorl-toothed fossil was a *steneosaurus*, a teleosuchid. The steneosaurus was a nine feet long semi aquatic reptile that spent most of its time in the sea, returning to land to rest or nest. The bronzy brown and green body was sleek and streamlined with a long, flat muscular tail, built for quick bursts of speed, its back lined with leathery rectangular plates, four slim limbs with partly webbed feet tucked against its body, which undulated side to side. Its long, narrow jaws with short, thin and sharp teeth suited to catching soft-bodied prey were of no harm to the temnodontosaurus.

A second steneosaurus appeared on scene swimming close to the seabed, silhouetted against the sun's rays which brought out the colour of its green/brown eyes with slit pupils positioned high. A shoal of belemnites scattered explosively behind the sea reptile like an underwater black cloud, one of which it nabbed as they swam past it and began to consume as it swam higher, the bend of its body accentuating the looping ascent. The steneosaurus and hybodus avoided each other, some had close collisions that didn't result in any bites that would render themselves as prey in the process.

For the moment, the temnodontosaurus wasn't concerned about the secondary predators, but the other member of its species swimming its way. It wanted this spot. The occupying temnodontosaurus beat its tail and swam head on towards its challenger; a battle ensued with their bodies slamming against each other. They turned around and their snouts crossed, miraculous that they hadn't injured their precious eyes. After unsuccessfully managing to inflict a damaging bite the two ichthyosaurs split off from each other and headed back out into deeper water, where they swam at full speed, darting well over 20 miles per hour. They had tight, stiff beats to their tails which was their prime method of propulsion, their flippers steering them like the sharks. The two temnodontosaurs went to the surface, the congregation of meranningdactylus scattering upon seeing their shadows.

The dorsal fins of the ichthyosaurs breached, their exposed fins tearing through the surface at speed, their bodies collided again and remained unmoved as though stuck.

They dived with their thrashing tails briefly exposed to the surface and began to ram and bite at each other, the moves were quick and drew small clouds of blood, but their speed made any evidence of injury appear invisible.

They circled each other in a spiral formation, the defender landed a bite to the tail of the challenger which slipped off, a beat from the fluke smacking against the skull briefly disorientating the defender, no vocalisations were produced, the only sounds were the churning of the water and the thuds of physical contact, this type of dynamic belligerence gave them an edge hunting other marine reptiles.

The two rivals turned sharply to the left then scuffled, the violence of their determination scaring off smaller predators. The defender sped up, this allowed its tail fluke to bump against the head of its rival. After curving around, the defender struck its challenger head on with a volley of body slams and pushed it deeper down, albeit with very firm resistance, the blood from the injuries became more visible and formed a thin cloud that encapsulated the two. After all the free battery, the rival eventually gave in and swam off towards the surface.

The victorious temnodontosaurus lingered for a moment, a slow beat of its tail swiping away a thinning cloud of blood then swam back into the lagoon it had claimed, the yellows, greens and aqua of sunlit shallows far more picturesque against the ichthyosaur compared to the sterile dark blue and purple tinges of deeper outer water. The temnodontosaurus headed for the largest concentration of coral, where it remained... A bloom of blood rolled out from its cloacae. This was a pregnant female, one that had fought for a spot to give birth. Her efforts might as well have been in vain; as always, the local predators were aroused—it was the soon to be born that were in real danger.

One temnodontosaurus pup was ejected, its eyes were twice as large as its mother and the dorsal fin had softer edges. It swam off to the left, its tail and flippers starting out their function for a life in the sea.

But it was seized by a steneosaurus from below. The mother pumped out more young in a steady sequence, but the accumulation of voracious predators were quickly laying a cruel waste to her efforts, as each one of her offspring were hunted down. And if it couldn't get any worse another predator from the open ocean had found its way into the lagoon to participate in the massacre: an *eurhinosaurus*, an ichthyosaur six metres long with broad and wide pectoral fins, a dark blue upper body with stretched glossy brown spots and a silvery white underside, colouration more resembling fodder fish than shark.

What distinguished eurhinosaurus from other ichthyosaurs was its sternly tapered skull and elongated upper snout, nearly two thirds longer than the lower jaw and lined with hundreds of small razor-sharp teeth that were splayed outwards horizontally. Though not preferable prey, the hybodus should be cautious trying to approach it as it steered towards a temnodontosaurus pup swimming out to the left, the deaths of two other fellow offspring by hybodus jaws distracting the other predators. The long snouted ichthyosaur locked onto the fleeing pup, and with a flick of its tail launched itself its way smoothly at lightning speed.

Rather than swim after and seize prey, eurhinosaurus took a more specialist approach to hunting; after it zeroed in on its target it thrashed its front about, where a single swing of its weaponized rostrum cut the pup's escape short, sawing into its side, the force of the blow caused its body to spin allowing the long snouted predator to casually swim back in and consume it.

As of now the mother temnodontosaurus had lost all the young she had birthed, and with the abnormally high concentration of predators within this lagoon she had risked her life for, the place had become all but a death trap. This mother's only chance of procreation now lay with her last offspring inside her, which she couldn't dispense. The tail hadn't even breached her cloacae. And the three species of predators circling her were eager to claim it. The stress of her failure and vulnerability combined with her exhaustion was starting to drag her down away from the surface, her otherwise streamlined and tight movements became hasty and erratic; a thrash of her tail for oxygen didn't get her too far, metres were reduced to feet.

Repeatedly, the mother weakly beat her tail desperately to reach air, her best efforts only allowing the mid front of her snout to penetrate the surface. With the deadly lack of oxygen getting to her brain, the mother's sensory interpretation of seconds were stretched to feel like minutes, heart rate elevated to the highest it had ever been. And of all the predators around her, the hybodus were getting closer, bolder—far too close that they had a bite of her wounded sections causing her to lash out in a futile effort, wasting more precious energy with clouds of bubbles scattering in mass, their volume increasing and concealing most of her outline and fragments of the predators visible between whatever gaps in the bubbles.

Her erratic thrashing caused her strained body to bend to the right, further than it had ever, causing a sprain that would cripple her ability to hunt. She unintentionally rolled over to the right, her tail beat slowed down before coming to a stop… Then she was completely still with the sea's current rocking her, her left eye staring up at the sun and mouth hung open, bubbles rising from it. This unfortunate mother temnodontosaurus had drowned. Spasms rippled through her body…and with no life left to propel it her body slowly began to descend to the bottom, her unborn young left to a no less ominous fate. The predators cautiously followed her body down to the bottom without attempting to get a mouthful of flesh, and a cloud of silt formed on impact with the seabed, her large eyes highlighted a ring of sunlight. Even if the predators didn't consume her remains, there was no guarantee they would be preserved.

~

In life there was success and failure, near success and near failure. In this present case, the mother temnodontosaurus struggling with her final offspring, the predators still circling. Above the flickering green and yellow surface light, appeared a bright white light, one perfectly encircling that already present spot in the sky that was the sun, and revolving without compromising the life-giving light already beaming down as though there were two of them. The spectacle wasn't enough to distract the mother from her disastrous labour. She tilted her head to the right.

Then the world froze, and was preserved in the moment. That event stored away not in a space where something could scratch it out. This happening was beyond tangible.

Then there was another capture. Something was heading towards the temnodontosaurus mother, and it wasn't making its presence known. The circling light above water vanished. Then there were splashes, from fish falling from beyond the surface a few short metres behind the mother. They were immobile as in dead fish, extracted from the sea only then to be thrown back in, how and why was not something to squander on.

The hybodus were the first to respond. They ripped their attention from the mother and diverted it to the free feast. They rushed in and gulped them down in a frenzy and nabbed further servings in multiple succession, which resulted in collisions and conflict with some individuals and the swift arrival of more sharks. The steneosaurus were slower and more cautious and the lone eurhinosaurus need not waste any energy swinging its bill as it turned for the wanton morsels. More fish rained down from above, the supply appeared infinite and leant a break to the efforts of seaborne predators. With the distraction, the mother temnodontosaurus was safe, for the moment. Something else was approaching her, homing in on her bleeding cloacae with interest, and the sunlit jellyfish that swam by in front to the left of the birth canal did not compromise that agenda, even as its near transparent gelatinous hood turned bright red briefly while it passed by the cloud of blood. The pursuer's prolonged focus and visual rocked and trembled to the most miniscule degree.

Then the temnodontosaurus' progeny was liberated from its incubation in one smooth movement, as though ripped out, as opposed to pushed. The phenomenally lucky new-born wasted no time and swam for the surface, energised for a breath of air, the witness of its birth still observing, but not pursuing and the surrounding predators distracted by the free bounty of fish. The new-born took its first breath, eyes briefly exposed to the rays of the sun. With her labour over, the mother temnodontosaurus went up for air without hindrance, the surface chaotic from the motion of the predators and flocks of meranningdactylus flying in for a piece.

After the mother dived, her eyes caught sight of her one surviving young swimming away into the sheltered maze of coral to the right and from there, an uncertain future. The mother then began her retreat for the ocean, her body lighter in the absence of her young, yet sluggish from exhaustion. Like her ancestors she felt no sense of care for the offspring after birth. No interspecies welfare. The pup had to fend for itself. No easy meal granted by vocal communication or signalling, benign or aggressive, and a barter of material. None of which, when acquired were wholesome or easy to digest. No additional proponents to ensure compatibility, just raw flesh, blood and bone. No guarantees of survival after that even. Efforts though remained canon.

~

Further west along the coastline, following the stretch of ragged coral that harboured any vulnerable life and predators alike, were a pod of plesiosaurs called *posidoniasaurus*, smaller cousins of rhomaleosaurus at four metres long. These plesiosaurs had bulky bodies with four large flippers, necks over a third of their body length with smaller heads, their jaw muscles weaker with the strength compensated to sustain the longer necks, evolved only to tackle small prey. Posidoniasaurus were a dominantly white/grey with soft black spots on their backs, the top of their heads were coated with that same shade, and their flippers bore bolder markings of such; from below they were camouflaged on the seabed. Both plesiosaurs and the pliosaurs had evolved from the same ancestor over 30 million years ago and had retained the same morphology with long necks, two pairs of flippers and rows of long, sharp teeth. But shortly into their evolution the pliosaurs split off when they began to evolve larger heads and shorter necks to accommodate a more powerful bite for predation, while the necks of their cousins grew longer and their heads remained disproportionately smaller.

The movements of the posidoniasaurus were speedy, graceful as well as hydrodynamic, and while only slightly slower than the ichthyosaurs they were far more flexible; able to roll about and bend and alternate their angles in an instant, their long necks chasing their small heads. They swooped like the pterosaurs did in the air, only far more fluidly, these acrobatics allowing them to catch fish. The flickers of sunray and their shadows on the seabed created an unappreciated spectacle. But the diet of the posidoniasaurus weren't limited to just fish. One individual snatched an ammonite, one that was small enough for it to swallow down whole then immediately dove down towards the seabed with an open mouth, where it sifted through the sand on the move, swallowing down stones to aid in digesting the tough shelled cephalopod.

Later during the day, the tidal current shifted with the coastal surface of water pushed back and forth at a perilous pace, the skies above darkened and the waters appeared grey above and below the surface while the horizon was a darker grey. Shapeless flashes of lightning flickered across the sky in random directions with rumbles of thunder following, increasing in their frequency after the flashes while waves smashed into the shore, chucking up coral and miscellaneous sea debris and creature unfortunate to get caught in the upheaval. The washed up front half of a juvenile temnodontosaurus with its jaws gaping wide open was no such casualty of the indiscriminate tides, having perished before the storm.

Sensing the change the meranningdactylus flew inland, some as far as they could from the reach of the storm, those that were too late to do that having risked their chances to fill their stomachs more sought refuge among the trees on the shores—anywhere that would shelter them. And other than flight, the four membranous limbs of the meranningdactylus were far more suited to the task of clinging to the trees than moving on the ground.

In the shallows, the posidoniasaurus dived and swam into deeper water to avoid the drag of the tides, a boom of thunder resonated through the sea, blue and white lightning briefly illuminated the foaming, bubbling waves on the surface along with everything else below, in every area the storm had influence. In one area, a rhomaleosaurus just below a school of fish, it didn't appear intent on attacking. In another, a temnodontosaurus giving birth, the blood cloud of her labour appeared black under the flashes, this one mother unhindered and successfully spawning her progeny in a smooth, chained sequence.

Each flicker of lightning showed a birthed pup swimming away—multiple young revealed within close proximity—and with no visible predators out to get them. One flash illuminated two eurhinosaurus darting into a spooked school of fish in opposing trajectories, the grey-scaled bodies of the fish shimmered a bright silver under the flash, with a disturbed ammonite caught in the centre that would be free from harm by them. With the hybodus though, the activity was more varied; the lightning would reveal near misses, or the process of a killing; one individual had snatched a fish and was shaking the prey apart, tissue and glistening scales scattering to the currents, these natural light shows highlighting just how close predator and potential prey were to each other. That was life flashed in a moment. There were no limits to what angle.

~

It was morning class break at college, and Emily was stood outside the building entrance having a cig with the hood of her blue Juicy draped over her head. The spot smelt strongly of weed, and it wasn't uncommon to have bored or pissed off students come out for a spliff on their break. And Emily hoped no giddy individual would pass her one and accuse her of smoking it, cuz she wasn't in the mood. The reason why was sat to her left on one of the dirty benches; this lass about her age with her son who couldn't have been more than four year old, moaning *"Memmey?"* and jumping about, each call out getting annoyingly louder like he had ADHD or summat. And the mother wasn't doing owt about it; she was just sat there texting on her phone like nowt was happening.

Following last week's incident at the Stanley Parker's Emily didn't bother intervening.

"*MEMMEY?*" The unattended toddler cried painfully loud. Emily hastily finished off her cig then went back inside, the child's calls got louder the further Emily went. Then there was a deafening shriek that must have been heard across the entire street.

"WILL YOU BLOODY PACK IT IN, KYLE?" The mother ordered. Then there was crying from Kyle, along with some words that couldn't be understood. *What a bitch!* It was good to get back inside the college lobby, which had a Christmas tree with simple red and gold tinsel stood up.

While awaiting Denise's return to class Emily was sat down, while about a third of the class was stood up. The closest next to her was Amanda Biggs, who had been off for a couple of days. Biggs was a 16-year-old midget, and skinny to the point of anorexic, her hair was dyed a platinum blonde, the natural dark brown roots showing, and worn into a tall bun. She wore blue fashion lenses over her brown eyes, and her makeup was so excessive; she had these thickly drawn on eyebrows, her lipstick was the palest pink, her foundation was so thick and washed out that it made her pale as a ghost, and the silvery white eye shadow and long, black fake eyelashes didn't help.

All in all, her face didn't look right! Amanda Biggs looked like a doll! What did she even look like underneath all that cosmetic? And what would she consider going for next? Botox? She was so young! It was somewhat tragic to think about, but no one was going to say anything about her in ear range. Amanda's reasons for being off class…? The speculation wasn't limited to bulimia or owt. Biggs never arrived to class in uniform, she had to show off what she was wearing before changing and it was always a combination of Uggs and designer leggings, which didn't always go too well together. Emily didn't find Amanda to be particularly interesting anyway. "Ghost girl" was an appropriate nickname for her!

Meanwhile, Beth Huxley was going on a tangent, this was common of her, and everyone in class could hear her whether they wished to or not.

"This cunt wouldn't fuckin' serve me! He said: *I were drunk*, but I were fuck all!"

Beth was so hormonal; she had revealed she had been banged up a couple of times, had admitted to shoplifting and constantly tried to give off this alpha female vibe to everyone. And because of that Emily didn't feel comfortable having a night out with her, and she was sure plenty of the lasses in class felt the same. But it was Jasmine Cartney that was making everyone's day; she couldn't stop laughing about summat, and it had everyone else laughing!

"The fuck's *gargalation process*!" asked Zoe Burton from her throat to sound mystified.

"I dunno!" Jasmine said with Emily resisting to tell her that it sounded like some procedure at the sewers to filter all the crap from the water or summat. But no one here wanted to hear that!

"Some fella in the queue at KayGee's were chattin' up me mates," Jasmine answered, "He must have been on summat cuz he were just sayin': *gargalation process!* And he were goin' on bout Koala bears!"

"I like them thingies!" Lauren Rotherford said with an endearing voice tone, the curved-nosed brunette and former gymnast, with a medium height sock bun and tattoo on the back of her right hand, could be random at certain moments, but other than that she was normal like everyone else.

"He were lovely though!" Jasmine said almost defensively then laughed. She was going to have a sore throat tonight! No surprise if she didn't come in tomorrow!

Isabelle Woodhouse arrived in class late. She had no bother from Denise as the Aussie had called in advance, and Denise had told everyone, with the class bantering on about the possibilities and reasons for such. Isabelle had a rough look on her face, like she had just been given bad news over money or visa matters, which concurred with that unanimous class speculation. And no one asked her why she didn't have a red streak in her hair. Isabelle sat at her desk while Emily observed the combing marks of the hair at the back of her head for her high ponytail, which were prominently visible and layered. She fumbled through her handbag, took out this folded up piece of paper then spread it out and pinned it up on the upper right corner of her corkboard mirror frame with some of the available pins stuck in. It turned out that it was a drawing of Isabelle herself, done from the left side while looking down with her high ponytail, though with the collar of a dark overcoat present, a dark, shaded background surrounding her face. The whole class was peering in.

"Who did that?"

"That's sick!"

"Where'd yah get that?"

There were a dozen variations of the same response going about the class. In response, Isabelle put on a controlled grin, but her cheeks blushed. She raised her eyebrows then answered, "This bloke at the bar."

"Someone fancies yah!" Zoe pried. And who could blame any bloke for wanting to do a portrait of Isabelle Woodhouse? Emily crept around the row of desks for a look and saw that it was indeed a very good drawing! Not perfect, as there were scribbled edges, sort of like them police profile sketches for suspects as though done in a rush, but summat you should feel bad chucking away. The artist had signed the work in a very stylish way; a **J.K.** with a ribbon-like effect done by maybe a white marker or summat in the lower right corner.

"How much were it?" Asked Amanda, her voice sounded like a childish babble.

"He didn't charge!"

The "arrr" of Isabelle's accent stuck.

"Were he fit?" Jasmine asked looking like she was ready to probe like half the class.

"He was okay…!" Isabelle delayed her answer.

"A bit weird though…!" She added.

~

At lunchtime, Emily went out front for another cig then went across the road to the deli for a chicken and bacon sandwich bought with the remaining change from the fiver Mum gave her. From there, it was a very normal day at beauty class, Jasmine having given up with the gargalation process stuff. After the 3 o'clock finish, Emily was joined on her way out by Isabelle. The Aussie was two years older than Emily, leaner in the thighs and had a different walk; it was confident like a gymnast before doing some crazy acrobatic in front of thousands of spectators. Aussies were an active lot. Isabelle went into her locker nearly halfway down the corridor to the right of class, grabbed a packed carrier bag then went into the ladies. Emily had to go, checked her appearance with her compact mirror, and by the time she exited the cubicle Isabelle had undone her ponytail and changed into her work clothes, which were a black sweater, light blue jeans and these really fit boots, which were black, over-knee height, made of suede, had short heels and brass studs. Isabelle wore them just about everywhere except class, and Emily wanted a pair, though didn't know what she could wear them with, this time of the year anyway.

Isabelle was combing her hair, keeping the centre partings straight.

"Where'd you get them?"

"They're from Moore's."

Moore's, the most popular place in town and a Thewlie exclusive, not a chain like Primark. And there was summat every lass wanted in Moore's.

"How much?" Emily asked her Aussie classmate.

"Two hundred pounds."

"Bloody hell!" Emily said quickly then added, "I'll have to wait until I start work."

"You doing bar work again?"

It sounded like Isabelle was offering her a job!

"Applying for Zaks and Marias in L.O.Z's." Emily replied.

"I like that bar!" Isabelle said, her pronunciation really emphasised.

~

Emily didn't head for her regular 175 bus stop, which was outside this smoothie shop outside the Longford Centre, feeling a bit adventurous she went west and walked a little further along Holden Lane up until the Bradshaw Post, which was an ancient pub for them older working class blokes. But that wasn't where she was going, in fact she went into Si Hong Suns, town's only Chinese supermarket, with an upstairs restaurant and adjoining Indian restaurant, it was also on route to a 175 bus stop on lower Furnivall Road a couple of blocks away. The supermarket was small with narrow aisles, and it was packed with foreign produce and busy so you had to move out the way for someone and were put off looking too long.

There was some Christmas decor put up in store probably to please the locals, and unlike Leeds there weren't many Orientals living in Thewlington, and Emily had always been curious about people from that part of the world despite the racist opinions of her peers. And Emily had been in this shop many times, on her own mind you. There was a very distinctive stinking odour about the place. Well…It really wasn't that bad, as in sick-on-the-floor-bad—it was summat you'd get used to quite quickly if exposed to for a few days, and Emily was certain that the source was durian, that spiky melon-sized fruit of infamy; and there was a batch stood up on a shelf and held back with cord.

There were so many weird things: yams, summat called **lotus root**, green vegetables that came in every shape you could think of, dried squid and fish, fridges full of tofu, fresh noodles of all shapes and thickness, dim sum, and all these instant noodles with these flavours Emily didn't know about, snacks that were seaweed flavoured, these sweets that had *bean paste* in them of all things or were green tea flavoured, and so many varieties of hot sauces that might make you consider wearing nappies for a few days! Emily left the store with a full carrier bag with Chinese lettering which, to avoid having a finger pointed at her with all them obnoxious Thewlies, stuffed into her handbag, though it really did overcrowd it.

She had been stood freezing in the dark, breathing ice clouds for nearly half an hour now on Furnivall Road with a crowd of commuters, earphones in so hopefully no one dodgy would come up and bother her. It was an unremarkable crowd of moody, miserable people Emily had become familiar with for most of college term, and sat a few yards away was this beggar mumbling for spare change, who had a badly done, unrecognisable tattoo on his left cheek and wore a black winter cap with earflaps. He was always seen suspiciously with a clean shave, wore some brand-new-looking designer trainers, and could be seen sipping away at a bottle of red wine he kept hidden underneath his coat. Emily didn't give him owt.

Then the 175 bus arrived, and there was another one behind it! Since everyone was getting on the first bus she went for the second and sat upstairs three seats away from the back, the fella next to her was quiet, which was a good thing… Halfway down Harewood Road, the longest main road in the city, and approaching the inner suburbs of Carlin Venture, which had the nearest police station to home, was an all-boys secondary school somewhere nearby, which you couldn't see from either side of the road behind the rows of houses. And all these teenage lads came thundering upstairs, making their way towards the back, unable to tone down their ravings and acting like bellends. This was the worst part of a college day! Listening to music didn't help, Emily's present track was the Saturday's *"Ego"*, the lads began stomping, whether stood up or sat down, and had to make their insufferable presence felt by every sense; they swore, said obnoxious shite, opened up bags of crisps and left a mess on the floor and seats, chewed with their mouths open, and thought it was gentlemanly to belch and get all gassy that Emily discreetly had to hold her nose.

Then the lads began pointing out people with scapegoating quotes:

"Who farted? Were it you?"

"Were it him?"

"Were it her?"

"No, it were you!"

"Fuck off! It were that guy there!"

Emily was kicking herself for not getting her driver's license sooner! This one lad, ugly and freckled as sin with prickly spiked blonde hair was like the leader, it was obvious as he was the worst of the lot, acting like he had summat to prove and stormed halfway down the aisle and started dancing, flailing, not caring that he would hit someone. He needed a slap to sort him out!

"K'at him!" He pointed to the bus's front window at some fella seen getting off on the bus in front, which sadly also had a bunch of lads causing grief to the passengers.

"K'at him!" The rest of his gang followed, pointing out to people unseen on the dark streets, their fingers switching between individuals.

"K'at im!" They deepened their voices, making a poor attempt to sound like a hard, thirty summat year old. Now, for anyone who wasn't familiar with the Thewlie dialect, "kat him" was supposed to mean: "Look at him!"

"*Kim!*" One of them said thickly with dread and was parroted back by a mate. No, these divs weren't referring to someone by name, it was a further downgrade of the previous downgrade. And it wasn't even Thewlie, too lazy to enunciate it was the simplest a sentence could get!

"*Im!*" One lad called out, sounding like he was gonna throw up and was met with childish giggles. The K for "Kim" was absent! It was truly terrifying to see language be degraded to such a low level—next thing it would just be guttural, constipated noises!

"She's fit!" One of the lads pointed at Emily, she just saw him in the corner of her eye as she looked away, saw that he had a brown bowl cut he probably had the piss taken out of at some point.

"She's *really* fit!" His mate said and winked. Emily looked away, and it wasn't too long until a crisp flew by her face. Though it was accidental it still wasn't right.

"Pack it in, eh?" Emily said without raising her voice having reached breaking point. The other passengers looked at her, and to piss her off more none of these lot had the decency to back her up, and not once during these journeys back had the bus driver kicked them off, or at least come up to have word with them.

"Ooooooohhh!" Hollered out multiple lads at once, which had several passengers frown visibly.

"You're a right tight knobhead you!" One of them addressed whomever had chucked the crisp, as though it was meant to make Emily feel better. She wanted to slap them rather than scream, but instead she got up and went downstairs and sat in the space next to a middle-aged woman who looked just as pissed off as she was. Upstairs the lads were hollering out victoriously, praising themselves on how they had made her move—*fuck off...!*

"Good God...!" The woman next to her said then looked at Emily.

"They'll *never* be men!"

~

The nightmare that was known as the bus ride back was over for one night. Back home Emily was calm, dressed into her trackies, for tonight it was a brown velour two piece. She made herself a cup of Jasmine tea and was munching away at a bag of Japanese rice crackers, one of five bags she had purchased from the Chinese supermarket, which had either salted, seaweed and spicy. And you know what? They were absolutely delicious; Emily was munching through her second bag already! At least she didn't need to worry about putting on weight as these were very low fat—she might just have to stop eating crisps from now on and switch to these. Sat alone in the living room on her laptop she was watching a Japanese drama film, with subtitles of course. There was no proper title for the film, the clip just said: **Kashiwagi Japanese film 2008**, as though that was simple enough. Kashiwagi, that was a funny sounding name – must be the director! It was a different film experience and dubbing could be a bit misleading and sounded hammy, but if you could be bothered reading the subtitles then you were getting the story, but at low volume, so no one nosy passing by didn't hear.

Anyway, Japanese film by this Kashiwagi was about some American gangster group lot that were pissed off about summat in Tokyo, and a gangster group there were angry about some family in L.A. and had gotten the wrong idea about some member of that family and had sent their son to see his cousin in L.A. to restore *honour* and some crap like that. Emily was halfway through the film, the film's protagonist was this tubby Japanese lad wearing a blue frat boy style jacket and yellow sports hat, walking down a steamy alleyway lined with packed rubbish bins. Emily knew summat bad was gonna happen. A gang of lads, dressed up like punk rockers, stepped out from behind the rubbish bins.

"Yeah, that him!" One of them pointed out then ran at him, turned out they were a bunch of bullies ganging up on him.

"S'up *kimchi*?" A black fella with shades and an ultra-thin goatee called out and giggled. The fat lad tried to run but didn't get too far. The punks surrounded him then grabbed him from behind and took both arms, there was this daft, quick paced drumming in the background.

"Yamada!" Tubby lad screamed. Subtitle: **Let me go!**

"Yamaro!" Tubby lad screamed and repeated. **Stop it!** Subtitle said.

"What's he sayin man?" Someone said with the gang laughing and giggling to it.

"*Yeh me gu!*" Tubby lad pled, eyes squinted and head shaking. Was that as in: "Let me go"? There was no subtitle. Emily snorted a suppressed laugh.

"Yeh me gu!" Tubby kid demanded looking like he was about to vomit, "*FAH YU!*" He spat. As in: "Fuck you!" Again, no subtitle. Tubby lad spat saliva at the closest fella, who just smirked, calmly raised his hand to his face and wiped off the spit, then wiped it viciously against tubby lad's sleeve.

"Fuck me? Fuck me?" The spat on bloke said back rather angrily, with Emily sure he was going to punch the tubby lad.

Then this other fella stepped in, he was wearing a black woolly hat and was cross-eyed.

"*Why not all of us?*" He said, giggled like a psycho then took off his hat. There was this thing on his head that flopped down the side of his face: it looked like a pink, rubbery snake/dildo thingy with a yellow eyeball at its end! It looked like it had come out from his skull… The gang members recoiled in laughter seeing it, while the cross-eyed punk started making blowjob gestures to tubby lad, that spurred on more laughs from his mates.

"Can I join in as well?" Giggled one of them.

"Oh God…!" Emily breathed now regretting she had clicked on the film!

"*IEEEE…!*" Tubby fella squinted and cried out hysterically. Subtitle: **No!** His efforts were getting him nowhere, and the director of the film had all these close up shots of every gang member, who all had dodgy faces; one of them had a massive nose ring. And *what* was that bloody thing on the cross-eyed lad's head? Then the film went to a shot of this other fella—maybe he was the leader as the shot was longer, he was a black fella with a curved nose and these really nasty eyebrows. He nodded his head at the drama and smiled.

"Perfect…!" He said.

There was this tall bald fella that stepped out from the crowd, he had a skinhead look to him and was wearing a muscle vest, even though the pair of earrings he wore was a bit queer. This bell and chime sound came on. The bald fella smiled and real *slowly* folded his arms and nodded in delight, like a pervert. Tubby lad paused, looking horrified by the sight of him then screamed.

Somehow breaking free of those lot restraining him, who looked really surprised. Tubby kid quickly looked around then picked up a rubbish bin, one of them old rounded metal ones, for some reason was empty, then charged screaming towards the bald fella in the vest, who was just stood there. And he allowed himself to be knocked out with a really loud clang, which you could tell a dummy was used for the stunt! Emily gasped with laughter. Tubby kid turned and faced the crowd and shouted, "*Bakayaro!*"

Subtitle: **Bastard!** He spat on the floor like it was the first time he had done so.

"You want more?" Tubby lad taunted. "Fah yu! You want?"

This black fella stepped forward with this dopey look on his face like he had just smoked a gram of weed all at once.

"He ain't the boss, samurai nigga!" He corrected with a very husky voice. Black people just had to say the N word!

Then this short fella with a mop of blonde hair, a *really* tight red vest and running shorts appeared from behind the dumpsters, his body lowered into a squat and walking sideways like a crab with both hands hanging down to the floor as though holding summat really heavy.

"Not boss-not boss!" He muttered intensely like a handicapped child with some monkey-like expressions.

He wiped his nose with his thumb, made the most stupid face and glared at tubby lad, teeth exposed, jaw moving about, lips moving in all directions and growling quietly. Then a shot of the sky, with a bird flying past for cinematic effect… Girly, puffy screams were heard, along with these suspicious sucking/chewing sounds. Whose were they…? White Japanese lettering appeared against the sky, but there was no translation below—*ok, that was helpful!*

The Japanese made a lot of weird stuff!

"Fuck me...!" Emily laughed safe in the realm of fiction and felt like heading to the fridge to pour herself a glass of wine. And before she could she heard the front door being unlocked then opened.

"Good God!" Mum was heard cursing, most likely due to the cold outside. Emily paused the ridiculous film and turned around, saw Mum step in, setting down two bulky bags of shopping on the floor. Her face was orange as an ice lolly from the bottled tan, her hair parted in the centre, she hung up the thick black winter coat she was wearing revealing a blindly orange velour tracksuit underneath. At first, Emily thought her Mum's trackie was Juicy, but turned out it wasn't, though it looked really nice on Mum, and Emily wanted summat similar, pink or red. And they looked good with Uggs. But Mum wasn't wearing Uggs, she was wearing these tall, black leather boots with flat soles, ideal for when there was snow.

"Where'd you get that?" Emily asked while stuffing her mouth.

"Got it just last minute at the charity shop before they closed—they just sold it to us!" Mum replied looking in the dotted, brass frame hallway mirror, constantly throwing back her hair which had evidently had some fresh treatment at the hairdresser's in that it was ultra-shiny and silky.

Emily half jumped hearing a bang against the window. Every year there was one for each house on the street by the local scallywag kids, but from snowballs, and there was no snow about.

"*A slag lives there!*" A child's voice could be heard muttering outside.

"Fuckin' little gits!" Mum cursed while checking herself in the mirror. Emily didn't go to investigate.

"Do I look nice, me love?" Mum asked sulking.

"You're lovely, Mum!" Emily answered spilling a bit of sarcasm her way. Mum was keeping up with that Essex lass personality, minus the poshness.

There was a knock on the door. Was it them mischievous wankers again? Mum immediately went for the door, quietly hissing incoherent words, opened the door and without her consent in stepped this tall, well-built fella wearing a leather jacket with a hoodie underneath.

"This is Bryant," Mum introduced.

"He plays rugby!"

Rugby player… Mum had slept with so many, successful or not. Emily had been very good at sports during school but never took any interest in them, and she had been to a couple of footie and rugby matches just to get a look at them lovely bums and muscles. This Bryant fella's face though was very rectangular, he had this dopey-eyed look and this ridiculously tall quiff! While he was certainly fit, as in physical, he wasn't fit as in handsome—Emily's version anyway.

"Alright…?" He mumbled as he passed by Emily without making those typical flattery remarks she had so gotten used to, then buried his face in Mum's bosom. Then he stopped and looked up at Emily dimly.

"This your lass?" He said with widening eyes.

"She joining us or what?" Bryant mumbled, Emily could smell booze on him and wondered how much he had had before coming here.

"Shut up yah thick cunt!" Mum laughed.

"She's me baby, she dun't want a bloke!"

Emily cleared her throat.

"Pardon?" She exclaimed and caught the smirk of her Mum's partner, which was wider than his eyelids.

Mum just grunted dismissively to her daughter's protest then began snogging Bryant, who liberally proceeded to grope her bum, while she murmured and unzipped her orange trackie top. Emily rolled her eyes away.

"In here?" Mum complained and started guiding her beastly partner into the living room, away from her daughter.

Emily went into the kitchen, opened the fridge and poured herself a glass of the rosé that was in then retreated upstairs to her room, where she did some homework on her laptop while listening to *closer* by Nine Inch Nails.

"Do us in will yah?" Mum could be heard moaning over the music. A smirking Emily frowned, owning an internet camera she could maybe start a vlog and upload this moment. But that wouldn't be right!

"Oh fuckin' hell!"

Hearing that from downstairs Emily took a sip of wine.

"Argh!" Mum screamed as if she had stubbed her toe. Emily laughed with a half full mouth and sputtered wine out from her mouth over her bed, glad she wasn't online! Men for yah!

Chapter 4

Tuesday. After getting out of bed, Emily crept around on her tiptoes, and somewhat cautiously as she got ready for college. During the simple journey downstairs to the front door there was no sign of Bryant, and Emily didn't want to so much as look at him or respond to a comment. Gangster fella wasn't sat on the bus, and in class Jasmine didn't have owt hilarious to say, though Beth Huxley was moaning on about how supposedly unfair it was that she was being denied access to college just because *the doorman were black*, though she didn't even have her ID to begin with. Denise had to tell her to calm down. But the subject of interest today was about Isabelle, who had that job done at the hairdresser's which had been meant for the weekend, she had a bright red/purple streak in her ponytail, which was really nice. And the Aussie still had her portrait pinned up. On the bus back home, Emily had no hassle from them lads, as she was sat at the very back with plenty of people taking up the seats in front of her for several rows. She could just listen to her music in peace!

Later that evening Emily was upstairs in her room on the internet, wearing her bathrobe and her hair wrapped up in a turban. She was drinking a can of cream soda and listening to Leona Lewis' *better in time*, while messaging Abigail Hartley, Denise's daughter, who was only just sixteen. Abby didn't look much like her mother; she was smoky dark like Cheryl Cole with big brown eyes, wore similar styled eyeliner and long brown hair, ruthlessly straightened. And she was a very good-looking lass. Emily was envious of all the new clothes Abby had posted in photos, with her smugly holding them up and posing with them.

Emily removed her turban, revealing dyed black hair. She had nipped up to Hoperwood Beck's shopping centre an hour ago for a box of hair dye. There was another event on tonight at the Stanley Parker's, fancy dress and discount booze on offer. Initially Emily didn't know what to wear. But upon arriving back home from town Mum, had told her a story about how she had gone past Garbot Arndale, and saw a mother and daughter pair, goth types all dressed up, and that she had liked their appearance. She had had a word with them, took a photo with them and gone off to do some additional shopping.

At least, Mum had some ideas for tonight! Halloween just gone by, Emily had gone dressed up as a Greek goddess, she had made her own outfit out of white duvet sheets, which she had cut up and sewn together, and that golden leaf decoration thingy they wore on their heads she had ordered long in advance. The outfit would have been better for summer though as it had been cold! After another two hours Emily was just finishing up, she had plenty of eyeliner and black eye shadow on already and was applying some moose to the top of her hair, which gave it a feathery texture and put a red rose clip accessory in her hair on the left.

She had borrowed some fake eyelashes from her mother, which Emily very rarely wore, yet went well with the outfit. She didn't have any black lipstick in her makeup kit, so she just stuck with bright red. Her outfit involved a black T-shirt with white graphic print under a grey/black denim vest, biker style with studs on the shoulder, which Mum had got her from Garbot Arndale today, though hadn't revealed the price of it, glossy black wet look leggings to imitate the look of leather, a thick, black studded waist belt for sophistication, and some black leather booties with short heels and solid buckles and thick, woolly black leg warmers. She didn't have them big chunky goth boots nor would she dare consider wearing them! Looking in the mirror it was quite the transformation!

Sure you don't wanna make your face corpse pale with white foundation? Emily thought as she turned left and right, inspecting herself from countless angles. She took her crucifix pendant out from under her T-shirt and let it fall in front of it. Satisfied with her efforts she went downstairs. Mum was sat on the sofa, her already dyed black hair had big corkscrew curls, she was blasting her hair with hairspray and the living room was saturated with the stuff that it was stinging Emily's sinuses. Mum turned around, she too wore red lipstick and fake eyelashes, though twice as long as the ones her daughter wore.

"Show your tits off!" She ordered (how many times counting now?) upon seeing her T-shirt.

"Erh, no!" Emily objected.

"I'm gonna *nick* 'em off yah one of these days!" Mum said then rudely added, "You're never gonna get a bloke!" Emily dropped her mouth open but didn't say owt back.

Mum's outfit tonight was far more revealing; a low cut black sleeveless top with a black leather waist coat worn over, really saucy cropped black leather shorts that revealed plenty of her arse cheeks, these transparent leggings with a thorn tribal tattoo print and long, leather black boots with the old pointy fronts and stiletto heels. Mum was the only person about who seemed to be wearing them, other than some of those Asian women you did see in town. Emily didn't mind wearing tight clothing or really high heels at all, but she couldn't walk in them stilettos, she had tried when her mother had bought her a pair on her fifteenth birthday, had worn them with blue denim. Them pointed fronts were just too tight on her toes and she had fallen over, nearly knackering her right wrist. Shame on the family!

A knock on the door, Emily answered and not too hesitantly. There was a tall woman stood there, outwardly looked like she was in her mid-forties, had a lovely figure similar to Mum's, blonde hair just short of shoulder length, with a fringe and a slightly wavy texture. She had a tense expression, her wrinkles masked with foundation and her makeup was simple and refined with blue eye shadow, mascara and pink lip stick and was dressed sensibly for a night out; a white denim jacket, a pink top of some sort underneath with all these black graphic characters, white jeans and her black suede platform heel boots made her tower a couple of inches more over Emily.

It was Mandy Nicole, her grandmother. She was 57 years of age, but looked 10 years younger thanks to an active lifestyle and careful diet, as well as a little bit of Botox, unlike Mum who went over the top with rejuvenation products, drank to excess and was aging too quickly for her comfort. And aside from a longer nose, pastier, blemished skin and green/blue eyes, Nan bore a stronger resemblance to Emily, her eyes were closer in shape, her jaw line identical, her breasts from age were naturally busty, the same size as her granddaughter's, and would probably look similar in forty years' time. And she hadn't had any implants, *leave 'em alone!* Nan would say. She was actually very nice to look at. Forget MILF—this was a grandma the lads would like to shag! Gorgeous ran in the family—what was Emily's child gonna look like? It was a very tender thing to ponder over.

"Y'alright me dear?" She breathed an ice cloud in Emily's face. Nan had a slow voice, like speaking the moment after doing a shot of vodka and had a steady Yorkshire accent. She looked at her granddaughter toe to head.

"You look like a *vampire!*" She commented without any emotion.

"Mum's idea!" Emily defended stepping aside to let Nan in, who gave her a kiss on the cheek.

~

The Nicole's took a taxi ride up to the Stanley Parker's each of them having to endure being chat up by the driver, who knew the way fortunately. Black Eyed Peas *I gotta feeling* was playing on the radio, and Emily regretted having not filled up her stomach properly this evening due to her being preoccupied getting ready over the sudden decision to go out tonight. She wanted a curry—a jalfrezi or korma would be nice, but it wasn't like Mum was going to stop off at some place before the pub. All three eating out together could be a bit difficult, if not boring; like Mum, Nan didn't like *anything* foreign and hadn't been any further than the Mediterranean and didn't speak any other language, except for a bit of Gaelic she had heard during her childhood. English was acceptable—mainly a carvery on Sundays, as was fish and chips, pizza, and them Italian places Mum didn't mind, but Nan was funny with owt spicy which was a proper shame!

The three stepped out of the taxi, there were plenty of people stood outside the pub having a fag. As always, the gorgeous Nicole family drew attention wherever they went. Although Emily and Mum's makeup tonight was already getting some ridicule, their outfits were concealed beneath their thick overcoats. They stepped into the Stanley Parker's warmth, Shakira's *"She Wolf"* was playing and the pub had its Christmas decor up, white Christmas lights nailed up on the bar and a small Christmas tree in each corner. Despite it being a fancy dress occasion, there was literally no one about in fancy dress, or anything that could be seen as fancy and that was just bad, if not embarrassing like a nightclub where no one danced! Emily felt a pinch of relief seeing Karl the barman dressed up; he had this ridiculously tall leprechaun hat on his head as well as a green cape with a massive buckle over his shoulders. Well…cuz he was a ginner! Emily unbuttoned her coat and saw a bunch of lasses queuing on the other side of the bar wearing angel wings and pink ballerina skirts—bet they were off clubbing in town later on.

There was another fella dressed up in a sailor's outfit on Emily's side of the bar, and stood further back was the Flibbigan's cunt, frowning more than usual when he could just piss off out of here for tonight if he didn't like what he was seeing. While the pub did serve food, people from neighbouring districts had flooded the place tonight, so it would be a wait—best to order a takeout later.

"Nice outfit Nick!" Karl acknowledged, ready to serve.

"Tah! Why aren't more dressed up?" Emily asked while Karl shrugged. Emily ordered two bottles of rosé and a packet of spicy flavoured crisps then looked around the pub, saw Mum and Nan moving to the left side of the pub for a place to sit, and then set her eyes on a table to the right of the pub beyond the pool table, right against the window with a view of the car park and the venue's high standing sign. There was a group of lasses sat there, the table cluttered with plates of food, crisp packets, pint glasses full and empty.

Emily brought over the wine and glasses for Mum and Nan, poured herself a glass, told them she would be with them in a moment then went to that table by the window. Feet away from approaching she heard childish hollering over the music, she knew was addressed at her. Emily sat down at the table, facing the car park directly, folded her coat up, revealing her outfit to the pub and received an assault of giggles and disses from the occupants of the table and patrons stood nearby.

"Halloween were like last month!"

"Ear Nick? You look like an emo!"

"I fuckin' hate emos!"

Couldn't anyone tell the difference between subcultures? These sad lot were Emily's mates, had been since primary school. Back then they were a lovely lot, nothing short of sisters for the ones she never had. Halfway through secondary school that quickly changed. Now they had changed too much for comfort. Yet still, they were all she had. Last time Emily had got together with one of them was two weeks ago—and that was the longest she had gone. She hoped that the absence would get longer and longer until they didn't even notice.

Starting to Emily's left there was Gemma, she was 20-years-old and quite lovely, her face smothered in fake tan, her serious-looking brown eyes treated with eyeliner so as to look like Cheryl Cole, her hair dyed blonde and pulled back into a tight ponytail that slacked her face up, allowing her massively hooped, chavy earrings to be seen. Gemma had two children, and had another one planned—her vagina was a bloody machine gun that shot out babies! Gemma had been married once, the marriage hadn't lasted more than a couple of months, and now she was asking her latest boyfriend to propose to her. Gemma's older half-sister Stacy, sat at the table's corner never left her side, unlike her sibling she wasn't attractive. Stacy looked like she was in her late-thirties, even though she was only 21, she had a curved nose, long filthy dark blonde hair parted in the centre, and was skinny as sin with the white body vest she wore showing off her tent pole arms, her right hand coiled around a pint. Like her half-sister, Stacy had serious-looking brown eyes, except they were beady in appearance and in an appalling constant state of aggression. She hadn't married, yet had two children, and at times Emily had babysat for her, free of charge, out of pity.

Heather, sat next to Emily on the right, was the only one who didn't have children to interfere with her life, was lovely—almost angelic with long natural blonde hair and piercing crystal blue eyes, that had a nervous, laughably quick motion to them like a bird's. Heather was a hypersensitive crybaby who had sympathy for others, yet didn't know how to manage it—badly enough she ended up being sympathetic for the wrong people, such as convicts. She was so gullible she had been taken advantage of. And she also went in the opposite end of that extreme; she had called the police and delayed a bus just because some lad had been chatting her up. Truth was she was a pitiful liability to anyone in her company.

Directly across from Emily was Jody, who was blocking most of the view of the car park with her wide frame. She was a joke. She might as well be wearing a costume with the way she looked; she was big—maybe 20 plus stone and absolutely horrible to look at. Jody's dyed purple hair was worn into a big pineapple bun, and her bulging double chin gave her a frog throat appearance, and her head seemed to be tilted back all the time with this judgemental look to her addressed at everyone…Even if she was going to need a wheelchair to move about soon. She had a massive plate of chips in front of her topped with an unhealthy amount of ketchup, a near finished piece of burger and several packets of crisps. Jody ate shite all day; snack food, stuff out of tins, cheap microwave meals and made the shittiest breakfast ever with nil effort, and it was that full breakfast crap *in a can* they sold at the supermarkets, unhealthy and horrid—and Emily hadn't managed three spoonfuls of that and had felt poorly for the rest of the day. Like most of the patrons in the pub, Emily's mates weren't even dressed right for tonight.

Wifey for lifey was playing, and a couple of shots of sambuca had been ordered. Emily was what you might call…a "well-rounded" drinker, one who paced herself, trying not to mix wine with lager and had a snack between drinks so as not to get tipsy too quickly or wee so often. She didn't find it funny trying to keep up with the drinking manners of the lads, who went absolutely mental, violent even and would chuck up, spewing sick all over the floor inside or outside the pub. Emily didn't want to know how bad it smelt in the men's room! Everyone at the table downed a shot, then Gemma and Jody did most of the talking, as they always did. The two spoke *absolute* shite, most of it so crude and offensive that some countries might not allow them to step off a plane. They thought Pakistan and India were the same culture, they had no plans to learn owt, a good effort of which would help dispel the bad reputation of young people in this part of the city.

Gemma, Stacy and Jody had scarily addictive personalities; they weren't afraid to knock on peoples doors for a cig or spare change, would hold up queues and buses, and if there was just one minor difference in price would ask the driver to "turn back" if they missed their stop. They'd get pissed in clubs and throw up anywhere they felt like, would gob off at bouncers and coppers and would report it proudly the next day to their mates. Emily managed her PMT far better than her mates, and thought of herself as being quite correct, politically, but without being preachy about it. During that time of the month she would rather lash out at some obnoxious cunt pissing her off than someone who was just being nice.

Emily had a pretty good vocabulary, got A's in English, history, religious education, had been good at science and excellent at PE. She had tried really hard not to cry watching documentaries in history class about the holocaust, the Japanese invasion of China and the rapes that followed, whereas everyone else in class just laughed, feeling safe that because they were foreign that it didn't matter. Emily made use of her brain whereas her mates had practically abandoned theirs…as they might do to the children they kept on having, finding out just how difficult it really was to care for them in the long run. But that was talking too deep. In this part of the city, talking eloquently was like speaking another language, summat that was frowned upon—renounced. Use your brain and you were gonna get the piss taken out of you, simple but totally uncalled for! Emily had to lapse back into chav whenever around her mates and anyone they knew. All of these lot at this table, except for herself lived off welfare, and it was these sad lot who couldn't be bothered getting work, and those with actual disabilities were suffering because of it. Fuck the DWP for granting welfare to these sad lot!

It was Jody's turn talking, and she was doing her "workout" as she called it, which involved flexing her disgustingly thick, flabby arms about. She thought wearing a brightly coloured sleeveless vest would make her appear somewhat more attractive.

"I were havin' a contest with these lads and their family, I were challenging them to a burping match!"

She spoke like she had brain damage.

"Lady burps! It's either gonna be fuckin' lady burps or manly burps that win this match! It's about which is loudest!"

How the others managed to go along with it was sickening. Jody felt the need to belch, and it was as bad as any bloke could. Emily was glad she hadn't eaten—she didn't bother eating any of her spicy crisps, preferring to wait as she watched the fat cow pick up what was left of her burger and ate it, while laughing.

"I were askin' me mate: what do yah thinks gonna cause earthquakes if you had one of them set up speakers? Lady burps or manly burps?" Jody was talking while chewing.

"And this lad were laughin' bout me on bout me lady burps! He thought it were right amusing—he looked turned on by it!"

This lad she was on about had real bad taste! Stacy was still as a statue for some reason and looking at the table with this irritable, awkward motion to her cheeks, like she was constipated or summat. Some bloke had actually slapped her in a bar in town a few months ago, and with a bitch face that bad Emily liked to think she knew why…

Jody put some more ketchup over her chips then burped—*shut up, will yah?* Emily cringed then looked to the car park over her wide, fat shoulders, not wanting to see Jody gobble down more shite, and in legendary good timing as she saw an *owl* perch itself on the pub's sign. *Hello!* Emily thought smiling on the inside, puzzled why an owl would choose such a loud place to hang out. The bird turned its head left to right and all them other angles a human couldn't do in quick motion, its dark, button-like eyes meeting Emily's for a blink.

She didn't mention it, even if it might just bring Jody's disgusting ramblings to a pause—as if she cared about anything other than food. Emily wanted to take a photo of the owl—it was so fluffy and cuddly-looking! She remembered a time during primary school when everyone was in assembly and a bird handler had come in to treat the class to a close up of falcons, hawks and owls. To Emily the owl was summat real special; it was the big eyes, short beak and the way it turned its head and the "who-who" noises, and when she came back home she couldn't stop talking about her experience with Mum, begging her to buy her an owl for a pet, wanting one more than a cat or dog. So as a compromise, Mum had bought her an owl soft toy!

Now it was Gemma's turn to be the centre of attention, and it tore Emily's attention away from the owl.

"…So he's like: *do you want a coffee with me?* And I'm like: what…*?*" She had a slimy voice that sounded like shite from some creature living in her throat, her eyes squinty, face creased up, teeth on her upper jaw exposed and her tongue hanging out. She might look nice, but when she made that face she looked like one of them lizards that had them big, scary fan things around their necks!

"Then he's like: *would you like a coffee?* And I'm like: YOU WHAT…?"

Gemma made a piercing and annoying shriek that made you want to jump off a bridge.

"I don't fuckin' like Chinese people!" She added. Poisonous words they were! And Heather didn't look too pleased; if there were Chinese people in the room she would probably panic and try to tell Gemma to calm down.

"Sure he wont Japanese or Taiwanese?" Emily intervened without making eye contact.

"You what?" Gemma barked with hostile eyes.

"What's the bloody *difference*?" Stacy said still frozen in posture with her perpetual scowl, looking like she would try to bite a fly if one flew past her face.

"Very different!" Emily said.

"Different *how*?" Stacy challenged without making eye contact and jerked her head forward dramatically.

"They all look the same!" Gemma sneered in defence while Jody giggled and stuffed her gob with crisps.

Emily wore a toothless grin, as though she was going along with it, but inside she was frowning and irritated. She couldn't fucking wait to leave these lot behind! She was joyful over the thought of having enough money saved up, leave without saying good bye to them and settle in a new home in one of the big cities, then change her number and email, then she could work on finding some more decent mates. While not a princess living in a castle, it wasn't a fantasy.

"I don't find that dodgy!" Emily said without showing any offense to what Gemma had said.

"You what?"

Her mate gave her this look that would have gotten her shot in another country—maybe Burma.

"A nice fella comes up to me and offers me coffee I'd go with him, unless I were busy." Emily said. Gemma waved her off then hastily turned to look at the others to conceal the embarrassment.

"Anyways, I were like: *WHO…THE…FUCK…ARE…YOOOU?*" She hollered loudly like a toddler that didn't get what they wanted, and even started pounding her hands against the table—*argh, just shut up! Who the fuck are you? Bitch!* Emily thought back upon hearing this symphony of shite! How do you let people get away leaving school like that?

"And he were like shittin' himself!" Gemma continued with Emily wanting to get drunk enough that she wouldn't hesitate to slap her. She didn't like calling someone a cunt, actually she never had in fact, but sooner or later she was going to say it to Gemma's face…maybe before their final parting?

During weekends and holidays, while avoiding calls and texts from her mates Emily had got out the city, took a bus into to Leeds by herself and even Bradford for a little solo adventure. She had chatted with as many people as she felt like, including foreigners, as many as she liked—hoping no one saw her doing that— and she loved it. There weren't enough decent foreign restaurants in town like French, Spanish, Japanese or Mexican, the latter she would die for. The last time she had had owt like that was in Leeds. And you shouldn't have to go as far as London for that, and that was expensive. A couple months back, Emily had been out in Manchester for a music event with Jody, Gemma and Stacy, and while wandering about the town she had spotted an advertisement for a Polish polka event on that night a couple of hours before the gig. And Emily really wanted to go. But her mates…they detested the idea, made her feel like she was insane, disturbed. But the real reason was because Jody had difficulty moving about.

Some fella wearing a white sports jacket with a pint glass came up to the table, he didn't look dodgy or owt, he said summat, whether polite or worth complaining about Emily couldn't hear. Stacy turned her head and glared at him.

"What…?" She greeted. The fella said summat—a repeat.

"What…?" Stacy repeated with Gemma turning to look, Jody too preoccupied with her food and Heather just sat with her eyes flicking about. The stranger spoke again.

"WHAT?" Stacy squawked loudly like a child with a tantrum, her tongue stuck out like her sister.

"No…! Go away…!" Gemma said lazily backing her sister up.

"We're fine." Emily said without being nasty or dramatic. Was a simple yes or no so difficult? The fella walked off shaking his head, and who could blame him? Emily felt like making an excuse to go out and have a cig, just so she could see the owl and maybe get a picture, as her mates were talking about football, or pretending they knew summat about the footie like these hopeless wannabe waggers.

"Jamie White's me lover!" Gemma said, her eyes twinkling with reflected light from the pub's Christmas lights.

"Fit bloke!" Jody said raising her left hand in agreement, then with the other crammed chips into her mouth.

"I love him…!" Heather said. Stacy said nowt and continued to scowl, her ugly gaze directed at the space to her left for some reason. Emily grinned and scoffed before taking a sip.

"He's a cunt!" She said.

"Ergh you! Don't take the piss—he's fuckin' lovely!" Gemma complained while Jody laughed with a full mouth.

To you he may be gorgeous, but he's still a cunt! Emily didn't say that though. Mr Jamie White was a role model for the lads, mid fielder for Chelsea and earning millions with fame and everything. But he was a cheater and wife beater who kept repeating and getting away with it, and there were all these stories in the papers about him getting bailed out which made sensible people sick to their stomachs. Not Emily's ideal soul mate, even in youth… She stood up.

"Where the fuck yous off now, eh?" Gemma grilled.

"Fuckin' chills Gem! I'm talkin' to me Nan!" Emily said back without looking at her.

"Yah talkin' to yah nana, man!" Jody said putting on a very bad Jamaican accent then giggled.

Invaders must die was playing and Emily grabbed her crisps, left the freak show and went to the bar for a drink. Karl's assistant who was wearing a red and white Christmas sweater saw her and signalled that she would be with her in a sec. Then someone pushed in to the left.

"I were here!" Emily protested, having to look up at the perpetrator who was this really tall, overweight lad with cropped dark hair, a very unflattering square head and boyish face, these beady brown eyes that really accentuated his bullying stare, he wore a white tracksuit, the flab of his stomach was hanging out and the top of his red underwear exposed. He had a proper chav vibe to him. He had a mate, a shorter, skinny, but still real tall half cast fella, he had a heavily stubbled face, a short afro, wore a T-shirt with a Reggae print, baggy blue jeans and white trainers and had a bruise on his right cheek as though he had been punched a few days ago.

Emily knew who these two were. The lanky bastard was Dominic Newby and the fella with the afro was Mazza Elmwood, the biggest pair of cunts in Barnothcroft. Newby was a kleptomaniac and thick to the point of retarded; he loved to diss and fight people but always got battered in the end, and being so tall and thick-headed anyone could take him down. Mazza was a serial bully who just liked to start with everyone, usually with blokes with girlfriends or family. Like Newby he got karma and loved playing the race card when he got arrested. News about the two sad acts spread across the district with every incident, with quite a few people shocked as to why they both weren't in prison and had the use of their limbs. Newby said summat to Emily, she couldn't make out a word but heard this childish blabber which was more than she needed to give him the evil eye.

"Fuck off, Dom!" She said.

"Stop nickin' stuff!"

Newby blinked, his tongue hanging out of his mouth like a child.

"EH…! What av I done?" He shouted, also sounding like a child.

Mazza stepped in, his posture wobbly and with a very aggressive look on his face, he was very noticeably pissed and couldn't even make eye contact. He mumbled summat and Emily didn't know if what he was saying was stupid or offensive. She just didn't want him or his mate around here.

"Piss off you!" Emily spat.

"You what?" Mazza barked trying to scare her.

"Fuck off!" Emily growled her answer while waving her left hand.

"Grow up you two!"

"You what? I'm fuckin' twenty one!" Mazza protested blinking.

"Ear, Dom?"

This hard-looking middle-aged bloke with a shaved head and leather jacket came up to the two.

"Off!" He ordered motioning his hand towards the door.

"Off, the lot of yah!"

Both Newby and Mazza turned and vacated the pub.

"Fuck sake…!" Newby mumbled like any twat did in these situations. But Mazza wasn't so forgiving and spun around.

"Why? That's savage, mush!" He complained then asked an annoyingly irrelevant question, "*Is it cuz I'm black?*"

Why did black people play the race card all the time? This was the main reason why Emily wasn't too keen on dating a black fella. And she didn't give a toss about what her mates or anyone else said.

"Fuck off!" The bald bloke scoffed, waving Mazza off.

"Fuckin' divs!" He added then looked at Emily with a very amusing smile.

"I saw him get brayed!" He confessed and coughed with laughter—*well hallelujah!* It must have been quite the sight! Emily chuckled.

"Cunt deserves it!" She said, half wishing she had been around to witness it then looked to the pub's entrance, where she saw Mazza gobbing off at some bloke with Newby stepping into view by his side. Emily grinned upon seeing some bloke step in from the left and slap the back of Newby's head and was rewarded with several laughs from unseen blokes.

"Fuckin' lanky knobhead!" One of them said then giggled.

"The fuck you doin'? Fuckin' divy bastard you are!" Mazza complained.

"Come on! You lot'll fuckin' get a back hand off us I swear down!" Another bloke warned. Growing commotion drowned out any recognisable speech from there, though a glass could be heard shattering, drawing even more attention outside with that lass behind the bar wearing the Christmas sweater marching out to investigate.

Nan was sat by herself at a high table facing the centre of the pub, calmly looking through her phone's texts, the drama of no appeal to her. She was a sensible lady who didn't like cussing, she had originally come from some place in South East Ireland she hadn't told Emily of when she was a teenager, and had lost the Paddy accent, but at the heart she was proper Irish; she drank Guinness like the blokes, dealt with shite like a bloke, but better and went to church every Sunday. Nan continued to wear her wedding ring, long after Grandad Rob had died when Emily were only three, and she didn't remember enough of him to feel any sense of sadness. Nan had had a long career as a professional hairdresser at the pricey salons, evidence of that she had on her person; her long fingernails were painted with red nail polish, the ring fingers painted silver, the right of which bore a ring with a massive golden oval face.

Emily sat down with Nan, shortly Mum appeared in the centre of the pub with a bunch of blokes following her like ball bearings to a magnet, which she was.

"Wish she'd wear a higher cut top!" Nan stressed.

"I wish she'd put her arse away sometimes!" Emily stressed back and began to eat her crisps, then watched as more blokes joined in, dancing around Mum competitively for attention, their biceps getting bigger with each new fella! More than half these lot, and a couple of others nearby had their phones out, some were taking photos of Mum. And she was letting them—posing for them! Portraits ok, but them lot were taking photos of her arse! They were gonna have wanks off them and post them online! Then the activity got more alarming; the lads were spanking Mum's arse. And she was spanking herself! *No fuckin' way!* It would be scary if she did this in another country!

"Oi! Fuckin' watch it!" Nan mouthed.

"She's a fuckin' *liberty* her!" One of the passing lads mumbled, drawing the attention of another lad who starred with a very eager, mischievous smile while Mum just kept this dim-witted smile. She was being far too friendly with this lot—if they had done that with Emily she would have slapped them clean across their face, no exceptions! Then again, Mum always loved attention from the blokes.

Mum came over and gave Emily a hug, nearly knocking all the stuff off the table.

"I love you baby!" She said holding on for too long with excessive kisses to the cheek. Emily always reciprocated.

"You're so lovely yous!" Mum sulked then messed about with her already messed up hair.

"She knows you do!" Nan said supportively, but Mum wouldn't give over.

"Deb's!" Nan complained with Mum responding by bobbing her head left and right.

"I'll just go…!" She remarked sarcastically, let Emily go then returned to the crowd, howling then dancing.

"My God…!" Nan cursed. About an hour passed, some patrons were clearing out, and Mum had found her alpha male: a massive fella with close-cropped hair, an orange tan and way too much upper body muscle, but had a hilariously friendly face. Though Mum was unfussy with blokes, they needed to have some qualifications: the blokes had to be in good shape and hard; near cage fighter hard and had a knob that worked. That was pretty much it. But Mum was also a cougar, her partners could be younger; the youngest had just been 20, and Emily was getting a bit concerned of having a potential stepfather her age…

Mum pointed a finger Emily's way, her freshly acquired partner turned and waved to her. Emily lazily reciprocated. Then Mum brought her partner to the table, her arm around his waist and not too far from his bum. Nan turned her head, looked at him with a blank stare and put her fingertips together, rubbing them eagerly.

"That your lass?" Mum's partner asked with a voice as goofy as his face, his eyelids flapping. Emily grinned and nervously looked away.

"She's fit as you!" She heard the bloke say and chuckled, giving him a complimentary, "Tah love!"

"Come…on…!"

Mum took her partner away to dance. While someone of higher class might think of it as a miracle, but to everyone else in this room it might just be blasphemous that Emily didn't have kids, like everyone else in these areas of Thewlie. But there was a simple answer to it all: she *always* had her partners use a condom, even when she was pissed enough to not get served at the bar, and there was like a lifetime supply in her bedside drawer she had collected from free handouts at the many club and gig events she and Mum had been to—so forget that sad excuse of not being able to afford them!

Then Mum and her partner returned again to the table, and with this lad with short blonde hair, nice eyes but a terrible physique, and he had his eyes wide and fixed on Emily. He obviously fancied her, but she didn't fancy him.

"Alright?" He announced with Mum's partner landing a palm down hard on his shoulder.

"Me stepson." He said.

"I'm alright!" Emily declined.

"We're okay…!" Nan backed her.

"We're talkin'!" She firmly added, her voice as sharp as one of them cheese cutters. "Come on…!" Mum begged loudly. Emily shook her head without looking at the two blokes.

"Come on! Let's leave me babes in peace!" Mum said cheekily then escorted the two away.

"Not your sort?" Nan said then looked down at her nails.

"I never liked that Liam or Danny…"

Nan was referring to Emily's previous boyfriends.

"They're not responsible lads them." Nan said before her granddaughter could. Emily didn't say owt. She had been in a relationship twice, both of them during secondary school. They had started out passionately, then quickly turned sour through immaturity, being overly competitive and the big no-no: irresponsible. The opposite of what Emily wanted.

"You're like Princess Diana." Nan said. That had to be a compliment. Emily was only a child when she died, and she didn't know much about her, other than nice things.

"I were gonna tell her (Mum) to name you Diana."

It was quite moving to hear.

"You can be a decent person." Nan added, and it wasn't like saying she'd be a superstar or owt, giving expectations for recognition of false skills. Nan brushed back her hair with her hand then checked messages on her phone. Emily ate some spicy crisps.

"Your cousin Freya, she's not right in the head!" Nan said peering over the frame of her phone. Emily had never seen her, not even a photo.

"She won't go looking for work!" Nan explained.

"She carries spicy stuff in her bag all the time. She don't like English food you see. She's into all that proper spicy foreign stuff."

"Weird…!" Emily remarked somewhat absently. Then again, who could be bothered looking for work?

"She drinks on a morning…" Nan said.

"What, *booze*?" A shocked Emily asked. Nan nodded gently.

"I wouldn't dare drink on a morning!" Emily shuddered.

"She's only fourteen!" Nan added. Not even the age of consent and boozing on a morning, *good God!* For a moment, the alcohol fuelling her imagination, Emily wondered what this relative of hers looked like. Freya was from Mum's supposedly accomplished older sister, Auntie Janice whom she had been estranged from for a very long time and lived far south.

Emily had always been hoping for a chance to see them and spend a day out with them.

"You alright for money?" Nan asked.

"Sound!" Emily said.

"I'm not planning on movin' yet or owt. Just waitin' for a new job soon."

She didn't want to burden anyone, there was more pride in it—she was a worker and a fighter.

"No new boyfriend yet?" Nan questioned with a steady stare, her eyes seemed to glow.

"Oh no…!" Emily answered, resisting the need to giggle, which she was sure pissed off some people. She liked her fellas to be interesting and a bit modest, but driven, committed and nice. None of them requirements existed in this pub. *Anyone here who isn't obsessed with football?*

"Every fella I've met…they're all the same!" Emily said then knocked back some wine. "Nowt interesting bout 'em." She finished. Emily didn't want to think of herself as being selfish, awkward or needy—pragmatic—was more like it. *Take us to the cinema each month. Pay the bill when we eat out. Don't belch at the table! And if you feel the need to fart, do it where I can't smell it! Don't cheat! If I'm chatting with an interesting bloke then don't get blooming paranoid! I'm not cheating on yah! And buy us a decent curry every Friday night! Maybe a bottle of wine? On me birthday though I do expect to go a bit mental—buy us and pop open some champagne!*

It wasn't asking for too much really! *And do pay the telly bill for us though!* Emily would buy her own trackies and trainers. But if she needed intimacy she needed it soon! *Make sure you han't drank too much—the knob needs to be working!* Bold but simple. She finished off the rest of her wine.

"You wantin' another drink Emily?" Nan asked.

"Yeah please!"

While fumbling through her pursue, Nan looked on at Mum, who was chafing her legs while bent forward, the act not going unnoticed with a phone camera flashing from the crowd, which illuminated the sheen of her leather shorts.

"Look! She's done it again!" Nan said then leaned in and whispered into Emily's ear.

"Don't tell her this," she said with Emily bracing herself, wondering what was coming.

"I love you *more* than her!" Nan said then gave Emily a kiss on the cheek before she could react.

~

It was just after midnight when Mum had decided to call a cab. Nan took a pricy taxi back home to Bramley Leeds. Emily didn't want to say goodbye to her pathetic mates, but that couldn't be helped as they came up pissed to the table, and took them more than five minutes to say bye and had to include plenty of disgusting comments. And Jody had to burp—she might as well start her own bloody video channel! Gemma had pulled some fella, and Stacy had fuck all to say about him as she was so drunk and moody and just wanted to go to bed. Mum's new partner had a name: Wiggy, and he was all over her every couple of steps, they stopped to have a snog and grope each other. Back home everyone was sat in the living room, the radiator on and a club remix of Red Carpet's "*Alright*" playing, which was great as a finishing track in a nightclub before closing, or while you were watching the sunrise.

Mum and Wiggy were sat on the sofa, Emily was glad she had stopped in at the off license before going out so she could have a glass with Mum before bed. Absolutely famished, she had ordered takeout on the taxi ride back, and just in time as the takeouts closed soon! Food came and was paid courteous of Wiggy. Emily had ordered a chicken jalfrezi, Mum wasn't bothered but Wiggy was more enthusiastic and had ordered a 12-inch pizza to share. Emily stuffed herself with curry, drunk she didn't care how she appeared, was reluctant to laugh and was getting tiered, glad she wasn't on her period. Satisfied with her meal Emily exhaled dwelling over tomorrow morning, how bad her hangover would be, if she could make it out of bed in time for college.

With that, Emily covered her mouth, held back a belch, got up and left the room.

"Where yous off?" Mum complained.

"She can stay!" Wiggy said with a high-pitched squeal element in his voice you could laugh at when not so pissed.

"She *should*!" Mum groaned drunkenly.

"Got college in the morning! Have fun you two!" Emily said expressionlessly, not sure or giving a toss if she sounded rude then went up into her room. Not wishing to see Mum and her mate get all rumpy-pumpy she removed her clothes, couldn't be asked brushing her teeth, then fell into bed freezing cold and wrapped herself up. But after a short while even she was defeated by temptation herself. She inhaled, shifted and rolled about. Then slipped her hand down her underwear. There was one in her memories—a guilty pleasure that had her blush, the redness on her face concealed by the dark.

Okay… Emily thought somewhat submissively. She rolled over, feeling good about herself. An actual body in bed with her would be nice actually. But she fell asleep before she could put a face to that body of pleasure.

Chapter 5

As static as it appeared in some areas, from still waters to an absence of cloud cover over an arid area, the world continuously moved on by. And it moved quicker than anything living on it around the sun that gave it life. Land once at the lowest point on the planet, had now become the tallest. In the air at one moment in history, altitude of no significance, several vivacious entities navigated through it at high speed and with aerodynamic efficiency, while travelling as a uniformed cluster then scattered. These aberrations were superficially solid, shapeless black one moment, then multi-coloured, then almost invisible. Or moved so fast that they could not be distinguished. From the perception of eyes about, these were not insects or micro-sized pterosaurs. Both suspects had wings. These entities did not.

On Laurasia, the northern landmass, the sun beamed down on the archipelago of islands that comprised the western end. Another ocean had formed beyond its shores and was starting to split Laurasia and Gondwana, vertically. Lands were divided. And with that were introduced new weather patterns, new climate schemes, new worlds and existential challenges. In this sector of Laurasia, the land was arid but fertile, the loose dirt had created a thick miasma from the movements of local fauna, in the background lingered a dusty orangey brown hue from the sun trying to penetrate through, the view of the horizon blocked out. The topography was dry, but lush with vegetation, and with some colour to the monotonous green dotted about from *angiosperms*, flowering plants, which were an impactful visual for anything that could register colour. The prevalent fern and coniferous greenery appeared brown or red under the current lighting, waterways glistened with orange with dragonflies hovering over the surface of the water, while the swampy areas appeared tarry. Anything a hundred metres away was heavily silhouetted.

As a vertebrate animal, having the advantage of flight allowed it to cover so much ground. One of these locomotors descended from the sky, as an ominous shadow onto a rise overlooking the banks of a river. Those that utilised the skies just got a whole lot larger. Homing in on the rise was a male *istiodactylus*, a pterodactylid, a member of a contemporary pterosaur design. In flight, his wings stretched five metres tip to tip, his tail was short, if not vestigial and the flaps of skin of older species didn't so much as connect the legs, thus freeing them. Possessing a neck longer than his predecessors his wings were narrower and slanted diagonally inwards, giving his form a basic star shape in order to counteract the dip of his head. As size went istiodactylus was sufficient in the competitive realm, so as long as matured. He had a long, sharply triangular bill, the end of which was flattened and rounded, lined with small, yet very sharp teeth.

The istiodactylus raised his wings and dipped his head further forward. He descended and refrained from beating his wings, his legs swung inwards 90 degrees and his feet stretched out, he stabilised the speed of his descent with a few micro beats of his wings and raised his head. The pterosaur's feet touched down on the rise, his wings spread horizontally then folded back as his body fell forward from gravity, his hands made contact with the floor, his fingers were positioned backwards in this stance. While flight lacked the challenges imposed by land, it still had its restrictions; too large to cling to trees and other surfaces the istiodactylus was grounded to an odd form of ambulation, seemingly cumbersome and inelegant on all fours. But in actual fact he moved about smoother than his smaller, long tailed predecessors, given the lack of membrane around his legs. Though he couldn't really run or chase after anything on ground, he could get by. Despite his impressive size, he amazingly only weighed 15 kilograms, as a result of possessing the same ultra-light, hollowed out bones of his arboreal ancestors.

There was more penetrating sunlight in this area, allowing for a less murky view of the pterosaur. His pelt was a soft grey, his wings were almost white, his bill a plaque yellow with small, blotchy black spots on the upper sides and a bold, elongated and pointed black streak on the roof. The fleshy pouch at his throat was pink with black spots and black and blood red patches encircled his perfectly round yellow/green eyes with piercing black pupils that dilated in the lower light. The male istiodactylus had a very daunting stare, the orb of the sun reflected in pricks of orange, the intensity periodically mitigated by his rapid but infrequent blinks that made his eyes appear cataract afflicted. He dipped the tip of his partly opened bill into the fur of his right wing arm and ran his teeth through it to scratch off an itch from some bloodsucking parasites invisible to him. Comforted by his groom he produced a hoot, it was low, deep but very audible with a bark-like characteristic to it. Then he remained silent, his sun glowing eyes focused on nothing.

Primarily, istiodactylus was a scavenger, his unusually arranged teeth allowed him to tear off bite-sized pieces of flesh off carrion, and his large size could intimidate smaller predators if need be. He moved towards the edge of the rise to inspect his surroundings. There was a glistening river system a few metres below, a low, rumbling ambience cascaded through the miasma with a bouncing/ricocheting effect between calls that could be felt tingling invasively against flesh no matter how far something could run. The whole ground level space was an ongoing musical chorus, punctuated by other unique sounds of varying tempos. On the west bank of the river, below the roosting site of the istiodactylus, another pterosaur landed, plunging feet first into the shallow edge of the river, its winged forelimbs limbs submerged and the ripples of the splash dying down, water fizzing.

The plunger was *kurstyailison*, a ctenochasmatid—essentially a smaller, distant cousin of istiodactylus with a metre long wingspan, though it had a longer neck and a sleeker bill, with sharp teeth replaced with long, compacted bristles limited to the frontal bill. This pterosaur had a fluffy white pelt with a delicate pink tinge that was bolder around the head and wing arms and black markings around the eyes, the bill for this female was a dull yellow, but the orange glow of the ambient miasma irradiated it. The kurstyailison was a filter feeder, actively seeking out small prey in the shallows, her bill opened and submerged, sediment and rocks below churned and disturbed as she probed and prodded about, all the while harmless to anything that couldn't fit down her oesophagus.

She scooped up water and sediment, and anything it harboured, algae and mini crustaceans, water spilling out from the gaps of her bristles, creating miniature waterfalls, a pouch at her throat bulging as her filtered catch entered. The kurstyailison vocalised, the sound she produced was louder and more flaring than the larger istiodactylus unwittingly beckoning down on her. A call from a fellow member somewhere had her turn her head to the left, away from the bank, of where a *bernissartia* was, heading her way for the water. It was a reptile with fairly long and low, triangular jaws filled with conical teeth that weren't particularly sharp, a long body and four limbs that were positioned in a semi erect stance, the partly webbed feet tucked below the body while the elbows and knees were bent outwards instead of fully sprawled.

Bernissartia was a crocodylomorph, archosaurs with a semi aquatic lifestyle which varied radically in size, shape and lifestyle. But this particular form wasn't unique, as many unrelated vertebrates had taken on similar body plans over the past 200 million years. Bernissartia though, was an exceptionally small member of the crocodylomorph clade; just two feet long, body covered in squared dark brown scales with sporadic black markings, a back lined with rows of armoured scutes, a softer brown underside and veiny amber/yellow eyes with vertically slit pupils. Its jaws were suited for small, hard-bodied prey such as the shells of molluscs and crustaceans. But the lightweight bones of a pterosaur as minute as the kurstyailison were not exempt…with a little effort, those neck vertebrate could be snapped.

Slowly, and quietly the bernissartia slipped into the water, the upper half of its skull above the surface, high-set eyes focused on its prey, the side to side tail and body motion leaving a soft, bending ripple behind it that didn't so much as disturb the filter feeding pterosaur, which was preoccupied as she looked up at the shadow of an unknown, larger pterosaur flying above her, its broken reflection sweeping past on the water. But in the end the kurstyailison spotted the crocodylomorph, which propelled itself for her, the pterosaur of which launched herself out the water by rocking forward onto her forelimbs, her wings raised above the water and her feet slapping against the surface, practically running on it, the action of which provided her enough momentum to take flight. She flapped her wings and gained height, with water spilling out from her bill, leaving a widely spaced trail of sparkling splashes that appeared disassociated with her benign feeding strategy.

Airborne, the kurstyailison's small form appeared insignificant when scaled up against the other pterosaurs soaring much further back against the orangey horizon, distinguished by their varied bill and crest shapes and sizes. There was land fauna about, and they weren't small but very large. Concealed partly by the miasma, they were the source of the background commotion; beasts with small heads, remarkably long necks and colossal bodies supported by four legs and long tails, others members of which were concealed by the surrounding tree lines. One of these anonymous behemoths strayed from the group and was heading towards the river with the kurstyailison flying past it, its slowly rising neck shadowing everything around it.

Approaching the riverbank below the perched istiodactylus was a herd of *iguanodon*, the quintessential fauna of the region. Adults were 10 metres in length, three metres tall at the hip and weighed over four tons, their heads were rectangular with short beaks, anchored to curving, upward angled necks and bulky bodies, a long, thick tail stretched out from their hips, short, dark scales ran along their spines. The iguanodon walked on all fours, their hind legs were muscular with three toes, their forelimbs were slender and shorter than their back legs, their hands had three tightly packed hoofed toes with connective webbing, their fifth fingers were slender and curled back around behind the exterior of their hands, while their thumbs were stiff and arranged into thick, cone-shaped spikes that pointed forward.

The iguanodon were mainly brown, but their coloration encompassed a brilliant palette of various shades of green, brown and yellow that would have reflected the surrounding terrain under normal conditions. The males were more colourful, but with the exception of size, that dimorphism wasn't apparent under the tinted lighting. Zealous browsers, they fed on leaves, twigs and cones, rearing up on their hind legs without hassle to get at higher vegetation if required, their spiked thumbs were particularly useful for digging. Accompanying them under their shadows were clans of smaller herbivores, the *common hypsilophodon*. Belonging to the ornithopod clade, they were distantly related to the iguanodon, but were bipedal and lightly built with longer, leaner legs, adults measuring six feet long and standing less than two feet high. The hypsilophodon had five fingered hands and short claws on their thumbs and first two fingers, small triangular heads with big eyes, and thinner, stiffer tails. Though they were covered in small scales they also bore a loose, bristly pelt, and under the miasma they appeared a deep, earthy brown.

The hypsilophodon drank at the edge of the river, their beaked mouths dipping into the water and heads tilting back. They communicated continuously through chirps and sequenced clicks. The young hypsilophodon weren't as uniformed in their behaviour, they hydrated in only a fraction of the time as the adults and were left to their own accord without attention. They ran about in frolic, exercising their hind legs while running into each other or jumping away evasively in all directions, sometimes they pecked at each other or mocked the act. One day they would need their legs to run for something other than play.

The young hypsilophodon were being observed in plain sight, the surveyors: *eotyrannus*, a pair of them, stood out dead in the opening as a pair of frightening silhouettes that they might as well just be running straight towards them. They were theropods, carnivores, 10 feet long and standing on two long legs with three clawed toes plus a smaller digit on the inside of the ankle that pointed backwards, balanced by a long, sleek tail, short arms folded almost like wings with some quills on the undersides and ending in three clawed fingers, the palms facing inwards. The skulls of the eotyrannus were low and oval in shape, dark, knobby scales lined the top of the snout to form a jagged ridge dividing the tall, circular crests above their large eyes, long, sharp teeth lined their jaws, concealed by scaly lips, their nostrils located at the end of their snouts sniffed the air.

Their bodies were covered in a primitive feathering for insulation in this dry climate. The female was a light, grey/brown and mottled heavily with small spots and thin, curving stripes, her underbelly a significantly lighter shade. The male had multiple rows of quills behind his head, a darker brown body with a more erratic body patterning that resembled a bed of twigs, the assorted palette of light and dark colours on his snout couldn't be discerned under this lighting. Either way, both sexes appeared as fiery as the sun's rays as it struck the surface of rock, hill or cliff face.

The eotyrannus vocalised through grunts underlying a sequence of rapid clicks, followed by a wetter noise, their throats throbbing and plumaged chests pulsing, the motion also ruffled the feathers long their bodies. The predators were targeting the iguanodon herd. Adults were impervious to attack from them, but their youngest members were at risk, and eotyrannus were opportunists. They stepped forward, a fleeting gap in the miasma allowed a shimmer of sunlight through which brightened their faces, their eyes were almost orange, their round pupils shrinking from the exposure, the yellow of the male's mid snout and the crescent arrangement of brown spots behind his eye sockets livening. The hypsilophodon paused and raised their necks, standing tall and in sudden, collective silence. The eotyrannus had lost the element of surprise.

The predators ran forward. But not at full pelt, their long strides left three-toed footprints in the dried dirt.

One of the formless flying entities witnessed the moment from above and moved down in to intercept them, for whatever reason. The female eotyrannus turned her head in its direction, but it moved away too quickly to elicit a response. She slowed down while her partner continued on, oblivious to the entity observing him aerially from behind.

Then he stopped on his own accord, his tail raised with his partner stopping a few steps ahead of him. The predators had mock charged, causing an upset among the nearby hypsilophodon clans with a succession of piercing clicks and squeals unleashed into the air as they scattered, light-footed and swift, some skipping or jumping before breaking into dashes which left behind dust clouds, their tails stiff and horizontal as they sped off.

The eotyrannus pair didn't give chase, they shook off dust from their plumage and inspected the fleeing prey for weaker members or strays. The lighter young iguanodon were also spooked, and reared onto their hind legs and dashed away bipedally, yet unsurely from the source of the alarm. The adult iguanodon though remained unmoved, their black eyes blinking in confusion at their surroundings but were fixed and guarded at their younger members. The eotyrannus pair were stood too close to each other, and a decisional conflict of engagement resulted in them snapping at each other, of which was witnessed from below by the airborne entity.

The adult iguanodon looked their way and slowly, unsurely approached them on all fours while creating a barrier for the young with their bodies. They consummated their approach with bellows that didn't require them to open their mouths, while some individuals further back reared up, gaining nearly three metres of additional height, which partnered fittingly with their thumb spikes flaunted for intimidation. For the eager eotyrannus, they had a choice of being crushed by an adult or having a thumb spike rammed fatally through the flesh. These smaller carnivores stood no chance. The eotyrannus walked around them to the right without straying.

~

The iguanodon commotion hadn't drowned out the song of croaks by the river banks, those associated with amphibians. One example hopped onto an algae ridden rock from the water: a *karlrana*, an anura—a frog, less than half a foot long, light green with brown spots on the back, a silvery white underside, a brown stripe outlined with golden yellow extended from the periscopic eyes then alongside the entire flank. Unlike ancient predecessors, the body of the amphibian was short, broad and compacted, the limbs were much longer while the hind legs were bent out to the sides, the spaces between its flat fingers and toes were lined with webbing, and there was no tail present. The amphibian's throat bulged and throbbed, its eyes with horizontal, oval-shaped pupils unflinching as the aerial entity hovered by it and stopped. The karlrana hopped forward on its rock without plunging back into the water. The observing entity remained unmoved.

For the past 70 million years, this group of amphibians had flourished, and while they were hardly apex predators and a fraction smaller than their ancestors, their unique method of locomotion allowed them to exploit a wider area. A highly productive group of vertebrates, where there was freshwater they thrived.

The water erupted into a cloud of white and the karlrana was snatched from behind by the jaws of the bernissartia, the near blunt teeth sank in easily through the amphibian's soft flesh. The armoured reptile shook it about, unintentionally bashing its body against the rock, then dragged it underwater, the ripples from the action fading. Another POV was completely focused on something in the opposite direction. Approaching the opposite bank from the spot of the karlrana's demise was another theropod: a male *baryonyx*.

Unlike eotyrannus, his body was fully scaled, nine metres in length, standing three metres high and weighing two tons he was formidable. His elongated snout was nearly a metre long, with a very crocodylomorphian character to it; it was smooth in texture, sleek and lined with nearly a hundred blunt, yellow tinted teeth, though not bare, concealed partly by short, scaly lips. A short, jagged ridge crest protruded from his forehead, his yellow eyes had round, black pupils focused on the water ahead, patches of muted blues, greys, white and browns surrounded the eyes, connecting the skull was a long, slender neck with a drooping, light shaded throat pouch and a row of short, scaly spines mapped along the entire spine.

Baryonyx owned a pair of short, muscular arms with three scaly fingers ending in fearsome black claws, the thumbs branded a thick and heavily curved foot long claw. His spine was notably tall and ridged, it peaked into a short hump around the hip region, melding in with the thickness of the base of his long, thick tail, his legs were relatively long and he did not possess the curved toe claws of the smaller theropods, they were almost flat and he had short webbing between his toes. His body colour was a soft, reddish brown but with some orange tints similar to the environmental miasma treatment and darker, spotted shading, the dark, greenish asymmetrical smears on the mid line of his body were from algae stains.

For now, the baryonyx preferred the routine lifestyle, where he waded into the river, calf deep and dipped his snout into the water, his nostrils positioned on the centre of his snout instead of the end allowed him to breathe doing so. A piscivore, fish exceeding a metre in length were the most common choice of prey. And they came steadily… He didn't need to watch for prey, thanks to tiny, black sensory pores at the front of his snout that were motion sensitive. The teeth of baryonyx were smooth but prickly-edged, those beyond the rear mid of his jaws were small, conical and abundant, the bulbous, downward notch at the end of his upper jaw held sharper, curved teeth that varied in size. The iguanodon had the baryonyx on the other side of the river constantly in their sights, there was no chance for ambush. But the fish eater was tame with his would-be catches.

There was something in the water. The baryonyx froze, the only motion coming from the last half of his tail balancing him as he anticipated a hapless fish to snatch. But the motion detected from the prey suddenly went out of range by one step. Of all things, it was one of the anomalous flying entities, rising up from the water, slowly. The baryonyx's tail lowered as the perplexed theropod looked up at it at the same pace. There was no water dropping off this thing, which looked like a distorted, translucent cloud of alternating colours. Prey or not, it was within reach, and the baryonyx's clawed fingers coiled and flexed readily. He lunged at it, the end of his snout made a soft, broken contact briefly, but nothing to bite down on. Startled, he emitted a guttural bellow. *What* kind of prey was that? He didn't see that the aerial entity was now floating statically below him, just above the water, viewing the picturesque, silhouetted underside of his jaw and neck, the ends of his air strafing claws coming into view. Then its view transitioned into a rear image of the bamboozled baryonyx.

The iguanodon herd was causing another kerfuffle with some members moving about, allowing the baryonyx an unobstructed view of something previously concealed by the walls of flesh; lying on the floor on its side was a static juvenile. A fresh corpse up for grabs. Smaller, flesh hungry pterosaurs appeared above in the near vicinity and circled in patience. For anything that consumed flesh, a carcass this size was always tempting, and it lured the baryonyx further forward, his lower body submerged further until his feet couldn't feel riverbed anymore. He had some buoyancy to him and a crocodylomorphian bend to his tail, though he mainly swam by kicking his legs, the webbing propelling him and his head held above water. The iguanodon herd saw him coming and began to stir-up another fuss. And there was something else in the water with the baryonyx: swimming in from his right was a *grindynatator*. Incredibly it was a plesiosaur, a marine reptile—a sea dweller.

While seemingly out of place, some plesiosaur species though journeyed periodically from salt water to fresh water, whilst others sought refuge as infants from the larger predators out in the sea. At just nine feet long and surpassing 400 kilos grindynatator was rather small for its kind with murkier yellow/brown shades and brown spots instead of cooler, oceanic colours, but in this river system it was freakishly large among other aquatic life, which it exploited through the lack of competition and threats. Orange, wavy shimmers of muted sunlight flickered off the grindynatator's body as it swam around behind the baryonyx, its long neck curving, then propelled itself up river.

A competitive situation was about to incur, but not from the aquatic reptile as it was unable to come onto land. On the rise, the istiodactylus also had his eyes on the iguanodon carcass, though he would have to wait until the mainly piscivorous baryonyx had filled his stomach. The eotyrannus, having spooked the herbivores at the river were cautiously closing in on the freshly deceased, keeping their distance without expending energy, though they did need them to clear the site. But they weren't the only ones drawn to it. Behind the swimming baryonyx, stepping slowly towards the water was a female *neovenator*. Seven metres long, over two metres high, gracefully built and weighing over a ton, she had a high, broad skull with short, keratinous horn-like crests in front of her eyes, rows of flat sharp teeth, a short, muscular neck and short forearms with three evenly-sized claws evolved for ripping into flesh with minimal effort while her muscular legs with clawed toes were built for running.

This new hunter on scene was a killer with a stern appetite for red meat. Adult iguanodon were not safe from her. The neovenator's nostrils dilated and closed, registering the scent of a corpse which she prioritised as much as breathing. Exposed out in the opening she remained still, her flesh covered in small scales, spines of alternating height ran along her back, her body coloration comprised of a brown, broken leaf patterning with thick, backward slanted bands around her tail, her upper snout was mottled with soil brown spots, the flesh around her eyes appeared as orangey and hazy as the outer rim of the sun and flaking coagulated blood encrusted her lips. The penetrating sunrays gave her a temporary golden sheen to her lighter shaded throat and underbelly. Her dappled flesh was camouflaged well against the greenery, especially effective from a distance. The iguanodon though were more focused on the baryonyx nearing the banks, they alerted his presence with cautionary bellows and slowly began to move away. The eotyrannus seized this moment and walked towards the juvenile carcass.

~

Upon reaching the opposite bank, ridden with equisetopsia that were the ugliest shades of red under the miasma, a shower of water fell off the baryonyx's body, the drops cutting into the bank's silt in dotted rows. He snarled, not at the eotyrannus that were indecisive about running in for a hasty mouthful of easy meat, but upon registering the scent of the rival predator across the river. Water raining off his body the baryonyx turned around, his clawed arms hanging down and his head lowering at the sight of the neovenator. The two predators faced each other off in a bloodless duel separated by the river. Agitated, the baryonyx emitted a low gurgle from his throat. Without a gesture or responsive sound the neovenator turned and moved on, heading east along the river. She wasn't going to swim across for this one. Though the iguanodon had cleared the river banks, the eotyrannus didn't get a chance to get a mouthful of flesh from the carcass as the baryonyx turned around and approached, his trailing wet footprints stood out boldly against the dry soil of the land and his long jaws gaping open in a threatening display. The smaller predators stood their ground, they would not risk a swipe from a baryonyx claw.

The iguanodon carcass was all his for the taking. His jaws gave it a go without hesitation, though…his teeth weren't actually evolved for ripping into flesh, that was a job relegated to his hands. His clawed fingers were able to pierce the flesh of the carcass, the strength of his arms was sufficient enough to break apart muscle, tendon and ligament. A couple of minutes of effort granted him a severed leg with a gush of blood that appeared dark brown under the miasma, trickles of it ran from the banks into the water, an invitation to any water dwelling predators that could access land. With a backward jerk of his head followed by a couple of cautious twists and yanks, the baryonyx swallowed the limb down, whole and managed not to choke on it. He probed his snout into the opened amputation wound and scraped out the exposed, softer tissues.

The impatient eotyrannus squatted down and rested, their heads held up high and eyes rarely straying from the corpse. The baryonyx, with a dripping, bloodied snout and hands looked back at them, checking they weren't making a move then resumed gorging on the carcass, his frontal teeth delicately tearing off flesh. An hour passed, and the shadows of pterosaurs of all sizes began to appear on scene, the smaller ones were closest while the bigger ones circled high above. With a full belly that visibly distended, the baryonyx lowered himself to the ground and rested for a moment, his jaws opened at a low angle, and a thrum made every time he exhaled. A tiny pterosaur with a semi-circular head crest flew past him, accompanied by several more, some of which were bold enough to land on him, an annoyance that cut his rest short. Then the fish eater got up, the blood from his feast coagulated and crusted on his snout, and began walking off, heading into the cover of the woodlands to rest properly.

The baryonyx hadn't stripped the iguanodon carcass bare, and with them softer duty teeth of his had left a bounty of meat, enough to satisfy ten eotyrannus. Seizing their chance, the smaller predators stood up and moved in. At the same time, the istiodactylus swooped down from his rise and landed in front of the iguanodon corpse, blocking it off from the predators, which he faced directly a few yards away. On all fours the pterosaur stood as tall as the two theropods, which weren't at all receptive to this competitor chancing their meal. When they got too close, the istiodactylus clapped his bill together, made a chortling noise in a doubled succession then reared up onto his legs spreading his wings, making himself appear even bigger in a convincing display of intimidation.

The eotyrannus stood their ground, their throats throbbing and heads turning, their arms lowering then folding back in. The male opened his mouth, baring his killer teeth and stepped as far as he dared keeping his jaws open while he made a hoarse rattling noise, his partner joined him and took a step further than him. Either scare off the pterosaur or wait was the current option. The istiodactylus audaciously repeated his intimidation display and went as far as to flap his wings, which sent some of the dusty dirt towards the predators. But all three animals had other problems; the neovenator, that had found her way around the river appeared from around a patch of woodland, stalling just before her left foot landed on the ground, her eyes blackened from both being shaded by her eyebrow crests and the shadows of the trees locked with the participants of the conflict, her lower jaw hanging open, strings of saliva dripping down. The istiodactylus spotted her first and jerked his head up. The neovenator approached, her body bending as she negotiated the turn. The eotyrannus were oblivious.

Seemingly second-class predators, like anything alive, or before them, their genes harboured the blueprints for evolutionary potential, one of which was nothing short of majestic…given the right conditions. But this branch and their descendants were an inferior design under the shadow of the older, more radically evolved theropods. Such as the one currently announcing her arrival with a closed mouth bellow. The eotyrannus quickly turned around, lowered their stances but kept their heads high then froze in posture, startled. Right now, all they could do was run. They didn't though, and challenged the larger theropod which stepped towards them fearlessly. The istiodactylus made the right move and took flight, all four limbs were required to push him off the ground, he gained altitude, banked right and headed north.

Below the pterosaur the marshes transitioned into coastal plains, though all in sight was still saturated heavily with orange, but thinning out with every metre. Flying was the fastest form of biological travel so far. Nearly two hours on the wing and the istiodactylus was flying over higher, inland terrain, the skies were now clear and visibility was one hundred percent, the grey of his pelt stood out boldly, along with some finer details such as the thin, dark slanted markings on his wings. On the ground was plenty of sparkling green lakes and accessible water sources, otherwise a preferable place to stop for a rest and hydrate. The istiodactylus descended down on a clearing, scaring away a clan of foraging *mountain hypsilophodon*. These were a northern species of hypsilophodon with longer legs, allowing them to run up steeper terrain, under the light of day they were a reddish brown with white spots along their bodies and white underbellies, brown eyes with sunray yellow eye patches and more muscular cheeks to tackle the tougher, more varied plant material of these lands.

When the istiodactylus dropped back on all fours the claws of his right wing missed squashing a two-inch *cockroach* on the ground, which skittered away. The highland hypsilophodon didn't run too far from the pterosaur, as a landing pterosaur was a common thing, so as long as it wasn't large enough to eat them. The herbivores resumed feeding. The cockroach that had evaded being squashed by the pterosaur ran for the undergrowth. Before it could conceal itself within the foliage it stopped, its antennae flickering, then turned to the left.

Where it was snatched by a *burchvitatherium*. It was a mammal. Less than a foot long with a large head, five clawed digits on each of its four limbs, its body was essentially a ball of fur with a short, slim fleshy pink tail behind it. The mammalia had evolved from the more basal reptiles, long prior to the great extinction 120 million years ago, despite having very little resemblance to their ancestors.

Set along the jaws of the burchvitatherium were multiple, variedly shaped teeth, scales were replaced with naked flesh and short, dense fur, a moist, fleshy nose with long, millimetre thick whiskers fanned out, broad, cartilaginous ears stood high at the back of its skull instead of holes and small, dark beady eyes reflected the sun as it chomped down on its catch. The burchvitatherium's pelt was grey with a soft brown tinge, three bold, bark brown striped markings stretched out and lined the forehead. This species lived in burrows, were mostly nocturnal with a high metabolism that allowed for a flexible hunting schedule. Burchvitatherium didn't lay eggs, they incubated young inside their bodies. As of now they were tiny fodders, living under the shadows of the land fauna. How could they remotely compete?

~

Thursday. Emily had done her best to get rid of the black hair dye last night; yesterday everyone in class was taking the piss out of her, and she was surprised she had even managed to get up for class in time, and had to do the rest of her makeup on the bus to town. Today her hair was dyed a medium dark brown, which really brought out the blue in her eyes and worked well with her college uniform. Fuelled by a modest breakfast of beans on buttered toast and a cig Emily put on this long black overcoat, though she wore her beloved blue Juicy hoodie underneath. She had to wear summat more appropriate for her feet in this weather; a pair of woolly grey cardy Uggs, though was hoping one day she could get summat nice like them boots Isabelle wore. She stashed her uniform's white flats into a carrier bag. Emily and Mum had put up the Christmas tree in the living room along with some plain white lights on the window. Some of the neighbours were far more extravagant; they had artificial snowmen, reindeer and fancy lights all over their house—and more than half the neighbourhood went to church anyway.

Halfway down the road to Beckett Emily noticed this *really* long queue of students stretching out the entrance in an L shape.

"The fuck's all this?" She said genuinely surprised.

"Coppers searchin' everyone!" A lad in the queue answered. What the fuck was this, an airport? Was everyone a suspected terrorist again? Emily scoffed then made her way to the end of the queue, which was like two bus lengths from the entrance.

"Oi? Some of us want to *learn*!" Some lass called out. How true that was…even if it wasn't for most! While waiting Emily had herself two cigs and felt dizzy from the overindulgence of nicotine. It took 15 bloody minutes for her to reach the entrance, and it was longer than them adverts and trailers at a cinema. And she was shivering!

A female officer ordered her to step through one of them metal detectors they had at airports. As Emily stepped through the metal detector beeped. What could that be now? She had so much metal on her person!

"Your bags?" The officer demanded with Emily handing over her carrier and handbag and removing her coat. Satisfied with the search the copper asked her to step back through the metal detector, where she set it off again.

"Arms out."

Emily did as she was told. She had been frisked at airports, but this was just too much! She hoped she didn't have to remove her piercings! A short wave of humility and degradation set in as she felt the officer's palms pat her down from all angles and other students smirking with Emily comforted by the reality that it would be their turn next!

"Thank you…" The officer said drearily without making eye contact. That was all. Emily wanted to curse; she mouthed a silent "fuck sake!" as she left then went into class. Only Alice was present, she had some fashion magazine laid out in front of her and was painting her nails red. She smiled at her and waved in an exaggerated way.

"You see all that out there?" Emily called out to her.

"Yes!" Alice said.

"Were you waiting long?"

"I come early, only took two minutes."

Though she was half-Geordie Alice spoke with a thick German accent. Emily sat down across from Alice and began to change into her flats.

"How'd you say: *pissed off* in German?" She asked her classmate. Alice looked at her, sat up a bit more and wiggled her fingers.

"You can say: *verarget!*" She replied.

"Das ist schiezer!" Emily said without caring if she pronounced anything right. Alice chuckled.

Lunchtime. The college cafeteria was teaming with students, loud, hostile and full of testosterone and competitiveness and whininess. Almost everyone had to make their presence known, and they didn't care how they would achieve that. Some would throw things at other people, some would laugh too loud, some would belch, some would stare at other students like Stacy then act surprised when someone confronted them. It was a battle for dominance. Emily wanted summat hot in this cold weather; they were serving cheese pizza but some excruciatingly indecisive bitch was causing a queue, so to avoid hassle, she nobly left the queue and went to the deli across the street from college and had a sweet chilli chicken sandwich with butter and salad, and sat in peace on one of four of the seats available at the place listening to an Alicia Keys album.

Back at class Emily waved to newcomer Justina, she was from Lithuania and despite her meaty limbs and height she was pretty enough with a square face, strong cheeks and a size bustier than Emily, her dark blonde hair parted and tied back into a medium height bun, the rectangular black frame glasses she wore in front of her gorgeous watery blue eyes suited her. Justina reciprocated Emily's wave with a friendly, perfectly white smile. Emily had yet to have a proper chat with her. Then all the class, except for Alice poured into the room.

"Alright Nick?" Beth Huxley shouted acting like she was the leader of the class, which she wasn't.

"Isn't our Nick *right* fit!"

Though her shout out had everyone gang up on Emily.

"She is!" Isabelle said somewhat enviously with the remark spreading amongst the lot, and it got Justina's attention with her chuckling nervously. Emily kept quiet, trying not to smile. But in the end she couldn't help it!

"Tah...!" She said.

"*Why* you still single?" Beth questioned in a child's voice while making a cringy face. Emily had an easy answer: "Blokes here are shit!"

Laughter followed, that was short-lived.

"What you on about?" questioned Beth.

"They are...!" Emily protested and felt like dancing about.

"You sayin' our fella's shite?" The normally silent Amanda Biggs had to ruin the moment, yet it triggered explosive, excited laughter. Zoe went up to Emily and started rocking her crotch back and forth.

115

"No! Don't!" Emily waved her away.

"She *has* got nice tits!" Zoe exclaimed.

"Sure you han't got implants or owt?" Beth questioned putting her hands on her own chest and shook them about tauntingly.

"No! But me mum has!" Emily said back. Another explosion of laughter followed.

"We all know that!" Jasmine said jokingly.

"Nick's fit as fuck!" Zoe called out. Then the classroom door opened with Denise stepping in.

"Has our Abigail been bothering you?" Denise asked Emily, it was what you'd call her mantra.

"Yeah Nick! Has she been givin' yah grief?" Teased Beth.

"No, she's really sorted!" Emily said back. Denise smiled without looking at her.

"Alright then…!" The tutor raised her voice, getting everyone to shut up.

"Any of you fancy volunteering as a *model* for the art department?" She said. Wolf whistles followed.

"Do we have to take our clothes off?" Zoe asked then giggled. Naked models, *how* did they cope?

"No! Just sit down and keep still!" Denise assured them. Laughter turned into silence.

"*Who* wants to volunteer?" The tutor asked without making eye contact with her class. The silence was broken with giggles and quiet commotion.

"I can see there will be plenty of flirting going on!" Jasmine exploded into chatter. No one had the balls to volunteer…

"Nick?" Zoe called out with a guttural voice.

"Definitely Nick!" Everyone seemed to cheer at once.

"Emily Cerina Nicole? Our most fab here!" Denise shouted out. Heads turned Emily's way.

"You wanna volunteer?" The tutor asked. Emily grinned and blushed.

"Alright then!"

~

The chosen one, Emily went to the ladies room where she checked on her appearance, made sure she was looking good. No flaking skin or

116

imperfections…no need for lip gloss or…further makeup… She tied the hair on the back of her head up into a medium-high ponytail, though there wasn't much to show but it was comfortable. The art department was upstairs one floor in the college building. Emily stood outside the entrance, messing about on her phone, ignoring all the lads and lasses passing by, the lads giving her whistles and making comments they didn't try to keep quiet. Soon Emily was greeted by a fella with a dark, severe flattop and pierced ear.

"Hello love!" He greeted with a Scottish accent.

"Ergh…I'm here to *pose* for them lot, or summat?" Emily said then was escorted inside. She looked about the corridor nervously which had all these drawers to the right, and coming her way was this fit-looking fella in his early-thirties, sporty-looking with ginger hair and stubble.

"Alright Joel?" These lads acknowledged as they walked past him Emily's way.

Joel smiled at her in a very welcoming manner. He looked like the sort of bloke students would look up to.

"Emily?" He said.

"Yes!"

Her uniform must have given her away. Joel guided her into the room to the left, unlike the beauty class everything was messy with dents, knife marks and paint stains on the tables, her white uniform made her stand out against all the casually dressed art students; half of them seemed to be alternative types. The students' chairs were arranged in a circle, large sketchbooks resting on easels set in front of them, in the centre was a clean seat, more fancy-looking than what everyone else was sat on that it may as well be a throne.

"Just sit yourself down there, Emily." Joel told her. Emily wished she could have worn summat more fitting, like a dress or an ancient Greek robe or summat? *Just sit down…* Denise's words echoed in her head.

"Shame Jack's not around!" Emily heard this lass say behind her.

"Is he even straight him?" This lad said. Without expressing it, Emily cringed upon hearing a wolf whistle from someone lucky enough to have not been seen by her, followed by several quieter ones and silly noises.

She nervously sat down on the seat in the centre and folded her right leg over, brushed her fringe away from her face then placed her hands on top of one another over her lap. Seeing all the contagious smiles from all the lads and whispers from the lasses made her crave a cig.

"She's fit as sin!" A whisper that didn't stay quiet—*oh God...!* Emily sat still, glad she didn't have to take her clothes off... Her eyes making a big effort to avoid the gazes of those around her, as well as the expectant smiles of the lads. She didn't entertain their hormones by winking back but merely returned the smiles with the cheapest of grins, while trying to make out owt dodgy in all the whispers going about.

Joel ordered them into silence without having to raise his voice, then had the class start drawing.

"Eye to pencil..." The tutor said holding up his hand with an orange pencil, and made movements accordingly. Emily wished she could put her iPod's earphones on to mute out the sounds of the lads blowing raspberries, that wasn't nice to hear! Every minute or so Joel uttered some advice for his class as he stepped in and out between the gaps of the students' easels, weaving his way around the circle and inspecting each one without saying owt. He stopped at an easel in the left most corner of Emily's sight, where he smiled at what this lad was drawing then moved on to the next. To be honest Emily was more concerned about one thing here: would any of these lot do her portrait nice? A boring half or so hour into the session and her bum was aching on the hard chair. She couldn't sit still for any longer.

She looked to the classroom window, like the ones in beauty class it was large, though mostly blocked out by the tall shelves which had so many jars and pots permanently stained with paint. Outside, the sky was still grey, and the rooftops of Oldmill Brig beyond it combined to create a hideous image. Sun would be nice, or at least some snow to cover it. Emily wanted to cover it up with some nice, colourful curtains or summat—ones with some of them fancy Indian silk patterns? If it could all be made like that for the whole district then there wouldn't be a problem; they had big mosques and temples built for foreigners in places like London didn't they? Emily could share her views on the district with others for a whole day.

"Okay...Let's stop there!" Joel called an end to the session. Emily continued to sit in place for what she assumed was another unnecessary minute. She blinked then looked at every student without making direct eye contact. They cleared up, checking out each other's works, commenting and all that. The dissing laughter of some students wasn't comforting—*oh no!*

"Ok! Let us see!" Emily said getting out of her seat to investigate. She only got to see a couple of sketches, and she didn't like any of them; too big lips, nose that was shaped wrong like some freak, too strong lines around her image, and what was with this dodgy chin? And the artists were giggling about it! *Why* did some of these lot even take up art anyway?

~

That afternoon back in beauty class Emily felt numb, on the edge of humility for the second time this day but wasn't going to kick up a fuss. Everyone was asking her how it went with the art department, and she was reluctant to answer; "bad!" was the most common reply. Was anyone cruel enough to post one of them sketches online with her name to it? Emily wanted to trade places with Isabelle Woodhouse, have someone do her portrait nice! The class were doing manicures, partnering up and taking turns painting each other's nails while they let music play, the current track was Lilly Allen's *the fear*. Emily let Justina sort her out, asking for a pink polish to her nails with a glossing. When finished, she held up her right hand and flipped it, wiggling her fingers.

"That's just fine!" Emily said then asked, "What's thank you in Lithuanian?"

"*Acieu.*" Justina answered. And it sounded like a sneeze!

Emily was ready to make a joke about it.

Then the bloody fire alarm went off, with that scary, blaring sound making most of the lasses in class jump and yelp. A fire drill! *Seriously?* So in-fucking-convenient with everyone having to stop what they were doing, walking out cursing with half-done nails and having to wait outside in the car park on the east side of the college building. The third moment of bad happening today! The sky was still grey and it was spitting it down, and it was so cold!

While trying not to make any contact with anyone or her clothes with her drying nails, Emily lit a cig and looked about the crowd, some bitch dressed like a tom boy in baggy jeans, trainers and short hair strode past her and screamed, dancing about like an idiot to get the attention of her mates. She scoffed at the dyke then resumed her passive watch of the crowd, she spotted them lot from the art department who had drawn her badly stood in a steeper spot of the car park to the west. And of all people, Gangster fella was there. His tie and leather jacket made him stand out like a shining diamond on a dirty heap of coal.

Emily was wondering whether she should walk over to just say hi, as she would with any other student who she thought was alright. She hesitated, as Gangster looked more pissed off than anyone else. He stood tensely with a hunched pose, delicately stomping on the ground with these sudden, short turns of his upper body and jerking, high movements to his shoulders. He looked like he was ready to rip off someone's head if they so much as spoke to him. Then Gangster reached inside his jacket pocket, probably for a cig like everyone else? Well, he was smoking alright. He put a *cigar* in his mouth—as if Gangster wasn't more exquisite than he already was—and it wasn't one of them small ones, but a fairly big one, short and fat like a sawn off chunk of broom handle! Emily had always associated cigars with old men—it was a first to see a young lad smoke one! The other students, smoking roll-ups or standard cigs were looking at him, smiling and saying stuff while others laughed. Though he had this grimace to his already tense features, he ignored them.

Then Emily was distracted by Beth Huxley.

"You got a cig Nick?" She asked, her fingers spread awkwardly like the whole beauty class from their still wet nails. Emily handed her a cig, though took her time doing so.

"Canada, their gonna make cannabis legal!" She spoke as though she was gonna reap summat from it here in England. Emily though just chuckled.

"They should just make all drugs legal!" Beth said loudly. Was she on summat already? Emily wondered.

"Make drugs legal!" Beth rephrased.

"And just ban all alcohol—cuz you don't need it; it just gives you a bad hangover!"

Emily disagreed on many levels.

"They tried that!" Denise said stepping in, having overheard before Emily could argue.

"Prohibition they called it. It didn't work—it put the mafia in business."

"What's mafia?" Beth said thickly.

"*Al Capone…?*" Denise explained with a puzzled look to her face. *Prohibition…*Emily didn't want to sound critical or begin some annoying argument, but not being allowed to have a drink at one time in history sounded insane. For children it made sense, but for everyone else…what the fuck? It wasn't right!

"I hope you haven't been taking anything today young lady?" Denise grilled Beth.

~

120

Friday, midday. Emily had a job interview for Zaks and Marias, a cocktail bar in L.O.Z's which was below the cinema. She was the right age and had had a decent amount of pub experience, a quick learner she could do up cocktails after just being told how to the one time only. The place was very posh-looking, the bar pearl white with a colourful stock of overpriced booze, the colours of the glass bottles lit up and cast against the walls in triangular streaks which competed with the Christmas décor, and there was a second floor space with a stairway to the right of the bar with a large chandelier dangling down. Immediately Emily knew this was going to be better than working at any standard pub or fast food chain! She was directed to a table near the bar by one of the staff. Last night she had dyed her hair a deep red, this morning she had curled it slightly for a change which gave her volume like a red cloud, and it looked nice.

Emily wore all black today: a thin black turtleneck sweater tucked into some black jeans, a black cardigan and tall black boots with short heels and buckles as it was so cold. Her outfit was smart, with a bit of sophistication, though originally she had planned to wear a suit, except she didn't have one. Mum had a couple of suits from her earlier jobs as deputy manager at one of the cosmetic shops in Lytham Arcade, across the road west of Longford Centre, but they were too large for Emily, so this alternative would have to do. Also, she removed her nose stud and mouth ring, unsure whether they were appropriate.

Emily was sat at a high table facing the bar, Owl City *fireflies* playing. While waiting, she took a peek at one of the menus in front of her and was surprised to find out that it was also a Mexican themed restaurant. Then this bloke approached the table.

"Is it Emily?" He said.

"That's me!" Emily smiled raising her right hand.

"I'm Thorold." The manager said with a very husky voice that had a semi posh part to it. Emily had been expecting someone tall, handsome and a bit awkward to interview her. Well, the bloke was tall…he had a pot belly and didn't look like he cared too much about his appearance, the hair on his crown had almost disappeared, his scalp shined, the ridiculous patches of dark hair on the sides of his head made his head look like an egg in a cup! He scratched his stubbled chin with these tanned sausage-like fingers while looking down at her with an unnerving look like he were going to eat her or summat! Then Thorold pulled out a seat across from Emily, sat his big bum down and opened up his folder, muttered some stuff, his finger pointed down and hovering over the page. And he had a wedding ring!

"So, Emily…" He started.

"What makes you interested in working at this venue?"

~

Whenever asked about summat, Emily had told Mister Thorold the truth: she liked X Factor, she liked shopping, she was a sensible drinker, she worked out, had had a previous pub job so was naturally good with people, she had no partner, no kids and was committed to whatever job she had… Thorold looked up at her with a glowing smile that looked out of place on his moody face.

"You start tomorrow!" He said. The interview was a success! Relief, excitement and a bit of nervousness to go with it overcame Emily.

"Yay!" She said innocently, even though she was legally an adult she still had the habit of saying that like a little girl whenever there was good news.

"Do I have to keep me hair natural colours or summat?" She asked Thorold who got out of his seat.

"Do whatever you wish with it!" He said and managed a lovely smile.

"Our staff have tattoos and piercings all over!"

That was a relief hearing!

After the interview, a happy Emily grabbed the same menu she had been looking at earlier, then went to the bar. Why not get a little taste of where she was working for lunch, Mexican style? One option was scrambled eggs with black beans, avocado slices, brown rice and homemade salsa. She ordered that with a coffee. Her food arrived just as her coffee turned warm enough to sip more frequently, artistically presented on a fancy white plate with a sprinkle of coriander over the salsa for décor. Before picking up her cutlery, she took out her phone and took a photo of her food, as she did with owt nicely presented. The beans were liquidy and a little bit spicy, the avocado slices had a neat, overlapping C shape to them and there was this green hot sauce brand they had unique to the place in the condiments tray on the table which Emily felt the need to drizzle over her eggs. Not including the coffee, the meal had cost her £5:95 and it was wonderful!

After leaving Zaks and Marias, she went into Longford Centre, which had a currently unused Santa stall for the children set up, *never had a dream come true* was playing. She went into a cosmetics shop and bought another box of hair dye, the same purple/red she had used like two weeks back or summat then took the 175 bus back home, sat in her usual spot upstairs far back to the right, the bus wasn't even half-full. While going through Carlin Venture, a familiar face from primary school, Lindsey Greensmith came running upstairs, she spotted Emily then came her way.

"Ay up!" She said then sat across from her.

"How yous been?" Lindsey asked.

She and Emily hadn't been mates, nor were they on any bad terms. Greensmith had nice, full lips coated with brown lipstick, though this didn't go well with her severely tanned face and long dyed blonde hair with very tight curls. She had potential when it came to natural looks, but didn't seem to know how to make herself look presentable.

"Why you wearin' all black?" Greensmith questioned.

"Interview! I got us a new job!" Emily cheered then had a chat with Lindsey that distracted her from the gathering crowd that came upstairs around Hoperwood Beck. Greensmith had nowt interesting to say. Emily said bye to Lindsey then got off her stop beneath that tree at Carnian Street, and while walking home got beeped at by some lot driving a white van. Since she was in a good mood today she smiled, amused with flattery.

Chapter 6

Monday morning, December 7th. Emily had had a rough but very pleasant start at work on Saturday, getting to know her co-workers was the best part of it all, though the roars of a boozed-up all male crowd had really done her ears in. Now it was all about balancing her lovely new job and college studies. Emily had gotten up early, had had a toasted scrambled egg sarnie with Sriracha for breakfast with a cup of coffee with milk and sugar. She had her nose stud and lip ring back in and was dressed in beauty class uniform along with her black coat and blue hoodie like last week, flats on today as it wasn't too cold, then a final spray of perfume before exiting home.

Emily had dyed her hair with the pack she had bought on Friday, though this time the result was a bit darker, any light that struck her hair really brought out the purple bit of the shade. There were no nights out planned for the weekend, just sat at home with Mum, gossiping over wine, though Emily had bought a pair of black leather gloves on Saturday at one of the charity shops at Hoperwood Beck. She didn't have work tonight, and was thinking of cooking some meat when she came home, maybe lamb; she dared to bring out the barbeque from the shed out back, though that would get a lot of attention from the neighbours.

While waiting at the bus stop, Emily was listening to *dare* by Gorillaz, and when the 175 arrived she went upstairs to the back and saw *him* again. Gangster fella was wearing the exact same colours, though his tie was worn higher and hair slicker, as if trying to make an impression, or had to attend a meeting of some sort. The bus moved. It wasn't Gangster's appearance that was so different today. He had a sketchbook out and was doodling real quickly, robotic, a bit like a photocopier. Though other people would see it as a bit creepy, Emily couldn't resist leaning in and peeking at someone doodling; her eye caught the picture.

"That's *really* good is that!" Emily said, for lack of better words. Gangster paused, lifted his blue pencil up and looked at her with this stare as though she was the only lass on the planet. He smiled with the left side of his mouth, as though the other side of his face was paralysed. The bus turned right into Hoperwood Beck and Emily had to hold onto one of the aisle poles to avoid falling.

"What you drawin'?" She asked removing her earphones and turning off her music. Gangster stopped and put his pencil in his mouth like a cigarette, then hesitantly showed her his drawing of a very *recognisable* bloke, the hair and goatee unmistakable!

"*Noel Edmonds,*" Gangster said with Emily chuckling, leaning in further to inspect the portrait, forgetting that she had nearly put her hand on his knee as she sat down while the bus moved, where she discovered for herself. Yeah, it was definitely *deal or no deal*!

"Can't stand him!" Gangster said saying can't in the American way. He was funny!

"I *like* him, but I can't stand him!" Gangster hastily corrected his remark.

"It's his sense of humour!" Emily said.

"And the way he dresses—like he's got ideas from someone we all know!"

Gangster made this sound, that sounded like an "ah" crossed with a cackle. Emily was sat down in the centre seat. Since all the bus's windows were closed the heating was at full, she removed her overcoat and sat on it, then faced Gangster and chuckled.

"I saw you smoking a cigar…" She said. He was looking at her as though confused.

"During the fire drill last week..." Emily reminded him as she put her phone away in her bag.

"Yeah…?" Gangster said as though being accused of a sin.

"They're relaxing."

Emily scooted over a seat away from him and got a better look at Gangster's face. He had brown spots scattered about his face, some faded, some partly whitened as if bleached, and these gold spots on the white of his right eyeball, that looked like them little bits of wrapping from sweets that got stuck on your fingertips. Emily noticed he had a green folder to his right, looked like one purchased from a bargain store.

"That your portfolio?" She pointed. Then there was loud, silly-sounding commotion from downstairs, which had Gangster look towards the aisle's stairway expectantly, sort of like a copper aiming his gun in the direction of a scream. "Yeah." He breathed.

"You mind if I have a look?" Emily asked. Gangster passed the folder to her without looking at her. In plastic wallets were portraits of people, some Emily kinda recognised: that fella from the Victorian age with the big beard—Charles summat—who invented evolution, and there was Michael Jackson, Posh and Becks, Jacqui from *Hollyoaks*, Stacey from *East Enders*.

And to a surprise that would surely make anyone's day: Simon Cowell, Cheryl, Louis, Danni—the X Factor judges were there! Emily's amusement was genuine, it wasn't every day you met someone with real talent.

"Everyone keeps talking about them—they're popular, so I kinda felt *inclined* to include them…" Gangster said sounding stupidly modest.

"These are fuckin' brill!" Emily said, almost as if complaining in envy then glanced back at the artist, who held up his pencil by the foot, looking at it with endearment. It was one of them refillable sorts, blue in colour with thin white stripes and a rubber at the end.

"I won't draw with anything else…" Gangster said, the way he held it up was like it was a weapon—sort of like them films where the character said that their gun or sword was "their soul" or summat. Well fair enough, if it helped him draw! Emily turned pages, where she saw *dinosaurs*, and other weird prehistoric animals.

"Wow! I really like these!" Her marvel was genuine—even more than seeing the portraits of familiar people. Who could draw dinosaurs around here?

"Drew them from the bones up." Gangster said with a lot more enthusiasm in his voice, he shut his sketchbook and put it into the laptop bag resting at his feet. Among the plastic protected pages Emily recognised a *triceratops*, some pterodactyls, a *stegosaurus*, them long neck *brontosaurus* or Loch Ness monster thingies, some weird crocodiles and big, weird-looking birds with big teeth and scary claws, some hippo/rhino thingy with weird horns and a sabre tooth tiger.

"I liked dinosaurs when I were younger." Emily said. She had begged her Mum to buy her them books full of them colourful pictures that always had you gripped at how weird and outlandish they were, and she had enjoyed them cartoon shows and CG documentaries on the telly.

"*Why* don't you now?" Gangster asked like it was a police interrogation.

"Cuz everyone moves on?" Emily said.

"Not me…" Gangster said and sounded totally proud of it, like them people that were extreme with their appearance and walked around in public, not caring with what anyone thought about them. Emily brushed her fringe out her face.

These dinosaurs drawn by Gangster looked very different from what she was used to seeing; instead of just scales they had fuzz, feathers, sags of skin on their necks like some birds did. Some of these Gangster had drawn were actually quite scary to look at, as they certainly would have been millions of years ago—*didn't he say he did them from the bones…?*

"Didn't know they had fluff!" Emily said.

"Argh…" Gangster cursed like a teacher to a pupil who had failed to learn time and time again.

"We were all spoon-fed inaccuracies…! They don't want us to learn."

Emily held back a laugh while putting an image to Gangster's words. She enviously flicked through more pages then stopped upon seeing summat that looked familiar, but at the same time not: it looked like a dolphin with big eyes Gangster really brought the life into, didn't have that fin on its back, had the body of summat like a crocodile, four flippers, and the tail had a sort of half fin to it.

"That one of them dinosaur dolphin thingies?" Emily asked.

"Yeah." Gangster corrected without looking at her.

"This is a *cymbospondylus*—means: boat spine. It was like a *transitional* specimen."

Emily couldn't process that David Attenborough language, as much as she was fascinated by it.

"Midway?" Gangster explained with Emily catching up.

"Like ape-men?" She said with Gangster grunting and raising his right hand, wiggling his bony fingers for emphasis.

"On them lines."

Emily remembered watching *Digimon* when she was a kid, that Japanese show with all the monsters with these freaky names transforming into summat bigger and weirder during every fight. Gangster seemed like that type of lad! He could be drawing for the producers or summat! Emily turned the pages and saw this meat-eating dinosaur on the left with what looked like a curving hair comb on its head, its mouth opened and sharp teeth exposed, the piercing detail of the eyes staring straight off the page like it wanted to kill the viewer. **Cryolophosaurus** was written below in the neatest handwriting ever—how did you pronounce that? The creature on the opposite page, titled: **hopolophoneus**, looked almost like a leopard, but had fewer spots, it was drawn in a stalking pose with its teeth exposed, and it had longer teeth that went beyond the lower jaw and this short droop below the chin.

"Glad they're not around!" Emily remarked.

"Why?" Gangster asked like it was so important.

"A *dromaeosaur* running off with your credit card?"

"I don't have a credit card…!" Emily said back.

"What's a dromaeosaur?"

Gangster held up his right hand and curled his index finger into a claw which he constantly flicked downwards, as if tapping.

"Raptors…?" He said as though she didn't know the first letter of the alphabet. Emily searched her memory.

"Oh them? They're nasty!"

Gangster was peering outside, there didn't seem to be owt worth looking at though.

"Obviously you like dinosaurs?" Emily openly said—a no-brainer.

Instead of a simple yes or no Gangster said, "The Mesozoic's like a sushi bar; it focuses heavily on the reptiles—the diapsids."

Emily had some idea what he was on about.

"You should be a writer!" She suggested.

"And I love sushi!"

"Same here." Gangster said, attention still fixed beyond the window.

"I love dinosaurs so much I eat them."

As in birds? Was that what he was on about? Emily chuckled.

"I like some marinated chicken with rice and homemade hot sauce!" Gangster said.

"I love a decent chicken tikka masala!" Emily spoke her mind. Gangster had nowt to say to it.

"They say birds evolved from dinosaurs." Emily continued the conversation, recalling a documentary.

"They are!" Gangster said with a harsh "ah" to his pronunciation.

"At least, you're up to date!"

He sounded critical.

"So when did these live?" Emily hovered a finger over the two drawings.

"I know there's like different time periods and all."

Gangster leaned in towards her without looking at her, his gaze fixed forward.

"Two words: *before God*," he said. While she understood, Emily didn't know how to react to that. She turned the pages, saw two meat eating dinos, both were strange and had these distinctive semi-circle things on their heads like them big, weird birds in Australian. Gangster pointed at the specimen on the left, called: **guanlong**…this dinosaur had short, dark fuzzy feathers all over its body except for the snout, throat and feet, its arms were long with three clawed fingers and feathers like a useless pair of wings, and guanlong probably would have been colourful judging from the heavily varied shading Gangster employed.

"*Gu-an-long*. North West China, mid Jurassic, Oxfordian stage."

It sounded Chinese the way he said the dinosaur's name. Emily didn't say anything, nor did she commit the sin of shrugging.

"One hundred and sixty million years ago?" Gangster simplified.

"A primitive *tyrannosauridae*—an ancestral relative of the T. rex."

"A great grandfather uncle or summat?" Emily said trying to engage decently.

"Precisely!" Gangster said nicely, flashing a lovely smile for a moment. The second dinosaur on page, called: **dilophosaurus**, looked similar to the guanlong, but it didn't have feathers but spikes on its back like some lizards, had a spotted patterning, a slightly longer snout, longer neck and four shorter fingers. It looked very familiar; as it had a pair of them round thingies on its head which Emily remembered from some film…

"*Dilophosaurus wetherilli*," Gangster said.

"Arizona early Jurassic, one hundred and ninety million years ago. They were six metres long, and no, they didn't spit acid!"

The last sentence he spoke with a firm sense of correction.

"You have *talent* I have to tell you!" Emily said enviously. Gangster sat back and relaxed his tense shoulders.

"Doesn't really get me anywhere." He said darkly, still not making eye contact with her.

"Aw! Don't talk like that!" Emily said back.

"You could get a job doing portraits!"

"Not my *type* of lifestyle!" Gangster said as if unimpressed then looked up at the bus's ceiling, for some reason.

"What *is* your ideal life then?" Emily challenged—this was turning into a good verbal fight!

"Me? Productivity, creativity, good food, a good sex life, dead or badly hurt enemies," he casually yet boldly said what most blokes were afraid to say.

"Be nice to bring them back in some way..." He abruptly added aiming a finger at his folder. By that he meant dinosaurs?

"*How* would you do that?" Emily asked expecting some mad, nonsensical reply.

"Advanced C-G media...along with some advanced AI, maybe...? Certified by paleontological experts and zoologists?" Gangster answered confidently then shuffled in his seat. Emily had an idea of that; maybe some sort of exhibition with massive screens and state of the art graphics and an interactive feature...? Summat the whole family would like?

The bus was coming downhill into Carlin Venture, during the day the repetitive grid of inner suburban housing could be seen spread out for a half mile on each side of Harewood Road as well as a few green spaces between them, which made the district look like a wooden artist's palette with random green splodges of paint.

"You look tiered." Gangster said all of a sudden. Emily turned her head and saw that he was looking straight at her.

"I' am! A bit!"

"Did your *cuckoo clock* not wake you up in time?"

That was random! Emily smiled, nervously chuckling with them amusing noises along with various images of the bird appearing out from the clock playing in her head from memory.

"*Why* would I have a cuckoo clock...?" She asked as meekly as her smile, aware of how cute she did sound. Gangster shrugged.

"I don't know what girls keep at home!"

A pitifully giggling Emily needed to ask him summat.

"Do you watch *Corrie* or *Emmerdale*?"

"What's that? A type of cheese?" Gangster asked almost instantly and blinked, looking really confused. He didn't sound like he was joking. Emily thought about it and really tried not to laugh. Come to think of it, yeah, it did! Like Wensleydale... She was familiar with the term ambivalence, where you had two different opinions about something. Gangster represented that. Emily surrendered to a cough of laughter—*have you even lived?* She wanted to tell him.

"You listen to any music?" She asked instead.

"Yeah, the sort that don't sound like recruitment tools."

You what? Was there any limit to his randomness?

"And I don't go to concerts." He said. That was just bad! Emily went to any concert for any artist she was a fan of, whenever they were in the country.

A bunch of lads came running upstairs, being loud and obnoxious on purpose for attention, nearly tripping over as the bus moved and laughing about it. Gangster didn't look impressed, he glared at them with that same hostility he displayed to the crowd during the fire drill assembly, and it was good the lads only sat near the front.

"They don't know it, but they're the luckiest pricks in the world!" Gangster said, taking a sudden turn to the dark side of conversation.

"They can just be loud and walk up and insult someone and walk away with their tongues and teeth!"

He fiddled about with the fingers of his right hand, tapping them against his knee then tenderly scratched the back of his neck.

"They're just young lads being themselves," Emily said trying to appease any upcoming sorrow.

"They're gonna have partners and kids one day."

Gangster stopped scratching then looked at her, his eyes said summat like: *you're one hundred percent wrong!*

"You *don't* have to be an asshole to be a father…!" He said with his mouth. But then again, so many dads were!

"Respect is the last thing they deserve!" Gangster continued his ravings. "They spot you, patrol your line of sight, target and follow you home, bring all their friends around, each one uglier than the last and full of shit!"

Then he mimed a gunshot with his right hand in the direction of the lads sat at the front, his expression bitter and lips pursued and retracting tightly in very apparent anger.

"They all get away with it!"

Good thing them lads hadn't seen that!

"You're not a chav are you…?" Gangster asked, his tone almost to the point of rude, his imaginary gun hand pointed up at the ceiling.

"No…!" Emily proudly exclaimed her denial, her mouth dropping open without the need to shake her head.

"That's good! Be a shame if you were…!" Gangster lowered his imaginary gun hand to his lap, then reached out with his left hand and placed it on the top of the seat in front of him.

"Harsh!" Emily said playfully.

"Getting your face dunked in stinging nettles for trying to get past the crooked slow dick in front of you, cuz you're in a rush *is* harsh!" Gangster bounced back, speaking quickly as he did. Emily's responsive chuckle wasn't meant for any offence or owt, on the inside she was asking herself whether that had really happened. Or had he seen it on telly or happen to someone else?

"Bullying, it claims more lives than terrorists." Gangster said potently, like some ending subtext for them TV adverts that were meant to disturb you and coerce you into calling a number for some organisation. There was a ring of truth in what he said, if you let yourself dive into deep thought. But no one would probably listen—here you got dissed and battered for it.

"Same with beggars and homeless." He added. Emily didn't agree.

"Them lot are just unfortunate people tryin' to get by." She had to say from her heart, but without making any commotion.

"Ah…!" Gangster snarled irritably looking away.

"People are always thinking about their situation, and not who they are as people!"

A courtroom type of argument was starting.

"You don't know what sort of person they were, *before* they decided to be homeless. No one ever talks about that!" Gangster said in defence.

"They could have been really nasty—why'd you think they're not afraid to go up to you, and mouth off when you don't give 'em anything? They're not intelligent and that bugs me! Nasty and unintelligent is the worst combination ever!"

Upon hearing several cars beep, a near collision, Emily along with nearly all the passengers looked to the right. Except for Gangster.

"Besides, this is Britain, not third world, as much as it wants to be."

He added. This debate could go on for hours with another person; a thick cunt, as Gangster was on about, would turn it into fun one moment then get violent despite not understanding what was being said. Guiltily enough, sometimes Emily envied them…

"Who'd you vote for this year…?" she asked.

That probably wasn't the best question, Emily had voted for labour. Gangster didn't reply, instead he went into his inner jacket pocket. And of all the things he could take out it wasn't another cigar, and it wasn't even a gun—some people must surely have joked about! It was one of them tiny Jack Daniel's!

"A bit early?" Emily coughed with laughter, her smiling intensified.

"I need to *fortify* my willpower…" Gangster said a bit depressively looking away from Emily as though she had a big mole on her face.

"At this moment, it's not very strong."

She couldn't help but laugh, having not heard anything like that from an actual person, other than some quote in a film. And Gangster looked like someone out of a film, and acted like he was in a film.

"What'd you like?" Emily remarked in response. Gangster looked at her with this indescribable expression she couldn't be sure meant if he were offended or puzzled.

"I'm not exactly *sure* yet." His weird reply was loaded with mystery. Did he have a girlfriend?

"Need some solution." Gangster added, blinking a lot as though he had summat in his eye then sighed. He raised the mini bottle in a toast gesture to the air.

"Cheers…!" Emily said frivolously and watched him swig down half the bottle, he gasped gently afterwards, his cheeks flustering and eyes watering from the burn of the whisky.

"I'd vote for the panda." He answered an earlier question. *Panda?* That was random! Emily looked at him for what seemed like an hour.

"Why…?" She chuckled awkwardly.

"Just bamboo, survival and procreation for them, and looking cute for us humans."

That was Gangster's answer.

"Why?" He said, eyebrows lowering slightly.

"Don't you like pandas…?"

It sounded like a diss, but it was the weirdest diss Emily had heard!

"I do like pandas!" She complained. Gangster was expressionless.

"Good!" He said strongly like she understood.

"People who don't like pandas are just assholes!"

Folder still in hand Emily flicked through deeper.

"So, you do anything else other than dinosaurs and people?" She asked and found out for herself after turning the page. There was a drawing of a mummy. Not a loving mother, but a dead body with wrinkles of dried decayed flesh over a skull, a perpetual grin from the exposed teeth, dark, empty eye sockets staring emptily off the page, the preserved skin appeared varnished and the body sat in a yoga position and dressed in some oriental robes.

"A mummy! I don't like them things!" Emily said with a heavy cringe in her voice, completely forgetting about the last bit of banter, images of mummies from books and documentaries flashing through her mind. They had always freaked her out.

"Then you're gonna love the Japanese!" Gangster interjected lightly as he screwed the J.D.'s lid back on and slipped the bottle back into his jacket pocket.

"There were these priests that mummified *themselves*."

What...? Emily would write that in big bold letters accompanied by several question marks.

"How'd you mummify yourself?" She asked in a surprisingly casual tone, despite how weirder things kept getting with her fellow passenger! Gangster's expression didn't change.

"Well," he started and held up his right hand, fingers making delicate gestures. "They undergo this thing called *sokushinbutsu*. It's kind of a phase of enlightenment to become one with Buddha. Takes ten years to complete and very painful, done in three phases. First: the monk trims his fat down to zero, engages in rigorous exercise and sticks to a diet of nuts and seeds for three years. Then for the next three it's just tree bark and roots local to his temple."

Gangster paused, looking like he was ready to say summat proper critical.

"And then he poisons himself with tree sap to get rid of bodily fluid and to make his flesh inedible to maggots."

He did! Emily shuddered while managing to look interested.

"After that he seats himself in a tomb, large enough so he can sit cross-legged and meditate. They give him a bell and an air tube. Each day he rings the bell to let them know he's still alive."

Emily's phone vibrated, and she burrowed her hand into her handbag. She wasn't ignoring Gangster.

"When the bell stops ringing, they seal up the tomb. After another three years, they dig up the tomb and see."

There was creepy and there was dead creepy!

"They didn't even need to remove the organs like the Egyptians did!" Gangster added. Emily continued looking at him even while she took out her phone, thumbing buttons. It was a text from Jody, the fat bitch of whom would make a fuss of this perfectly lean and interesting fella. She immediately put her phone away and gave Gangster an apologetic look and smile, which he didn't see as he was looking forward with his eyes scrolling about as though there was a fly somewhere.

"And the monks, they sit in that position until they expired; in total devotion to their cause. But in the end most just rotted. Others, well…"

He ran a hand through his smart hair.

"They became Buddha incarnate, mascot of a temple or village. There were like only a handful out of the hundreds that tried."

He stopped, Emily was about to comment.

"I can't help but admire that. Unlike these lot…" Gangster started again, his eyes aimed disapprovingly at everyone else on the bus. He then looked humbly at Emily.

"Eerie!" She said, not mockingly.

"I'm surprised a young lad here even knows that!"

Though Emily didn't glorify the macabre, this brief lecture was maybe the one exception. She wasn't gonna tell anyone for as long as she lived!

She turned the last page of Gangster's folder and saw the scariest abstract she had ever seen; a monster, summat masculine with really wide shoulders and long, muscular arms like an ape stood up. It had chunky, fingerless boxing-glove-shaped hands, a small, stumpy head with no neck and a gaping black hole for a face. It was uglier than all seven sins combined. Gangster's shading of the skin was so expertly done so you could not ignore this sickening texture, the sort you saw from them tiny cameras that went inside the body and showed you what went on, and the mix mash of crudely depicted but very apparent female body parts; its chest was made up of the nude backs of two, headless women sat in a foetal position side by side. And *what* was it that Gangster had drawn over the crotch? A football with the obvious texture of the inside of a tangerine over it? That was a world away from his lovely animal drawings, and Emily didn't want to look at it any longer.

"That's scary!" She said lightly without breaking her tone.

"Wouldn't want to have nightmares of that!"

She didn't need him to go into detail. Gangster smirked on the right side of his face, while running his right thumb down along the rim of his tie. Then Emily carefully shut the folder with her left hand and pointed a finger downwards at it.

"That's really impressive!" It was a modest compliment.

"Wish I could draw!"

Gangster furrowed his eyebrows. Emily handed him back his folder, he leaned over smoothly putting it away into his laptop bag, the zipping sound muted so as to not sound like summat ruder on a bus full of people. Now, it was time for a more *normal* question.

"So, where you from like?" Emily asked Gangster to break the silence. "Singapore?"

"No." Gangster denied and shook his head.

"I didn't wanna say *Chinese* in case you get offended an' that!" Emily explained. Gangster grinned.

"Better than Taiwan!" He said a bit harshly as though he didn't trust anyone.

"I get bullied a lot for that."

"Aw, you…!" Emily said tenderly.

"You're sweet!" Gangster said—*I know I' am!*

"Aw! Tah!" Emily laughed.

"I'm a *luk khrueng*."

It sounded like some ancient tribal term—like someone important—like a guard of some sacred place.

"Half-Thai, half-English." Gangster added more pleasantly.

"Not *half time*! I know it sounds similar it's because most people wish they were retarded!"

More strong words! Emily smiled in defiance.

"Am I retarded?" She challenged.

"No!" Gangster said and smiled perfectly.

"You're diligently thoughtful."

Thank Goodness for that!

"I went to Thailand this summer." Gangster shifted to summat positive.

"Were it nice?" Asked Emily really wanting to know.

"Could've been better." Gangster replied then smacked his lower lip to the left, the peak of his lower right canine pressing below the flesh of his lip.

"I do like being half-English—it was the English that coined the term "dinosaur"."

Emily didn't have anything to say to that bit, though she was secretly surprised and mildly expressed interest with her raised eyebrows and bobbing head.

"I wanna go to Thailand," she said, figuring out how and when she would get around to doing that.

"I really like Thai food!"

Gangster grunted pleasingly.

"Always some place to eat there, any time of the day. You don't have to worry about queues," he said coolly and confidently.

"Unlike here…"

A silence ensued.

"Well, I can cook some of it!" Gangster quickly broke it, then looked away awkwardly as if Emily had bad breath or summat.

"I like massaman and green curry," Emily said.

"I love me curries!"

"Had them for breakfast on many occasions, here and over there…" Gangster said with his fingers rising to his chin.

"Haven't cooked them though."

Though he didn't express enthusiasm like a curry lover, he opened a new area for conversation.

"Can you like…cook pad thai?" Emily asked him.

"*Pad thai?*" Gangster said back musically with an accent sounding like he could speak the language fluently and nodded. After watching the world go by from the bus window, he turned to look at her.

"A *speciality* of mine—I have my own little version! I cooked it in my mom's restaurant."

His mood brightened more, like there was hope or summat.

"Your mum owns a restaurant?"

While Emily's keenness showed in her widening eyes, Gangster paused, his posture sinking slightly.

"She's worked at a lot…Leeds mainly." He spoke slowly and with discomfort, then sat up straighter.

"Nam tok neua." He said, the words pronounced with a heavy accent, probably saying summat related to family; like a brother being a certain character and a sister who had this sort of role…

"What's that?" Emily asked.

"A real spicy beef salad, good with sticky rice and whiskey!"

He had changed the subject.

"I like spicy!" Emily said.

"You'll like this then…"

"How spicy is it?"

"Might be a little…bit too much…" Gangster tugged at the buttons of his shirt. "Not recommended as a main course!"

The last sentence had a lot of energy to it; his voice had more energy and personality, and he didn't seem to care that it might piss someone off or make them feel insecure.

"So which one of your parents is Thai?" Emily enquired.

"My mother." Gangster replied.

"Ah! Thai women are right pretty!"

Emily had watched them documentaries. Gangster though grunted like the remark was poisonous.

"So many *dickheads* go there! You can't even talk to them! You speak Thai and they get mad!" He said almost angrily and raised his right hand, wiggling his fingers at his crown.

"Just like cops…" He added. Emily didn't get that last bit. She didn't know what to say.

"I *do* respect law and order…!" Gangster said hastily, almost in a panic as though he psychically sensed Emily's discomfort and didn't wave any corresponding gestures.

"Just not *this* one!" He cemented a surprise finish, just before a lass with two little girls came upstairs, one of them red faced and crying hysterically—nails on a chalkboard annoying—and the mother doing nowt to appease her child. Like the lads that came upstairs earlier, Gangster really didn't like it, and again made it obvious; his eyes widening and flaring with contempt at the crying child like it was one hundred percent her fault and could just swat her, as casually as a fly pissing off someone.

"Argh, fuck!" He snarled quietly.

"A whiny child comes onboard, let's all feel endeared!" He complained.

"You alright…?" Emily asked him aware that this could get uncomfortable.

"Children are *dangerous* to the group!" He said and took out his Jack Daniel's.

"Someone with a baby wants refuge and their begging and guilt-tripping you to get into their *secure* space…"

Though she wished she didn't, Emily actually knew what was being said. But it wasn't summat people were ready for, nor were they willing to provide a *solution* to it.

"In the end, everyone gets caught!" Gangster said ruthlessly.

"But the baby can't help it!" Emily said, her counter argument seated in the boat of common sense and humanity…though she was sure she couldn't get through to him. There were far worse things people could say. And do.

"That's the most dangerous thing about it!" Gangster said unscrewing the cap of his whisky bottle.

"And everyone acts like they're pure and innocent from everything."

He raised the mini bottle to his mouth but hesitated.

"Babies…infants…" He said, while Emily looked at the head of the wailing little girl who had calmed down, her Mum actually patting her, "…they die every day; some get blown up, get these viral pathogens and die slowly, they get torn apart and eaten by animals."

After that devastating quote Gangster tilted his head back and drank, finishing the bottle.

"And I'm suddenly the bad guy! I don't decide!" He said and rubbed the back of his right arm.

"Though it'd be better if I did than some PC hippy!"

Emily had heard so much horrid banter in her life… But none so honest, none with so much passion and without having to swear every few seconds. Even though she was still deeply, utterly disgusted by it.

"You have some strong opinions, me love!" She said automatically, regretting she hadn't sounded politer. Gangster grunted.

"What do I call you…?" He asked. Emily replied, but the little girl had decided to cry again and drown out her words. "Come again?" Gangster requested and eyed the noisy child.

"Emily," she answered him.

"But everyone calls me Nicole."

Gangster grunted, put a finger to his chin and grinned.

"You look *more* like a Nicole." He complimented before she could ask him his name.

"Tah!"

"But I think you look like a Katie also!" Gangster added. Emily jutted her lip forward, while she tried to…process what information she had received. The nasty, anti-humanity stuff from a few seconds ago seemed to have died down. "You religious or something?" Gangster pried with Emily wondering why he'd bring that up.

"Catholic," she said proudly.

"Not too devout—laid back and all!"

Gangster though didn't look impressed, he blinked tightly, searching for something to say. Emily had summat to say.

"You Buddhist?" She asked him, "Thais are Buddhist, right?"

"I don't follow any creed, but I respect Buddhism."

He had the attitude of someone who could never be pleased, no matter how hard others tried.

"It's the marijuana of religion; it never did any harm."

That last part was hilarious but interesting, though most would just laugh without thinking about it.

"Can you do mine?" Emily asked, referring to her portrait and Gangster, who surely knew what she were on about looked at her, and made these weird movements with his head.

"Me portrait?"

"I...don't think we have time here..." Gangster said sombrely and looked about, turning his head at short, tight angles with a strong, straining look of thought.

"If I had a photo of you to work from, then I could do it at home," he said, a condition Emily thought about...

"If you don't mind..." Gangster said reaching back and taking out his phone from a pouch on his belt at his left side, like where a copper kept his gun, it was unusual but nowt to fuss over.

"Alright then!" Emily accepted his terms. His phone, despite his suave dress ironically was not one of the latest models, not a touch screen but summat in fashion maybe three or four years ago. He slid off the cover for the phone's camera with his finger and raised it with Emily smiling, not showing too much teeth and posed.

"Ok...three, two, one." Gangster counted. Emily held her pose, the bus didn't make any sudden, picture-ruining jerks.

The photographer's thumb pressed down on the button, no distracting flash came. Gangster inspected the photo and grunted pleasingly.

"I can work from that, Nicole!" He said her name very cleanly, like how gentlemen said madam then turned his phone around with Emily leaning in to see her photo which wasn't bad at all!

"That's alright!" She commented. Though Gangster was probably gonna wank off to this trophy tonight, which was sorta sweet. But only if the promise

140

was fulfilled though. How many fellas who had laid eyes on her had fantasies about her each day? Hundreds. And the people behind CCTV weren't exactly honest themselves with all the groping security at the airport, and now there were these X-rays coming into use that allowed people to be seen naked, which was very off putting and concerning.

"I'm gonna call you: *Venus.*" Gangster said putting his phone away back in its pouch without looking her way.

"You what?"

Emily thought she heard him say "penis". But she quickly realised that wasn't the case.

"Why?" Emily asked giggling while wearing a puzzled look.

"Because you might as well be!" Gangster was insistent.

The Roman God of beauty and love… Quite the compliment actually, even if other people were gonna diss her for what it also sounded like. Emily blinked and raised both eyebrows. Her day had been made!

"You're so random!" She said, people looking their way.

"*Your cheeks are adorable!*" Gangster said ignoring them. No one had ever said owt about her cheeks before, and a blushing Emily widened her eyes and looked about, her smile as unbalanced as a seesaw, no one was looking their way. It didn't take her too long to figure out what he meant.

"Yeah! My cheeks are a bit full and that!" She said, putting her right hand to her right cheek.

"There should be coked-up *mariachi* playing in the background with that look of yours!"

Gangster held up both hands, his fingers fiddling about and miming a trumpet while be made similar noises.

"What's mariachi?" Emily needed to know, having heard it mentioned many times before.

"Mexican music? Those really big hats?" Gangster elaborated, spreading out his hands above his head a foot apart and mimed playing a guitar.

"Oh yeah! I'd love to go to Mexico! I love Mexican food!" Emily enthusiastically remarked as memories of bits from films and TV programs came back to her. She was just about to tell Gangster that she worked at a Mexican restaurant.

"I envisage you…" He said before Emily could speak, and put symmetrically cupped hands to his face like he was using binoculars. "…Eating spaghetti Bolognese!"

She didn't get it one bit, but she had a crystal clear mental image of what he were on about. Any other lass would go mental!

"I love spaghetti, you!" Emily interrupted.

"I make us own from scratch!"

"A bob cut!" He said with a girly child's voice, pointing at her hair. For someone with such a serious face, he did produce the most adorable expressions!

"I do have a bob cut!" Emily said back and brushed back the bangs of her fringe.

"Why you name Emily?" Gangster shot back at her with an even more infant tone to his voice. That was such a weird question!

"*Why* is my name Emily?" Emily said back thinking about it, her eyes widening and expression sulking. Could any bloke be more random than that?

"Cuz me mum named me…?" Emily said innocently enough.

"Adorable!" Gangster said as if Emily were summat fluffy and cuddly—like a panda. Then she asked him a very important question: "D'you have a girlfriend?"

"No," Gangster said without moving his lips.

"Get one!" Emily said cheeringly.

"Get online! Soon you'll be having kids!"

Gangster looked unsteady, he went into a blinking spell, his jaw moving about for a moment before coming to a complete still.

"I'd…like a daughter…" He said almost as a whisper, there was grimness in his voice. It was only then that Emily realised she had arrived in town and was just yards away from her stop. This must have been the quickest bus ride into town! Seeing them lovely drawings had really made her day! As it would for little kids; they'd love them, framed and hung up in the classroom. Emily asked herself *why* children liked dinosaurs the most, before they would move onto like football, makeup, reality TV, booze and drugs and cars and plastic surgery.

"It's our stop! I'll see you later love!" Emily announced and threw on her coat. Gangster sprang up out of his seat, he was taller than Emily by an inch or two.

Then he slouched forward a couple of degrees, he had a very distinct stance you could see in a crowd. Emily walked forward, other people stepping out into the aisle in front and behind her as she headed for the stairs.

"I'll have your portrait for you, Monday." Gangster called out promisingly like some gentleman who guaranteed a reliable service. Emily turned around and saw him with his laptop bag strapped to his back instead of hand carrying, and half the passengers looking at him, only for a sec though.

"Alright!" Emily said and saw Gangster smile warmly her way. She didn't even get his name.

The alighting passengers moved slowly, and continued to even as they stepped off the bus. On the footpath of Furnivall Road, Emily went into her bag for a cig, lit one up then looked around and saw Gangster walking up road on the other side of the street. He looked back at her and held up his hand. Emily smiled and returned it. If she saw him in college next time, she thought she'd join him for a coffee or summat. Emily put her earphones in, *bad romance* playing. While walking through Isherwood Centre, Emily passed by a jewellery shop, she stopped and backtracked, engraved on a gold ruby ring. Rubies were her favourite of the gems. And at two hundred and thirty quid she couldn't afford it! It would make a nice present.

Chapter 7

Tuesday. There was another event on up at the Stanley Parker this Friday, but Emily had work for the rest of the week after college, and Christmas was coming up along with a bit more clubbing, so she needed to make money for then. At least, these evening hours were short. She was stood behind the bar at Zaks and Marias dressed in her work uniform: a plain black polo shirt—you had to wear a black top of some sort—the rest was more relaxed with dark blue skinny jeans and some black trainers. She had removed her mouth ring but kept her nose stud, her polo shirt she wore untucked and buttoned all the way up with her crucifix showing for sophistication, her hair unstyled, the purple/red colour being the highlight with her head looking like a fruity, berry flavoured lollipop from behind.

Emily had a work mate, Chris who had been here for nearly a year now, she was a five foot midget, wore her blonde hair up high in a topknot and she happened to be quite a looker; her all black, skin-hugging, cat woman choice of work outfit conveyed that. She got a lot of attention from male customers, but mainly due to her short stature, remarks of which could be heard over the music, though not as much as Emily when she stepped out from the bar, going back and forth to fetch glasses and cutlery from the tables. So far she hadn't had any verbal hassle from the male customers, whom were monitoring her bum as she moved from table to table.

Every hour or so a crowd came in and April, the deputy manager, wearing a fairly loose fitting black turtle neck sweater would be bobbing out from behind the bar, informing the two bar lasses of the profits gained so far: *four hundred, four hundred and forty six, five hundred and two* etcetera, and usually complaining about the lack of in regards to the time of day. April was in her mid-forties, slightly taller than average with a lean, almost athletic figure, long dark blonde hair, a parted fringe and a mid-height ponytail, her glassy, grey/blue eyes seemed to shine like gems against her desert sand tan face, her high cheeks were

144

sunken and her jaw was very defined, not like big or owt but really emphasised her clean, white smile. She looked amazing for her age. There was a couple sat by the window, their baby was crying, and they were giving it plenty of attention, trying to pacify it and gently cradling it. Emily couldn't resist gliding over.

"Aw you!" She said consolingly and leaned in.

"Wanna try?" The mother said welcomingly instead of causing a fuss, and held out her baby and actually let Emily cradle it.

"Usually works!" She said and continued to rock the child back and forth until the mother wanted her back.

"Thank you!" The mother said, Emily hearing her and her partner squeal gratefully in awe, accompanied by a second thank you, and her partner appeared to be such a happy chap! Emily had always had a knack for pacifying infants; originally she had considered working in a nursery. The couple had thanked Emily again before she went back behind the bar, no tips though but that was ok.

Emily was put on her dinner break by Thorold, who was only around behind the bar, sat on a simple chair and busy on his laptop, and not sat upstairs in a fancy chair watching everyone on multiple security cameras like some villainous overlord. The Killers *smile like you mean it* was playing while Emily sat down on her discount dinner break with a pulled pork burrito and coke, which was lovely although the portion should have been maybe a third larger to satisfy her appetite; she had been starving. She helped herself to some more of the venue's green chilli hot sauce, which she splashed over the last third of her burrito, then was approached by the on-duty security staff, Marvin his name was. He was Emily's height, lean, in his fifties, had big ears with these deep creases all over his reddened, rubbery-looking face. He wasn't the best-looking bloke. And he didn't look after his teeth too much; they were yellowed and like the white and black keys of a piano, the blacks being the gaps from the teeth he had lost from excessive smoking. He sat down across from Emily, uninvited and started talking. It didn't take him too long to get into uncomfortable stuff.

"I were workin' in Lytham Arcade last year, they've got like twenty cameras in there and three security on the floor, and these Romanians…Latvians…or Polish—whatever they bleedin' were—came in. There's this woman, she's in with a four year old and a fifteen year old and they split when they come in. And we're all watching 'em." Marvin spoke aggressively, his brown eyes wide all the time to make an unnecessary glare, the creases on his forehead deepened with every tick like they could fold over each other.

145

"There's a thick post in front of the entrance—"

"Yeah, I know where you mean." Emily said abruptly, stressing her irritation.

"It's deliberately wide so we can wait with our back to it and they tell us," Marvin tapped on his ear as though he had an earpiece. "And he tells us: *three, two, one, they're coming!*"

He raised his thumb, flipped it down then made a fart noise like a child would. Emily was about to lose her appetite.

"So I stop 'em, and it's just them kids!" Marvin said.

"Oh dear…!" Emily blankly remarked before she took a bite of her burrito.

"Turns out the mother's just left her kids and fucked off down in the basement! And I were watching that footage. She walks straight into a locked door with all these bags and we stop her! It were over a fuckin' grand of stuff she had in her bags!"

Marvin raised a thumb and pointed it over his shoulder.

"*Get back inside!* I tell 'em and have 'em put in detention! Over there they cut your hands off for stealing! Here," he pointed down at the table. "You'll live, but I'll just cap your benefits!"

Then he did that same fart sound again—*bloody cut that out will yah!*

Believable as that story was, Emily couldn't tell who was worse, the shoplifter using her children, or this obnoxious security guard who seemed to like what he was doing a bit too much? She didn't need to hear any more of this.

"Marvin?" He was called over by April.

"Leave her alone yah pilac! She's new here!"

She had a rough, commanding, drill sergeant-like voice with a Leeds accent, and it was enough to have Marvin get up out of his seat and leave, though he was still looking at Emily, even as he walked backwards! Thank God that was over! Some people were just awful with conversation.

Back on the bar a small crowd had come in, and it wasn't a nice one, a bunch of college age lads and lasses, most of them were on the chavy side, but they mixed in with a couple of alternative sorts, summat that only happened in the city and not the suburbs. Though there was an extra hand on the bar April stepped in and monitored the lot.

"ID 'em all!" She instructed as she walked by Emily. One of the lads stood slouched against the bar and was trying to chat up Chris, pitifully enough he kept calling back to his mates sat at the table for support, while Chris wore a fake smile. Plenty of cocktails were ordered, among them were two long island ice teas and a strawberry daiquiri, which Emily found therapeutic in making, probably because of the shaking bit, the energy and focus involved that distracted from the clientele.

Twenty or so minutes in and the group were getting louder, they started singing, whistling and pounding their palms against the table.

"*Shut your fuckin' mouth yah numpty!*" One of the lads said casually to his mate while looking on his phone's screen then cackled loudly. Them same lads chatting up Chris didn't give up on her, boozed-up and swearing like their life depended on it wasn't the best way to pull a lass. They looked Emily's way with cheeky smiles and waves, the start of an onslaught of sexual gestures to come.

"Don't serve 'em anymore alcohol!" April said discreetly as she walked past behind her. She knew the trade, her assessment was smooth. Two of the lads approached the bar, one of them whistled annoyingly while waiting.

"For fuck sake man!" His mate blabbered loudly looking back at the group, just as Emily approached. He turned back around, didn't look surprised by her presence, then asked for another round.

"I can't serve yah." Emily said abiding April's instructions.

"Why not?" One of them asked unsurprisingly. This was the worst part of the job, after toilet checks.

"You're too loud and yah keep swearin'."

Emily braced herself for a mouthful of abuse and options how to handle the situation and look cool doing so, if owt bad kicked off then she'd have to push the panic button under the bar counter, far less obvious to the offender than having to phone the police. But the lads and his gang left without having to take the piss, except for one of them who was still sat at the table where them lot had sat. Then April walked behind Emily.

"Alright me love?" She enquired to her wellbeing.

"Yeah, fine!" Emily assured her.

"Had much worse back at Hoperwood!"

The incident was earlier last year, at her previous pub job where she had refused service to a female customer off her head on summat, who had called her a *bitch* and had knocked several empty glasses off the counter which hadn't half made her jump. She had had to phone the police, and seeing that the customer had picked up another customer's drink and chucked it at the counter, luckily she had been so pissed the glass had only shattered below the counter. And instead of walking out and taking her chances, the customer had picked a fight with a bloke who had stepped in, she had slapped him then had been pinned to the floor and restrained by other helpful customers until the coppers arrived. The drunk lass had been arrested and Emily had given a statement to the police fresh after the trauma, which hadn't comforted her in anyway, nor had helping her fellow staff clean up all the glass and shite left behind. She had drunk a full bottle of wine just to get to sleep that night.

The lad from that rowdy group that was left was sat quietly by himself, not causing any hassle and likely embarrassed by his mates. He came up to the bar, April approached him.

"What you havin' me love?"

She was friendly and flashed him a tight smile. He asked if he could order a bottle of cider.

"Yah *can* love!" April said. From there, the one member of the crowd just drank in peace and went on his way. Seven O'clock, kids had to be out, the general pub rule as the more explicit things got, in town it was more apparent than the suburbs. The lights on the bar dimmed down, the music was turned up more, and customers came in steadily, usually dressed up like they were gonna head off to a nightclub later. Emily was left on her own behind the bar, cleaning up glasses, Shakira's *she wolf* was playing. Two Asian blokes in their mid-thirties with army style crew cuts, clearly on a binge came up to the bar, all chatty. One of them was wearing a thin gold chain around his neck, while his mate wore a really suave silvery watch.

Emily put her cloth down and approached them with a smile.

"What can I get you me love?"

She got no answer, and it took the fellas a while to decide.

"What is this called?" The fella with the chain pointed at the Flibbigans pump, which seemed really out of place in a Mexican place.

"Flibbigans—Flibbies." Emily answered without trying to get into conversation.

"Why?" The fella with the chain asked and smiled widely.

"Mmm?" Emily grunted keeping her smile.

"Why is it called *Flabby*?" The fella with the watch grilled.

"Why do they have *stupid* names here?"

Still smiling, Emily shrugged at the otherwise hilarious question.

"I dunno—I just work here…!" She said unable to help laughing halfway through her sentence.

The two blokes ordered two pints of Flibbies, Emily poured them, they paid and they cheered but remained stood at the bar, gossiping among themselves in their own language. It didn't take them long to get all chatty again.

"She is *beautiful*!" The fella with the watch pointed out. Emily flattered him with a smile.

"You have a boyfriend?" The fella with the chain asked her. Again, Emily just smiled.

"You *want* a boyfriend?" The bloke's mate pointed a thumb at his own chest then at his mate.

"You can have two!"

Emily chuckled.

"No…!" She said keeping a smile.

"Why not?" The customer asked with Emily's expression shifting awkwardly as she struggled to answer, wondering if she would regret serving them in a few minutes. They didn't stray too far from the bar though; stood at the nearest table and left her alone while she cleaned up the bar and reported their…*charming* conduct to April.

Done cleaning the bar Emily took a moment to check her texts while thinking about summat to order for supper when she got back home, also she thought about Sunday, hoped Mum and her had enough for a Sunday roast at the carvery down Hoperwood Beck.

"Thank you love!" The fella with the chain called out, interrupting her while his mate waved frantically.

"I love you…!" The mate called out and blew her a kiss. Aside from not tipping, that was rude, and Emily didn't have time to react, as both of them were exiting the bar with their pint glasses!

"Ergh…excuse me?" She didn't quite call out and was ignored, the blokes moving further away.

"Excuse me?" She called out hopelessly and watched the pub's doors close. Emily scoffed, frowned then chuckled. Even with her previous pub experience she didn't know what to do in this sort of situation, and it showed upon her face— *fuck me!* There was no Marvin about as well, despite making his presence and powers very well known earlier on! *Oh well…* She informed April, who shook her head with a glassy-eyed grimace.

"Where the fuck's Marvin when yah bloody need him?" She complained— *my thoughts exactly!*

It was 10 O'clock. Emily had had no reprimand, but an early finish for her. At least, there was no closing duty for her tonight, that chore was given to Reese, one of her male co-workers who worked in the kitchen, a lovely fella with his hair tied up into a bun on top of his head. Instead of waiting out in the cold and catching the last bus home Emily was afforded the luxury of a paid taxi ride home. But for the later hours though—late night travel was not summat she was looking forward to for the rest of her working days. She was knackered! But not enough to just fall asleep the moment she reached her bed. Mum wasn't up to greet her, so Emily got herself comfy into a plain grey tracksuit while she ran through her college course work, she turned on her laptop, put in her earphones. Still feeling peckish she got on the phone and ordered a chicken chow mein from the Chinese takeout behind Hoperwood Beck. If she had some fresh ingredients and a recipe, she would have tried to cook it herself. Her full belly was making her tiered, and she didn't want any booze so instead she cracked open a can of cream soda. This brand, called *Langhias*, had a very distinctive pink and white can and had been her favourite non-alcoholic drink since she was a kid, though her mates asked why she continued to drink it and how she could handle the vanilla taste. Some habits never died.

She went online while listening to Beyonce's *crazy right now*. Abby had messaged her several times and was live. Emily said **Hi**, then struggled for summat else to say. The usual faceless banter followed, and Abby never hesitated to reply like she was on an upper. And Denise had told Emily that Abby was a coffee freak!

Met a fella yesday Emily messaged.

U seeing him? Abby enquired.

No, Emily thumb typed, grinned and hesitated.

4t emerdale was a brand of cheese!

WTF? LOL! Abby replied with a smiley face. With another day of class and work afterwards tomorrow, Emily needed to get some sleep!

~

51 million years had inched by since a cataclysmic event had fallen from the skies, murdering over 70 percent of life on the planet. In this new age the earth continued to rotate, as it had through the chains of eras and periods and stages over the eon. The geology had transformed. Grand mountains miles high, had

formed at a southern point at the expansive sector of Eastern Laurasia as an ancient, sub continental piece from the east of the Central Gondwanan continent drifted towards it, and pushed up the sea floor, altering weather patterns. The once grand and long enduring Tethys Ocean had ended, having closed off through Gondwanan's central continent via collision of another drifting piece of it leading to a rather chunky, southeast angled peninsula now giving Laurasia some more features.

There were now four primary oceans on the planet, the Arctic in the north which was cooling, the Atlantic dividing the oceanic gap between western most Laurasia and the two near identically sized separated Gondwana continents, the Indian below the subcontinent now connected to Southern Laurasia and the largest was the Pacific, another rendition of the long gone Panthalassa. The Western Laurasian continent on the other side of the Atlantic was almost joined up with its Southern Gondwanan neighbour, volcanic growth would complete this land bridging in due course. The eastern most section of Gondwana had recently split into two continents: Australia and Zealandia, the latter which was less than half the size, and was being engulfed by the sea.

There was green all over the planet, but with a difference; ferns and cycad no longer dominated the floor but standing bladed plants bearing flowers that produced grainy seeds. *Poaceae,* or grasses had appeared around 110 million years ago, as a peripheral species in small varieties among the ferns. But against the constant shifting of climate their resilience had led them to become the dominant form of plant life on the planet for the past 40 million years. On the main West Laurasian continent, where there were once masses of islands, there was now an established continent joined up to the rest of the great land mass to the east.

On its coastline, mighty grey Atlantic waves crashed violently against shallow coastal cliffs, the fizz of water inaudible and dominated by the continuous, remorseless roar of the waves. Some of these waves had such character that they resembled part of an animal as it moved across the surface. This cryptic distortion could amass several proposed species. In spite of the cold grey skies, it was still temperately warm. Piercing honks and clicks filled the coastal air, and the waves didn't succeed in muting them out. They were the sounds of a soaring flock of *gehatanornis*, local avians.

Birds were archosaurs, in actual fact their evolutionary trajectory had derived from the late theropods over 150 million years back, though they didn't so much as resemble them. Excluding their small size these archosaurs had short, slender keratinous beaks with no teeth. Outwardly they looked more like the bygone pterosaurs, had long, slender wings but with sharper, pointed ends, the wing made up of the entire arm, less than a half of the entire wing length and bore a single, atrophied finger. The flight membrane was made not from skin but feathers, each fibre interconnected and wind resistant in place of scales, (a discreet ancestral connection) which was limited to their feet, their legs of which weren't connected to the flight membrane in anyway. Analogous to the pterodactyloid pterosaurs of past days the birds had short, atrophied tails but with a fanned out crest of feathers in place, helping them steer and stabilise in flight. Unlike the pterosaurs though, the birds were not quadrupeds and had their legs tucked against their body and were mostly concealed by their pelt, giving their bodies a simplistic oval-shaped appearance with wings from above and below.

The gehatanornis were just over a foot long and had a four feet wingspan, their smooth, fine plumage deceptively made them appear twice as bulky than they actually were. They were a cold, dark brown/grey all on top from head to their tail feathers, pure white on the underside, sternly round, bright blue and black forward facing eyes and slate blue bills with dark, scratch-like markings and a downward curving, spiked tip at the end of the upper bill. The males had brighter bills, a bold, black stripe around their eyes stretching and tapering down to a point just at their necks and brown specks on their chests. The diet of gehatanornis was reliant mostly on the ravaging sea, they glided, with their wings outstretched and their heads dipped down, where they received upward gusts of salted water droplets. They spent most of their time on the wing, hovering over the updrafts caused by the tides, allowing them to stay airborne without having to expend energy in this environment as they navigated around the coast in search of food. Several of them broke off from their wind draft soar and dived, their short necks extended and straightened and wings folded.

The birds plunged into the treacherous grey water, the bubbles of their impact instantly erased by the waves. Below the surface tides they spread their wings, where they swam down a dozen metres deep after schools of small fish with stunning efficiency, propelled by their light blue/grey feet, with heavy webbing stretched between four, long, thin toes, the longest on the interior which got shorter along the exterior to form a triangular arrangement. The gehatanornis surfaced with their catches and floated, riding the vicious drifts while swallowing it down. Some of the seabirds took flight shortly afterwards, their webbed feet running on the uneven, rolling water surface as though it was land. This remarkable hunting tactic had been witnessed before. But the versatile gehatanornis were a fraction of the size of another seabird that swooped down and dispersed those in the air without a shadow to cast upon them under this sunless sky. It was a relative of theirs: *pelagornis*, and there were more of them soaring against the gloomy horizon, keeping away from the smaller birds.

Once insignificantly small and living under the shadow of flying reptiles for millions of years, the birds had now claimed the skies. Pelagornis had a body length of nearly two metres and a wingspan of seven metres. Nothing this large had flown in the skies for over 50 million years. Like the pterodactylids, pelagornis was a long-range traveller with a global reach. But these birds were unlike any other; as if size wasn't enough to astonish, the pelagornis owned a foot long bill oval in shape, dark grey in colour with a dark blue gloss, had a black curved tip on the upper bill like the gehatanornis, each side of their beaks were lined with cruelly sharp, prickly, calcified extensions of the beak that resembled teeth, giving the birds a gnarly expression that concurred with their orangey eyes with piercing black pupils.

Like their smaller relatives around them the pelagornis had long, narrow wings, but were proportionately longer by a quarter. The backs of the birds, their upper wings and tail feathers were a dull shade of brown, mottled thinly with black feather outlines, black tip feathers lined their wings while the wing tips ended in an isosceles shape of bold, jet black, the heads, neck and underside pure white, the males had pink/orange coloured rings around their eyes. In the long stretched evolutionary mindset, that couldn't possibly pause or recount for a viewer, some features and adaptations had evolved independently in unrelated lineages, for related niches however. An ongoing procedure of convergent evolution that had succeeded repeatedly throughout history. Upon spotting a sizeable school of fish, the pelagornis descended to the surface, several gliding past each other in unintended X-shaped formations with the gehatanornis flying out of their way, some still on the water hastily so.

And just in time, flocking off honking as the giant birds crashed onto the grey waves without diving.

They floated, paddling with their large, pale pink webbed feet which were over a foot across and came to a slow, stabilising by raising their long wings then folding them giving them a broad, bulky mass a metre across not seen in flight. The pelagornis bobbed with the waves, looking very comfortable in doing so then dunked their heads below the water. A feeding frenzy had ensued. Being so large made it difficult to pursue small prey under the waves, yet they were able to do short dives, though they weren't as fluid as the gehatanornis, their wings breached the surface and caused more disruption in the form of bubbling clouds that quickly concealed their view of prey. It was a messy, chancy business, and that was why such wicked teeth were required, to snatch and hold onto larger fish prey. Though squid weren't an uncommon by-catch, and their slippery texture wouldn't let them slip out of a pelagornis' bill. During feeding the birds made an erratic succession of honks that increased in their pitch, they were deeper than the gehatanornis and the waves did little to drown out the collective coastal ambience. Below the surface commotion though, it was a different story.

Several short, stumpy fins from a pod of *squalodon* broke the waves in a uniformed forward rolling motion. They were cetaceans, mammals that had taken to the water and had become fully aquatic. Three metres long, bulky in every way that they were slender with glossy, furless, streamlined body plans packed with muscle for maximum hydrodynamic propulsion, tails ending in a horizontal fluke with a notch at the centre. Wide, curved pectoral flippers steered them, the tiny, functionless remnants of what were once hind limbs remained present in the form of flower bud-shaped protuberances.

The squalodon had bulbous foreheads, a singular hole on the top, small, beady black eyes which were set low and close to their jaws, which were long and slender and armed with large, sharp, triangular teeth with double-edged serrations that resembled that of sharks, slightly yellowed in colour and were larger towards the back. The squalodon had blue/black backs the upper mid tail region of which stretched forward to form a slanted band, accentuating the lighter dusky grey sky shade on the entire underside, the ends of their snouts blushed with the same shade as their backs and ran along the lips. Like sharks they had a dorsal fin, though shorter and more curved, but unlike them the bodies of the cetaceans undulated up and down as opposed to side to side.

Another remarkable incarnation of convergent evolution, the squalodon resembled the ichthyosaurs, though they lacked the large eyes of their extinct, reptilian counterparts. Instead they navigated these dull waters through an alternative means: through a uniquely evolved organ housed within that distinctively pronounced forehead of theirs, the cetaceans produced sequenced clicks and squeals as they communicated with members of the pod, the sounds deflected off whatever they struck and echoed back, relaying an image whatever the weather and light. These clicks were periodically broken with some piercing, otherwise unsettling shrieks resonating faster through the water than air. Regardless the squalodon were musical creatures, each individual had a unique song to form a type of intraspecific language. And as of now, they might just be bunched into the hierarchy of most intelligent life on the planet. One member of the pod took a breath then descended, diving forward elegantly.

Nearby, lingering on the seabed, not being inconvenienced too much by the current was a *metaxytherium*, another marine mammal, a sirenian. Over three metres in length and weighing 700 kilos it was covered in thick, dark grey blubber, had an oval-shaped body with a wide, conical trunk. Like the squalodon it had lost its legs and had a tail with a horizontal fluke with a notch, its short, circular pectoral flippers retained nails, a direct clue to a land ancestor. The metaxytherium had these bulbous pouts mapped with short hairs on its snout, that overlapped the end of the lower jaw and spread out widely. Despite its utterly bizarre appearance, the metaxytherium was a benign creature, as its docile brown eyes inferred, and as a consequence of its slow movements parts of its body had become home to colonies of barnacles and algae. The marine mammal was attracted to the small bits of plant matter, partly buried under the sediment of the seabed, which bloomed into grey clouds as it made contact. Despite thriving on a diet of sea grasses, small shellfish that couldn't escape the metaxytherium's mouth were grinded down with batteries of small teeth.

Kelp was abundant—forests of them grew in vertical, flat, spiralling rows moving with the current, and like with wind that ravaged the trees of land, a substantial portion of it would be ripped off, but carried back and forth with the waves. But the kelp wasn't a singular plant but a collection of algae, it was an ideal food source for herbivorous marine life, as well as a resource; it provided shelter to some marine life from predators. With its thick blubber, the metaxytherium was almost impervious to attack by a small separate pod of squalodon diving down and darting its way.

Though the irritation through harassment was still unavoidable, with the shark-toothed cetaceans intentionally colliding with it repetitively from various angles, the metaxytherium exuded no audible response to the squalodon exercising a behaviour known as fun. Their commotion was deafening to the bulky sirenian, which submitted and swam away, heading for seclusion within the swaying forests of kelp.

Cruising against the background was this bulky grey figure, which disappeared from view behind the towers of marine foliage. Its body was as grey as the gloom, with muted dark spots and a white underside that made it close to invisible in this murky, chaotic coast. A small fish passed by its wide, blunt snout with a high, almost domed forehead, past its round, black opaque eyes, set deep into leathery flesh then quickly swam along its body, past its short, easily identifiable dorsal fin and a large caudal fin beating steadily to the side, two paired rows of ridged keels running horizontally along the thick tail, steering it against the current.

~

After their frolic with the metaxytherium, the rogue squalodon surfaced for air with a sprout of water jettisoned from the holes on their heads. They submerged then slowed down before coming to a complete stall, the current bobbing them about. They had sensed a disruption among the schools of fish, their clicks became more frequented and accelerated in their pitch, they swept their heads tightly in every direction their compressed neck vertebrate would allow. Something was coming at them from the depths at speed. The clicks of the squalodon turned into wails that cascaded and relayed with every individual in the area, turning the shoreline water into a matrix of fear. With a beat of their tails, the cetaceans scattered. The feeding pelagornis on the surface witnessed the source of apprehension from above, their commotion alerting those attempting to dive, to abort and stay clear of the water. The giant birds dispersed and took flight in different directions, the outer half of their wings dipped through the sea, but were immediately raised clear of it without hindrance for flapping while their webbed feet slapped against the rolling surface as though they were running over them.

Two squalodon leapt over the waves, their communal klaxon shrieks reduced to guttural squeaks when exposed to the air, then blared out and ripped throughout the coastline when they submerged.

And just in time as the surface water exploded thunderously, partly revealing a large body as grey as the water turning to the left, a thick pectoral fin and white underside exposed briefly before sinking back under, the churning water turning the local surface area white and the waves erasing the disturbance in an instant. The attacker had missed. It turned to the right, seemingly at a slow speed, the tip of its dorsal fin momentarily cutting through the surface as its mass descended. With stealthy calculation, the predator circled the parameters of the squalodon pod, which were regrouping a couple hundred yards west, then thrashed its tail for speed.

The cetaceans shrieked and scattered for the second time. The hunter breached the surface again with the squealing squalodon leaping and diving over the waves, it was another miss. The predator dived again and rerouted for the area of coast where the cetaceans were reassembling. It found its opening and initiated its third attack. While zeroing in the waves of this spot suddenly became rougher, and it was enough to disorientate one of the swift, hyper alert cetaceans off course for a split second. But not the hunter from below. And this time it didn't miss.

One of the astray squalodon emerged flailing and crying having been caught by the tail, clenched within the jaws of an enormous head nearly as wide as the cetacean was long. The predator owned several dozen rows of massive perfectly triangular teeth the best part of a foot long, muscle red/pink gums flaunted as the jaws peeled back. With a thrash to the right, that revealed the pink and white tissue of rolled back eyes, followed with a downward motion in the opposite direction the killer disappeared back under the depths with a mighty splash, bloodied water pouring out from two metre high gills, creating a growing spot of red on the surface of the water, only to be washed away by the waves in a blink as though the violence had never occurred. Only marine creatures could get a full view of the predator after the bubbles faded when it submerged.

Impending death could and would remain a mystery for most that encountered it; the unlucky squalodon not being one to look death in the face. The perpetrator of this demise was *megalodon*. At 15 metres and weighing over 50 tons, this shark was the largest predatory fish to have existed so far, and the most formidable predator to have evolved since the explosion of life 526 million years past. Any challenge to its might it was receptive to, and there were plenty of candidates in the world's oceans. The sharks were no longer prey.

Something appeared over the mega shark's kill site; it was translucent like jellyfish but had no shape. Though it was starting to take on an octagonal shape, but with none of them sharp, identifiable outlines, and there was a horizontal revolving motion to it with a phasing in and out visibility event analogous to an image perceived while blinking. It descended a few metres in a perfectly straight line despite the coastal drafts and crisscrossing seabirds around it. Safe away from the shark kill site, one floating female pelagornis had spotted the beckoning object and took flight, initially with the intention to investigate it, like the other birds. Until for some reason it vanished from sight, this thwarting the trajectory of the female pelagornis, that headed north, flying along the coastal rim and cliffs overlooking the shores, fish bones and the carapaces of shellfish littered the ground near the edges where both gehatanornis and pelagornis were roosting. Some birds stood dancing, both species raised their long wings and took cumbersome steps with their wide, webbed feet. Curiously, among the litter was the shell of a small *ammonite*, but it wasn't comprised of keratin but of stone. Those unique cephalopods had perished during that extinction event from the sky... And smelling of fish from the dried fish bowel stains on it, it wasn't too much of a surprise why this fossil had been snatched up and joined the pile of waste.

The female pelagornis beat her wings and gained height. Around her other seabirds were taking flight or landing in even numbers. The cliffs, coupled with the updrafts of wind-facilitated take off, so their long wings didn't come into contact with the ground and impede it. Should these conditions cease then it would spell the end for the larger seabirds. Right now this barrage of wind and waves was shaping the environment. One cliff face left of the female pelagornis was crumbling, sending large chunks of rock falling into the sea, only just distracting her and causing her to veer off right a few degrees while scattering all other coastal birds on the wing. The female pelagornis banked to the west and flew inland, the cold blues and greys of the coastline transitioned into green.

~

Rays of sunlight beaming out from the cloud clear brought out warmer yellows and oranges of landscape features, mountain ranges and peaks appeared on the inland horizon. There were droplets in the air, the aftermath of rainfall along with the chained orbs of sunrays and multi-coloured bend of light on the horizon were of no significance to the pelagornis, just a visual distraction. Below the bird was a sea of wet grass growing out from muddied soil, the giver of life providing food for a new host of terrestrial life. But woodland was still more than plentiful, with broad-leaved trees mingling with once prevalent conifers and flower-bearing shrubbery. Mammals were abound in these lands, especially ungulates which moved about on hoofs, like the grouping of *heorotheleas* below the dripping canopy, which were ruminants—deer. These shy, quiet creatures were flourishing and were a staple woodland fauna.

Standing nearly three feet high and four feet long and weighing over 40 kilograms, they were long limbed quadrupeds stood on an even pair of hooves, their skulls were low with moist, dark brown muzzles, their bodily pelt reddish brown/grey with white undersides, the sides dappled with horizontal rows of white spots and a cloud of bushy white fur for a tail. The heorotheleas held their heads high whenever not browsing, had black eyes with eyelashes on the side of their heads and oval-shaped ears with motion to them independent of the other, always alert of danger. The young heorotheleas had bolder flank spots and a lighter, fluffier, almost blonde coloured pelt. While the males stood out from the females not by their larger size, but the monumental pair of structures that grew out vertically from the top of the heads. These antlers were a foot long at the base, tree bark brown with a delicate wood groove texture, each of which parted into curved, front and backward facing prongs over a foot long, for use by the bucks in seasonal mating.

Sat at the hooves of the heorotheleas was a *gineveralepus*, a lagomorph—a hare, a foot and a half long, five kilo critter with whiskers and memorably long and wide incisor teeth, exposed through the pouted upper lip which had a continuous up and down motion, long ears that stood up straight, the pink interiors exposed, big black eyelashes lined eyes on the side of the head, alert like the deer. This gineveralepus sat with its legs bent and arms stretched upright, backside sloped and broadened its fur an intriguing blend of beige, black and brown and with a small fluffy white tail. A plantigrade, meaning that it moved with the metatarsals of the foot bones planted on the floor, instead of hooves it had paws, and the gineveralepus moved about by hopping along the floor through heavily muscled thighs, and it could accelerate this locomotion if danger was spotted. While seemingly insignificant against other life forms, they were extraordinarily hardy creatures, inhabiting every type of environment on the connected continents of the planet, and happened to be highly prolific breeders; a gineveralepus could produce a dozen offspring a month after mating and could repeat this process shortly after. A male could produce over a hundred descendants within a year.

Grazing on the plains were a band of *nornskers*, equines which outwardly appeared similar to the heorotheleas but were not related. They were twice as big and three times heavier, their skulls were longer, the neck and body was bulkier, the skin thinner and tree bark pelt finer with longer fur around the cheek area and behind each limb. The face and neck area were darker with a faint black stripe running along the spine and extending outwards into short, black stripes on the upper body, the belly was a lighter brown, this same shade wrapped around behind the muzzle and a near black shade covered the lower end of the legs against the mud covering them from treading on the plains. The tails ended in a bush of long black hairs that swished about continuously and strips of black, erect mane along the neck provided a majestic character to the animals.

The nornskers were a different type of ungulate, completely adapted to open environments; instead of possessing an even set of hooves they bore three of them, the middle was the largest, of which they remained balanced on was wide and circular with a smaller, atrophied set on either side of it that didn't touch the floor. While they grazed, they often made gruff puffs and brays, shaking their heads and flinging off droplets of water of recent weather from their manes. Grass wasn't the most nutrient rich plant about, but it was the most abundant and owning a set of teeth with thick enamel, coupled with the ability to finely chew countered against the surprising tough, micro construct of the material. As small as it was, grass to be put simply: was bad for the teeth.

Distant from the equines and browsing on some shrubs near the forest edge was a not so likely relative: *scortculmeneus*, a bulky, squat thick skinned mammal two metres long and a ton in weight with an arched back, not much fur on its dull grey/brown body, short legs with circular feet with three, wide semicircular toes covered in mud, lips triangular and heavily creased, a maroon pink patterning on the forehead and a short, smooth keratinous horn on the snout for this male. Scortculmeneus were rhinocerids, horned-nosed mammals that were not the ideal choice for challenge and were very common, though they were excruciatingly slow breeders, with a gestation period of nearly two years for just a single offspring, and were not particularly shrewd animals.

The scortculmeneus raised his head, spotting the pelagornis which had no intention of descending down here, as her destination lay further north beyond this mountainous island. She was flying over the edge of a short ravine on the edge of the plains, when motion to her body froze, though she was still gliding. Nature had no concept of a negative art visual, tinting an anomalous freezing of a creature one moment in time. Conscientious or not, things still did and will continue to happen until the extinction of consciousness. The pelagornis rolled over to her left and began to descend, her wings forced up into a soundless clap that bounced back. With no wing movements to correct this fall, gravity commandeered her and brought her down to earth. The notion of one freak phenomenon being more outlandish than the previous wasn't categorised lightly in the realm of sense. The pelagornis continued to fall. And her descent hadn't gone unnoticed.

~

Treize—the pair of grey/green eyes surrounded with white ocular tissue long and black eyelashes blinking, fearless of falling from any height were observing, following the pelagornis down. *Douze*—the dew on the grass and the tiny, multi-coloured orbs they emitted irrelevant to the worm navigating the blades. *Onze*—the swarms of blood sucking mosquitoes in the woodlands over a pool of brown water. *Dix*—the tiny black birds perched on tree branches with a fourth toe on the back of their feet for gripping, which was the most common adaptation for inland species. *Neuf*—the falling pelagornis was witnessed over the tree lines by another female pelagornis heading in the opposite direction. *Huit*—the rock covered in bright green moss. *Sept*—the nornskers on the plains were on the run, galloping. *Six*—there was another rainbow fading above the prevalent one. *Cinq*—the caps of grey fungus that colonised a fallen tree. *Quatre*—the concealed swamplands within the woodlands, where some heorotheleas were springing instead of galloping. *Trois*—the gineveralepus that appeared from a burrow in the grass. *Deux*—the female pelagornis disappeared from sight as she passed by the edge of the ravine. *Un*—the plantigrade foot coated in a tall layer of brown, leathery animal skin landing down before a scortculmeneus, which had it turn its head in that direction. All unrelated events registered.

The body of the female pelagornis smacked against the white rocks of the ravine, a stream flowing by muted the sound of the impact. A puff of loosened feathers erupted into the air and formed a cloud, each quill slowly swaying and settling, her bulk had flattened, some of her teeth had broken off and shot out like crumbles of smashed rock, every inch of her skeleton was shattered with ruptured organs, the blood that had escaped from her body had exploded out and stained the rocks, the splatter had a distinctive shape to it. The pelagornis hadn't experienced any pain, as she had perished minutes before impact. This ravine would be her final resting spot. As far as an observer could interpret, her remains would not be preserved, nor memory or association of her encounters. According to the technicalities of geology she never existed.

~

Night fell, and above the pelagornis corpse was a near cloudless purple sky with brightly twinkling stars, and shooting stars, near missed collisions of small, outer space debris streaming past the atmosphere in the form of rapid white streaks. As beautiful as it was, nothing could distract anything hungry from the pelagornis corpse. An *eldracanis* came scurrying the corpse's way with a trot motion. It was a carnivora, this order of mammals had become an explosive success, dominating all of Laurasia and were doing well in the recently connected central Gondwanan continent, quickly becoming the top predators of their environments. Eldracanis though was an exceptionally small creature with a weight of only three kilograms and body length of 18 inches, almost half of it comprised of its bushy tail.

The eldracanis had a long snout with a slender, firm triangular shape, a black, moist nose, whiskers and triangular ears with black tips. A digitigrade, it moved on its toes with long legs built for running and clawed paws, its pelt was a light grey with black spots and black markings on the face, especially effective under low light. Smell was highly developed with eldracanis, allowing it to navigate darkness, further aided by its forward facing eyes to give it binocular vision. While omnivorous, a freshly deceased bird was a big break from the effort of preying on young gineveralepus. The eldracanis opened its mouth, revealing some formidable canine teeth and jagged rear teeth, its tongue sliding out as it panted. This freakish death and the phenomenon that had bestowed the pelagornis was little more than a free meal for this eldracanis. And it too had eyes on it, those from a small head attached to a long, alarmingly slender and scaly body with dark bands and a lighter underbelly with leathery, overlapping horizontal scales, body undulating in fluid, curving sideway bends stealthily under the dark.

At six feet long, *atorsavium* was an above standard size for a serpent in the Northern Hemisphere. A permanently fixed, vertically slit-eyed stare with a forked tongue that flickered and retreated frequently from a gap at the tip of the snout, corroborated its field of vision: a red/orange and yellow blur of the eldracanis's body, a heat signature with the surroundings a cooler blue and purple. The serpent could practically see in the dark. These legless reptiles had been around before the extinction from the skies, their unique form had allowed them to survive the event, by slipping into tight sheltered spots of any sort. Environmental heat was responsible for great size in most reptiles by default, but now up in the shifting northern latitudes drifting towards the northern pole, the climate was starting to get much cooler for these cold-blooded creatures; subsequently so many species had shrank in size and adapted to brumation through the colder months, similar to hibernation for warm-blooded mammals, but with less body fat reserves required.

Within range of the eldracanis the atorsavium silently raised its head, along with nearly half of its frontal body off the ground. The serpent opened its jaws widely, baring thin but sharp, backward curving teeth, inch long, near translucent fangs extending forward and bulbous pink glands behind exposed. Constriction had been the main tactic of killing prey, but lately some serpents had adopted venom, a potent resource against the brute of teeth and claws as there was competition about; and poison saved energy and reduced the risk of injury. Good thing that seabird had fell where it had; as this famished snake was pregnant. An additional fortune as well: this posture of the hunt had been captured in time. *Casser!* The owner of the green eyes blinked.

Chapter 8

Wednesday. Emily had come back from lunch a bit sooner than usual and had the classroom all to herself. She played *warrior's dance* on her phone and took out her sketchbook, along with an oversized pencil—it was one of them novelty ones and had a massive pink rubber on the head. She should be using this extra time to be getting along with some class work revision, but instead she got on her phone and did a search on her internet, looking for dinosaurs she could maybe *try* to draw... *So what's it gonna be then?* Emily thought. There was tyrannosaurus, triceratops, stegosaurus, brontosaurus, pterodactyl—she didn't know how to spell the latter—that one that sprawled like a crocodile with the weird semi-circle thing on its back (whose name she never got up until now) called **dimetrodon**, and them Loch Ness monster ones... Summat that looked sick anyway. But there were so many others to choose from, some images were brilliant while some were outdated, some were boring or just shite, they had a dinosaur for every letter in the alphabet, and some of the names sounded dodgy— if not racist; a long neck one called **nigersaurus**, and this one with a bony cap on its head called **pachycephalosaurus**—summat you wouldn't dare say out loud in this place!

But in the end Emily wanted to draw the most recognisable dinosaur, and it ended up being stegosaurus. She found a real decent digital rendering during her search then slanted her phone against her handbag placed on her work desk, got the picture to stay on, "hand-eye-coordination" required as she began to sketch. When it came to applying makeup, she could do just about owt, but drawing was summat else. She wasn't pleased with her progress so far, the dinosaur's proportions were off, the legs too blocky and them spiky thingies on the back were so bloody difficult—that it called out for a frustrated grunt every time summat went wrong! There were smudges all over the paper from all the rubbing out, unsightly grey fingerprints were visible from the perspiration from gripping the pencil too long, the spikes on the dinosaur's back looked like they were smouldering from the accidental smears of lead. How did these artists do it?

The classroom door opened and Denise came in.

"You drawing something, Emily?" She asked then almost immediately danced her way towards her and peered over her shoulder before she could react.

"That a stegosaurus?"

"Yeah, not that good though!" Emily replied—*should I call him Fred?*

"That's fine!" Denise dismissed as she walked around her.

"That was me Abby's favourite when she was little! We went to America just to see them skeletons."

Emily wanted to go!

"Our Abby loves animals—she rides horses." Denise said. That was interesting! Emily always wanted to be around animals, especially the fluffy ones, but she had never had any pets as Mum wasn't keen on it.

"Aw, I wanna ride horses…!" Emily sulked. The door opened and half the class poured in. Emily immediately folded her sketchbook.

~

After class finished for the day Emily went into town, she had an hour to kill before work and wanted to get some light cosmetics shopping done. She was walking down Hemmingway Street, via Kirby Square and in the direction of the train station. This was where all the banks and posh bars and restaurants were, all the business people and lot that were loaded lived here in the fancy flats. And there was a permanent population of beggars and rough sleepers about who knew that; on every block, either sat in a doorway or next to an ATM was a beggar, and you would always see a big issue seller or three. There was this one fella though that Emily knew, he had a big, brown beard, bushy brown hair, wore a rainbow coloured woolly hat, green overcoat and had a hippie look to him.

"Hello Dean!" Emily greeted him and passed him a quid, which he was thankful for. Dean had been living on the streets for two years, he was a genuine.

This part of town had a reputation: on this street, mixing with those who were unfortunate were frauds, dickheads who already had benefits, a home and happened to make more in a day than what the hardworking person made in a week. Emily had heard that there was some pilac who approached foreigners only, because they didn't know what to do, and would end up giving him notes, while one dickhead only approached young lasses. If she knew which ones were fake she was likely going to point them out, scream out to the public and shame them cunts!

Emily made a left turn into lower Kimmeridge Street, there was an open space for lorries to park with their deliveries, in front of it were three tall white posts stood in a row to the right with some rain withered advertising stuck to their lower segments. A big black bird flew towards the centre post and perched, its back to Emily, then hopped around one eighty and looked down at her. Emily stopped. She didn't know if it was a crow or raven; she didn't know how to tell one apart. She took out her phone, turned the camera on and began to zoom in.

But the big black bird flew away.

"Bollocks!" She cursed and turned around to her left, where she saw a building with army recruitment posters advertised. Emily couldn't help but fix her eyes on it. She was the right age, reckoned she was fit enough for training, had the right mentality and wanted to make a difference in the world. She could see herself in army uniform, with her picture and honours framed and hung up proudly on the wall.

She approached the recruitment centre and entered, inside were more posters and a TV screen mounted to the wall with video advertising, there were four desks with lads sat down having a one to one with fellas in camouflage gear and berets. Emily felt a sting of nervousness not sure who she was meant to be approaching.

"Can I help yah, love?" A tall, groomed fella in his thirties in uniform came up to her, his hands behind his back.

"I'm thinkin' of joining…" Emily answered, her nervousness spilling out. The fella looked at her, but not in a condescending way.

"Thinking, not *absolute* just yet." She added. The army fella lowered his head into a gentle nod, turned around and fetched a pamphlet from the desk behind him.

"This has all the info," he said as he handed her it.

"When you've made a decision just fill in the online form!"

After doing her shopping down in Kimmeridge, Emily went to a coffee shop up street for a latte and sat down and read through the pamphlet in bits, with a blueberry muffin to munch on. She didn't want to get hurt in the service, nor did she want to hurt anyone. She was terrified about the toilets, the showers—the lack of privacy and the screaming in the face by the drill instructor. But there was surely more to it than that—why did so many people join the army without being forced to? Emily gave the pamphlet a more thorough read, went back to certain paragraphs. After a decision, that lasted a few minutes after she had finished her coffee, Emily shut the pamphlet and stared into space. There were other ways to make a difference... And she didn't want owt to happen to her hair! Well, she thought she could do one of them training courses on a challenge show though!

~

After work, Emily had the taxi driver drop her off at the foot of Carnian Street; there was a copper, his vehicle's lights flashing while he tried to calm down some bloke who had caused an accident and was blocking the road, arguing with another bloke, the owner of the car that had been struck, how and why Emily didn't know and it made her nervous about other people on the road when she got her driver's license. Walking down street, the lights from the vehicles further back allowed her to see a crow/raven feasting upon some road kill on the cobblestone, a flattened patty of meat, crushed bone and the distinctive spikes of what was obviously a hedgehog. The bird pecked and pulled away a string of meat, causing Emily to shudder. Weren't them black birds day time birds or summat? Emily didn't know—and films that showed them as man-eaters weren't the best source of information.

Emily arrived back home, Mum was sat at the kitchen island with her left side facing her. Her hair was swept back into a high and tight ponytail, she was wearing a black turtleneck sweater that looked brand new and these light blue jeans and them black pointies she had had for years. She looked proper moody. Well, she was on, and had probably been held up by that accident outside, and hopefully there was nowt to piss her off! She was looking at some letter.

"What kinda bleedin' language is this? Scottish?"

"Let us see!"

Emily walked forward, Mum passed her the letter, hoping she would maybe get some clarity. She pursed her lips and cackled after seeing what the fuss was about.

"Fuckin' hell!"

It was a repair job for the lack of pressure of cold water in the kitchen sink, not that Emily had been bothered by it to begin with. On the letter it said: **Conf**

order 6151988 for matt for ooh com 09 12 2009 add on. And there were alternative language options on the back.

"I don't think it's in any other languages, Mum…!" Emily said while actually trying to investigate! Mum snarled and started rummaging about in her handbag, not finding whatever it was she was after she shoved it aside a few inches and growled.

"C'mon Mum! Cheer up—it's almost Christmas!" Emily insisted, took her phone out and pointed it at Mum who looked her way without smiling, though Emily had already taken several photos.

"Fuck it! I'm off back to the post office in the mornin'!" She stood up and went for the fridge, the click of her heels as harsh on the ear as her mood.

"You wantin' a glass?" She asked.

"Please." Emily replied. With a glass of rosé in hand, she went up to her room, changed into her PJs and turned on her laptop. There were no messages from Abby, allowing her to browse freely on YouTube. She found a clip titled: **Kashiwagi English film 2004**.

So Emily clicked on it, the video uploaded and showed a downward panning shot of a Yorkshire village then came to a still with a bloke stood at a bus stop smoking a cig, a steep road to his side. He wore a green jacket and had short greying hair, a drooping, chiselled jaw and piercing blue eyes and checked the time on his watch. The most normal thing to do at the bus stop. There was this bloke running down the hill his way. There were no words from the bloke smoking, no narration or owt. The fella that was running was odd; he was wearing a hoodie, a turban, had a long, scraggly beard like that cunt responsible for 9/11, but he was white and freckled. Not so normal.

Thirty two seconds in and the bearded bloke stopped in front of the fella who was smoking and slouched over, hands on his knees, panting loudly. The bloke smoking didn't pay him any attention. But in the end he turned his head his way.

"You okay, mate?" He asked. The fella with the turban held up a hand.

"Just a sec mate!" He said with a Cockney accent. His panting turning into hyperventilation.

"You sure you're alright mate?" The smoker asked. Turban fella held up his hand.

"I'm sound! Just gimme a moment!"

Then he began to stand up straighter.

"I'm alright…!"

Then his back was perfectly straight. He exhaled.

"I'm alright…!"

Then he stepped towards the fella smoking, and it looked like there was a friendly conversation about to take place, or at least a request for a cig. Then he put his hood over his head, and did it slowly, like someone who was about to do summat nasty.

"*Do you suck dick?*" He asked, suddenly he had an Asian accent to him. Emily snorted and gasped, while a very brief image appeared: a single frame of a horrifically detailed bronze statue of a drag queen in a dress, mouth wide open and arms stretched above his head like a rising ballerina, and there were a pair of perfectly round pillows on the ground, positioned to look like a knob. Then came another frame image of a fat bloke laid back with a gas mask over his head, man boobs and a hairy chest, he was just wearing pink underwear and had his legs spread. Emily questioned her sanity for the same amount of time. Definitely not normal!

Without asking for a repeat, the fella smoking the cig shook his head without making eye contact with the proposer. Then the fella with the beard just sprinted off, the camera following him. Emily exploded into laughter and paused the clip, having choked on it. Superbly abnormal!

She resumed the clip.

"*C'm here yah fuckin' bellend!*" Some bloke shouted and came into frame, running after the fella with the beard. Then a farmer with a hammer joined him.

"*Stay away from us fuckin' sheep!*" He warned.

"Good God!" Emily coughed, tears threatening to spill down her cheeks and ruin her makeup. Then there was what looked like Arabic writing on the screen in white font, which quickly faded into an English translation: **Don't be something you're not!** Followed by another Arabic sentence: **Asshole!** A quietly giggling Emily drank some wine.

~

Thursday. Class was done and Emily was behind the bar checking the pumps for gas levels with a reader. Anyone coming in for a pint was gonna be disappointed for the next hour. Then of all people, Zoe Burton walked in, Emily having seen her less than an hour ago. Zoe had chunky blonde highlights in her hair, her overly pouty lip brightened up with cherry red lipstick, she was wearing a long light brown coat over her class uniform and some mental Uggs that were thick as tree trunks and with proper fluffy rims as though they had come off a polar bear or summat!

"Alright Nick?" She greeted and ordered a bottled lager with lime. Zoe was planning on going out tomorrow, except she didn't know where to go or who to go with—fair enough her mates were all busy—and she asked if Emily was out. Zoe could tag along with her anytime, if Emily wasn't skint that was. While chatting, Zoe constantly kept throwing back her hair in admiration, she didn't order any food or another drink, and that was the only eventful thing about the shift. Emily was just over an hour away from finishing work, when she got a call from Mum. "*Just* two hours…?" She remarked and covered up a yawn.

"Yeah, I guess…!"

Emily had finished work, but she had been offered another job: babysitting, a fairly common thing for her since secondary school. Fortunately this would not be long at all, and she would be sitting for a mate of a mate of a somewhat close mate of a sister's mate of Mum's whom she was on good terms with. No need to get changed tonight. The taxi dropped Emily at the address of the job, number 231 Carnian Street was a block away from the very end of the street. She knocked and was greeted by both parents: the mother, Terri, a fit brown-eyed, twenty summat brunette who worked as a cook at some bar in upper Oldmill Brig, which was posh unlike the lower part of the district near college, and the father, interior decorator Brad, Terri's second husband, tall and black and sporty.

Francesca, Terri's first child, stepped into the hallway, she was white, eight years old, had bushy brown hair and her mother's beady eyes, she bounced up and down, overly happy to see Emily again. Emily had never asked how old Terri was when she had had Francesca, but reckoned she had been pushing it.

"You changed your hair again!" Francesca called out shuffling towards her.

"I know!" Emily said as she removed her trainers then went into the living room. There weren't toys all over the floor, there had been in the past with Terri making a fuss every time she returned home, now it seemed the kids had learned to clean up. There were plenty of framed family photos on the wall and a cabinet shelf with school certificates and trophies and plenty of DVDs and video games. Oliver, Francesca's younger half-brother was sat quietly in front of the massive telly playing his video games on the PS3. Brad and Terri left, but not before encouraging Emily to persuade her to get the children to sleep. Good luck with that!

Emily made herself a cup of tea and sat down on the sofa, keeping both kids in sight. Francesca talked *a lot*, but Emily wasn't really listening, her smile seemed to suggest she was though. It was Oliver who was getting her attention; the games he was playing were pretty bloody violent; he was going around shooting people, firing missiles at them and blowing them up. He shoved the controller in Emily's face, begging for her to have a go. He should definitely be asleep! Just to avoid a fuss Emily took the controller. Oliver saved his current game then went to multiplayer mode, a split screen.

"You're him, I'm him!" He pointed at the left side of the split screen. Next thing they were running around in some warzone, both characters onscreen in military gear. Emily wasn't sure how she was meant to control the character, pushing the sticks about confusingly, firing a machine gun all over the place, her bullet metre dropping and not knowing who she was meant to be shooting at— *good thing I han't joined!* Though Oliver might do in a decade's time!

"I'm gonna get yah!" The lad promised joyfully, telling Emily things like "I've picked up an AK-47", "an M4", and "Mossberg shells" and a "claymore" and an "RPG"—things a soldier should know! The split screen and all the moving about was disorientating, but aside from that the game was awful and showed Emily's character being shot to death or blown up into bloody pieces with the screen being tinted blood red with computer graphic lettering letting everyone in the room know that she had been killed.

"Oh dear!" She said.

"You're dead!" Oliver cheered victoriously and repeated it.

"Again!" He demanded with a roar. Did Francesca have to go through this? As far as Emily knew, the relationship between half-brother and sister was sound. Emily wanted a sister, younger or older. To her there were just summat about being an only child that just didn't feel right, other than getting Mum's love one hundred percent every time.

Emily had to listen to Francesca while half-heartedly preoccupied trying to kill Oliver's character onscreen. After being killed summat like 25 times, Emily got the hang of the controls, her eyes trained and focused on both screens. She quickly figured out how to switch between weapons, and there was a mini map in the upper corner of the screen that showed where she and her opponent was. She was ahead of Oliver, and had picked up a rocket launcher. Upon spotting him, she fired a machine gun and ran about, unrealistically side to side like crazy, to distract him. She backed up and went behind the corner of a building and backed up further, waiting for him to come around, using his overconfidence to her advantage. The moment Oliver's character appeared Emily switched to the rocket launcher and fired at him, his character blew apart into several flaming, pixelated pieces with a hazy CG blood shower. For the first time, he had been defeated!

"Gottcha!" Emily said then slouched forward and sighed in relief. She went into the kitchen for a glass of water and upon return Oliver begged her to play again, but Emily politely refused.

"Do us a handstand!" Francesca begged. Emily had taken gymnastics class when she was much younger, wanting to learn how to do somersaults and tumbles like acrobats, whom made it all look so easy. She had learnt handstands, headstands, hand walks, cartwheels and front flips, but could never get around to doing back flips, and after a failed attempt had left her with a traumatic lump on the back of her head and in pain for a week, she had dropped out of the classes, with plenty of persuasion from Mum though. Emily fetched a cushion from the sofa.

"Stand back then—so you don't get hurt!" She ordered the kids then put her head against the laid down cushion, rocked her body forward, knees tucked against her body, arms and palms straining to support her so she didn't tip forward while her legs unbent and slowly pointed up at the ceiling. A couple of seconds in and she was feeling the blood rushing up to her head, and uncomfortable she stood back up, her face hot and red with these silver fly thingies in her vision—gosh it had been a while!

Francesca cheered then tried to imitate her, with Emily dissuading her before putting on her coat and going outside into the cold for a cig, vowing the rule of not smoking around children, like some parents did. She turned her head to the window, keeping a vigilant eye on them rather than be careless and let something happen.

She hoped there were no one dodgy walking past, stopping to chat to her then walking up to her then inside where the kids were. No one walked by, and that had been a good fag! Once back inside there was more hassle.

"Let's go carol singing!" Begged Francesca.

"No, it's too late!" Emily said with Oliver letting loose a "ha-ha". And you couldn't really blame him!

"*Come on Ollie...!*" Emily ordered him, with him shaking his head and having to stop his games. Francesca wanted to watch TV, but Oliver wasn't having it. What was there for a child to watch this late anyway? It was after midnight when Brad returned with a happy smile on his face.

"Why they still up?" He asked, his jolly tone and smile masking his disappointment, then asked for a report.

"All good" that he was happy with and handed Emily twenty quid in hand. That was enough for a simple night out tomorrow with Zoe, that was if she was willing to make the journey over here—it wasn't enough for a night in town though.

Emily walked back home, the streets were quiet with the exception of some music or TV heard and with only a few dimmed lights seen beyond the curtains down street. Mum was sat in the living room, her laptop on the coffee table, she was wearing her silky robe and some silvery pyjama bottoms, her hair was combed back and damp from what had to be a recent shower. She was smiling, rolling a glass of wine in hand, her smile was slowly getting wider with her head bobbing slowly, a finger from her other hand winding around a lock of her hair. She didn't even ask how her daughter was.

"Who's it now?" Emily called out.

Mum said fuck all and continued to play with her hair, horny emails or summat preoccupying her.

"Alright me babe's?" She said just as Emily turned her back and grunted, feeling the need to sit back and live a bit.

"Any wine?" She asked.

"You what?" Mum said.

"There any wine?" Emily repeated.

"In the fridge!"

Emily poured herself a glass, took her time doing so, after a sip she floated into the living room to check on Mum.

"Who is it now?" She asked. Mum said nowt and folded her legs, her expression was daft, like it had been lazily drawn on. She typed.

"He's from London," she said. "I'm seeing him tomorrow!"

Wonderful!

~

Friday. Emily was off college today, and she had been woken up early by a call from April telling her that the bar wouldn't be open today cuz of some "plumbing problem" that had left the ladies room flooded. No work today either, nice. After getting up Emily went out for a run, wore her hair back as usual, she was wearing a two piece, light grey spandex gym outfit, the bra covered up with a plain black trackie top without a hood, and them black and red trainers she liked to wear while proactive. This weren't about looking pretty, but as always it didn't stop the stares, honks of cars and muted out whistles. The Chemical Brothers *the salmon dance* was playing through her iPod's earphones, and Emily was expecting some snow or sleet to fall.

While running around the back of a Sancrott neighbourhood, which had rows upon rows of wooden fences facing a field beyond some towering trees, a partridge swooped down from the right and perched itself on a fence. Emily, summat like three metres away, stopped and impulsively went for her phone to take a picture of the plump bird.

But like the crow/raven thingy in town the other day the bird flew away, camera shy—*bugger!* And there were no pear trees as far as the eye could see! There was nowt worthy of taking a photo for the rest of Emily's run.

Back home she showered, wore her hair back again and dressed into a grey trackie with a thick pink hoodie over as it was nippy even with the radiator on. While sat down at the telly, sipping away at a cup of tea she thought about what she could do for the rest of the day—she was struggling to make a decision on what to make for lunch. Emily loved those cook shows, was fascinated by all these desserts they made from France, Germany, Austria and Denmark, which gave her sweet cravings. She hoped these cooking shows didn't get boring in the future though. She bought recipe magazines whenever she could, as having to rely on quick microwave meals and takeouts for convenience after a busy day were slowly ruining her health, and she had a spice collection in the kitchen growing at about the same pace a 40-year-old bloke collected tools for his garage.

Emily had been one of the best in her class at cooking, she could cook a brilliant shepherd's pie from scratch, was quite good on the barbeque, but would like to know how to do a steak medium rare on the frying pan. Back in school they didn't do curry while in cooking class, but Emily reckoned with a bit of practice and some better cooking equipment she could master curries. During an advert Emily went into the kitchen and fetched the latest food magazine and became focused on a spaghetti with meatballs recipe. She had cooked pasta countless times, though with a readymade sauce most of the time. Right now her growing appetite yearned for pasta, but this time she was gonna do the sauce from scratch. She put on her trainers and coat and went out to do some shopping at Hoperwood, she didn't care about tonight anyway. The hedgehog road kill had been cleaned up by the council, but there was still a smear on the road.

There wasn't a lot of choice in the Sainsbury's, but Emily got what she needed: a small tub of minced beef, spaghetti, canned tomatoes, some tomato puree, onions, garlic, dried breadcrumbs and some of that grated cheese in a tub. Back home she played music on her phone while she sorted out her shopping, OMP *heaven is a half-pipe* playing—she remembered everyone singing this while she was in year five. Emily had bought a bottle of discount red wine to go with the pasta and to add to the sauce, though everyone she knew of would go against it, but if it was authentic, it had to be done and that.

Emily brought her laptop down and placed it on the kitchen island so she could watch a YouTube cooking demonstration. She was watching it a second time. No, the clip didn't have a plump, overdramatic, singy Italian fella with a massive chef's hat in love with his own voice, and giving you a lecture between bits. The bloke was an American, wore an apron, was tall, lean with a bald head and a jutting chin and looked like a sensible chap. And he had a proper dodgy voice.

"Foyerst, seesan yoh tomaytoes with sallwt..."

First season your tomatoes with salt he meant. He sounded like *Elmer Fudd*! The chap put the tomato sauce on some meatballs he had resting on a plate. Emily had already made some seared meatballs herself, draining on a separate plate, which had required the breadcrumbs to make. In that same pan, she had made the meatballs in, she was sautéing two small white onions she had sliced up and three sliced cloves of garlic in olive oil. You had to love the smell of garlic cooking!

Carefully, Emily watched the greenish oil as it began to brown the onions and garlic then sprinkled in a handful of Italian herbs and chilli flakes, her nose relished the collision of odours. She transferred them to a large saucepan, where she impatiently dumped in her canned tomatoes, a half glass of red wine and two bay leaves. She couldn't help have a cheeky glass and a cig as well—chefs would complain—while she watched the bubbling brew of red sauce, which she stirred and tasted every few minutes. So far it was going well. Emily went back further on the clip.

"Ayudd in a teaspoon ow suugaar fowe guud maysure!" The chap on the clip instructed, Emily paused it then did what was recommended, "adding a teaspoon of sugar for good measure", tasted for clarity, then skipped forward on the clip, looking and guessing where she had left off. Unsure where she was she just let the clip play and watched the chap take a fork to his plated tomato sauce and meatballs, which were mixed in with spaghetti, winding it up and eating the pasta.

"Ayand they Leord av mercay!" The chap praised the Lord, and after taking his time eating the spaghetti, ate a meatball.

"Leord av mersaay!" He said again with such intensity like his life depended on it! According to the video there was a different way of cooking the spaghetti; the pasta and the sauce were tossed in together towards the end and mixed together, which didn't seem right after Mum's tradition of mixing it separately. Emily was plating her food, thinking of her Italian heritage, wondering if her grandparents would accept her. It was an exciting mystery she was gonna be dwelling on for as long as she was stuck living the way she was. Then Mum came home, cussing on the phone and stepping into the kitchen with two big shopping bags as expensive-looking as the silver necklace she was wearing with that orange tracksuit she had bought not too long ago, her hair shinning from another fresh salon job.

"For fuck sake I'll call you tomorrow, *matey*!" She shouted then ended the call. Emily didn't need to ask who it was and why she was raving on. Mum exhaled loudly and put on a smile.

"What you cooking? Smells good!"

"Spaghetti with meatballs." Emily answered. Mum hummed, leaned over her shoulder and slowly wrapped her arms around her daughter's waist. Emily could smell booze on her; there was surely a bottle or two in them shopping bags. Emily offered Mum her plate before she could have a taste herself. Mum took a fork and dug in without saying a word.

"How is it?" Emily asked.

"Good!" Mum said in an exaggerated way while nodding.

"This all mine? I'm starvin'!"

Chapter 9

Later evening. Gemma had texted Emily to tell that she and the lot wouldn't be going up to the Stanley Parker, but were now going to the Toarcian Palace, though it sounded like a castle some fairy-tale princess needed rescuing from, it was actually a proper sorted pub/restaurant on the far edge of Hoperwood, not within walking distance though, nor was it the sort of place you'd make it through a night with just twenty quid. But Mum, like the super Mum she always was, had given Emily an extra fifty quid—how generous, but all the while suspicious. Not complaining though, Emily got herself ready, straightened her hair, wore a magenta pink, sleeveless vest that came down to her bum, had cute, ruffled straps and all these gold studs around the medium height neck line, some cream white jeans that were tapered at the ends and the same white platforms she had worn back when that slag back at the Stanley Parker had had a go at her. Mum offered to drive Emily up to the Toarcian before heading off to town to see her latest partner from down south. She was never going to be short or sexually frustrated!

The Toarcian Palace was a lovely place; from the outside it almost looked like a hotel, it was three stories high, its walls were plastered a ceramic brown and its name presented in big brass letters on the front. It was a popular place for visitors to town and had a car park for at least thirty cars. The last time Emily had been here was when she treated Mum to dinner for her birthday back in March 21st. The outside had some green space, all the trimmed hedges and trees had golden Christmas lights on them, and there was a large beer garden with them heated lights that provided warmth for when you were out having a cig which was just nice—that's why Emily didn't bring a coat.

She went inside, the pub's heating smoothening the goosebumps that peppered her exposed flesh. The atmosphere was brill, everything was clean, polished and smelt nice like a hotel. The ceiling was white, there were posh chandeliers dangling from it, the floorboards were a varnished brown and there were these large, potted plants about. The Toarcian looked like the sort of place that should be by a river or summat, but there were nowt to see other than the dark main road, its traffic and Christmas lights from a few businesses across the road, which was a shame. The staff were smartly dressed in white shirts and black waistcoats. Emily looked about and didn't see any of her mates, guess she was the first one here.

She went to the bar and ordered a bottle of rosé and was asked for ID by the barman, who provided a quick, quality service as though she was priority. Emily sat on her own in one of these booths, having a look at the menus with her bare arms soaking up the pub's warmth. Enrique Iglesias's *do you know* was playing, it was a favourite Friday night track. Emily texted Zoe, telling her where she was, but really didn't want her here with her mates though. Gemma and Stacy arrived too soon for comfort, and they weren't even dressed properly; Gemma was wearing a blue fleece, these limey green trackie bottoms and black Uggs while Stacey was wearing a light blue blouse with blue skinny jeans and white trainers, her hair was pulled back very tightly. She looked like a surgeon! There was no Heather though, even though Emily had texted and welcomed her.

The horrible sisters sat across from Emily, grabbed some of the oversized white menus and immediately started complaining about what there was and wasn't on the menu. Emily wanted a curry and began her search, the food at the Toarcian was ace, though mostly it served English; last time here Mum had been going on about how brill the shepherd's pie was. Sundays they did a carvery here, but at fifteen quid per person it was dear—summat royalty could afford. A half glass of wine in and Emily hadn't made a decision, put off by Gemma and Stacey's indecision and the need to make remarks about some of the other customers. Then Emily was tapped on the shoulder, and surprised by the quick arrival of Zoe, who was dressed properly; a black choker, a black, long-sleeved, off shoulder top, white jeans and a peek down at her feet discovered these boringly grey peep toe wedges that might have worked for summat else.

"Love yah top!" Gemma said looking pleased to meet her, Stacy not so much. Zoe squeezed herself in next to Emily and the two began to catch up on gossip.

Everyone at the table was drinking, still deciding on what to eat, then of all the people that you didn't need turning up, Jody shambled in wearing a thick, knitted purple sweater with all this Christmassy embroidery, the topknot bun she wore her hair up into had a chopstick through it. Legitimately there was no space for Jody at the table, and embarrassingly, she fetched a chair from another table and loudly dragged it, screeching against the floor towards the table with everyone in the pub looking her way. Then she began to get chatty with Zoe.

"You go to college with our Nick?" She screamed accusingly.

"Where'd yah live?"

"Badmington Moor." Zoe replied.

"I live near there!" Jody said, sounding like they were instantly mates or summat. Of course Jody could not walk there and needed a car ride to get there. And that was a matter of fact. Jody was the first to order food, and it was a plate of chips with a jug of gravy she just poured over—*yuk!* Emily wasn't listening to her as she was busy chatting with Zoe, but in the end it was unavoidable as the fat bitch and Gemma got into some laughter.

"Would I *fart* in public?" Jody shouted as though accused then chuckled as she grabbed a handful of soggy, browned chips.

"All the bloody time!" Gemma said, Zoe giggled, but it wasn't genuine. Jody stuffed her chips into her gob. Emily frowned, bracing herself for the next repulsive thing she did.

Cascanda *what hurts the most* was playing and everyone at the table had made a decision what to order for main course: curry. Gemma, Stacey and Jody went for chicken korma while Zoe was more adventurous and went for a chicken jalfrezi. Emily wanted summat different—summat that had more chilli indicators on the menu than Indian—summat that would make her nose runny with the cold and that. There happened to be a Thai option to the menu here temptingly enough; green curry with chicken and jasmine rice. On the menu's appetisers, Emily's eye fell across tempura, spring rolls and fish cakes.

"C'mon, you order!" Gemma demanded pointing at Emily. Zoe couldn't get out, as she was blocked by Jody's *irresponsible* body mass. So Jody had to get off her arse, which took nearly thirty seconds, and she had to do her sad arm exercises. Emily squeezed out to place her order at the bar.

"What'd you order?" Zoe asked a very normal question upon her return.

"Thai green curry with spring rolls."

"The fuck you orderin' a chinky curry for?" Stacey grilled without looking at her, scowling at the table she might as well slam her face against. Emily didn't say owt and topped up her glass.

"Next thing yah know our Nick's gonna be shaggin' a chinky fella!" Gemma had to sensationalise it for some reason.

"Ergh, *fuck off*!" Emily said back without shouting, still pouring her glass.

"You whaa…?" Gemma blabbered with her tongue hanging out.

"How's that any different from shaggin' a black fella?" Emily challenged. A near silence followed in which Zoe looked at her for a moment then back at Gemma.

"That's *racist*!" Jody laughed.

"You fuckin' takin' the piss, Nick?" Gemma started with Stacey turning her head and glared at Emily for dissing her sister. Emily screwed the bottle's cap back on and placed it back in the bucket while managing to grin.

"Jamie White's Pakistani!" Emily added, needing to *retaliate* you could say.

"He's English!" Gemma defended.

"He's English-Pakistani!" Emily corrected. Stacey wouldn't stop glaring.

"So what if he's part Paki…?" Gemma said back—*fuckin' hypocrite, you!*

"I love Jamie White!" Jody said with a retarded-sounding voice.

"I want im to massage me bum!"

Emily did not just hear that! Zoe rolled her eyes while Stacey mumbled summat and shifted about uncomfortably in her seat. Emily resisted the urge to ask her if she had any bowel medication she had forgot to bring with her! Food arrived, all curries had yellow rice, poppadoms and naan bread sides—that was more food for Jody, the plates of which were cluttering the table. Emily's starters arrived, four spring rolls with some sweet chilli sauce and some shredded carrot and cabbage for decoration. You had to love spring rolls! They were crispy on the outside, tasty but steaming hot on the inside, and as always Emily couldn't resist taking a peek at the inside of them. There was sweet corn, cabbage, some clear, jelly-looking noodles and some sort of minced meat. She needed to learn how to make these at some point.

While the group got stuck into their food, Gemma and Jody were talking with their mouths full, and Gemma had to be a bitch by letting rip a loud belch that would scare the devil, if not the appetite.

"Fuckin' hell!" Jody complained and was likely gonna scare away half the people eating here already!

"You're fuckin' disgusting!" Zoe said fearlessly. Jody though threw up her arms and started clapping.

"Yeah man!" She cheered with a Jamaican accent.

"She does epic lady burps!" Gemma told Zoe with a full mouth.

"Cheers Gem!" Jody thanked then tore off a chunk of naan bread and dunked it sloppily in her curry. Stacey said fuck all, she was prodding her food suspiciously with her fork as though it was a dead rodent that might just spring back to life.

Atomic Kitten "*It's OK!*" was playing when Emily's green curry arrived in a white bowl on a posh, curved plate with white rice in a dome shape to go with it, the curry had some coriander leaves and red chilli slices for garnish. Immediately she dug in and mixed it, the curry was lovely and creamy and coconutty, though she didn't feel it was quite spicy enough. Could she get some chillies with that to spice it up? A few seconds later the same waiter that had asked for her ID earlier gave her what she needed. Emily stood out even further with her mates as she was given a tray of condiments that interestingly included four brown ceramic jars.

"Sick!" She said trying to fit it in on the crowded table. All the jars had these small, white spoons which Emily had a snoop with lifting up the lids, discovering chilli flakes in one jar, what looked like sugar in the other, this brown watery sauce with chillies and a clearer version with larger chillies. It looked neat!

"The fucks all that shite?" Gemma complained and leaned in.

Emily dabbled with the odd condiments; the clear, watery thingy was sour, vinegary and a bit sweet...the brown watery stuff was salty and a bit spicy and garlicky. Adventurously, she dumped a tablespoon worth of each onto her curry and doubled the amount with the chilli flakes until she was satisfied. Emily shoved three spoons of rice and curry into her mouth before she felt the heat, her nose runny and the mucus finding its way into her mouth, which she wiped away with a napkin that needed chucking away quickly as it wasn't glamorous! Her tongue became swollen and her eyes on the verge of becoming waterfalls, but she felt good—she was on a chilli high! But like an addict Emily wanted more, and against her better judgment dumped more chilli on her curry for another buzz.

She had a look at the menu again for inspiration, telling her prying mates she was searching for drinks, the pad thai caught her eye, the pad kee mao, the tom yum soup... Emily wiped her runny nose with the back of her hand, discreetly searching for a fresh napkin, some parts of her face felt sore from contact with the chillies.

"Is it too hot?" A smiling Zoe asked.

"Yah gonna throw up?" Gemma said having to take the piss. Emily gasped then replied, "In a good way!"

She finished her plate, Stacey left a half plate—no wonder she was so skinny! *Black Betty* was playing and Emily went to the bar and ordered another bottle of rosé.

"Come on! Let's get shots!" Gemma was heard shouting.

"Let's av 'em!" Jody said then clapped.

"I'll get 'em," Zoe said—how nice of her—then came up to Emily's side.

Shots were poured on the counter, five shot glasses lined up together and filled up with one professional sweep of the barman's arm, as Emily had been taught to do at Zaks and Marias. She didn't ask what sort of spirit was being served, and not caring about having to do them all at once with everyone in the group she chucked the shot down her throat, judging from the aniseed flavour, it had to be sambuca. Gemma wasn't too pleased by Emily drinking solo and Jody demanded that Emily "bring the shots to the table". Gemma wanted a group photo and asked this random fella walking by to take their picture, he didn't want to but Emily asked nicely, and in the end they all leaned in together. Everyone in the picture except for Stacey was smiling—she was a proper killjoy! Emily didn't want to be around her.

She went off to the loo to clear her nose, then on her way back she bumped into that same barman that had been serving her.

"Alright?" He said. That's when Emily stopped him and freely felt like asking a question.

"Would…It be possible for me to thank the chef?"

"I can ask him," the barman said then took her to this staff only entrance near the pub's east side entrance, thankfully away from the eyes of her mates. Emily wasn't waiting too long before the door opened and a hot, fragrant waft of stir-fry poured out along with a short, lean fella in chef's uniform, brown skin and balding black hair with a comb over.

"This lass wants to thank you!" The barman said and the chef widened his brown eyes, smiled in genuine appreciation while nodding quickly.

"Hello! What you have?" He asked with a thick accent.

"The green curry." Emily said.

"Khaeng khiao wan?" The chef said. "You like?"

"Oh yeah, it were lovely!" Emily replied then didn't hesitate to say, "Could I ask you summat?"

~

More booze down her gob and Emily was friendlier—she chatted with almost every person she came across, and was getting wobblier on her heels with each passing minute. *I should be so lucky* was playing and she was stood at the bar waiting to get served. There was a right fit bloke stood to her right, saying a few words to her and even bought her a shot of vodka, which they downed together. Emily gave him a kiss then thanked him for it. Jody had spotted it, and was saying summat nasty about it as she shambled up to the bar.

"I'm friendly!" Emily complained merrily. Jody's belly flab slammed against the counter.

"Why don't yah chat him up, lesbo?" She dissed loud enough for the barman to hear, and he grimaced, likely he wasn't gonna serve her. Emily didn't say owt and went back to the table.

There were people dancing in the space in front of the Christmas tree left of the main entrance. Gemma, Jody and Zoe went there. And it didn't take long for Jody to get out of breath and perspire; anymore and she was going to have a heart attack. Once she took a time out and went back to the table, Emily joined in. She liked dancing, Spanish tango she was interested in, but she needed a partner for that. She didn't like break dancing as it was too in-your-face, sort of like Gemma was doing, bouncing around and waving her arms about like an idiot and butting in with the other dancers. Zoe was more modest and slower and nervous with her moves, Emily had more motion to her arms and turns to her hips. No blokes were coming over, put off by Gemma who was screaming more shite and trying to irritate everyone else. Then it was back to the bar with Zoe, who bought her another sambuca, and Emily went back to the booth to pour herself another glass of rosé, Jody was saying summat she didn't understand and giggling. Zoe rescued Emily by asking her outside for a cig.

"So fuckin' cold…!" Zoe complained even with them warm lights on as she fumbled through her handbag for her cigs. Some bloke gave them both a free cig, and he was chatting them both up. Emily was so mellow she didn't even need to try and get rid of him, nor did she care about her pronunciation of words.

"Cheers for the cig love!"

She still had the decency to say thanks and give him a hug though. Back at the bar she had another sambuca shot, courtesy of Zoe, the smiles of the barman seemed wider than they should be. Maybe he fancied her? At the booth Gemma had her arms around Stacy who looked demonic and was cussing. Zoe was proper lively, talking fast and giggling. And the booze was making Emily choke with laughter at it. Zoe was fucking brilliant!

"Argh, I fuckin' love you…!" Emily babbled with a near sore throat and pounded her hand on the table not too loudly.

"You love her?" Gemma shouted, letting the whole pub know while leaning into her face. Jody was giggling, bringing her fat hands up to cover her mouth, the flab of her arms obstructing most of the view beyond her.

After a while, everyone except Jody went out for a cig, Gemma and Stacey went to a different table. It wasn't too long before summat kicked off.

"You whaa…?" Stacey shrieked. Emily turned around and saw this bloke smiling at Stacey, other blokes gathering around.

"Fuck off…!" The same bloke said back as though she were nowt.

"You tellin' me sister to fuck off?" Gemma backed.

"Fuckin' knobhead!" Stacey shouted throwing her skinny arms about, "Bastard!"

Whoa! She was losing it!

"Fuckin' anorexic skank!" The smiling bloke added, gasps of laughter followed with the bloke looking away and beginning to mess about on his phone.

"Eat summat! Bun's av plenty of calories!" This other bloke among the crowd taunted and had the lot giggling. There were all these empty bottles on the table.

"Fuck off yah bastard!" Stacey howled and swiped the bottles off the table with Emily and a couple other lasses yelping in surprise at the near deafening crashing of broken glass.

"Fuckin' hell!" Witnesses, including Gemma, said unanimously. Emily didn't bother stepping in and concealed her smirk, which she let Zoe see but had to secretly gesture for her to refrain from showing it. Staff came out to confront Stacey, and she caused a scene with them, her words were unintelligent and very witch-like, and the laughs and disses from the crowd didn't die down. Emily and Zoe hurried up with their cigs and finished them in only half the time than normal, and not wanting the anti-social sisters to get them involved, they went back inside.

"Oh me God…!" Zoe laughed, letting loose her smile she had kept restrained.

"She's got some proper issues!" Emily told her.

Jody wasn't at the table. Emily topped up her glass and drank. It was just her and Zoe enjoying themselves for a short while, up until Jody returned to the table, though she would be better off leaving with her dysfunctional mates.

Outside, the volume of the commotion increased and Jody was being annoying.

"What's going on?" She asked, and annoyingly continued to ask whenever one of the sisters shouted, as if she couldn't get up to investigate. Then there were cheers from the lads outside, the sort you'd hear when a footie match was on in the pub. Emily ignored the calls and texts from Gemma, good thing they were off—too bad they couldn't have left before she got tipsy! Zoe bought Emily another sambuca, she didn't need to get one for Jody but she did anyway, and it tasted even worse; she choked and nearly gagged.

At the table, Emily's head was elsewhere, she was tiered, her hands felt like they were miles away, her vision tumbling to the side. She drank some wine to get rid of the sambuca taste then swallowed back hard, she didn't want to go out for another cig. Jody was talking shite again, and Emily felt sick looking at her and would probably chuck it up if she did any of her lady burps. She wanted to go home.

"Y'alright?" Zoe asked her. Emily was about to tell her the truth.

Then Jody interrupted with a loud belch.

"Pardon me!" she said.

Next thing Emily was crouched by the toilet on her knees, puking up the contents of her stomach into the bowl, not caring if her jeans were dirty. She didn't want to look at it! Once she felt she had gotten rid of it all she wiped away vomit from her mouth with the back of her hand. Shame! That was a lovely curry!

"Fuck sake Jody…!" She moaned then flushed the toilet, and disgustedly ran her fingers through her hair, checking if any vomit had got in it. Emily stood up and fell back against the cubicle wall, she fumbled about in her handbag for her phone and tried ringing for a taxi. She couldn't press the keys properly, her vision switching like pages being turned in a book. As she went to unlock the door she nearly fell against it.

"Fuckin' hell!" She cursed staggering, without giving in to have to call for help.

~

Saturday morning. Emily woke up safely in her bed at 56 Carnian Street, her head was aching from all the booze. And bleeding hell, her tummy was hurting! At least Mum wasn't up early in need of a shower. Emily was really regretting the booze-coached decision to top so much chilli on last night's meal. At least, she didn't have to start work early! The thought of Mexicans, Jamaicans, Indians—all them cultures eating proper spicy food all day, shoving whole chillies into their mouths like it was nowt, and people doing all them spicy challenges begged the question—*why do you do this…?* Emily wouldn't include this in a diary though! Fucking hell no, she would not be sharing this God dreadful experience with anyone! Emily went down into the kitchen and drank two glasses of water, then lay back in bed until her insides felt normal. Hydrated and comfortable enough to step out into the world, which just welcomed ridicule and misfortune, she put on a navy blue and white striped trackie, hardly her favourite though and she didn't care how she looked. She went for a run without her iPod, but only half distance and felt good, not having to hold back vomit.

Emily stopped in front of her home's gate, wishing she had brought her cigs along. She couldn't quite remember all the ingredients from last night's pad thai request, so she went on her phone and browsed through the internet for recipes. According to the recipe a chicken pad thai required chicken, eggs, unsalted peanuts, carrots, bean sprouts and rice noodles, this tamarind thingy paste, fish sauce and a lime… But another online recipe was different and mentioned all this other stuff Emily didn't think she could afford never mind find: dried shrimp, tofu, preserved turnip, Chinese chives. It didn't say owt about carrots though. Better off sticking with the original recipe. The Sainsbury's at Hoperwood Beck wouldn't have them ingredients, so it was a trip to town then, and Emily had a bit of extra money left from last night, thanks to Zoe getting half the drinks. Distracted by her search, her panting masked the noise of her front gate opening.

She stalled as this bloke walked past her, he was a short, skinny black fella with a fortnight's growth of stubble, wearing a dark grey body warmer and had a light grey hoodie over his head. Immediately Emily didn't like the looks of him. And…had he just come out the bleeding house?

"Yah don't av tah be scared of us lav!" The stranger said unflatteringly, revealing some ugly yellow teeth and bright red, gingivitis-ridden gums, and his first two upper teeth were missing, broken.

"I'm *really* scared!" Emily bounced back with a very even, flat delivery. She went back inside, cautious as though being followed, she looked back and watched as the fella raised his arms and howled loudly like one of them monkeys in the Amazon rainforest. Safe inside she locked the door then peered through the peephole. He wasn't loitering about, but she heard him howl again—*fuckin' hell!* Emily silently cursed, shaking her head and wanting to kick that dodgy cunt's head in. Was that how he had lost his front teeth? It wasn't unreasonable to believe. How drunk was Mum to have fallen for a creep like that? Emily wanted the whole house boarded up like in them films that had gunfights!

She went upstairs, planning on having a proper serious word with Mum about this cunt. She opened her bedroom door, her Mum was wrapped up in a grey king-size duvet and had her back to her.

"Ear, Mum?" Emily half shouted then tapped her on the shoulder.

"Bloody…hell…!" Mum muttered.

"Were yah shaggin' him?" Emily started.

"What…?" Mum rolled over, her eyes not open. She didn't have a bruise on her face.

"Were yah shaggin' that cunt just then?" Emily retorted.

"No…it were his mate…he couldn't get a taxi…" Mum explained. So both had slept in the same bed as her? That was just careless—it could have gotten out of hand!

"Leave us alone…!" Mum begged without any effort and rolled back over. Emily shook her head—*well thank fuck for that!* With a slight bit of peace of mind Emily showered, dressed casually in a cream brown sweater, blue jeans and kept her makeup simple, her hair tied up into a small, high bun without any real effort. Her overcoat and some tall black Uggs on, she needed the exotic stuff for her Thai meal tonight…

She sat upstairs on the 175 at the very back on the right. There was this little girl sat with her mum, staring at Emily over her seat four rows from her.

"Mummy?" She kept nagging, pointing Emily's way.

"What?" The mother said without raising her voice.

"She's *beautiful*!" She said, eyes making contact with Emily's—*aw, bless you!* The heads of passengers turned her way.

"Sorry!" The mother apologised.

"She's fine!" Emily assured her, waving. In town she went to Isherwood Centre and bought spring onions, some ready to cook rice noodles, unsalted peanuts and a Chinese stir-fry vegetable pack and a single lime. She bought a cream soda and drank it on the way to Si Hong Suns supermarket, and upon

187

turning the corner onto Holden Lane she had accidentally bumped into crybaby Heather. On her own, Softie could be managed, except she wasn't alone. And of all the people you wished you'd never run into, Bethany O'Mare was with her.

If you wanted the definition of skank, then look to Bethany O'Mare. She was a midget with this round head and pointy chin that gave it a pear shape, her thin, wavy brown hair pulled back too tight and in a bun and wore massively hooped earrings, that could get caught on something. She was anorexic with legs like toothpicks that could snap if she tripped. And her fluffy cuffed brown Uggs looked out of place like a toddler wearing their dad's boots, or as though she had stepped in two mounds of shite! But all them physical flaws of hers could be ignored, prince charming could come and take her hand if she didn't act like a bitch all the time.

Emily didn't want these lot going into Si Hong Sun's with her. Crybaby Heather was so nervous, looking like she was going to have a panic attack, and Bethany—cry-me-a-bleedin-river—she was worse than both Gemma and Stacy combined! There was no way of getting rid of her, she had to have her own way; if she came up to you on the street asking for change she would follow you if you refused, if she did summat to piss you off she wouldn't apologise, if she took summat from you she wouldn't give it back, and she was one of them sort of people that had no issues holding up a flight and making everyone else suffer. Interestingly, she and Stacey had had a catfight during a summer party that neighbours had called the police to split them up. Bethany O'Mare was a bad person.

"…So I need this…tamarind paste thingy…" Emily muttered peacefully to herself looking at the shelves for some products in English among all these other far eastern languages in colourful lettering, while keeping a budget in mind, the fact that their prices weren't listed properly was just taking the piss. She carefully filled her basket and went further back to the store, where there was this sweet, sharp odour about, nowt unpleasant but still odd.

"It fuckin' stinks in here!" Bethany complained, sounding like she was gonna throw up. All the time Bethany kept droning on with an intensely cringed-up expression, "What's this?", "Not for me!", "I wouldn't fuckin' eat that!"

She got paranoid when this bloke appeared around the corner to investigate, whatever it was that was pissing her off.

"What you lookin' at?" Bethany barked, the bloke didn't look away and moved on like nowt happened.

"The fuck's this?" she continued, taking her paranoia out on a tin of what Emily only just caught on the label as catfish.

"Come on…don't!" Heather complained, looking around wondering if they were all gonna get kicked out for racist comments. After getting everything she needed, Emily went to the till to pay, embarrassed by the dysfunctional pair behind her.

"That looks like shite! Would you fuckin' eat that?" Bethany mocked while looking at the cashier who ignored her.

"Why'd you even go here? You cookin' summat shite?" She asked Emily with a cringe showing her crooked upper teeth, looking around for another victim—*why do you need to be such a bitch?* Emily also felt like saying unable to resist a look at Bethany's ghastly lower body. She couldn't squeeze a baby out through them horribly narrow hips! *C-section for you!*

"Just summat new," Emily replied without sounding like she gave a toss and was pleased when the cashier asked for the charge, which wasn't over budget. And to whine horrible Bethany up, Emily decided to stop in this café behind the supermarket, alienating her further. Crybaby was on her phone, really burying her attention in it and typing very quickly. The place was small, with white walls and tables, some Chinese décor which was red with gold lettering which Emily quite liked, and a counter displaying a rainbow of colourful cakes and other desserts. Still feeling the effects of her hangover, Emily ordered this Chinese lager in a green bottle and a slice of *green tea* flavoured cake that had this light green, fluffy-looking sponge topped with whipped cream with chocolate sprinkles on top.

"*Why* you drinkin' a fuckin' Chinese beer this early?" Bethany sneered— *and I'm a bitch cuz I han't been arrested?* Talk about irony! Emily smiled and picked up her lager.

"Fuck off!" She said more than ready to deal with the consequences then drank.

~

Back home and feeling much better, Emily arranged the pad thai ingredients from her shopping trip on the kitchen counter. Even though she had brought her laptop down to watch a YouTube demonstration, this wasn't a familiar way of cooking to her; no wok or super-hot gas cooker, just the average frying pan on an electric home stove as always. Girls aloud *untouchable* was playing while she prepared her ingredients, slicing spring onions, regular onions, garlic and chicken, grinding up the peanuts with a rolling pin still in their packet. Emily needed to make a sauce for the pad thai, which required tamarind paste concentrate, this thick brown stuff she had bought today. She put some in a bowl, a dip of the finger revealed a weird, sour and bitter taste; summat you'd maybe put into a curry. The internet recipe said to mix some ketchup in…not very Thai as well as some Sriracha, which was sorted. Emily assumed soy sauce would have been used, but the internet recipe and the chef from last night said to use fish sauce, which smelt fishy, but there was summat good about it. She put a drop of that on her fingertip, tasted and cringed lightly over how salty and strange it was then put some in the bowl.

Emily put some sunflower oil into the largest frying pan she could find then put the hob on at the highest heat. Chicken, onions, garlic and the stir-fry veg pack, which included cabbage, carrots, bean sprouts, water chestnuts and peppers went in the pan.

The oil sizzle on contact was so vicious and frighteningly loud that it made her jump, the splashes of oil on her wrist causing her to yelp, swear and recoil. She didn't know how them chefs could cook so fearlessly over a fiery hot wok! Emily added the rice noodles along with that tamarind mixture, which looked nice as it cooked and mixed in with the flat white noodles, giving them a delicate bit of brown contrasting against the colourful vegetables.

Convinced they were cooking well she pushed the noodles to the side to allow some space for three eggs, which she scrambled in the pan with her spatula, which was becoming overcrowded with stuff spilling out onto the hob and floor. Then she added the spring onions and crushed peanuts and delicately stirred the heaped amount, cursing as more spilled over. Emily forgot to add some sugar, which she did at the last minute of cooking, palm sugar was what the Thais used normally, but it was too expensive at the oriental supermarket, but the chef from last night said normal white sugar would work. She turned off the cooker and put half the portion for herself on a plate.

"Okay…" She said flexing out her lower lip, took a fork, wrapped the noodles around like spaghetti and bit down, getting a nice crunch of vegetables and soft noodles, tasteless at first then some flavour came. She grunted with satisfaction. The noodles were a bit sweet and salty, and the crunchy peanuts made them proper savoury, but they were missing summat though, Emily didn't know what. She didn't have them ace condiments for last night's curry to experiment with. Actually, she had forgotten the lime. Having had pad thai at a fancy Thai restaurant in Leeds Emily remembered a lime wedge being served, which you were supposed to squeeze over. She cut the lime she had bought in half then squeezed the juice all over the noodles, the taste had improved, it was a bit sourer and had brought a balance. But there was still summat missing. She didn't hesitate to squirt some Sriracha over her noodles and mix them in. The result wasn't perfect, but it was still better.

Emily finished her plate, wanting to eat the rest in the pan, but saved it for Mum, who just happened to come in.

"What's with the Chinese stuff?" She asked, almost as if heading an interrogation over the smell and mess of unfamiliar, opened up ingredients scattered all over the kitchen. She went for a fork, lazily fished out some noodles from the pan and ate a decent mouthful. Mum actually trying summat foreign for once was unrealistic!

"Lovely that!" She said. Did she mean it though or was it a white lie?

"You cookin' chinky now?"

Emily smiled.

"It's Thai…!" She corrected.

"You can have that." She offered her plate.

"No, you're alright! I just had lunch!" Mum declined.

"Yay!" Emily cheered.

~

Sunday. It was sunny outside, but that did nowt about the mid December chills. Emily had done a couple of sit-ups and stretches before getting ready to go to church across the road with Mum for Sunday service. It wasn't a weekly thing, just went more like every fortnight, and Mum was pretty much the same about it. It was all about community and keeping in contact with people so you didn't get isolated or labelled as weird by the neighbourhood. Emily wore a white blouse, black work trousers, her crucifix exposed while Mum was wearing all black, as though she was going to a funeral. Except she still looked provocative as usual; she was wearing a short black leather jacket with a sweater that had a normal height cut thankfully, her tight trousers and her tall stiletto boots concealed by the pews. The only time she wasn't dressed sexy was when she was asleep, but that depended on whether she had fallen asleep drunk in whatever it was she was wearing before then.

The church had mahogany tiles, the stain glass windows stood out beautifully against the pure white walls and there was a fairly fresh scent of paint as though it had been done during the week. There was no church pipe organ as the indoor space wasn't that large, but there was a piano to the right corner of the altar, but no one to play it, usually it would be played by Misses Scorey, who had played during assemblies at primary school. But she was off ill today. The local vicar, Father Adrian Kirkdale was young, quite handsome, in good shape and looked more like a high school teacher than a man of faith. He played footie and had actually been around to both Emily's primary and secondary school to coach the pupils. As with each service, Father Adrian held a sermon with the Lord's hand being relevant in the subject.

"Mister Caudiverbera," the vicar awkwardly pronounced with an educated voice, "Were a butcher in Mexico with a shanty house with a backyard facing a swamp. One morning, while fetching water to do the laundry, the head of a *crocodile* appeared."

Mutters among the congregation began, along with some swallowed back laughter. Was this gonna be about some animal attack, like them American shows with dodgy, over-excited voiced narrators describing the aftermath?

"Mister Caudiverbera was petrified. Weighing three hundred pounds, he knew he couldn't turn around and run!"

Amused laughter swept across the gathering.

"Instead the crocodile just floated there, staring at him."

Father Adrian lifted his hands off the altar podium, gesturing accordingly then smiled.

"Mister Caudiverbera—a devout Christian—braced himself for what he believed would be his end: being a crocodile's lunch, or at least a limb of his would be!"

More quiet laughter came about.

"But no!" Father Adrian exclaimed and smiled, his blue eyes whipping back on everyone as though he was an emcee.

"The crocodile walked out from the water onto Mister Caudiverbera's backyard, then it just stopped and rested. Mister Caudiverbera went back inside and came out with a broom. He tested it, prodded the crocodile with fear. That failed and he tried to lure it away by throwing chicken into the river. But it just stayed there."

This might just be the most interesting preaching Emily had heard in a while; most of it usually involved the Lord's blessing being involved in simple things like a cup of coffee, a sweater purchased from the charity store that was coincidentally similar to a celebrity's seen on TV, or a decent lottery win that allowed a whole family to dine out.

"But the fear subsided over the hours," Father Adrian continued, "Mister Caudiverbera got closer and closer, to the point where he could reach out and touch it. It was night and it still refused to move, so he left it then went to bed, but told his family: 'not to go out onto the backyard.'"

Did summat bad happen overnight? Did the crocodile crawl its way into the bloke's house while he and his family was asleep? Emily was wondering.

"The next morning, the crocodile was still there!" Father Adrian answered that. The congregation chuckled, and it must also have summat partly to do with the vicar constantly pronouncing that Mexican bloke's name.

"Mister Caudiverbera couldn't just get someone to put it down or move it. So he fed it offal and chicken bones from the market he worked at. But the crocodile still wouldn't leave."

Further laughter from the congregation.

"In the end he tested his faith and began to sit with it and pet it, like it was a dog. And for weeks after that, the crocodile remained in his backyard. It would move around a little bit, it would slip back into the water. But it would always come back."

Father Adrian paused and spread his hands apart on the podium.

"We all know crocodiles kill hundreds of people every year. Another irony here is that during *damnation ad bestias*," Father Adrian slipped some Latin in. "The condemnation by the beasts, the Romans had fed Christians to crocodiles they brought over from Africa."

Emily's secondary school history teacher had told the class that Christians had gruesomely been fed to lions, wolves and bears. But crocodiles weren't mentioned, and no one other than the smiling, giggling lads had wanted to hear more.

Emily slowly turned her head towards her Mum, who had her eyes on Father Adrian, smiling and raising her eyebrows, trying to get his attention. As friendly as Father Adrian was to his flock, she was not gonna be banging him! The vicar adjusted his priest's collar with his left hand.

"Mister Caudiverbera told the townspeople about his affair, and people from neighbouring towns came flocking to his house, just to see him with the crocodile and take photos. Mister Caudiverbera was able to make a small business out of this and get some extra money; he was able to build a pond for his latest addition to his household, where everyone could see it, do some improvements on his house *and* he was able to fund a decent education for all four of his children, which was a grand load off his back. All was going better than he could have ever imagined."

Father Adrian paused again, began preparing himself for his next delivery of lines.

"But one day Mister Caudiverbera woke up and found that the crocodile was no longer in his backyard. He thought it had just swam off for a bit, so he waited. Hours passed and it didn't show up. Days passed, people were asking him where it had gone. Then weeks. Then months. He knew it had left him for good."

It wasn't the best of endings…but it wasn't a sad one. What would Emily have done if she had a crocodile stay in her backyard? But she would have to be living in some ideal place in the tropics—as if! Father Adrian lifted his left hand off the podium and raised an index finger to the church's ceiling, his warm smile sustained.

"Historically, a crocodile is a bit of an ender of a believer of followers of his *(Mister Caudiverbera's)* faith, one of which became a blessing in disguise. For many people across the world just fetching water from the river an encounter with a crocodile is a death sentence, going as nature—as *some* people might say—intended, the way of things."

Then Father Adrian looked around, chuckled and held out that same hand, which he flipped, palm facing heaven, as though he was apologising for summat his flock didn't know of.

"My ancestor was *William Buckland*, he too was a priest—a Dean actually, for West Minister nearly two hundred years ago. But he was also a geologist and a scientist, during a time when it was becoming more accepted in society."

Father Adrian put his hands together.

"He was one of the very first people who founded palaeontology, the study of prehistoric life—*dinosaurs*, which…some of us do love as kids!"

Emily grinned. That was as ironic as his sermon, if not more so! And Emily wondered if she descended from anyone great herself.

"How *magnificent* is that?" Father Adrian said but didn't get much of an applause. Some bloke coughed continuously while others whispered.

"Okay, lets finish off today with *Here I' am Lord*." Father Adrian finished then everyone stood up, hymn books ready and pages turning. Everyone was singing, this hymn had been sung all the time during primary school, and during year four Emily had been asked to sing the lead for choir. Mum and Nan had seen it and were very proud with Nan recording it and sending them a tape of it. It felt off singing it without the backing of the piano.

~

After mass Mum decided to stay, she was chatting with a neighbour Misses Dixon at number 74 Carnian Street, and Emily was told to go on ahead to the carvery pub at Hoperwood Beck ahead of her. Outside, Emily lit a fag and was texting with a file of church goers behind her, beginning to split and part ways, but most of them were heading her way. Emily couldn't be sure if there was gonna be another service before Christmas, her life was just getting too busy for God now. He should probably help her make time. Across the road was this group of lads heading in the opposite direction, all had cropped hair, wore football shirts and were drunkenly singing an anthem, pausing between breaths to holler abuse at pedestrians on the other side of the road, most of whom were elderly and ignoring them.

Emily couldn't stand it. Imagine if this was a funeral procession? Oh yeah, and there were savage cunts out there who were empty enough to do that.

"Ear?" She shouted back at them.

"Pack it in!"

"Calm down!" One of them divs said with his mates giggling.

"Yeah, calm down, love!" Another one of them said, looking ready to leg it if Emily eyed him. Instead of doing a Stacey, she gave them the finger.

"Fuckin' hell!" Most of them cheered.

"Fuck off, yah sad twat!" Emily bit back hard like them honey badgers that supposedly didn't fear owt.

Half of the congregation were heading to the pub, which was actually more closer to Sancrott and around this dodgy corner where you couldn't see it if

195

driving, and its sign was worn down slightly and needed a paintjob. Inside though the place was very normal, and surprisingly spacious, Bill Withers *lovely day* was playing and the waft of freshly roasting meat stirred the appetite; Emily hadn't had breakfast and was famished! The pub's patrons included a mix of locals of all ages and a bunch of old blokes in tweed caps and jackets, *Del Boy* stereotypes. They were either proper passive or just loudly obnoxious, all say for this one bloke: Sergeant Peter Malthus. He was a widowed seventy five year old army veteran who had been stationed in Singapore and Hong Kong during the fifties or summat, and had travelled the Far East; China, Japan, Indonesia, Thailand, Vietnam, Taiwan (he had said), which was just incredible!

Peter had cropped, silvery grey hair, always wore a green army style overcoat, and a *very* moody, unapproachable face with intense blue eyes staring down at a pint always seen in front of him along with a tin of loose tobacco, which he would be busy rolling and storing away. And Sergeant Peter Malthus was a God-hating bloke who despised everyone; his neighbours, his neighbour's dog, the postman, his relatives, his own children and grandchildren, his mates, even his old army comrades. This pub hosted Remembrance Day events and Sergeant Malthus would be seen in his service uniform, nobly enough.

Well, he loathed everyone except Emily; he had been a regular at the pub she had worked at before the arson attack, he had always been nice, whenever she waved he would return it, he kept the swearing to a minimum, had left her tips and had even smiled. For anyone else he would either ignore or tell them to piss off, and if they got lippy he would get up and confront them. And old Peter could still fight; apparently he had been barred from nearly every pub this side of Thewlington because of decking anyone who pissed him off or backed him into a corner. Good thing them wankers outside the church weren't here causing a fuss! Upon spotting Peter Emily waved to him and he smiled and tenderly returned the wave.

Several tables had been reserved for the congregation, and everyone was sat chatting, eating, drinking booze…and talking the same shite pretty much. Emily had ordered roast beef which she just loved along with horseradish and plenty of veg, and for the sake of dieting, she went for mash potato instead of roast spuds which were cooked in dripping, though she had to have a Yorkshire pudding and a glass of rosé as well. And the Yorkshire puds here were brill! For some reason, Jody appeared and actually joined the congregation, squeezing in the spare seat towards the end of the table, even though she believed in fuck all, but it was just for the company and food, which was decent quality, unlike her table manners, and she had to refrain from them disgusting lady burps with Mum around, as she had told her off to her face one time.

Jody kept trying to talk to Emily, calling out from the further end of the table, and annoyed by it she made an excuse to leave the table and went out for a cig. She went on her phone and searched her messages, then all these people poured outside, complaining about the cold and the clicks of multiple lighters going off all at once as they lit their cigs. And Jody lumbered out—*for fuck sake!* And she didn't even smoke.

"Why were yah shoppin' for Chinese stuff!" Jody asked, sensationalising it, it was obvious that bitch Bethany had grassed her up!

"It were *Thai!*" Emily corrected without looking at her, though she did spot this smartly dressed blonde lad, five years old who stopped to her left and was just stood looking up at her with his chocolate stained mouth hanging open. It wasn't a look of innocent child curiosity, it was someone who wanted to take the piss. Their parents and their mates told them what was acceptable and what was dodgy; that it was ok to throw stones and eggs at peoples windows, and that being polite and investing in a decent future was for queers. This lad had no sense of reason. In ten years' time, he was probably gonna end up turning into a really nasty twat.

"Don't be starin' at her!" This lass in sports trackies and Uggs stepped in, she was miserable, obese, freckled, her face drained and blemished with acne and sores from a vitamin D deficiency, her hair frizzy and worn back in a bun. She grabbed the gawking lad by the hand, he complained as she took him away. Obviously she was the parent. Emily didn't say owt this time. Jody started talking, but Emily wasn't listening and just said, "Yeah?", "Oh really?", "Bloody hell!" In that order to make it sound like she was listening. She quickly finished her cig then went back inside, thinking of what to have for pudding while Jody pathetically tried to keep up with her. Mum came up to her side, glass of wine in hand, looking all merry and tipsy, already.

"Alright me love?" She asked. Emily grunted then had the courage to whisper into her Mum's ear, "I fuckin' hate this place…!"

And she had work tonight, but it wasn't a late shift.

The bus into town wasn't frustrating, thankfully as Emily hadn't been stood out in the cold under that tree for more than a few minutes. Two hours into the shift she was given toilet check duty. The loos in Zaks and Marias were dodgy in the way they were laid out; the gents were upstairs in another building, while the ladies were difficult to find; it was like someone had decided to build a maze then had changed their mind. The only way you could find the ladies room was by following these small women signs, which no one paid any attention to, and it got annoying when hundreds of lasses kept coming up to the bar when busy and asking where the loo was in the middle of service. Emily checked the gents, unlike most places the loos here were very clean, no piss or shit smell; urinals had fragrance tablets, soap dispensers with hand lotion at the sinks. Not long after her check of the gents she was in the store cupboard downstairs filling up a bucket with water to clean the ladies.

"*Wembley!*" She could hear some bloke shouting in the men's room.

"Wembley!" He called out again, his words slurred.

"We don't give a fuck!" Some other fella said.

"We don't give a fuck…!" Wembley fella parroted, obviously drunk. Emily chuckled. She wasn't serving him!

~

Monday morning, December 14th it said on Emily's phone's screen. Last week of college before Christmas holidays. Unlike yesterday it was a pretty drab, grey sky day with a promise of rain to come. After getting herself ready Emily was walking to the bus stop, checking on her appearance with her compact mirror, listening to *cool* by Gwen Stefani.

"Yo?" Some fella shouted across the road, she looked that way and saw Dan Ellerbe, a classmate from secondary school, who just happened to be heading in the same direction as her at the same time.

"Ear you? How yah been?"

Emily smiled and removed her earphones. Dan Ellerbe jogged across the road. He was a tall, lean lad with a goofy, long face and big, blue-eyed expression, but he had a nice hair style, his blonde hair styled into a crew cut with these flicks to his hair not as severe as other lads went for, and he went for the chavy look with his trackie bottoms tucked into his socks and was carrying a drawstring gym bag. While Dan looked athletic, the truth was he was lazy as fuck; his local takeout was around the corner of his street, yet he had to have them deliver every time or have his brother collect!

Emily hadn't seen much of him since he left secondary school for work, but she had always had a good time around him when she did. Dan Ellerbe was brilliant while drunk, as Emily had had the delight of witnessing being invited to a secondary school graduation party he had organised last year. Dan hadn't gotten into any trouble she had heard about, a bit ironic as he fit in with all the dickheads! Dan was coming into town also. They got on the 175 bus and went upstairs. The first person—the only person they saw—was Gangster fella, sat at the back to the left. Emily smiled at him, he saw her and had to return the smile. But he seemed to freeze, then looked away for some reason. Emily only just remembered that long chat she had had with him last week, and wondered if he had he done her *portrait*? In that case Emily was gonna sit at the very back as usual, but Dan chose the last seat in front of the back and sat next to her on the outer seat. They talked a bit, two more people came upstairs, Gangster didn't say owt flattering to start a conversation.

The bus went downhill on that drop of Harewood Road when passing by Carlin Venture then uphill, and Dan—bless him—had butterfingers and dropped his gym bag which slid backwards from the friction.

Emily looked back and saw Gangster scoop it off the floor without looking at it, he got out of his seat and handed it back.

"Cheers mate!" Dan said and giggled. Gangster just grunted, he didn't look too happy…And Emily didn't like that he wasn't either; he didn't even look at her.

"What's Santa getting you's for Crimbo?" Dan asked.

"I wanna red handbag!" Emily told him. Then Dan had slippery fingers for the second time—Emily couldn't trust him to hold owt for her! And Gangster caught it, again. He looked proper tense, like a dog you had managed to piss off all of a sudden without knowing why. Dan thanked him again.

Gangster didn't make a sound and kept his eyes on the floor. Emily actually wanted him to get up and sit on the seat across from them; she expected him to call out summat weird to get her attention. Did he hate her now or summat? She didn't look back at him. Only one other person came upstairs, this was oddly quiet for a Monday. The bus turned into town and at the foot of Furnivall Road multiple rings of the bus bells went off. Gangster walked past and awkwardly stretched his arm back and handed Emily summat: a piece of paper in a plastic wallet rolled up like a scroll with a piece of string tied up in a simple bow holding it together.

"This for us?" Emily said. But Gangster just walked off and went downstairs so quickly without waving or looking at her. For some reason, Emily knew this wasn't his stop.

She unrolled the paper he had given her—*oh my God!* And staring back at her was the most amazing drawing of herself. Dan gasped and froze with big wide eyes.

"That's *really* good is that!" He marvelled, taking it without damaging it for a better look.

"He shoulda charged yah for it!"

Emily couldn't say owt and looked towards the stairs.

"That's class!" Dan said and delicately passed it back to her while she stood up and went towards the window to her left and looked down at the pedestrians, the bus slowing down. People walked out, normally. Gangster didn't walk out. He ran out as fast as a wasp flying out from a crevice then slouched over, looking really pissed off like he was gonna punch the wall and knacker his knuckles. *What were that just then?* Emily was asking herself uncomfortably, legitimately ready to make a fuss over it.

"What's up?" Dan asked. Emily didn't answer. Her and Dan? All that…? Emily had given Gangster the wrong idea. While walking she paused on the inside, no rising body temperature.

"You alright?" Dan asked noticing her down expression. Emily felt like running as far as she needed to. But she didn't. Emily swallowed back gently and told a fib, "Yeah, I'm alright!"

Chapter 10

Monday morning, December 21st. It was the two-week holiday off college, Nan was nice enough to wire her a hundred quid, and Emily had already done most of her Xmas shopping at Hoperwood Beck. *The bird that flies over a warzone, the fly that witnesses a murder, the rat that heard the security codes.* Those lines she remembered the best from a science fiction book she had quickly finished over the weekend, she had also watched several interesting documentaries, so naturally her vocabulary improved. *Conglomerate, procrastination, subjective…* She didn't know how and when she would include these new words into conversation though, as there was no one to engage with that sort of banter. That seat at the back of the 175 bus was empty…

Emily had bought a few doughnuts at Isherwood Centre, obviously she wasn't gonna eat them all but it would be nice to share with the staff at work when they came in. At Zaks and Marias, the Spice Girls *to become one* was playing, half the class during college and secondary school had been singing it whenever it came on. There was no Marvin about, he had been fired for stealing, and that was nowt surprising… Emily was the only one on the bar, drinking some orange juice from a straw, she cringed from brain freeze from all the ice she had regretted chucking in then picked up and bit a chocolate sprinkled doughnut.

Then this bloke came in, Emily put her drink and doughnut down. The customer was a middle-aged bloke, tubby but suavely dressed in a navy blue suit with a light blue shirt, his potbelly bulging out. He had a double chin, stubble, but his heavily greyed brown hair was nicely parted at first style length, though it looked greasy and he walked with a very straight back with a plod to his steps.

"Hello my dear," he said, his belly touched the counter as he inspected the pumps with a dopey-looking squint.

"I will have a pint of…" He pointed unsurely at the pumps. "Do you have any *English* lagers here?"

"Flibbigans?" Emily answered and flipped a pint glass up from under the counter.

"One of them please," the customer spoke slowly, and had a deep voice with a posh, intellectual BBC accent. Emily poured him his pint, he placed a crispy clean tenner on the counter. She placed his pint down.

"How's yah day been?" She asked the customer, he coughed, but covered his mouth with the back of his right hand.

"How has my day been, young lady...?" He rephrased, he had this moody look to him and wasn't quite making eye contact.

"I went into the Isherwood Centre for some shopping yesterday, and I purchased a *royal pudding*. It cost me a prestigious four pounds, and it was a satisfyingly portly pudding—the kind you would normally get around Christmas."

His words were as smooth as his distended belly.

"Yeah?" Emily said as she turned around to get his change while listening.

"I heated it up in the microwave and dressed it in some custard, I made myself from Madagascan vanilla pods, and I was utterly disgusted and disillusioned by this substandard, *half-baked* pudding that I went to complain to management. I told him: *the prestigious title of this product placement is utterly disingenuous!*"

As she placed the customer's five quid eighty pence change down, Emily watched him lift his full pint and delicately suck off some of the foamy head then swill a gulp.

"I assumed that having the title of royal pudding inferred that it was manufactured by, or at least affiliated with the bakers of the royal family..." He said. *What...?* This bloke was so boring, but hilarious at the same time! Emily wouldn't mind listening to him for a couple more hours.

"In the end I got a refund, and I had to palm the manager's integrity, as he had been leeched by other dissatisfied customers previously."

"Well, that's good!" Emily couldn't say more. Royal pudding fella grunted dismissively and drank.

"As it was branded a *royal pudding*, it should thus be structured with the disciplinary approach of royalty."

He went on again—*bloody hell!* Then he gasped. And it was a slow, precise gasp.

"So, do you have a boyfriend...?" He asked her.

"No." Emily answered.

"And why is that?"

"The lads are just arseholes!" Emily replied, feeling a bit shite by her choice of words.

"Not *all*." Royal pudding fella said. "There are plenty of fine chaps out there who are exceptionally charismatic with plenty to offer."

"Just not in the mood right now." Emily said.

"That is your prerogative…" Royal pudding fella said steadily. *Prerogative…* Emily needed to look up that word—she was sure she had picked it up while reading. Royal pudding fella drank, guzzling away without any further conversation. Emily distracted herself with her phone for summat like five or ten uninterrupted minutes, looking at Abby's posts who was wishing she was eighteen so she could get pissed and see an Ashanti concert in Leeds. Royal pudding fella grunted, which prompted Emily to spin around, where she noticed his glass was near a quarter full.

"You wantin' another?" She asked him. Royal pudding fella took a sip and shook his head.

"I'm good!" He said. "You get out there and *discover* yourself a decent gentleman!"

His words were encouraging, but a bit too ambitious. Emily giggled.

"You are a fine young lady with unprecedented potential, and I must say: *very beautiful!*" Royal pudding fella said before she could begin to say owt.

"Awe, tah…!" Emily said and noticed the customer's change was still on the counter.

"The proof is in the *pudding…*" He said then finished off his pint, the glass he shoved forward on the counter, then he lazily held up his right hand.

"Farewell to you my dear," he said then turned around.

"And to you my love!" Emily said then giggled again. Someone mentioning "pudding" would never be the same again! She didn't have anyone to share this experience with!

"Your change love?" Emily called out. The customer looked over his shoulder.

"That's for you my dear…" He said. Emily put the coins in the charity jar and spread out the note.

"Aw! Tah…!" She said then discreetly stuffed her five pound note tip into her bra—*its mine!* Her eyes whipped around the place to check for witnesses before she drank some of her orange juice.

Over an hour later Chris and April came in together, and Emily was allowed on her break, she had a cig outside the centre, felt bad having to refuse giving change to a beggar as her purse was left inside, then she sat down with a breakfast burrito, spiced up with that lovely house hot sauce and was hopeless at restraining her laughter as she stuffed her mouth.

"*Royal pudding!*" She dissed and cackled covering her mouth.

"It were a royal pudding! Your prerogative my dear!"

Her imitation of that customer's voice wasn't so good. Emily had this cute vision of the fella sat at a table alone, he probably had one of them long dining tables surrounded with vintage paintings and a grandfather clock behind him, and he would be sensibly eating summat posh with summat like port or brandy for drink with a napkin around his neck. *Bless him!* Emily giggled with a full mouth she covered with the back of her hand. April noticed as she passed her by.

"What you giggling on about?" She asked with a big, curious smile.

"A bleedin' royal pudding!" Emily answered, hopelessly trying to put on the voice whilst giggling with tears beginning to swell in her eyes.

"It were shite!"

"Oh? I bloody love them!" April said back. Emily was back on the bar, when these two college-aged black fellas came in, and…*oh my God!* They were dressed up like rappers; tracksuits, massive chains, hats and all!

"Alright love?" Emily greeted them. The fella on the left smiled.

"This some place we can *chill out* man?" He said with an exaggerated Jamaican accent and a very white smile, the oversized shades he was wearing were summat to laugh about—summat else to make Emily's day today! She didn't answer though.

"What can I get you me love? You got any ID?"

~

Christmas Eve. There was plenty of snow about, the rest of Yorkshire had had it for nearly a week now, but it looked like Thewlington was gonna get a white Christmas. Mum had done her essential Crimbo shopping both locally and in town, running about and joining the queues not too organised, and had got back just an hour ago, she like her daughter had bought summat for Nan. They were gonna be paying her a visit tomorrow for dinner up in Leeds and joined with her older sister Auntie Moira and Nan's ex son-in-law Nigel, who had been married to her daughter Auntie Janice. Nan's other daughter, Auntie Sinead was going to be there and hopefully Emily's younger cousins Luke, Suzanne and Owen, whom she hadn't seen much of but had always gotten along with while growing up. Emily had been given the chore of wrapping up the presents, which she placed under the Christmas tree as an easy reminder and for the sake of that seasonal nostalgia. It was evening, and instead of having a quiet evening from all the hassle, the Nicoles were heading off to a Christmas event on at PLC Valentino by the river in town, and both mother and daughter had been given free admission for a private party.

After the gift wrapping, Emily had been passing time laying belly down on her bed in this long-sleeved body suit she had bought at Moore's during the weekend, it was a summer berry red and had buttons on the front down to the belly area and was proper comfy, but the sort of thing for lounging about indoors only, but you could go out for an errand with a coat on. Emily was sipping away at a cup of tea infused with mulled wine spices, it was like a limited seasonal edition that smelt lovely and tasted nice. She had been bored shite, had lost interest in watching the same shite on TV in her free time; she wanted to watch some documentary—summat interesting about another country, and wouldn't mind all of it being in another language so as long as there were subtitles.

She didn't know where to start and had been boredly browsing on her laptop, having to uncomfortably change the way she sat multiple times. Then she found a name she recognised from the title of the clip: **Kashiwagi| Door knock scene**—*him again?* She clicked on it and the clip loaded up to a door with a normal knock and this Asian bloke answering it. It opened up to a shot of this white bloke with curly dark hair, who was dressed up like one of them annoying people selling stuff with the shirt and tie and all.

"Hello?" He said and smiled creepily.

"Hello…?" The homeowner said back. Both blokes had English accents.

"Would you like to buy some porn DVDs?" The knocker asked. There was a pause in which the camera went to a shot of a tree outside the home, which was one of them semi-detached properties.

"Excuse me…?" The homeowner said, confused as anyone would be.

"Porn," the knocker said. "It's three for forty quid!"

"No thanks…" The homeowner said instead of telling him to fuck off. The seller's creepy smile widened.

"Conventional fanny's not for you, maybe you like senior or extra virgin?"

Emily blinked and scoffed.

"Mate, I need you to leave please…" The homeowner said nervously.

"May I use your toilet?" The knocker requested. Then there was a left side view of the homeowner, who looked like he was pissing himself. And who wouldn't if someone was trying to sell you summat dodgy like that?

"No!" The homeowner said. Then the knocker tried pushing his way in. The homeowner pushed him back and wrestled with the door.

"Come on! I've got the shits!" The knocker pleaded while giggling like a nutter.

"Fuck off then!" The homeowner said back and things got rougher, and there were these shots of the door opening and closing with the knocker licking his lips with these widened eyes.

He managed to barge his way in and sent the homeowner staggering back.

"I have to feel at home!" The knocker scolded as he entered, showing that he was wearing a blue satchel similar to a postman. The next shot showed **PORN TO BE INDEPENDENT** printed in big bold yellow letters on his satchel—*fuck me!* Emily couldn't help but get it!

The homeowner looked around, surely looking for summat to fight off the intruder. The camera went to this shot of a jar with a clear liquid, which he desperately ran for and picked up.

"What you gonna do…?" The intruder taunted and he put his hand on his crotch, his smirk widening that it squinted his eyes and caused creases around them.

"Anyone else live here…?" He asked then giggled.

"Don't worry! Your goats are safe with me!"

Then there was this proper close up shot of the homeowner's eyes, it was like millimetres away and all wide and scared—and who could blame him with a nutter like that invading his home?

"Yes!" The homeowner said then chucked the jar at the intruder. It shattered as it hit him in the face, causing him to flinch.

"You're gonna have to do better than that!" The intruder responded. Then it went to this shot of a white oriental *lantern* for some reason…

Then the intruder's face was smoking, sizzling and melting like candle wax. That stuff in the jar was acid! The detail was gruesome with the peeling skin and exposed muscle and all, his hair melting off in clumps. The intruder screamed, but not like he was in pain though, more like he was having fun. He staggered blindly about the place with his hands over his face while the homeowner ran towards the stairs, supposedly he was going to go up, lock himself in a room and call the police. But no, he grabbed hold of the sphere-shaped knob at the end of the stair rail and yanked it off as though it was a bowling ball. Below it was a pole, and more of it revealed as he continued to raise his arms, a concealed…*whatever* it was meant to be, the homeowner gripped hold of the base with both hands and swung it at the intruder like a club. It knocked him straight out and the camera showed the fall.

The homeowner tossed the secret hammer thingy to the side, and it made a proper loud, clingy racket.

"That's for Burton Bames yah *silky* cunt!" He said angrily then kicked the intruder proper hard, where wasn't certain as it was an upward shot. The next shot showed the intruder coughing up a fountain of blood that spilled out over his burnt face, the hair behind his crown was spared.

"Fuck you…!" The intruder spat and wheezed, "Fuckin' birthmark maker!"

That last bit Emily needed subtitles for, but wasn't gonna bother. The victorious homeowner hyperventilated then leaned in.

"So you know: she's my sister!" He said then smiled the same way the intruder on the floor had. "We've been havin' it for a while now!"

The intruder coughed up more blood. Then it went to this random shot of a frying pan with oil sizzling proper aggressively. Then it was back to a shot of the intruder's fucked up face.

"Okay bacon man!" He said intensely.

Was there owt normal with this Kashiwagi director or what? Emily went to the next clip and was appalled that it was another full Kashiwagi film. **Bad people who do bad things** it was called, and that was just a daft, lazy title! The clip began with this young Chinese bloke with a shaved head smoking a cig at a bus stop in some urban setting. He turned his head to the left and there was this Asian bloke balding at the top with a big, ugly mole on his forehead stood with his arms folded, glaring at him. The smoking fella grinned then nodded.

"They do not invent the bar for no reason…" He said summat quite memorable in an American accent. The fella with the mole continued to glare at

207

him. Emily skipped forward reckoning she'd give this film one last chance. The film was on a scene with some people in business suits sat at a conference table, writing down on notepads.

The projection background looked interesting with bright green jungle and everything. The next shot showed a vile-looking bloke, who looked like he would vomit at any second, look up at the camera, then it showed a slightly upward shot of one of the suited blokes touch an earpiece.

"Ok, let's get tuned in," he said with an American accent. "I believe our onsite anchor, former US Army sergeant major and former Democratic advocate and former chief advisory, administrative lobbyist to Herman Beltrami and a former football coach…"

He kept going on, and he looked like he was trying hard not to smile.

"…And also former secretary of state advisor to the president of the United States of America, Rob Beefman has something to tell us…"

Then it went to this shot of some middle-aged bloke in a grey suit with upward slanted eyebrows and some big city buildings behind him.

"We don'ts likes immigrants," he said very quickly and angrily in a cowboy accent with these big, intense eyes.

"Fuck off, y'all!"

Nope! Emily shuddered, closed the page and took her near empty cup downstairs.

"You want a cup, Mum?" Emily asked her mother, who was wearing a bodysuit she had bought her identical to the one she was wearing, only it was plain black and she didn't button up so much. Mum was sipping away some wine, checking her emails, smiling. Emily couldn't wait to meet this new one from down south!

"Are we getting ready?" Mum said.

~

The Nicoles were taking the taxi into town, but first they were stopping in at KayGees on Hemmingway Street, a block away from Garbot Arndale as it was like two hours or summat before the event on at PLC Valentinos. Mum was in her element, proper exposed with no coat to cover her on this freezing night, wearing some plain black ankle high platforms, a black, thin strap vest with a sheered detail on the sides and no bra underneath, these red spandex hot pants and matching woolly stockings, both of which had been given to her by whomever was running this show, and to exacerbate the kinkiness Mum was wearing a black stripper's hat like the ones coppers or traffic warden's wore. Mum had tried viciously to persuade her daughter to wear the hot pants and stockings, but Emily was like: *"Ergh no! That's not gonna work!"*

No, she was more conservative, wearing a black biker jacket with a red Christmas tree vest with a glittery patterning underneath, these loose, fluttery red trousers that were more ideal for summertime, but went with the festive scene with tights underneath, and for weather's sake she wore black suede high heel boots she couldn't tuck in. For makeup tonight: wing eyeliner and red eye shadow with some silver glitter, red lipstick, nails painted black which was a lovely contrast to the outfit. Her hair was three quarter parted on the right with two hairpins on the left side to hold her hair tucked behind her ear in place. KayGees was an old building, its bricks black under the night, its orange sign with red letters outlined by purple, glowing light. Mum paid the driver and yelped when she opened the door, struck by the cold. Mum went out first with Emily scooting out behind her, the heels of both Nicoles touching the sludgy brown snow, grit and litter ridden pavement.

That Pitbull song, *I know you want me* was heard playing, the queue thankfully wasn't too long, but Mum hooked Emily by the left arm and dragged her straight to the front of the queue, with all these wolf whistles from lads and blokes aimed at her and her saucy outfit.

"Ear Nick?" Emily heard among the queue and turned her head without stopping. Oh yeah, Stacey and Gemma were joining them for the earlier part of the night, they were stood at the middle back of the queue. But they were gonna have to wait. As always the two antisocial sisters weren't even dressed decently enough; cheap jeans and Uggs for Gemma and unexciting skinny jeans and trainers for Stacey. At least, they weren't wearing trackies!

As Mum went to the front of the queue, the bouncers stepped aside, getting a good look at mother and daughter. The head doorman was Ron, he was a short black fella with a proper muscular, almost refrigerator shape build. There was no way you could start with him and get away with it.

"Let us in Ronny!" Mum called out. The doorman grinned and opened his massive arms as though he was an oversized teddy bear and gave Mum a cuddle.

"She's a right *fine* lass is your girl!" He complimented with an oddly giddy voice for a hard bloke, as was the case every time the two Nicoles were at a regular venue.

"Cheers Ron!" Emily thanked as she walked past him without being ID'd, as she had since she came here on her eighteenth birthday.

There were three floors to this venue, there was VIP on the third floor which Emily hadn't had the privilege of going in, and there were some big renovations being done around the place, there was crime scene tape and white, paint splattered drapes from floor to ceiling to the right on the way to the first floor bar. As the two turned the corner to the left the lights were dimmer, red, green purple/blue club lights flashed and any and all chance of conversation was drowned out with every step in, with Mum having to shout down Emily's ear. Emily didn't hand her jacket in at the club's cloakroom, couldn't be bothered with the two quid fee. Arriving at the dance floor bar Mum got some fruity alcopops to get them started, with the hopes there would be some decent blokes about inviting them to champagne.

Emily looked towards the dance floor entrance, where her two unwanted mates appeared, Stacey's glare under the flashing lights as she entered was demonic—no bloke was gonna buy her a drink! Gemma and Stacey were hanging about away from the Nicoles, effortless doing their best to look unappealing. Mum and Emily danced a bit, Gemma and Stacey were still stood in their spot, gawking at mother and daughter, their disses unheard under the booming music. Mum hadn't found a bloke yet and she had drank two bottles. Emily went out for a cig, the dodgy sisters weren't joining. Outside in the cold and scruffy, litter-ridden open she stood having her cig in peace without anyone coming to chat her up, Ron wasn't on the door and Laidback Luke *move the house* was playing, which made her want to pop a pill against her better judgement. Then she heard female commotion at the entrance, where a tall, very muscular bouncer with short, spiky blonde hair and a square-shaped head stepped out, with Stacey in his grip. He was dragging her out. Summat had happened, Emily didn't know what but she was smiling on the inside and didn't want to get involved.

"Let go of me fuckin' sister!" Gemma screamed and appeared outside a frame of a second after and was moving all over the place like an excited puppy, one that looked like it could pounce. An unseen bloke obstructed by the big bouncer and the queuing crowd said summat.

"Fuck off cunt!" Stacey called out and was met with laughter from the queue.

"Go on!" The bouncer said and continued to walk her out onto the street.

"Don't fuckin' touch us!" Stacey screeched. *Bye-bye!* Emily thought, wanting to wave but pretended to look concerned.

"Alright, just go on now!" The bouncer urged then turned around, a grin instantly grew against his square face.

"Fuckin' psycho perv cunt!" Stacey shouted, looking like she was going to rush back in.

"K'off you!" The bouncer shouted, sounding like "cough".

"Argh? You're a Giberford cunt?" Stacey said back. Gemma laughed. The bouncer turned around.

"Argh, K'off will yah? Yah barred!" He warned.

"Both of yah!" He added and pointed towards Gemma.

"EEEEHHH…?" She said back in protest. The bouncer was from Giberford, a neighbouring district to Barnothcroft, and it was obvious. There was only one way to tell a Giberfordian from other Thewlies: Giberfordians were too lazy to pronounce F words! And it was the roughest place in Thewlington, full of chavs and wannabe gangsters, no one was clean from drugs, and people just loved to bully, rob and hurt everyone.

"Argh…!" Gemma said from her throat.

"We've gotta fuckin' go!" She said slowly in a child's tone, her voice so broken from very obvious intoxication.

"You gunna come down later en, Nick?" She called out to Emily who was almost out of ear range.

"They won't let you in Valentino's dressed like that!" Emily told her and took a pull on her cig.

"You what?" Gemma shouted. Emily scoffed, and the Giberfordian bouncer nearing her was heard chuckling.

"Fuckin' hope not…!" He muttered. Emily had to agree!

"C'mon Stace, let's go somewhere else!" Gemma said then turned around, staggering left and right and put her arm around her sister.

"Bye Nick…!" Gemma waved with Emily returning it casually while smoking. *Thank God!* Shortly after Stacey was heard shouting at someone around the corner, a bloke who replied with: "Fuck off! Skinny skank!"

Déjà vu! Emily snorted with suppressed laughter then went back inside.

Mum got another round of drinks before they walked down to the docks, Mum braving the cold and all the attention. They stuck to the left side of the street with Emily asking if she had witnessed what had gone on with Stacey. She hadn't.

"That bloody Stacey can never be civilised!" Mum said. Across the road was this bar called Burniston's, which the Nicoles hadn't been in yet, mindless cussing spilled out from its entrance along with the familiar sound of bottle glass shattering and the steamy white gush of a *fire extinguisher* held by this bloke chasing out several aggressive lads, and it seemed to be effective, though it didn't stop them gobbing off.

"Fuckin' hell!" Nearly everyone on the street said in varying tones of voice.

"Useless bloody bar staff!" This lass stood feet away from the entrance called out.

"Ear? Burniston's fuckin' shite! You'll get murdered in there!"

Mum put her arm over Emily and pulled her in towards her.

"No one's gonna murder me baby!" She said, then with her free hand she wound and curled a lock of hair.

At the docks was a rainbow of neon nightlights from all the bars and clubs, the black river reflecting them in smears. The Nicoles crossed over the bridge along with other club goers into Clayton Square, and it was a square with patches of cut grass that appeared orange under the glow of streetlights, and had no barriers whatsoever around the edge to prevent drunk people from falling into the river, and this wasn't an uncommon story in the newspapers! There were all these fancy bars, restaurants, hotels and flats about, a few blocks away was this luxury hotel, the Travistok—a place for loaded tourists and celebrities—mainly football players. PLC Valentinos was a few yards left of the bridge, it was four stories high but made taller as it was on a storey high rise with a larger beer garden, and there was a *massive* queue of people all wanting to get in the warm, and like back at KayGees, Mum jumped queue and handed Emily one of two white guest pass cards with red lettering. They were let in, but Emily had to show her ID to the doorman, much to Mum's annoyance.

The event was upstairs on the fourth floor, Mum complaining about the walk up in her tall heels along the way, the corridor had this fiery orange effect against the walls black under the low light, and there were two barriers to go through with a butch female bouncer watching the entrance and requesting the guest cards for inspection. Emily removed her jacket, had it put away in the cloakroom before entering and not into a dark room with colourful lights but a normal, well-lit spacious area with gold decor on the walls, Chanel's *dance* was playing. There was this big, tanned bloke with slick, black hair wearing an expensive-looking white shirt and a lilac tie, whom waved to the Nicoles as they stepped in. Mum trotted towards him, gave him a hug, and a kiss on one cheek then another on the opposite. Emily didn't know who he was but was sure he was the reason they got in for free. She didn't follow her mother and remained stood, looked around, thinking she wouldn't stand out much from a crowd whenever that came.

She was proved wrong; stood about and bickering excitedly were six other lasses, all ranging in age from early-twenties to like late-thirties and very attractive, like standard practice. Most of these lasses were wearing them same red stockings and hot pants Mum was wearing, along with kinky footwear—all high heeled, black tops and all but with different designs, mostly revealing. None of the lasses were carrying a clutch or purse, and some of them had their mobiles tucked into their red stockings, this lass with long wavy brown hair had a Santa hat on and this lass with really nice long straight blonde hair and wide cheeks was wearing a white feathery wrap around her neck. Emily thought she stood out in her covered up legs, until this other lass who was wearing a short red dress, black PVC leggings and black knee-high boots with pointed fronts and tall heels appeared to the left and joined the group. So, that wasn't too bad then…

Mum called Emily over towards the bloke, who kissed her on both cheeks also and introduced himself as "Fergie", who turned out was the organiser of the event. There was a bar with this one lass behind it, and every lass in the room went towards it at the same time after Fergie told them that there was a complimentary first drink on the house. There was a bit of wait, mostly because the lasses were ordering cocktails one after the other, and when it came to her turn in line Emily had a vodka with ice and a can of energy drink, which she mixed herself on the spot to save time. She wasn't sure who she could talk to, as everyone was gathered in a cluster a step away from the bar, talking quickly and loudly over each other, trying to be heard, Mum included.

There was this lass stood at the left end of the bar away from the group, she was a little bit older than Emily, was wearing glossy black platform heels with a single, thin ankle strap, she had large blue eyes, hair long, platinum blonde with wavy curls and she was excessive with her makeup and had a beauty mole above her left lip, which really exacerbated that. But she was a really fit lass with an amazing body, had these long, toned legs like a model, these natural-looking breasts and looked like that actress that were really popular from the 1950s. And she was staring at Emily, who was considering having a friendly word with her about it after a swill of her mixer.

Then Mum stepped in between the two and turned her head the blonde lass's way.

"Dawn, this is me baby!" Mum introduced her, the lass started messing with a lock of her hair.

"Oh hi…?" She said lamely. Dawn had an annoyingly sassy voice, and made these hand gestures, urging for Emily to keep some distance like she thought she was royalty. Emily didn't think she would be getting along with Little-Miss-privilege tonight. Then Fergie ordered the lasses to get together against the wall and pose for a "warm up shoot", where a photographer dressed only in a T-shirt, jeans and trainers came in, and made it very clear that he liked what he was seeing with his cheeky smiles. All nine lasses stood together and posed with their hands on their hips, were told to say "cheese", then turn around and look over their shoulders at the camera, smile included. Emily wasn't gonna do owt else like that again.

The ever so popular Eric Prydz and Boon remix of Pjanoo *precious love* was playing, and from there each lass had a couple of individual photos taken of them, that Dawn lass really liked it and was seen posing for like ten minutes or so— and she even sat down on one of the seats as though she was a hired model. Then it was Mum's turn. She was enjoying every moment of it, posing, bending over and showing her arse more than necessary, whining up the photographer, and she tried to invite every other lass in tonight's uniform into shot, Dawn especially, as if to see who was fitter, sexier. Emily of course had to be included, a shot of which Mum kissed her on the cheek was necessary. Afterward the photographer handed them all a card with a web address where they could find the picture, which would be going on the kitchen wall, as always.

Emily hadn't been photographed on her own yet. She stood sipping away on her mixer, waiting for stuff to begin, not wanting to be left alone with anyone boring or dull. Then the lucky photographer found his way towards her…

"A photo of you me love?" He insisted. Emily hesitated then guided him towards an empty space of dance floor, away from the bunch of skimpily dressed lasses.

"Alright then!" She said then smiled. She had a couple of photos taken and posed according to the photographer's requests. After a minute of posing, Emily stopped.

"Ok, show us!" She demanded with the photographer lowering his camera from his face, pleased with what he was doing. Emily was shown the photos—which she was also pleased with. A playing club remix of Corona *baby baby* got turned up with the lasses whooping, Mum being the loudest of the lot.

When the room started filling up with people, Emily felt a bit more secure. The people coming in, the lasses in particular weren't dressed up as daringly as the nine *star* lasses, but there were more lasses to blokes. Mum pulled Emily in with the other skimpily dressed lasses dancing in the centre of the room. Then the music got louder, the lights dimmed and became saturated in a dark blue, then all these crisscrossing, epilepsy-triggering lights flashed, any and all activity in the room from there witnessed like snap shots. Emily had no sense of time as she danced with her Mum, kept bumping into people who were trying to get a look at her, thanks to Mum who was saying summat to them that couldn't be heard. Emily just wanted to dance.

There were free shots being served on a tray by this lass wearing a Santa hat, Emily took one and gladly downed it, it was vodka with a cherry flavour, which was ok. Another mixer from the bar and she was friendlier, but there was no point in conversation with Mum drifting away into the crowd and the music track, Jack Beats *labyrinth*, Emily was fine dancing with to cancel out chat ups, which she didn't want tonight. She went to the bar, which took her ages to get served, and had an alcopop because it was easier dancing with one in hand. She looked about the crowd and couldn't even spot Mum or any of the skimpily dressed lasses among them, so she bought another drink from the bar, including a shot of vodka on the spot. Emily's clothes were soaking with sweat from all the dancing, and the booze was beginning to get to her head. She wandered about, tried texting Mum but didn't get a reply. For such a fancy place there wasn't a balcony to go out and have a cig, and Emily wasn't going all the way downstairs for that. Although it sounded like defeat, she wanted to go home.

On her way to the loo, she bumped into that Dawn lass, who motioned her towards her with her finger—maybe she knew where Mum was about?

"Seen our Mum?" Emily asked.

"She's back there," she answered pointing to a corner left of the crowd.

"You want a line?" She asked.

"Charlie?" Emily said, unable to help the tempo of her voice in this state. Dawn put a finger to her mouth to hush her. Emily nodded quickly. Dawn led her to the club's unisex toilets, which wasn't packed. And even though there was an African male toilet attendant, Dawn had Emily come inside a cubicle, the door she closed and locked behind. Crammed inside Dawn went into her black leather, designer clutch and took out a little button bag of white powder, which Emily had done a few times and managed not to get too keen on afterwards.

"Not too much!" She quietly urged. The toilet lid wasn't ideal, but Dawn had long fingernails, which she dug into the powder, and offered to Emily's nose. She snorted as quietly as her mind would let her then wiped her nose and watched Dawn have her own fix.

"Merry Christmas!" The blonde said with Emily forgetting the time.

"Love your tits!" Dawn said with Emily just noticing that the lass had breasts that were a size shorter than hers.

"Why you out with yah Mum?" Dawn asked critically, putting the palm of her left hand to her bust and waved her right hand about.

"I wouldn't *dare* go out with me Mum!" She said thickly. Emily didn't know how to respond to that, not sure it was an insult or owt. Then she felt a rush from the coke, like several coffees all at once and this bleach-like scent in her sinuses, and she felt better and forgot the question asked of her. She snorted and wiped her nose again. Why not stay a while longer?

Emily and Dawn went back to the dance floor and sought out Mum, squeezing in between the drunkenly ignorant crowd. When Emily found Mum, she acted surprised like she had found her daughter after a month long search, reached out and hugged her then brought her back into the group of skimpily dressed lasses. Mum passed her a shot from the table they were all gathered around, all the lasses toasted and downed the shite, howled then danced to that Calvin Harris *I'm not alone*. It wasn't long before one of the bar lasses came around with another round of shot glasses and filled them up with vodka. Another shot and Emily would have lost the groove if it weren't for the naughty stuff, she was energised, the music she could feel in her bones and she wanted another line more than a drink, but didn't feel like asking Dawn who was absorbed into gossip that couldn't be heard.

Mum, already boozed-up, went hunting for blokes, and soon enough she had several of them intrude in on the group (which didn't seem a private party anymore) from the rest of the main crowd. As always she became the focus of competitive blokes trying to rush in and be seen more than the others, scarily to the point that it seemed that a fight could break out, though there were more people bouncing about and Emily couldn't see what was going on. She hoped her Mum's new boyfriend from down south didn't find out! Emily, merry from all the stuff in her system just danced, not wanting any bloke to make a move on her. She had a competitive edge to her though, as she tried to out dance people near her, older blokes giving her a lot of dodgy chat ups she couldn't fully hear and had the decency to not tell them to piss off, a trip to the loo being a break from all that hassle.

Emily felt like calling it a night, the coke had saved her from ruining it, but she was starving and needed to eat. She ceased dancing and said bye to Mum, who was shouting out stuff to her over the music, which she couldn't hear. With her right hand, Emily made a phone gesture to her ear, which had Mum mouthing stuff inaudibly.

"I'm off!" Emily shouted hopelessly with Mum repeating her muted questions in confusion—*bloody call or text us?* Emily thought irritably pointing to her phone's screen, which Mum nodded multiple times in response, then left the room, collected her jacket and went outside into the cold on her own, which wasn't summat she was concerned about.

Emily left Clayton Square, lit a much-needed cig, went across the bridge, admiring the multi-coloured lights reflected against the black water for the second time, then headed for the nearest fast food place from the club, all of which were on Hemmingway Street. Emily moved along with a herd of blokes and lasses heading in different directions, and through safety in numbers and drunkenness they were overconfident, yelling abuse at other people across the street they would regret if reminded by a copper in a jail cell the next morning. Emily wasn't bothered, all the excess booze made her close to fearless and she had the energy to punch anyone who started with her.

She was walking past the gay bar part of town before lower Kimmeridge Street, passed this beggar sat down shouting abuse at anyone who didn't give him any change, then passed by this bar called Barry's with a line of all these people walking out, kicked out for closing. She heard banging against the window to the right, wondering if it was some lads trying to piss her off. There was a lad alright, he had a big chin, a big forehead and a big quiff to make things worse, and he was pounding both hands against the glass, *growling* and showing his teeth like an animal. Emily couldn't decide whether to laugh or give him the finger. Too off her head she went for both, flipped him her right middle finger without any expression then walked off chuckling. It was like summat out of that dodgy Japanese Kashiwagi film—or had this lad been watching too many of them, perhaps…?

There was a bit of a crowd in the Mackies, but the queues were being quickly served; they were gonna close early at some point. Some bloke was complaining about the toilets being shut cuz of repeated acts of vandalism, which Emily didn't need to hear with a rapidly filling bladder!

"I shall report this!" The furious bloke threatened then stormed out. Then there was further commotion with some knobhead breaking off from the queue.

"I'll fuckin' av yah! I'm fuckin' Belfast! I'm fuckin' Glasgow!" He threatened stupidly like a wannabe gangster, and he didn't have a Northern Irish or Scottish accent but a Thewlie one. He picked up a chair then ran towards the counter with it held above his head, which had a couple of lasses scream and move out the way.

And he slipped on some napkins left conveniently on the floor the chair falling onto his chest.

Emily coughed with laughter while lads hollered out "fuckin' knobhead" memorably at full volume. That would look good on YouTube! The epic fail div stood up slowly, looking confused and fortunately he hadn't appeared to have knackered his nose. *Fuck this!* It was too rowdy and crowded and Emily hadn't spent more than two minutes inside. She went back across the road to this place around the corner from the Garbot Arndale called **Oktay's**, it was one of them Asian places that sold sheesha, which Emily just loved smoking during secondary school holidays. There wasn't a crowd around and there were these two big chunks of meat on these vertical rotisseries on display almost carved down to the spit. She ordered a doner kebab wrap with chilli sauce, salad and garlic mayo, which she ate inside in the warm, it was meaty, crunchy, spicy and delicious—chomping down on a kebab when pissed was just brill!

Her ruler-sized kebab was really nice, and it didn't taste like that cheap, frozen shite they sold mostly on street corners. And she couldn't help giggling, it was a penchant of hers or summat. When there weren't other people about and any loud music, her drunkenness did seem to make her appear nutty as fuck! But at the same time: friendly!

"Are you okay Miss?" The balding Middle Eastern fella behind the counter asked her.

"Sorry! I just laugh for no reason sometimes!" Emily said covering her mouth. Taxis parked on the rank charged too much, calling them ahead was cheaper. It was a technique she had learnt from Nan, though Mum didn't really understand it. Emily phoned up the taxi company and asked to be picked up at the bus station which was only a few short blocks away. Before heading off, the fella behind the counter was kind enough to let Emily use the loo, and she was really thankful for it. He locked the door the moment she exited!

No tissues on her, she had to wipe away the snot from her nose with the back of her hand, which was bloody gross, but not that she was bothered about it, and with a satisfied stomach and alcohol sloshing around in her system she wasn't concerned about anyone coming up to her, and it helped that the taxi was waiting for her when she arrived at the bus station.

"You weren't waiting long were yah?" Emily asked the driver who shook his head.

"Good night?" He asked with a smile as she climbed in back.

"Lovely!" Emily replied and the car pulled out onto the road. On the way up Harewood Road, she got a text from her concerned mother. **U OK?** It read. **Fine in taxi goin home, have fun! XXX** Emily replied. At her street she went into her clutch, fumbled about for the right amount of change for the driver, which took her a while, she apologised, the driver was fine waiting and he didn't overcharge. Inside Emily went straight to her room, stripped off her clothes down to her bra without turning the lights on and went straight to bed.

~

Christmas morning. Emily was grateful she had ate before dozing off so she had less of a hangover, and she needed a proper appetite for Nan's Christmas dinner! Emily got up, checked the time: 10:27, drank a glass of ice-cold water that didn't manage to give her brain freeze, searched the house for any other blokes Mum might have invited back. There was no one lurking about, and Emily peeped into Mum's room, she was snoozing away and alone, which was good! Emily looked out the window, and yep, there was snow all over the place, a winter land feel appropriate for this time of year. She dressed into some new white and double black striped trackies she had bought with the money Nan had sent her. Emily tied her hair back, had another glass of water then went for a jog instead of waiting like the children of the neighbourhood to open up their presents, the will.i.am and Cheryl Cole track *heartbreaker* was playing on her iPod. There was a fresh, fluffy layer of snow on the pavements, but the roads were clear, so she ran on them instead of the pathways for the next half an hour, waving to people, some of them she said a friendly Merry Christmas to.

Upon reaching the back of Sancrott, she decided to extend her run and went up to the edge of Badmington Moor. There was this spot of snow-covered grass behind a primary school, the sort that would be used by local kids playing footie, where three dogs of different sizes and breeds came running up to Emily! She stopped, saw that there was an elderly bloke calling them back. They were friendly fortunately, rearing up and putting their wet paws on her.

"OK-OK!" Emily complained trying to give each doggie the right amount of attention.

"Sorry love! They don't bite!" The owner assured her. Not even remotely traumatised Emily leaned over and tried giving each of the bloke's pets a rub around the cheeks. After the dogs and their owner left, Emily bounced about on the snow to get her rhythm back then ran, passing by some snow covered hedges, where she turned her head and saw a robin, perched on top—that was just perfect for the season! She stopped, went for her phone and tried taking a picture of it, but the bird flew off. If only she could get them to stay!

Emily got back and was just about to prepare herself a small breakie from yesterday's shopping when Mum, dressed in her night robe came into the kitchen shuffling towards her with open arms.

"Merry Christmas me baby…!" She greeted with pouted out lips and kissed her, then went to the fridge, where she took out a bottle of champagne.

"Where'd that come from…?" Emily asked, not recalling such a luxurious item being present among the last minute shopping yesterday.

"Fergie at Valentino's." Mum replied. Emily chuckled.

"Did you get a room that late?" She asked without sounding sarcastic.

"No time for a room!" Mum laughed. Emily didn't pretend to know what she was on about.

"He were loaded…!" Mum added and held up the champagne. "He gave us a Christmas present!"

~

Christmas at Nan's had been lovely, as always each year. Emily had gotten a new phone from Mum, along with some clothes and some perfume from her aunt's which was nice. Next year Emily was *"gonna have to help cook"* with Nan (that was her demand) which she was up for. The Christmas dinner was brilliant, Nan always bought dear, quality stuff—everything from the meat, veg and condiments were fancy and could only be bought at them pricey venues, and as always, she made sure Emily had some pigs and blankets and honey roast parsnips at the table. Nigel had given Emily and Mum a lift in to Leeds and back, and they had a few presents to take back that required the boot of a car to hold. Emily had work Boxing Day, her hours were keeping her busy until college started; she couldn't imagine herself having a boyfriend right now, or what he would have given her for Christmas. Was there any way he could keep up with her schedule and course work?

The morning after work Emily was sweating herself out, peddling like a psycho on an exercise bike she and Mum had been given for Christmas by Nigel, which was much appreciated. Emily had put the thing together, though that required a visit to Hoperwood for an adjustable spanner. After her hour-long workout, Emily went onto the website given by the photographer from PLC Valentinos and checked out them photos. They were alright, she printed them out, trimmed them with some scissors and pinned them on the kitchen wall. Emily had work in the afternoon, and Zaks and Marias was pretty dead—nowt eventful—and she had New Year's Eve off, and just in time; there was an event on at the Stanley Parker, and she didn't have work until tomorrow afternoon which was convenient.

The Nicoles were in the taxi, and Emily's outfit for the occasion tonight were a pair of black, peep toe wedge heels, some pink, wet-look leggings with hollowed out openings that showed off bits of leg from ankle to below the hip around the front and sides. They were a present from Mum, as was the fluffy, rabbit white faux fur coat she wore for the cold, although left it unbuttoned cuz it was uncomfortable with the seatbelt against it. Her makeup for this night was a bit more than normal with plenty of foundation and some French nails, the bangs of her fringe were all fluffy and feathered up and she wore the back of her hair up high in a radish shape. Mum's hair was tied back into a mid-height sock bun, which was a bit severe, and she was wearing her tall, black pointed front boots with a red, long-sleeved jumpsuit with lots of matching embroidery, but the whole outfit was sheered, almost translucent—good thing she was wearing lingerie, which was bold red to correspond with the jumpsuit. Chipmunk's *oopsy daisy* was playing on the radio as the Nicoles stepped out, the driver was unable to resist a lengthy stare at Mum as she left; her red thong was visible. Emily did not approve of that!

There were a bunch of lasses stood smoking outside the pub, most of these lasses were far too wide to be wearing dresses or wet look leggings, Gemma and Stacey and crybaby Heather were there among them. The best looking of the lot was Carla Bean, she was Emily's age, gorgeous, lean, straight-nosed, freshly tanned, wore plenty of makeup, her long dark hair in corkscrew curls and was wearing a short, glistening sequin red dress with black slip-on stilettos. Despite her luscious appearance, she wasn't very lady-like, summat she had gotten from hanging around too much with Gemma and Stacey.

Emily hadn't seen Carla in a very long while, and she didn't miss her. She was the closest thing to an *arch enemy* of Emily's; during secondary school the lads could be heard asking whom they thought was fitter. Carla was flattered by those who chose her, not that Emily was bothered, but in the end the lads preferred Emily because she wasn't toxic. And that pissed Carla off, and had her engage in all that passive aggressive behaviour afterwards, though it hadn't been enough to get Emily concerned as Carla hadn't engaged in any cyber bullying with her or any pranks gone too far or owt.

Politeness was blasphemy to Carla. She wasn't afraid to go for a wee around a corner in public view, weren't afraid to scream, slap any random bloke or use him as a scapegoat for summat she or anyone else did and would say that she was "a girl" if they got pissed off. And she had this notorious habit of chucking unwanted shopping into the baskets of strangers, which would have them end up being accused of stealing, Emily didn't know how many times Carla had done it, but it didn't seem like she wanted to quit it. Carla screamed then broke off from her mates and trotted up to Emily, she had proper nice makeup on for tonight, mostly smoky shaded, but it was a shame about the extra-long fake eyelashes though, and to add to that, her figure hadn't been achieved from working out. She (like Stacey) just didn't eat right and while she looked fine right now, it was only a matter of time before she ended up with her concerning figure.

"Nick? Fuckin' hell!" Carla greeted with a big white smile then turned her attention to Mum then back at Emily. She looked down at Emily's partly exposed bust.

"Love yah tits!" She said—*well yah can't have 'em!*

"Can we stop goin' on with us tits?" Emily nagged. Carla giggled.

"You look like right slutty tonight!" She said to Emily's face and Jody, who did not need to be here, just suddenly appeared and was smiling with this other lass next to her who dared to laugh.

"Must have got that from yah Mum!" She added. Emily chuckled.

"What were that Carla?" Mum enquired as she came up to Emily's left.

"You're a right slag, Deb's!" Carla said boldly.

"I'm fuckin' proud of it!" Mum blasted back sarcasm instead of starting a fight and everyone who heard was laughing. Mum took Emily by the wrist.

"Don't be dissing me baby!" She cautioned Carla who bobbed her head and smirked with an "I'll have yah" sort of look.

Inside it was packed, half the crowd were dressed decently and there were kids still around. Emily looked around, hoping there was no one dodgy about… No one as far as the eye could see, except for the dodgy Flibbies cunt who was frowning at everyone enjoying themselves. Emily found a free table for two and removed her fluffy coat, any and all wolf whistles she didn't need to hear but saw from the pouting of lips from lads and blokes. She was wearing a black top underneath, another gift from Mum, a low cut with all these silver studs around the rims, the pub's coloured lights reflecting off her top's studs, had an abstract graphic design of a large ruby with a ghostly front view of a red elephant and a red moon behind it, its right tusk curving around the moon and all these other weird thingies that couldn't be identified.

Don't upset the rhythm was playing when Mum came to the table with a bottle of rosé and two glasses. Carla was seen dancing, getting her attention from blokes as she threw her arms up in the air and whooped. She was expecting competition. But not yet. After two glasses, Emily felt like getting up and dancing casually with the crowd, though she kept away from Carla. Not counting the passing of time Emily was approached by this fella, she turned around to avoid his gaze but felt hands around her waist. She didn't react or return the favour and continued dancing while he said stuff to her she couldn't hear, but in the end she spun around and kissed the bloke on the cheek then went back to the table with Mum. Eagle-eyed Carla was watching her all the way. She didn't appear to like what had just happened. A smirking and gawking Jody was stood with her back to the bar clutching a pint with both hands.

"*Lesbo!*" Her diss could be heard over the music.

"Piss off!" Emily mouthed without showing anger. Jody looked awful; the long, sleeveless purple dress she wore wasn't appropriate for her figure!

Mum ordered another bottle and Emily had another glass. Carla was still glaring at her, as were other lads and blokes hoping to have a chance with her. Carla was letting them come up to her and touch her, only for her to turn one bloke away then move onto another, repeating—*and she called Mum a slag?* Emily ignored the stares and took her time with the glass while helping herself to a packet of pork scratching. Once done she got out of her seat and approached Carla, eyes focused only on her and not the lads who cleared a space for her, the dance floor appeared orangey from the mixing of festive lights shining above. *Bring it on then, Bean!* Emily thought then erupted into a dance which had the lads whistling.

It must have been half an hour into all the activity and Emily was sweating; she didn't know having left her phone in her bag at the table, and Mum had a bloke at the table sat in her seat.

"Shots, Nick!" Carla shrieked then gestured for Emily to the bar while *heads will roll* was playing. Barman Karl served them, Carla requested sambuca and she was buying. After getting the horrid stuff down her gob, it was back to the dance floor to out-dance and out-charm each other. Then Carla gestured Emily back to the bar for more shots, this time Emily bought the round. Then there was more dancing, but after only a fraction of the time previous Carla insisted on going back to the bar for more shots—*for fuck sake!* But this time she requested two shots of each and was paying for it again. Carla did one after the other, trying to show how hard she was, oblivious that she was spending a fortune. After chucking down her second shot Emily coughed and wiped the spills around her mouth with the back of her hand.

It was back to the dance floor for a groove with the classic Steps track *deeper shade of blue* only to be ripped away again by Carla for more shots, thankfully it was just singles. Dance, more shot offers, dance then more shots. How long had they kept this up? Emily kept dancing regardless of the world going hazy, she had to endure this competition. Between the gaps of people she spotted Gemma and Stacey, who were arguing about summat with Gemma throwing her pointed fingered right arm all over the place. Then Stacey looked Emily's way, her unfocused glare was devilish! Then Carla began to slow down, she staggered into the lads who were all too willing to help her out, she turned Emily's way with a sickly expression without looking at her, and on her heels she awkwardly ran out of sight with her hand over her mouth. Could only mean one thing… Emily held out her hands, clapped and cheered—*Nick wins!* Then she immediately brought her dancing to a slow. She wasn't feeling too good, not ready to vomit or owt though, but she would if she continued to dance.

Emily wasn't gonna have a miserable end to the night like at the Toarcian Palace, she needed to sit down. She went to the table Mum and her new mate was sat at, but they were absent. Emily poured herself a glass of rosé, a sweet relief from the sambuca, then checked the time, and bloody hell it was twenty to midnight! She was just gonna sit and rest, in her seat she looked about for Mum but couldn't spot her amongst the walls of people. Before she knew it, people were all getting excited, some groups calling other members over to their tables and spots to join each other. Emily checked her phone, it was a minute till midnight. Mum came around just in time with another bottle of rosé and her partner who was a lean fella, athletic, in his thirties with spiky hair and a pockmarked face.

"I saw yah! You're a good dancer!" He said.

"Tah!" Emily responded passively. Honest to God, she didn't know how many sentences she could process from here.

Then everyone was chanting the countdown, and Karl shouted "Happy New Year" and rang the bar's bell. *Here us lot are in year 2010 now…* Emily thought bitterly before her mother lovingly wrapped her arms around her and practically squeezed the life out of her and wished her a Happy New Year. Around her was deafening whopping and whistling, clanging of glasses and patrons were giving out hugs and kisses with mates, family and random strangers. Everyone was happy. Emily poured herself another glass, unsure if she could manage another after that. Then Mum's partner tried speaking to her.

"What were that?"

Emily couldn't hear, and she was wasted enough she couldn't be bothered trying. Apologetically she left the table, forgetting her fluffy coat and went outside into the cold for a cig, the porch packed full of smokers and the sweat from her competitive prancing didn't help. Emily was able to get the attention of some lasses for a chat, but they were so pissed they had rudely short attention spans.

She felt alone…The truth was she was alone. No fellas coming to chat her up and none of them pathetic mates were coming up to her which was a bonus in her hammered state. The bangs of local fireworks were heard along with explosions of colour witnessed against the midnight sky, a view she couldn't enjoy with these lot about. She stepped out onto the car park and distanced herself from the crowd. A wasted Emily was hungry, and she knew what she wanted. *Any place that does a kebab open—any place?* Snacks from the bar could not substitute! She was going to shout her thoughts out. Confident from her drunkenness she could go about the pub in search of a solution; she would offer a kiss to any bloke for it!

After her cig, Emily nipped back inside and fetched her coat and phone with Mum and her partner asking her if she was OK. Emily staggered back outside and walked up to one of the car park's lampposts, then made a call to the place she normally ordered takeout from. There was no answer so she made several more calls in desperation, hoping someone would pick up. And in the end someone did answer the call...and Emily ordered the biggest kebab they had available and wanted it delivered to the Stanley Parker, while not bothered about what tone of voice she was using, as if she could remember.

With the cold stabbing her through the openings of her leggings, Emily trotted across the car park and nipped back inside. Mum and her partner weren't at the table, and the people clearing the pub made it less of a hassle for Emily as she went from spot to spot looking for Mum. She couldn't find her. Emily couldn't see Carla about, the show-off was probably still throwing up. She checked her phone and discovered several missed calls from Mum, she called her and went outside again so she could hear better, but got no answer. Her phone rang, it was an unknown number, turned out it was the delivery driver asking her to come out and he was easy to spot; an Asian bloke getting out of a white hatchback in the car park with a paper takeout bag. Emily went up to him, paid him and wished him a Happy New Year.

Inside the bag was a massive kebab wrapped up in foil and white paper, as the porch was packed she took her kebab with her to the pub's sign in the car park and stood under its light, where she stood out as though it was her own spotlight and she didn't give a toss as she devoured her kebab; any disses from them lot on the porch were rewarded with her middle finger. Emily realised her kebab had other meats in it amongst the doner, she was sure there was chicken tikka in there along with shish kebab and summat else. Demolishing this kebab was like another challenge for the night; how much of this meat combo could she get into her before getting into her soft, warm bed for a long, uninterrupted sleep.

Music tracks were changing and more people were pouring out of the pub, done for the night and though her legs were trembling from the cold Emily didn't care, or that a pissed off Carla might come out and have a final go at her.

"What you doin' out here?" Mum called out walking towards her with her arm hooked into her fella, her night's objective clearly fulfilled. Emily shuddered.

"We off?" She asked almost begging with a full mouth. And thank God they were quickly in a cosy taxi heading back home! Emily was allowed to wolf down the rest of her kebab in the taxi and Mum's partner was asking her more questions, but with a satisfied belly Emily was more than happy to answer. Back home Emily fell asleep, undisturbed by whatever frolic her mother engaged in. No more binge drinking for a bit!

Chapter 11

Spring. Emily was listening to *can you meet me halfway* while waiting for the bus under that big tree. That seat at the back of the bus upstairs was empty… That fella from down south Mum was seeing had let her go shopping, and more dearly priced stuff was filling up her wardrobe! In class today everyone was nodding their heads and parroting that addictive *riverside motherfucker* song. Every young person was snorting that M-Kat crap, or alternatively and cutely: meow-meow like the cat. It was horrible stuff that gave them very brief buzzes and terrible comedowns, and it had them gurning constantly for some reason.

Gemma had offered Emily a sniff of it, which she refused because it smelt God awful; it being plant fertiliser was obvious, and it was cheap as fuck, but worse: it was legal and was going around college. Loads of people had gone to hospital, some didn't turn up for class on Monday several times in a row; Beth Huxley was one of them, and it was obvious with her irritability and continuous swallowing back which had everyone take the piss out of her, usually by saying *meow-meow*.

Emily didn't have work tonight. But in that free time she was gonna have herself a workout. She had a gym membership now, it was for the one in Hoperwood Beck further down from where all the shops were, but still local which she visited three times a week, or four depending on her work schedule. Emily had bought a few gym outfits, and she was gonna be buying more for this new routine of hers in the upcoming weeks with her work income. Her outfit for today's workout was a very dark red, racer back gym bra with matching leggings, not too eye catching from a distance, her black and red trainers were alright with it, her hair swept back and pinned up messily at the back and earphones in. Emily was proper hitting it! And she had a bloody good playlist to work it to on her iPod, courtesy of KayGees that had handed out a free mix on CD to Mum and Emily and other clubbers on their way out last week.

Right now Emily was working on her bum with a bar bell with a 30 kilo load held up over her back, doing pulsing squats where she squatted down on the spot with both knees then stood up, stretching and squeezing the buttock muscles. The lads were giving her specific area of her workout looks and passive-competitively occupying the spaces next to her, whenever they could. After very brief rest with some loosening stretches, Emily went onto lunging squats with the same barbell weight on one knee, stood back up then squatted down on the other knee while moving along. She did four reps of ten squats, had another breather then was on the sit-up machine, to keep her road flat stomach flat, but without any bloke ripped definition. After her ab workout, Emily did a few more stretches while putting up with more chat up lines.

All pumped up she didn't have to return them all, and felt more than confident enough to take them on in the boxing ring if they wanted. And with no makeup, her hair scraped back and sweat dripping down her face, she looked a bit scary! Then it was a lay back on the workout bench for the bar bell hip thrusts. Emily slanted her lower body down at the end of the bench, where she balanced the barbell, reduced to a 20 kilo weight on her lower abdomen, lowered then thrust it back up and repeated, which had her back aching. Then she sat her bum down on the hip abduction machine, spreading her legs then closing, a breather and a stretch then it was onto dumbbells, 10 kilo weight and starting off with forward raises.

Initially the gym instructor had recommended the kettle bell, which was heavy as a bowling ball, where you had to lean down and grab the handle with both hands and swing it forward, then resist the momentum as it came down. But Emily was too scared, feeling she would lose her grip and that it would fly across the room causing someone else injury! After another breather, where she texted her classmates, she went onto the treadmill for her cardio, which she timed for half an hour, exactly. She really wanted to go swimming, but that meant going into the leisure centre across the road from the memorial in town each time. Again, she had to balance all this!

Emily had spent an hour working out in total—that was the average duration—and she was knackered, her gym clothes darkened from perspiration and feeling tighter! She had to take a selfie of herself against the gym mirrors, her arms were about a half centimetre thinner with some definition, her collar bones had a light wiry texture starting to ripple over them without looking unsightly, her beautifully flat stomach had a groove beginning to develop down the centre, which accentuated her belly bar. Emily had to turn down the offers from the lads and older blokes to go with them to the pub to eat/or and drink. It was time for some food! With burning, aching limbs and a spine that felt like it was gonna give way Emily did some shopping at Hoperwood, no microwave meals on the list, as she was gonna have them in moderation as part of her New Year's resolution, which she was sticking to very well.

Back at home she showered, didn't bother combing her hair and dressed into some trackies, then put on the hob and made two poached eggs, which she seasoned with garlic powder and cayenne pepper, cut up some avocado chunks, because avocado was like so…*good*, dressed a salad she had bought with olive oil, black pepper and lemon juice and served it as fancily as she could on a boring white dinner plate. Emily aimed to start her morning with a hearty breakfast, eggs of which would be among them—and there were three times more eggs in the kitchen than usual. But sometimes that wasn't possible, aside from time and not being able to resist the occasional can of her childhood favourite Langhias cream soda, for instance.

~

It was a dry sunny Friday, but not hot enough to walk around town without a coat. Emily had put on a few pounds, but that was muscle she had gained from her workout routine. Today she was halfway through her monthly episode, her hair was swept back with a bit of a quiff and held by hair spray and a few hairpins, which gave her an edgy look. She wore that biker jacket she had worn on Christmas Eve with these red leggings with a black floral print with a silver outline and these tall, black suede booties, similar to those Isabelle Woodhouse wore, but with cowboy tassels on the back and heels. Emily had work this evening, and would have spent her day working out rather than chilling at home, when she got a text from Mum who was in town and gonna be meeting that loaded fella she had been seeing since Christmas. Emily hadn't even seen a photo of him yet.

The place Mum was at was further up in Kirby Square and Emily was listening to Jason Derulo, the song playing was his cover of *I'm ridin' solo* while she tried finding the place. Everyone on the streets of Thewlie's financial quarter was dressed well; plenty of suits and a lot of designer stuff. After a 15-minute walk from the bus stop, that took her close to the edge of town, Emily found the place, which had a dark blue Aston Martin parked outside. It was a wine bar/restaurant, its wedding white sign had silver italic writing that was unreadable under the bright light and its front had a short concrete flight of stairs, a few white tables and a spiky metal fence painted white, that was only waist-high and quite dangerous—what if there were children running about?

Emily entered and immediately the heads of people wearing suits turned her way, looking at her a little longer than what was considered sensible. She wasn't dressed right, and she had her nose stud in; she expected some fella in a suit coming up to her and asking what her business was here in a French accent. That didn't happen though. The place was clean, a bit too clean actually; the white surfaces reflected the light outside and was overbearing like one of them secret government labs in Sci-Fi films that were doing dodgy stuff to people, and Emily's dyed red hair stood out.

The laughter of a woman nearby she thought was aimed at her compelled her to turn around and face her, but she had her back to her and walked on searching for Mum.

She quickly found her sat on a table for two and there was champagne in a bucket on the centre of the table, her legs folded and angled outwards for everyone to see. Mum was very polished today; her lips glossed red/pink, face fine with foundation and mascara with grey/blue eye shadow, she wasn't wearing her dimple piercing and her hair shined almost reflectively and she had a trim to her fringe, an expensive-looking job from the hairdressers by the looks of things. Mum was dressed like she worked in retail fashion; a plain blue V-neck sweater, these tight, plain blue trousers that were slightly brighter, tucked into these tall black riding boots with a golden bar detail around the heels. It was a nice outfit, and Emily noticed that it matched her hair and eyes. The padded red coat hanging on the back of her chair didn't go well with it though. Mother and daughter were dressed in contrasting colours that stood out against this white, polished place and the other patrons in their suits and all.

"Love your clothes, Mum!" Emily said. Mum hummed.

"Waitin' for our Geoffrey," she said and held up her hand, inspecting her fingernails which had had a professional manicure job done.

"Have some champagne!" She encouraged while Emily took a seat from the table across her. Mum waved for a waiter.

"Get us another glass for me baby, love!" She said a little louder than necessary which drew unwanted attention from the other patrons who didn't seem to like someone of Mum's character being here. Emily took off her jacket, she was wearing a short, dark tan dress underneath with a black short-sleeved top underneath it.

After the extra glass arrived Mum filled it up, Emily took a sip, really appreciating the fruity, bubbly beverage you only had at every special occasion.

"You eaten?" Mum asked. "You can order summat—whatever you want!"

The smile she made was almost unrealistic. Then this bloke in a dark blue suit came to the table, he looked at Emily, then looked about the place.

"That's *my* seat!" He exclaimed with a posh Cockney accent.

"Sorry!" Emily said and jumped out of her seat, she would have to stand now or summat. The fella in the suit didn't bother fetching a seat for himself from the nearby tables.

"Geoffrey that's me baby!" Mum intervened. Emily tried hard not to frown while looking at him—*oh my God...!*

He was a tall, slender fella, tanned and bald on the crown with patches of grey hair on the sides of his head, he had no looks to him at all and didn't look like he could batter another bloke! Basically: he was unqualified for Mum! This wasn't what Emily expected, she was thinking of some wealthy boxer with a polo shirt, gold chain around the neck and a shaved head.

About an hour passed and Emily had finished her second glass of champagne, food had been ordered. Emily ordered a chicken salad with spinach, cherry tomatoes, rocket leaves and grilled peppers with dressing, it was posh but had no flavour and there was no hot sauce to spice it up, so she resorted to putting salt and a ridiculous amount of pepper on it just to get some taste.

"What do you do, Emily?" Geoffrey asked and blinked in an odd way, as though he had seen summat proper dodgy.

"Didn't Mum tell you?" Emily said.

"No! She doesn't tell me anything!" Geoffrey answered with Mum chuckling. It sounded like a harmless bit of sarcasm.

"I'm doing a beauty course." Emily said.

"You going on to University after that?" Geoffrey asked his tone similar to an adult reminding a child that they would go to jail if stealing as an adult. Emily chuckled in the face of it.

"Need money for that!" She said.

"Emily wants to travel!" Mum said before Emily could.

"How many blokes you been seeing?" Geoffrey questioned. Emily pretended she hadn't heard that, she rolled her eyes down and could see Geoffrey's foot stroking Mum's boot.

"None right now!" Emily said politely and helped herself to another glass of champagne.

All the chatter between Mum and Geoffrey became muted from there as Emily drank. The geezer wasn't thick, he didn't look violent. But you didn't need them traits to be a cunt. Geoffrey was talking about Mum coming to one of them fancy events where everyone wore suits.

"I don't have one of them fancy receptionist suits!" Mum complained then took the dripping champagne bottle from the bucket.

"We'll get one tailored for yah, Misses blue!" Geoffrey said, referring to Mum's clothes and ran his hand along her shoulder down to her knee.

"Fuck me! We're gonna need another Geoff!" Mum remarked and poured what was left into her glass.

The champagne arrived, the waiter paid no attention to mother or daughter, a towel wrapped around the bottle as he uncorked the bottle.

"Enjoy!" He said then left.

"What do you want to do?" Geoffrey continued his questions.

"After college…" Emily said. "I *was* thinking of being a nurse."

"Why?" Geoffrey asked with this patronising tone and even had to lean in over the table.

"Because…I'm good with people…" Emily replied.

"In what way are you good with people?" Geoffrey said trying to start a fight.

"I'm nice. I care about people." Emily said.

"*How* does that make you a nurse?" Geoffrey said. Was this a bloody interrogation or summat?

"It…dun't make us a nurse, cuz I haven't even applied for a course!"

"Then why'd you want to be a nurse?"

Emily scoffed without making a fuss, she didn't need to hide how pissed off she was.

"I were interested in joining the army," she said. Mum gasped out in laughter, leaned back and slapped Geoffrey on the shoulder.

"The army?" Geoffrey said, blinked then chuckled. "The army?"

"Yeah?" Emily said with the tip of her tongue. Geoffrey scoffed through his nostrils. Mum giggled and took a drink of posh beverage.

"Do yah have any army experience?"

Geoffrey was really taking the piss with Emily's tolerance, and she could outlast him in a fight!

"No!" She said, and before he could say owt she added, "Cuz I'm at college?"

"And why haven't yah been?" Geoffrey asked and did that weird blink of his combined with a smile.

"*Why* haven't I been what?" A confused Emily said. "*Where* should I be then?"

At the bar, Emily would have more power than him, and right now she needed to say summat to him.

"Piss off...!" She mumbled then chuckled. She had had enough of him.

"What was that yang laady?" Geoffrey asked and leaned in across the table an inch, not doing too good of a job to sound hard about it.

"What...?" Emily said back without raising her voice and noticed people looking at her.

"*Fuck off!* You can afford a posh lass!" She said wondering how much trouble she would get in here. Posh git recoiled and blinked, looking stunned. There were a bunch of astonished "huhs" and "ohs" from the crowd, followed by silence.

Mother and daughter left the place, but not without a final word with the waiter instructing them both to leave in an overly polite way with Geoffrey easily being held back, only by the waiter's palm at a distance. Outside, Emily constantly looked back to see if Geoffrey was following or if there were any coppers coming to get them. On the street, Mum got a few looks from people, mostly over her bright blue outfit. And she covered her mouth and started laughing. They stopped in an overpriced bar a few blocks away and had another drink before getting a taxi back home. Mum hadn't been flirting with any blokes, even though plenty had been looking her way—*a first!* Mum was just venting over Geoffrey, and Emily had plenty of things to say herself about the wanker.

Black Eyed Peas *Imma be* was playing on the taxi's radio. The driver, as with any ride was giving mother and daughter looks in the mirror and taking every opportunity to get flirtatious with everyday questions. Mum was too pissed to notice, and Emily was too pissed off to give a toss.

"I don't like him, Mum!" Emily said referring to Geoffrey. "He dun't understand us—he thinks we're bloody peasants!"

Mum just grunted, closed her eyes and leaned in sleepily against her daughter, who felt like having another drink once she got back home; a full bottle of wine actually. There was quiet in the car for a few minutes. Emily noticed the driver looking at her and her Mum still lying against her.

"I'll av a baaycon baatty!" Emily mimicked a masculine Cockney voice, which had Mum sit up.

"And a fackin' rowsay lee my lav!" Emily added. "Caz I'm a caant!"

Mum snorted then broke out laughing. The driver was seen smiling, trying to contain it and ended up snickering.

"He *is* a cunt!" Mum said referring to Geoffrey and continued to laugh.

~

Emily was getting ready for bed, lying back on her bed stretching, while listening to N Dubz *I need you*. There was a knock at the door, which Emily wouldn't be answering. Mum answered the door and immediately there was some commotion from a bloke. And it was that Geoffrey! Emily didn't make out any words but she knew it was him from that accent.

"*You're a fackin' bitch!*"

That Emily heard, and she stopped stretching.

"Never fackin' talk to me like that again Debbie!" Geoffrey said. Mum was heard laughing as though she was watching summat stupid.

"Yah *mogwom*!" She giggled. Mogwom was a Thewlie term for someone who was proper thick—as in retarded, it used to be said all the time. Anyone who failed to answer a question in primary school class was called a mogwom. But it was not said anymore because of political correctness.

"What's a mogwom?" Geoffrey asked. Mum giggled.

"Means yah thick!" She replied.

"Stupid am I?" Geoffrey remarked.

"Bad manners!"

He sounded like Michael Caine.

"Geoffrey?" Mum repeated, drunkenly said incomprehensive words between each mentioning of his name and laughed.

"Silly fackin' cow!"

Geoffrey interrupted, "Yah bladdy rude tart, Debbie!"

Emily crept towards her bedroom door and opened it slowly and quietly as the hinges would allow.

"Bad fackin' example! Bad fackin' example!" Geoffrey stupidly repeated sounding like the first bit of a certain nursery rhyme.

"You're a cunt!" Mum said brilliantly with a giggle to follow. "You've got a wife and grandchildren!"

Wow! That was some exposition! As for *bad example*…what a bleeding hypocrite!

"Bad manners Debbie!" Geoffrey blabbered. Mum laughed and it was a lazy, comical laugh.

"Did you just drive here…?" She asked.

"Cuz you sound like you're fucked!"

Oh dear…!

"Shat ap you stupid bitch!" Geoffrey rudely said back, *how fuckin' dare he!* Mum laughed.

"Geoffrey?" She raised her voice.

"Shat ap you stupid bitch!"

Then Mum screamed hysterically.

"Shat ap you stupid bitch!" Geoffrey repeated. Was this a fight or a bad comedy? Then summat shattered downstairs—*what the fuck?* Emily reacted and tore open her bedroom door without taking a step further.

"Debbie! That was very fackin' impressive!" Geoffrey remarked.

"You think you're ganna be fackin' super stars, you and your daughter?"

Hearing that Emily immediately stormed out of her room to the top of the stairs.

"Don't be talkin' shite here Geoffrey!" She shouted. Then there was silence, which was broken by Mum laughing.

Emily just had to add summat there, "Go back to your wife, yah cheatin' bellend!"

~

Summer. The days flew by quickly, and it seemed to be only when the weather was enjoyably hot. The World Cup 2010 was coming, and there wasn't really anything of interest being shown on at the cinema, and Emily's mates weren't the best sort of company to go with. The last time she had gone was summer last year to see the sixth Harry Potter film with Gemma, Stacey and Heather. All the way through the previews and a fifth or summat into the film, Gemma wouldn't stop talking and had upset customers, security had come in, Stacey had had a go at them and she had been escorted out along with her sister. And Heather, who hadn't made a fuss, had decided to follow the horrible sisters instead of staying with Emily, who had got up and left shortly afterwards, though hadn't joined the two gobby sisters. Emily and Mum were in town, but with no extra pocket money bonuses from Geoffrey who was long gone, but Emily didn't need that, she had her job and had gotten a promotion to team leader.

Today she was wearing a black, ribbed vest with white linen, summer trousers with drawstrings (like a lot of the lasses did whenever it was hot out) and white trainers. Mum had gone off to a pub while Emily went and did a bit of clothes shopping, which she hadn't had much of a chance to do because of work. Thewlington had this women's clothes shop called Moore's on upper Kimmeridge Street. It was spelt: **MOoREs** in a white lettering with a thin blue outline, and it was named that because you wanted to buy more; every lass came out the shop with full bags. It happened every time! A typical visit here took at least half an hour for Emily, but other lasses could spend over an hour; because there was so much stuff to look at. That Kesha *tik tok* song was playing while Emily picked out stuff from the racks, inspected it and from there either tossed it into her basket or put it back. Emily saw this lass with two full baskets walk past her, which had her turn her head and raise her eyebrows in empathy.

~

The World Cup was on, and that M-Kat was still about, but the police were trying to crack down on it. Inside Zaks and Marias Lilly Allen's *not fair* was playing, and today England was playing against Japan, the bar was at overcapacity, there were three times more staff behind the bar, the customers were roaring and the very obvious meow-meow users were swallowing back and grinding their teeth. Aside from the deafening noise and repetitive orders, it was bad enough that the customers wouldn't move out the way when Emily was on the floor with a tray full of glasses, and she had dropped glasses.

"YAAAY!" She was met with from whatever group had spotted or heard it. And it wasn't even amusing! England had won two over Japan. But so what? It didn't keep the customers happy!

From there the days were like: Emily going to the gym, going to college, going to college, going for a run. At one point, she had a weeklong crush for coleslaw on them partly baked baguettes you put in the oven. Mum had invited her to the Stanley Parker one night. Then Emily had a thing for jerk chicken, which she had studied and made her own chicken leg and wing marinade for overnight, and baked after her workouts. Gemma would phone up to talk about shite, and in college Jasmine Cartney would be laughing about summat, Beth Huxley would be pissed off about summat. And with so many morning starts at work, Emily had missed out a lot on church. That's what the days were like. And there was another queue outside college from the police searching everyone, which was aggravating.

Then it was England against USA. Usher and will.i.am *OMG* was playing, tensions were high and there was twice as much security around, L.O.Z's had all these zigzagging barriers about, and there were several police vans parked about the block. Inside it was calm, and Emily had remembered certain patrons from previous matches. Then the customers kept coming in until security wouldn't allow anymore in, and once the match started there was a roar of excitement. Emily had been working in the back away from the bar, unpacking crates and washing glasses, and she hadn't seen the strike, but she had seen the sudden cut to some car advert as she put bottles into the fridge. And the reaction of the patrons caused several glasses to be smashed, a few stools to be knocked over and a chair to be thrown in the direction of one of the tellies. It was a draw from what April told Emily, the crowd was inconsolable, several police came in and Emily didn't have to give a statement.

~

Day after day from there it was the same bloody thing. Tell everyone you knew about the footie, go to college, go to the gym, go to work, have a pleasant glass of wine once back home, sleep, wake up and not skip a morning's run before college, because the weather was so nice. It was June 23rd, and today England was playing against Slovenia. The single goal victory for England wasn't enough to keep the crowd happy, the roars of mindless profanity were deafening, Emily's ears were ringing—she hoped she didn't get that tinnitus thingy. That proper catchy Ms Dynamite and DJ Zinc *wile out* song was playing while Emily was fetching glasses from the cluttered bar, and was unable to shut out the commotion from this tubby fella in a grey T-shirt with glasses and a fresh-looking crew cut who seemed unhappy being confronted by Josh, the tall, lean Jamaican dread lock wearing bouncer, his thick arm outstretched holding a phone, filming him.

"I'm Irish!" The bloke exclaimed. "I support England, I'm not with these destructive cunts, I'm Irish!"

He had an Irish accent alright!

"I have respect for English culture! Don't affiliate me with these cunts—that's just disrespectful—I'm Irish! I'm just here for the sport! I don't wanna be in a feckin' pickle cuz of 'em!"

Josh just stood there smiling, and tried reasoning with the angry Irish bloke, but he didn't seem to be getting anywhere.

"*I'm Irish!*" The fat paddy kept saying and did the same downward pointing gesture with his other arm. Half the staff were distracted and looking his way. This was going to be the talk of afterhours!

Summer holidays were coming and Emily wasn't getting her hopes up for going on holiday abroad. It was a Sunday morning when Emily came into work, Thorold had the staff come together for a meeting about the next footie match: England against Germany. There was a crowd waiting outside minutes before opening, and to make things more stressful there were German exchange students among the crowd. And they were lovely people! When local English fans came in the bar became crowded, with Emily constantly on the lookout for trouble, overhearing questions between customers like "where you from?" always got her on edge, as did playing or the whistling the *Great Escape* tune. *We're gonna win, and you krauts are gonna get battered* was the message…

Well, as it happened England had lost an incredible four to one against Germany. What was that all about? Emily had expected a culture clash, but no Germans were beaten up and there were very few glasses broken. But there were plenty of England fans crying—big, muscled men actually crying! After so many weekends working behind the bar with a footie match on, Emily had become desensitised to it. This fella stood waiting to be served had tears spilling down his face.

"You alright…?" Emily asked, though she meant it sarcastically. The tearful customer nodded quickly. While pouring him a pint Emily noticed this lass texting, who was in absolute tears as though she had heard news of a lover who had died. Faithless *insomnia* was playing, and someone had put up the volume when it came on, which was understandable. Emily wanted to dance to it in relief for the World Cup madness soon-to-be dying down for another four years…

~

There was no college for over two months now. Emily could just focus on her job, pouring pints without any footie madness. After a month, she couldn't wait to get back into college and get further in life. In the meantime, she continued her gym workouts, donated a bunch of old clothes to charity, shopped for new clothes—gym clothes more than often—so she would come into the gym in a different outfit each time. Emily's hours during the World Cup had earned her a break, and during late July she had treated Mum to a weekend up in Whitby, she had begged—and proper begged Nan to come along with them, but she couldn't make it, which had her gutted. They had drove up in Mum's car just after midday; they should have gone *much* earlier as there was plenty of traffic on arrival at the beach, and it was evening by the time they found parking, but there was no sunset yet, the sun was still high and could be watched setting later, lying back in plenty of time.

Emily had booked and paid for a room in a hotel facing the beach, which was packed with screaming children running around, and all these half naked adults of all ages with figures from the gorgeous to the repulsive glowing under the sun, whether you wanted to see them or not. For Emily, the smell of the sea coming at her was a big break from the smog of the city and she got to wear a bright red bikini with white rhinestone studs that had been resting in her drawers for ages while she bathed and topped up another layer on her summer tan. Mum had massive shades on and was wearing a zebra print bikini with an untied black frock spread out where she lay. While Mum was having it lazy, Emily couldn't resist fetching an ice cream from the van, that was like a hundred yards from the street behind where they sat, which she held in her left hand while wading happily into the green/brown sea, feeling sand and gravel beneath her bare feet but didn't dive in like a thousand others around her, as she hadn't tied her hair back.

Hip deep in water Emily remained stood and jumped, yelping like most young beachgoers around her at the waves coming at her, while not getting her ice cream splashed with salt water.

"Argh!" She grunted and stopped upon feeling summat lodged between her right big toe, hopefully not a crab, shattered sea shell or piece of junk tossed into the sea that would cut it. Emily lifted her right foot up sideways, as high as the motion of the waves would allow, slouched down and dipped her right hand into the water and delicately pulled the object out from between her toes, managing not to fall over as a wave washed around her. It turned out to be a rock the size of a two pence coin, the seawater dripping off it.

"Oh me God!" She said excitedly, upon realising that it was one of them proper obvious fossil snail-like thingies that were so familiar. But what were they called again…?

Emily shook water off her discovery as she made her way back to join Mum and inspected it, holding it up to the light.

"Found an *ammonite* there, love?" This old bloke walking to her left spotted her, and he didn't have big man boobs and a massive belly like half the blokes on the beach.

"I were gonna say! Forgot what they called 'em!" Emily said then licked off some ice cream.

"That's a *Jurassic* one!" the bloke added with Emily only just remembering that Whitby was a popular place for them fossil hunters.

"Oh? How'd you know?" Emily asked wondering if he was one of them experts.

"Whitby's on Jurassic bedrocks," he said. And that was easy to take in. Emily grunted pleasingly and closed her hand keeping the fossil safe, as it was an ideal souvenir for this beach visit.

Emily went back to join Mum and gently dried her find down with the edge of her beach towel and put it in her purse. Then she looked towards the pier and the lighthouse far to her left, the brightness of the horizon was starting to dim down, with a brownish tint to the coastline. Seagulls, coming east behind the pier, were changing their course and flying straight towards her, and the way they slowed down and jerked as they flew over Emily made her nervous, with her hoping they wouldn't take a cheeky crap on her head. And she had been shit on her shoulder once, fortunately no one but Mum had seen it then. They were gonna get changed at the hotel further back on the street, then go out and investigate the local pubs. But first they needed to eat, and there was no arguing about having *fish and chips*—you had to have fish and chips at the beach! Who would dare ban summat as delicious as that? A tasteless knobhead, like the one that had tried to ban booze in America.

While Mum was having a shower Emily, wearing a white and pink floral dress for the night out in town, ate her fish and chips sat on the balcony of the hotel room, which conveniently overlooked the beach, the orangey red orb that was the setting sun was the main focus with seagulls flying past it, and there was less racket from kids as people began to clear the beach for the night. It was a tranquil sight, made perfect by a box of fish and chips on the table, which Emily had with salt, vinegar, curry sauce and mushy peas. She didn't need ketchup. Emily picked up a chip, dunked it in the curry sauce and bit into it, gratified by the crunch which the vinegar hadn't spoilt. Then with a partly greasy hand from all the chip munching, she held up her phone and took a shot of the Whitby coast.

Chapter 12

Sunday, first day of August. M-Kat (thank fuck!) was no longer a legal high and the police were cracking down on it. There had been enough trouble at the bar with young people under its influence. The anguish of the World Cup was long over, and there was a gay pride march on in town. Emily and Mum were planning on spending the rest of the day in town, and Nan was coming down later. Instead of taking the bus, Emily walked it into town along Harewood Road while Mum got herself ready. She wasn't exactly dressed for an outing though, she was in gym clothes: a pair of white trainers with black running socks, a sleeveless bra with matching spandex shorts that were high-waist, concealing her belly bar and half of her tattoo. The gym outfit was a bold, citrus yellow with a lighter coloured pane with a sheered feature around the legs which stood out against her naturally tanned skin.

Emily had no clutch or handbag with her, but a black leather fanny pack with her bank card, ID, house keys, phone, cigs and lighter and a mini makeup kit and compact mirror, just in case owt happened to her face. Her hair wasn't straightened today, it was swept back, clipped on her crown and pinned on the sides and tied into a neat bun, she wore a pair of dark shades, a thin gold necklace around her neck with her crucifix and a gold bracelet on her left wrist. Her hair dye had faded and her brunette roots were showing as she had been too busy to dye and maintain it, and she was glad her top was sleeveless as she couldn't have sweaty armpits showing!

After passing by Kirkbrit Park, Emily looked upwards to a circling red kite against the clear blue sky. And no matter how hard she tried she couldn't snap a decent photo of the lovely bird. There were trees with bright, yellow/green leaves by this fenced off parking space on her left, where she witnessed the silvery glints of smaller birds flying by between the gaps of the branches, that were no doubt the prey of the circling kite. It was a good long walk, and Emily's flesh had healthily soaked up the sun's rays and she wasn't knackered when she arrived in town.

She stopped for a moment to stretch, lifted up her shades and propped them up on her head revealing her makeup, which she kept simple today with mascara and plain lip-gloss and yellow eye shadow to match her outfit. Emily headed west, passing by the bus station and headed towards Kimmeridge Street. She decided to stop at this pub with an outdoor beer garden and terrace. The pub was busy and there was nowhere to sit outside, people were shooing away wasps and looking at Emily who stood out among all the normal summer wear. There was plenty of space indoors, at the bar she ordered a pint of cider and browsed through a menu for summat to eat; she was in the mood for a toasted sandwich, but the pub sold homemade sausage rolls, which she couldn't say no to.

While sat in the corner soaking up the sun's rays from the window, she had to endure all the stares from blokes of all ages, but she hadn't lost her appetite because of it. The sausage roll was just brill and tasted much better than a shop bought one! Mum had called asking where she was, and had arrived not too long after Emily had finished her cider, her hair worn in a high quiff with a medium height ponytail. Mum, gracefully tanned from a summer of basking, was dressed far more fittingly for the summer outdoor occasion, and would be allowed into a nightclub in a black short-sleeved top, with a low V-neck, the bottom front which she knotted to show off her belly, these grey/gold loose fitting trousers with a black leopard spot pattern and some sandals, her dimple piercing back in her cheek.

Mother and daughter went down to where all them gay bars were on lower Kimmeridge, the road was shut off, a train was seen going past on the overpass, and below it was a massive crowd with a float with massive speakers in the centre of it with David Guetta and Kid Cudi *memories* playing over it. There was a pub on the left side of the street, there were extra seats put out for the outdoor area that were placed on the pavement and road of which were littered with plastic cups and other disposable crap. Mum ordered some rosé and sat on one of the seats on the road. It wasn't too long before Mum had some company, and no, it wasn't some bloke she would take home, but a gay fella called Adam, tall with a horrid, flabby stomach nearly a foot out, and dyed bright blonde spiky hair and a mixer in hand. Emily was stood up having a stretch when Adam came up to her.

"You look like a *lemon!*" He said to her with that exaggerated voice. Emily smiled, spread her hands down to the floor and posed.

"I love it!" She said.

"You work out?"

"*A lot!*" Emily said hoping that this chat was gonna be pleasant with Mum making a few friends and not getting into any drama.

"*You gay?*" Adam asked her.

"No!" She easily answered without taking offence, unlike the next question.

"Then what yah doin' here? It's pride!"

"Leave her alone!" Mum complained and landed a hand on Adam's shoulder before she could say owt that might…upset him.

"I'm just askin'!" Adam screamed and really exaggerated the queer element of his voice. Emily didn't sound welcome.

~

The big, giant fairy (or BGF for short!) took them to this other bar just metres away on the same side of the street called Barry's—which sounded proper bloke-like! The doorman allowed Emily inside, but not before asking for her ID, they went upstairs into a comfy indoor seating area next to the overcrowded balcony. Barry's was a fancy place and had a foyer surrounding a posh chandelier overlooking the downstairs bar, there were all these dimmed down multi-coloured lights just getting ready to come on when it got darker. They went to the bar for some drinks, Emily had herself a strawberry cider with plenty of ice. BGF introduced Emily and Mum to his mates, which were two other blokes and two lasses, Emily though was expecting some lasses with cropped hair and masculine builds to be present, but that wasn't the case.

She sat across from these two lasses separated by a coffee table, one of whom was attractive with a peroxide blonde bob cut, red lipstick, a white vest with black graphic print and bold pink skinny jeans and black, white laced skater trainers. Her mate though didn't do much about her appearance; her baggy blue jeans had all these massive tears, and she wore chunky, white platform sole trainers, a black sleeveless, *Iron Maiden* vest, she wore no makeup, didn't straighten her long, wavy dark blonde hair and had these big, black framed glasses.

While Mum chatted away with the fellas, both these lasses starred at Emily instead of trying to start an engaging conversation. The one in the pink skinny jeans sipped a mixer while her mate with the specks was giving her a creepy, unwavering stare while she ate from a packet of crisps.

"You gay?"

She broke her silence to ask Emily that.

"No," she replied sensibly as she had been with BGF.

"She's me girlfriend!" The lass in the pink skinny jeans said addressing the staring lass with the specks. Guess she was the *male* in that relationship? Again, Emily didn't appear welcome.

A staff member brought some courtesy nibbles to the coffee table: a small bowl of olives in oil and herbs, with the pips still inside. Emily didn't mind olives…it was just them brown ones, which she spotted among the green and black ones like an insect on food. She swallowed back, felt cotton mouthed and had to look away, while beginning to break more sweat than she already had in this heat. The lesbian couple were talking like she didn't exist, and instead of complaining and trying to bait attention Emily was relieved. All these "progressive" liberties people took seemed to be getting more extreme each time. She used the distraction to get out of her seat—*fuckin' brown olives!* Explaining this phobia was going to be difficult. Black olives on pizza, fine. Them stuffed green olives with salad and feta cheese, fine. But them brown olives…they were like kidneys, and though Emily was fine with liver, she dreaded kidney!

When she was a child, Emily had been at a dinner at Nan's, where she had cooked a large steak and kidney pie, and upon peeling back the pastry her fork had discovered among the gravy a large piece of kidney that just didn't look right. It had actually scared her, no screams or owt, but it had shaken her up; the kidney skin was shiny, smooth and fleshy, and it had had images of human anatomy flashing in her head like several punches to the face. It really didn't help that there was a human body poster in class—it was just *offal*! Pun intended!

Emily wasn't able to eat Nan's pie, and had only eaten vegetables and dessert afterwards. Just looking at a brown olive to this day reminded her of that moment and filled her with dread, the same way some people didn't like seeing someone prodding an eyeball, licking their upper teeth and other stuff like that. But that daft phobia didn't stop Emily from going on holiday around Spain though, where she had seen olives more commonly. She had never told Mum about it, but whenever there was a mixture of olives at the table she tried not to look at them too hard, and when she left the table out of panic no one had been able to detect any sort of pattern, or remember it.

Emily went to the ladies then checked on her appearance, the sweat had caused some of her lotion to appear in white blobs across her forehead. She wiped her face with some tissue and didn't bother touching up any of her makeup. She went back to the floor and saw Nan stood by the seating area where Mum and her gay company were. Nan had a red lipstick lip, her hair was longer, she had a brassy sheen to it and a bit of waviness, her bust strained against the plain, orangey red jumpsuit she was wearing with a single drape shoulder and champagne gold platform/sandal heels. Nan looked elegant, like a VIP attending some red carpet event, very lady-like, except for the faded black tattoo of a Celtic cross on the back of her exposed left shoulder. Each of the Nicoles was dressed up so differently it was mental! Emily and Nan helped each other to a hug.

A high table was available where everyone could sit, so Emily didn't need to look at them kidney brown olives.

She sat next to Nan, away from them obnoxious lesbos, whom thankfully left the olives at the coffee table. Mum was sat across the table with BGF and his mates, and she appeared to be enjoying herself. A massive menu with each dish being four quid minimal didn't put Mum or Nan off from ordering though, and it took over half an hour for the food to arrive. Mum had a Caesar salad, Nan had steak and ale pie and Emily, cheating on her diet, decided to have a peri-peri chicken burger with spicy seasoned chips and a spicy mayo, as there was no curry available. The food here was ok, but the portions were just regretfully small and overpriced!

BGF tried chatting with Nan, but she wasn't talking to him so much—she blanked him without showing a shed of guilt or discomfort in doing so. That dodgy lesbian pair were ignoring Emily, Mum and Nan—everyone at the table actually. BGF left shortly, his two mates were still sat at the table and not causing any problems, filling his place was this other gay fella Mum had invited to the table. This fella was proper orange tanned with white bits showing where he had missed, he wore a lilac shirt unbuttoned all the way down to his spleen with thick streaks of purple/blue war paint against his chest, and he had an even more piercing gay voice and even more exaggerated hand gestures—they were almost like an opera conductor's.

Like BGF, Nan didn't seem to like him and occupied herself with her phone. Nan was more talkative after a couple of wines, to the point she was laughing.

But she was only talking to her daughter and granddaughter. Them un-engaging lesbians had left, so Mum came to sit further up the table. It was dimming outside, and the coloured lights inside Barry's were starting to get brighter. Nan enquired about Emily's workout routine, and even showed off her biceps, the gay blokes didn't appear to be watching.

"Don't build 'em too big!" She warned her granddaughter. "You've already got a perfect body!"

MGMT *kids* was playing as Emily went to the balcony for a cig, squeezed herself in between people and put up with plenty of comments about her outfit. She pressed her belly and leaned carefully into the rails of the balcony where she could see a crowd below, that were being cleared out by event security staff in red polo shirts, most were decent but some were just shouting at people, which wasn't professional and didn't take an expert to figure that out. One of the obnoxious staff was this tall fella with dark hair and a square head who was just proper in love with his authority, although he didn't appear any older than Emily, people were seen frowning over him after he passed them by. Hopefully when they left Barry's this tosser didn't get too enthusiastic about his job around Mum, because she might just slap him without a care in the world. Safe on the balcony Emily didn't give a toss.

"Move off!" The square-headed knobhead barked at someone unseen behind a wall of clearing people. There was some commotion, and it wasn't "fuck off" or "wanker" and that. The wall of people cleared and Emily froze for a second, squinting upon spotting—of all people—that Gangster fella from back near Christmas. Such a small world this was! And even though it was boiling he was dressed *exactly* the same way as Emily had last seen him: blue shirt, purple tie, black trousers, black leather jacket and a belt with a very distinctive buckle. Why did she remember him above all other people? Because no one dressed like that? Gangster was just stood there, like he had a right to, not staggering about pissed, vomiting or bothering others.

"I won't tell you again!" Square head shouted at Gangster.

"*Watch it square head!*" Gangster said back, and Emily was shocked that she could hear it over the crowd.

"You what?" A clearly offended square head stepped forward.

But Gangster jumped to the left, like an animal that had been startled.

"Don't touch me!"

That could be heard, as well as him seen spitting aggressively near the shoe of the square headed fella.

"I'm not gay!" Gangster said with countless heads turning his way. And he didn't like it. He turned around and began walking away.

"Oi?" The square-headed security fella called out. Gangster raised his right hand and waved him off like he was a fly.

"Oi? I'm talking to you!" The security fella tried to bring him back. Gangster turned around.

"Go away, *paedophile*!" He shouted back and spread his arms, welcoming a fight.

"You what?" Square head said as thick as a chav. Gangster made this ridiculous sound and parroted back what square head said in a proper mental way and repeated.

"Don't touch me!" Gangster said and pointed a finger from his left hand. "You don't touch people!"

Then with that same hand, he flipped the middle finger.

"I'm twenty! Asshole!" he said. "Try it, I'll rip it off!"

Emily didn't hear that properly. Gangster spun around like a dancer and walked off, marching almost.

"Come back here!" Square head ordered with several more security staff walking up. *Fuckin' hell!* Emily thought to herself and didn't see what happened from there, and it wasn't like she could just go down and ask questions anyway.

She went to the loo, and upon turning the corner into the corridor there was this big lass, butch and all with muscles to her big, tattooed arms instead of flab, and she was wearing a sleeveless hoodie, the hood draped over her head. Upon seeing Emily, she squinted her eyes.

"Ear *you*?" She said loudly and strode Emily's way. "You gay?" She asked.

"No…!" Emily said feeling like she was backed into a corner; this lass could crush her if she hugged her!

"Oh? I'm gay," the big lass said, keeping her voice down—*good for you!* Emily resisted saying.

"Have a good day, love!" The big lass said, walked past her and landed a hand down on her shoulder. A shuddering Emily couldn't help but smirk—*the fuck were all that about?*

Emily got herself another strawberry cider then went back to the table. Them fellas, were gone, Mum was sat next to Nan, but there was this other fella sat next to her with bright red hair in a moppy bowl cut, a white turtleneck sweater, despite the heat, some black skinny jeans and white trainers. Why was that sort of outfit so familiar…? This red head fella was gayer than the previous fellas! Mum was enjoying his company, laughing after everything he said. He asked Emily loads of questions, which she didn't mind as the booze was making her so inviting.

"Oh? Yah doin' a beauty course?" The mop head said, got off his seat and shifted it towards her. That's when Emily realised he was sat far too close.

"Why aren't you with your boyfriend?" Nan asked him with a blank expression. It was a fair point!

"Oh? He left us!" The red head answered, squealing almost, then turned his head towards Emily who was inches away.

"What you's doin' tonight then, love?" He asked then reached in with Emily feeling her left bum cheek get pinched.

"OI?" She screamed and swung her hand his way, not caring where it hit. There was a bit of noise from the impact, and she had struck him on the jaw, which he clutched, blinking and staggered back out of his seat, which fell attracting plenty of attention with the perpetrator looking proper surprised. What was he even thinking? And there wasn't any blood on his mouth.

"I'm a woman! Fuckin' fraud bellend!" Emily said angrily and adjusted the waistband of her shorts without looking at the pervert. There was cheer in the room, Mum was laughing, even though it wasn't the best way to react to this violation. A pair of male bouncers quickly appeared, one white and the other Asian and Emily was tense as fuck. The fraud was taken by the shoulder by the slim Asian bouncer.

"What've I done?" He complained. "You're just bein' homophobic! All you Pakis are queer haters!"

"Shut up! Go! Go!" The heavily accented bouncer said back without hesitating. The red head was escorted out while squealing, "*I have rights—I have fuckin' rights!*" over the background commotion and music.

"Get him away!" Nan ordered without raising her voice but expressed her anger.

"Oh…you're done! You're fucked dickhead, fuckin' with me baby!" Mum cheered raising her drink to her lips.

The white bouncer was English, overweight and too muscular and asked Emily a few basic questions about the incident while Nan got out of her seat and put her arm protectively around her neck, looking at the bouncer as though he was about to make a very bad, unfair decision.

"You're alright," he said so casually in reassurance. "I'd have done his face in!" He added on the verge of chuckling. A bloke would not have gotten away with that. Important thing was that Emily hadn't got done, and it served that prick fucking right! Mum was smiling, clearly pleased while Nan had this composed look on her face wearing neither a grin or frown, but she seemed happy in her own way.

"Fuckin' hell…!" The bouncer was heard mumbling as he left. The Nicoles were allowed to stay, but Nan insisted that they "leave this *dodgy* place".

Outside Emily saw the mop headed pervert, surrounded by several bouncers and them event staff, and it didn't seem to bother him.

"*WELL GO ON THEN…!*" He shrieked, it was mental, child-like. "*DO FUCKIN' SUMMAT ABOUT IT THEN!*"

Most people were seen either frowning or laughing, a good bunch of them were filming him on their phones. Emily really felt like saying summat.

But Nan put her arm over her shoulder just in the nick of time and walked her off up street.

"You'll knacker his nose!" She said without any chuckles or laughter to follow. *I bloody wish I did!* Emily thought. "Ear yah cunt?" Mum called out. "You gonna touch kiddies next?"

She giggled afterwards but her outburst seemed to have gone unnoticed. She also put her arm over Emily.

"Fuck that knobhead!" She said then kissed her on the cheek.

The Nicoles turned right at the end of the street and went to KayGees, Ron was at the door and Emily was allowed into the club. The place was packed, and fuelled with an energy drink and vodka mixture Emily had herself another workout dancing to TV rock and Ruddy *in the air*. Nan was a very energetic dancer, even more so than Mum, although not as vocal. An hour into the dancing all three Nicoles hugged each other with a drink in hand. Emily wasn't gonna let any cunt touch her—next time they'd get a broken nose for sure! But slapping a pervert and not getting into trouble for it today was so gratifying though.

~

September 7th, first day of college second year. It was damp having rained last night and there was no sun, just grey, cloudy sky—a compliment for anyone who hated class. Along with her handbag Emily carried a small gym bag, she planned on going to the gym on her way back. This was going to be a daily thing. To look good for her first day Emily had given her hair a touch up. She and everyone else in class had to wear a navy blue uniform, but there were no matching flats though, so black flats had to do. Tao Cruz *dynamite* was playing as Emily entered class, it was the same room, but there were more new faces than familiar ones in class.

Beth Huxley and Amanda Biggs were still here, but Alice was gone, Zoe was moving on to work she had in Leeds and the lovely Isabelle had gone off back to Australia—Emily would like to go over there and pay her a visit. Jasmine was still here, though she didn't look so vibrant. That perpetual, lively smile of hers was toned down to a fleeting, timid grin, as though the realities of life outside the classroom were catching up to her. There was another lass who was fulfilling her role last year, though she wasn't as attractive or funny; she was a rather plain-looking lass with short, blonde hair shaved around the sides—she looked like a dyke to be honest, and she was proper gobby.

The blue uniform for this year was dodgy, not because of the colour but because every lass was wearing different footwear with it; Uggs, trainers, flats of different colour—it didn't match. And if it couldn't get any worse Denise had left. This new tutor was only a few years older than Emily and skinnier, mediocre pretty with long, strawberry blonde hair, and she was wearing the black uniform, but with chunky chestnut Uggs. What on earth was going on? It was so awkward, if it wasn't for the uniform than she would have been mistaken for a student. Before any tutoring could begin—along with any hint of how difficult the new course could be—the class were all summoned downstairs into this dark, depressing room with a projection screen that had the college logo displayed. There were a couple of other classes present as well, there must have been three hundred people present, and with no seats, everyone had to sit on the floor—good thing the new beauty uniforms weren't white!

Then this middle-aged woman came into the room. Emily recognised her, having seen her several times around college in passing, she was skinny with a very narrow face, unattractive wore these big, round glasses and dark, dirty blonde hair in a wide, severe bob cut. She was wearing a dark green sweater over a blouse, a long, pleated grey skirt and was wearing…loafers, *honestly?* She was one of them women that didn't make any effort with their appearance, and it made Emily shudder. She looked like a nun! She stood in front of the projector and cast a large silhouette against the screen.

"Hello, I'm Helen Marsh. Welcome to your second year at Beckett," she said, and blah-blah it was all that induction speech stuff from there.

"Put your hands up if you have a phone." Helen ordered. Plenty of hands were raised, Emily's included.

"Put your hands up if you *don't* have a phone."

That was Helen's next demand. Emily lowered her eyebrows. Some students were reluctant to raise their hands, which appeared slowly…with laughter following from the masses. Was this really *necessary*? Was this to have other people take the piss out of others or summat? This had to be the most unpopular woman of all! When was the last time she had had a decent trim or a shag? Emily thought, as she didn't see a wedding ring on her.

"Anyone claiming EMA?" Helen asked. Plenty of hands were raised.

"If you attend each day for every term, you will be awarded a bonus at the end of each term."

That dodgy woman's speech had plenty of stirring commotion sweeping across students.

"Anyone claiming ALG?" Helen asked. Only a few students raised their hands, given that they were older than the rest. Emily didn't raise her hand.

"ALG does *not* get a bonus." Helen responded.

"*Hah-hah!*" About half the gathering laughed with Emily making a face in response to how daft this woman's choice of words was. Does anyone here have an MP3 player? Does anyone live off welfare? Does anyone have a partner? Emily expected them questions, but thankfully they weren't asked by that silly woman.

Then the headmaster, whom Emily had never seen before appeared. He was a tall fella with grey hair, glasses and dressed in a dark suit.

"You might have seen me about, but I didn't have time to chat with you!" He said, Emily wasn't listening to him, as this get together was just an assembly to insult certain people.

"Fuck me!" Emily said along with half the class after they left that dodgy room and headed for the cafeteria, where she bought a latte then went outside for a cig. She was going to call smoking quits soon as she could, but the stress of life was making that difficult. Emily had a chat with her new classmates, all expressed how pissed off they were with that session with Miss Helen Marsh. But any further conversation from there was short-lived, the banter became muted. Other students started bickering with others, which quickly turned into arguments, which turned into proper conflicts almost escalating into brawls, but unlike secondary school it didn't escalate into a proper fight with more alert staff intervening. Emily felt she had *outlived* all these lot, as though she was a granny. She quickly finished her cig and left these new peers of hers then went to class.

Coming her way down the corridor on her way up to class Emily spotted this fit lass, she was very lean, had strong facial features—she looked like she was from somewhere like Lithuania or Russia. Her brown eyes were big, she had a beauty spot on her left cheek, and like Emily her makeup was done well, though her face had a bit too much foundation, which made her look pale like Amanda Biggs, her long, straight hair was worn back into a high ponytail that shined a trumpet gold, but it was dyed and was pulled back a bit too tight that it made her appear a bit like a bald bloke. The coat she was wearing was gorgeous, it was fluffy with a gold brown and black animal print and had a thick hood, her leggings were indigo with a glossy silver flower patterning with black outlines, and she was wearing black, suede platforms with stiletto heels and silver studs.

This lass looked like a celebrity—or some reality TV star—and accompanying her were these two other lasses, none of which were as fit as her. The lass on the right was as plain looking as them low calorie rice cakes tasted, and dressed just as boringly in baggy brown cargo trousers, trainers and a black T-shirt with a print of some unknown band on it, while the one on the left was obese, wore ripped jeans and Uggs, her thin, frizzy, dyed purple hair pulled back really tightly and wore no makeup or owt to disguise her unsightliness.

"Where'd you get them leggings from?" Emily asked the lass in the fit leggings. All three lasses stopped, the one in the leggings in question smiled with her two mates giggling.

"Somewhere you *can't* afford!" She said. The lass in the leggings had a middle class voice similar to Denise's, but unlike the tutor this lass was just plain rude. The fat lass with her giggled instead of saying summat nice.

"I fuckin' love 'em!" The lass in the leggings said in a dodgy, deliberately deepened voice then walked off with her unattractive mates following her, laughing as well.

"Why am I like that?" The posh, privileged bitch in the leggings called out.

"I fuckin' love 'em!" The fat bitch parroted her leader. Emily lowered her eyebrows—*fuckin' hell!* Did that just happen? She asked herself. Them dodgy lasses were laughing and Emily was unable to stop herself from looking back after four steps, and she didn't try to appease her glare, and didn't care that all the other students passing by saw it.

On her way to the Longford Centre bus stop, Emily had stepped on this loose tile on the pavement, which had sprayed water collected from last night's downpour all over her leg.

"Fuck sake!" She cursed. Bloody useless council not fixing things! At the gym near home she put on her workout gear, which was a two piece, leopard print with a racer back top which made her stand out among the other lasses in the gym who were wearing bolder, more basic gym wear. Emily had planned on having a relaxed workout, but the piss-taking of the first day at college turned it into fury, with the addition of getting an instructor to let her throw a bunch of punches at the pads to vent her rage for her last workout, that privilege bitch's face in her head, which she projected on each pad she struck.

Emily growled, threw the final punch then slouched forward and held up her hand not wanting the instructor to slam the pad embarrassingly down on her head.

"I'm done!" She gasped. It had been a 90-minute session—longest so far. Emily didn't talk to anyone afterwards, didn't use the gym's showers and just marched up into Sainsbury's and bought some lamb chops. Back at home she showered and had a go at cooking the lamb medium rare on the frying pan and served them with mint sauce, broccoli and some cold new potatoes she had boiled last night to mix in with salads because they were healthier. The end result of the lamb though was almost well done, but it tasted fine enough and went well with a glass of wine.

~

The course work at college was more demanding than a workout, and with no ALG to help her travel to and from college there was too much conflict with work that paid… Emily wasn't enjoying her course nearly half as much, work at the bar was far easier. These lot in class weren't as sorted as last year's, and if things couldn't get any worse Beth Huxley had become the centre of attention, everyone was just into her ravings. And there was no one to compete with her.

Amanda Biggs just got more extreme with her severe appearance; her foundation was thicker where you could see all the bits and her face paler—she might as well just use baby powder! The new elites weren't as fit as the previous, and they had childish attitudes. Emily felt *side-lined*—yeah, that was a good way of describing it, and she felt like the only adult in class. This new tutor, Warren her name was, had an annoying giggle to her, which she made after nearly each sentence so you couldn't follow her, or simply just didn't want her to open her mouth. Not setting a great example there!

Then in October Jasmine (former star of the class) had quit, for someone as vocal as her you'd expect a dramatic and tearful goodbye. But no, she was just gone and mean gossip spread about the class on that day. They didn't like her, because they were divs without charisma. Emily had texted Jasmine, it turned out that like herself she had had second thoughts about college and was doing bar work in Leeds full time. Hopefully she enjoyed it as much as Emily was.

All them annoyingly familiar and repetitive festive playlists were heard again around early-mid November in all shopping centres, and towards the end of the month there were some organised student protests across the country, against the government cutting their student grants, which was just *wrong*! For fuck sake, Emily wanted to join the crowd with a sign of her own in hand and block a few roads to get the message across, but she had work this evening; at least she was getting more in her pocket.

For Emily's twentieth birthday, she went into town with Mum and Nan at this posh place called Bar 44 on Hemmingway Street by the train station, that was part of a flat complex where only the loaded could afford. She had no mates to come out with her, so she had rang up Zoe but she was busy, cry baby Heather couldn't make it and there was no bleeding way she was bringing Jody, Gemma or Stacey along. Lasses would have a coach of supportive mates around for their birthday. But family was all Emily needed. Tonight she wore a short, coppery pink dress, one shouldered on the right, a massive 20th birthday badge pinned to her left breast, white platforms and her hair curled. Mum for once was wearing a dress, a long-sleeved, short white dress with a medium height neckline and her kinky tall black pointed front boots. Nan was also wearing a dress, though it was a plain black knee length dress with a slit on one side and them same golden platforms she had worn during gay pride. And Nan was paying for all this, so Emily could treat herself tonight, which was such a rare occasion, and there was a chilled bottle of champagne shared about.

She ordered sushi and mixed tempura for appetisers which was just lovely, the tempura mix included battered and deep-fried shrimps and various veg, the best one was a massive chunk of battered avocado. For main course: pork chops with mash, baby carrots, green beans and apple sauce. Nan being fussy had lamb racks, which was fancy while Mum had this chicken and bacon carbonara pasta that was presented in an artistic mound, both shared a mixed platter of baby quiches which were served on a small, multi-layered stand like at a wedding. And of course Emily couldn't resist taking photos of the food at the table! And the highlight was a yummy fairy cake with a lit sparkler that had happy birthday written in chocolate sauce on the fancy white plate.

After Mum embarrassingly sung happy birthday (drawing the whole restaurant's patrons their way) she hollered, and gave her daughter a year's worth of kisses then a present in a shopping bag: another tracksuit for her wardrobe, but unlike any other she had had before; it was a *proper* gorgeous bright, hot pink velour trackie with gold rhinestone patterning on the back of the top, which she could wear out in town during spring or autumn. Nan had bought her a pair of ankle-high, chestnut Uggs and a hundred quid voucher for M&S, which was just nice of her. After dinner it was off to KayGees, Ron wished her a happy birthday and the Nicoles were allowed to jump queue.

While dancing to *"DJ Got Us Fallin' in Love"*, Emily was having a change of heart about college… And she made up her mind after a glass of wine. She didn't feel sad or owt as there simply wasn't a group to say goodbye to—never mind worth seeing—and Christmas was coming around the corner, and this course wasn't helping her financially. So, she quit… Full time bar work, more time to make money, extended hours. The only thing from there related to college was her doing her makeup, nails and hair, though that routine was long before! Emily learnt more while pouring pints and having exchange of words with customers than being in class, and when new pint glasses came in she felt excited and eager to pour one, it sounded weird but it was part of the trade; some people were excited to take a crap, some were eager to do a line of coke. Everyone's *prerogative* as a charming tubby fella once told her.

~

Then it was another Christmas. Emily didn't get to go out for Christmas Eve, but she had had an after work Christmas drink with the staff, April among those

257

which she really enjoyed. After a Christmas morning run, it was off to Leeds for Crimbo dinner at Nan's with the family. Nan's place was in the suburbs, was semi-detached and almost cottage-like in appearance with a good-sized front and back garden, the inside was cosy and she had a vintage fire place with a fire going. It was a bit of a small Christmas at Nan's this year; Auntie Moira wasn't down today, she was joining her later-in-life children Luke and Suzanne who also weren't coming because they were having Christmas with the parents of their partners.

Auntie Sinead and Nigel were present, so was cousin Owen, Sinead's lad was a handsome bugger with cropped blonde hair and had a college look to him; and it was fitting as he was doing business studies at Leeds Uni. Owen looked just like his father Tyler, whom Sinead had divorced a long time ago, but could be seen on the many framed family pictures on Nan's living room wall. As with every Christmas, everyone was dressed reasonably well. Owen was wearing a white, designer shirt, Emily was wearing a black, long-sleeved jumpsuit with a Christmas holly accessory in her hair on the right, Nan was wearing a festive, red, green and white, wide collar sweater with a black vest underneath, and for once Mum seemed to be dressed sensibly in a thick black sweater right for the weather, if it weren't for these really shinny grey trousers with a black snake skin print. As if she was gonna pull today!

Auntie Sinead was a natural blonde, but she had dyed her hair dark brown and wore it in a bob cut, had blue eyes and was gorgeous like Mum, had a triangular jaw but a more squinty-eyed look, but she was less concerned with her dress sense and was wearing a baggy, cream brown rollover sweater dress. Nigel was a tall fella in his late-forties with a wide build, he had reddish hair and was balding on top, wore a light blue shirt with a navy blue body warmer and grey trousers. He looked like the boss of a factory. His wedding ring, which he still kept, gleamed under the light like some holy object. The bloke was seen as family to the Nicoles, even if his ex-wife wasn't regarded as so despite her blood relation. The family was sat in the living room, warming up by the fire, chatting away and catching up on stuff, opening up presents while sipping on some of Nan's warm, homemade mulled wine. The best Crimbo present today Emily had was a black leather jacket which had these pink rose petal details on it from Nan, that would go with her casual wardrobe.

At the dinner table was more food than you could eat in a month, a bottle of chilled champagne was passed about between guests, classic Christmas music playing and not the stuff you kept hearing every year when you had to go out shopping. Before anyone could dig into the turkey and trimmings, Nan raised her glass, signalling for everyone else to follow.

"Merry Christmas!" She said and everyone at the table reciprocated, clanging their glasses.

"Cheers!" Mum said out loud then knocked back a generous gulp. Everyone helped themselves to the festive food, passing around the dishes and trays of meats and veg and condiment jars.

Then Emily had a question she wanted to ask.

"When we gonna see Freya?" She said before shoving a piggy in blanket into her mouth. There was a brief pause from everyone at the table, from Mum most noticeably.

"She's in one of them wards in town." Nigel answered. He had a Dublin accent.

"I couldn't spend Christmas in a ward!" Remarked a frowning Owen.

"I don't want Janice round!" Mum warned wagging a fork.

"Why? Did she do summat?" Emily asked referring to Freya. Nigel produced a short sigh while he mixed the vegetables on his plate into gravy with his fork.

"There was a neighbour playing football with his lad at eight in the morning. She went up to him, told him to pack it in, he said: no."

Nigel chuckled.

"He was Paki, a chavy Paki—she hates the lot of 'em!" he detailed shamelessly. Emily shuddered quietly hearing that. "She slapped him about, got arrested!" Nigel said.

"Good God!" Sinead said grumpily and had a drink.

"He was being an arsehole! Had problems with that bastard for a while!" Nigel revealed. "He kept ignoring her, kept on playing football then she just went up behind him and hit him!"

"He shouldn't have provoked her…!" Emily said in pity.

"She proper did him though!" Nigel said. "She got him in the hamstring, he couldn't coach for a week!"

"Bloody hell!" Owen said.

"He wants to sue. She's already been committed! She got off lucky cuz the neighbour were there as witness. And even she had had enough of him!"

"Freya's not right!" Sinead said. "She shouldn't be drink-in' on a morning!"

She placed some comical emphasis when she said drinking.

"How long's she gonna be there for?" Emily asked.

"Couple of weeks. But she can go out and about now into Leeds—I took her out to lunch a few days ago." Nigel said. "She gets real worked up when anyone laughs around her!"

"She won't like us then!" Mum remarked and burst into laughter before knocking back a glass of bubbly.

"She had a fit around me once!" Owen joined in.

"Me and me mates had our lasses about in town, and they were just laughin' and shoutin', and she were just weren't havin' it—so she goes up to our mate's lass," he held up and pointed his knife in a threatening way.

"She's off her tits swearin' and going up to her face like she were gonna murder her!"

Nan shook her head.

"She's never gonna get a bloke!" Sinead said. Emily though wasn't so critical.

"Poor lass!" She said while Owen chuckled with a smile. "I'd like to meet her one time. Wouldn't want a night out with her though!"

Nigel bobbed his head about and made wavering grunts.

"She's a tricky one is me girl!" He said without frowning. "She's fine with a few cans and a kebab!"

"Like us!" A chuckling Emily couldn't resist inserting.

"She writes poetry. Loves her lions, them sabre-tooth tigers—it's always *big cats-big cats* with her!"

Nigel gripped his champagne glass.

"I wanna take her to Dublin zoo, see the tigers!" He said and took a drink. To be honest, Freya's interests didn't sound too odd.

"How is Janice anyway?" Emily asked Nigel with caution and noticed Mum looking at her.

"She's got her issues," Nan replied. "Hope Freya doesn't end up like her!"

"Well, it's not too late…!" Emily said.

"Bloody hell, can we change the subject please!" Mum urged and the commotion dyed down comfortably.

"New Year's resolution, Emily?" Nan asked her. Emily brushed her hair back and picked up her glass.

"Travel more?" She suggested from her heart. "Quit the cigs…?"

"Good idea!" Owen remarked.

"Achievable!" Nigel backed.

While Nan was preparing Christmas pudding, Emily and Mum went outside into Nan's backyard for a cig, and cuz it was freezing Emily put on her new leather jacket.

"I love that jacket!" Mum said enviously. Nan's backyard was nice, although the flowers in the long, raised, white concrete flowerbeds to the left of the yard were all dead for the winter the bed of grass on the right was trimmed with the grey sky above having nowt to beckon down upon. In summer, the flowerbeds were colourful with pansies and roses like some stately home, and there would be tables and chairs set out along with a barbeque. Nan had a rather large green house on the far right end of the yard, where she grew vegetables and herbs, particularly rhubarb, carrots, tomatoes, green beans and turnips, mint, parsley, sage and chives. Emily wanted a place like this in the future.

"I don't like Freya!" Mum said without keeping her voice down. Emily chuckled.

"Dun't sound like we're gonna see her now!" She said lightly.

Chapter 13

Urban structures stood out boldly amongst even spots of green space against clear, unpolluted blue horizons as though they were healthy stalks of plants. These structures were unlike anything seen before, and though they varied in size, their basic appearance was monotonous, a sterile laboratory white with dark windows. There weren't any eyesores in sight. The concept would be scoffed at, and any resulting "proceedings" denied—interpreted as ill oriented fantasy. The sterile white pathways were devoid of litter and used by consistently lean people of various ethnicities dressed in similar clothing to one another, but with some personalised aspects to them, usually in the form of embroidery or a badge (a bird, a fish, a dog, a flower, a creature of fantasy—various symbols and totems).

In one sector of this setting, there were these transparent panes a hundred feet high that separated civilisation from the natural world beyond, acting as harmless barriers. It was all green beyond the glass, plant life, tall and healthy miscellaneous growths of it asymmetrically arranged to assimilate a natural look. Among it were these vines, as thick as drainpipes, the darkest green in colour but bore no leaves. And there was animal life also. Moving down street alongside the pane on the left alongside the pedestrians on the white pavements was a *bear* the size of a bicycle with dark, chocolate brown pelt. It didn't look like a renowned species like a grizzly, and to make it stand out further: it had this yellowish patch on its forehead shaped like a sycamore leaf.

This set up wasn't a zoo and one's word was to be taken and upheld without any *opinion* interjecting. Security and association was priority without any harm to the other. Observation and esteem were the end results. The focus of the viewer was a family, the mother pushing along a buggy, the unseen baby facing the parents, which was standardised. The mother was white, in her forties, of average height, say for the fact that she wore black high heels of the platform variety. She was of an ideal figure, highlighted by her silky grey, long-sleeved, form-fitting jumpsuit with a thick, black waist belt, her hair was long, straightened, dark brown and centre parted, she looked happy with her green/brown eyes gleaming against mercifully shallow wrinkles, accentuating her smile.

The mother held a red rose with a trimmed, thornless stem in one hand the other she pushed her child with, which she looked down and inspected. The father was also white, he was a tall man with short, feathery white hair and was as attractive as his partner with stern, masculine features that included a square jaw, pointed nose, pronounced cheeks and stubble. He was dressed all in white: white shoes, white trousers, a white polo shirt, though there were small touches of purple to his shirt collar, and a purple caricature of what appeared to be a *Christmas tree* in place of a logo.

As this ideal family walked by the bear with the distinct marking one of the peculiar vines among the foliage moved. Not like from being dislodged by a breeze of wind or being disturbed by a small animal. The vine turned out to be animate. It bent like a snake to the left and the green shade began to fluctuate into different, alternating shades in a kaleidoscopic, chameleon manner. The viewer panned in the direction of the father, who was stood still, looking at the viewer. He had eyes *purple* as amethyst. They were really alluring, his smile not so much. He knew what he was looking at. Unsettlingly his smile grew, almost as if he could walk forward and put his hand through the viewing lenses. That he could not do. But he did have an impact nonetheless.

~

Alyona had her eyes closed, thinking. She opened her eyes, which were green, wide with a narrowed, oval accent, lined with long, dark eyelashes. This numerical gauge in the lower right corner of her vision began to decrease as she was presented with a new setting that consisted wholly of water. It was sea to be exact, and close to the surface, the screen flickering with colour, as if indicating the presence of something: a *helicoprion* in this case, said thing being viewed from the rear right as though being tailed. It looked like a shark, but it *wasn't related*, someone had told Alyona.

With a body length of seven metres, the helicoprion was up to orca size, counter shaded with a light grey/white underbelly, the upper body a blue/grey with white spots, some of which were elongated horizontally. It had a pair of sharply triangular pectoral fins, a dorsal fin and a crescent tail fin, the rear lower body fins were shorter than sharks and the body was longer, almost eel-like. Then the view switched to a frontal right shot mere inches away from the helicoprion's snout, which was short and high but pointed and tapered, its eyes were big, not as bold as some familiar species and had a lighter eyeball tissue, sort of like them bizarre deep sea sharks.

It was an unsettling sight as it cruised by the viewing source with its eye rolling back. Alyona noticed its lower jaw, which was what made it stand out most, maybe from anything else in existence; it possessed not multiple rows of razor sharp teeth but a singular row of partly backward curving triangular teeth, arranged into a circular row with red/pink gums exposed, giving it an asymmetrical swirl appearance compacted towards the back of the jaw. It looked like the biological equivalent of a circular saw. History was so impressive. The future, far less, if stuck to conviction.

"*Magnifique!*" Alyona said with a French accent. She was stood in a pitch-black room as featureless as the centre of a black hole.

She was watching the animate vine on the screen a few feet in front of her, which was frameless like a projection screen except clearer than the brightest of days. Alyona was a petite child with long black hair in a centre parting, her bangs framed the sides of her face while the back of her hair was tied up into a high ponytail with a hairclip that had a large green gem in the centre and a sharp prong on either side that pointed backwards resembling antelope horns. She wore a silky black, oriental robe with silver embroidery, a black sash with all the loose ends tucked in, silky red pants with similar patterning, although gold and wore black, oriental pumps with black socks, the ends of her pants were tucked into black leg warmers. Alyona held up and waved her right hand, flashes of colour appeared against the void around the screen, which began to take on the outlines of frames either square or rectangular in shape and of varying sizes. She spread both her arms outwards simultaneously with her palms facing forward, in response one of the rectangular screens to the right widened to the precise size as the one displaying the helicoprion and displayed a live image. Then from below, her entire body was enveloped in a concerning instant by a watery aurora.

~

There was no singular land mass formed beyond what the screen showed. All the mass was still rising from the oceans. In one equatorial area, a stretch of enormous mountain range ran along the Kasimovian horizon. On what little land there was present was infinite greenery, a seemingly endless expanse of ultra humid swampland and forest. On this one equatorial spot a visual provider cruised forward above the surface of an estuary in the direction of a forest of *lepidodenron*, which were a contemporary species of lycopsid, scaled barked green/brown giants that (on average) towered in excess of over a hundred feet above the ground. As mighty as these plants were, they had short life spans and after expiring they fell into the swamps in the masses, the accumulation releasing noxious gasses into the atmosphere, contributing to this steamy environment. Above the water, oxygen—one of life's givers—was at the highest it had ever been. Swarms of insects close to being opaque like storm clouds, only tangible were teaming in abundance every few metres. No spot was free of them, and the buzzing of their wings was the chief source of noise in the forest aside from the chirps and croaks of other unseen inhabitants.

Flying above the lycopsid forests were swarms of *meganeura*. These insects were apex aerial predators with two pairs of transparent foot long wings, big orangey red oval-shaped eyes the size of golf balls, these pincer-like mandibles, their two feet long exoskeletons were a deep, iridescent blue, which shimmered under the sun, highlighting cobalt blue, black and purple tints, and small white spots around the thorax, the dark, thin hairs on their body and legs, their glistening brass wings adjusting in intervallic beats on the spot, the reddish brown vein details visible.

The meganeura buzzed loudly and ominously as they beat their wings, which reflected the sun in glints, like the twinkles of stars did in the night. They had visible gender dimorphism; some members of the swarms had these curved pincer-like clasps at the end of their foot long segmented abdomens. Another visual provider observed a meganeura flying past one perched on top of a lepidodenron stem, the perched individual beat its wings, producing a loud buzz in a sequenced rhythm. It shifted position, its six legs raised up and lowered with the end of its abdomen flexing while another meganeura flew past it.

One meganeura landed on a stem adjacent, dark clouds were sweeping its way from behind, a blinding flash of lightning followed by the racket of thunder caused several meganeura to take off. A bolt of lightning struck a lepidodenron, igniting a spark. Having so much oxygen in the atmosphere, along with all the other combustible substances in the foul forest air carried a very adverse side effect. Smoke billowed rapidly around the struck giant's trunk. The smouldering thickened quickly into an opaque cloud.

Then the lightning-struck lepidodenron was set ablaze in a glow as bright as the sun, though the light didn't take eight minutes to be noticed from ignition, but seconds and the thick humidity did nothing to appease it as it spread with tongues of stretched, oxygen aroused flames making contact with plenty of closely packed lycopsids and procreated their blazes into an inferno. For the past 120 million years, plants and oxygen have acted as fuel for these wildfires on what had once been a barren, breathless planet and were now anything but uncommon, nor were they short in their range.

A mile away from the growing blaze one of the visual providers was fixated on an *arthropleura*, an arthropod. It had a small head with a pair of flickering antennae and behind it were thirty segmented armoured carapaces over a foot wide each coloured a dark brown/red with small and blotchy black and yellow spots and hair-like filaments sticking out between the segments. At two metres long, it was the largest arthropod on land, and might just be the largest terrestrial creature. The arthropleura crawled rather quickly along the damp forest floor on several dozen legs that made soft clicking noises, leaving a distinctive, trailing pair of imprints in the soil, its exoskeleton was covered in plant spores which it had unwittingly collected from its interaction with the foliage and was now spreading them about the forest as a vessel to new locations. At this size, arthropleura had no natural predators. Not on land anyway.

The arthropleura stopped at the foot of a lycopsid, the base of these giants were notably wide in comparison to their trunks which were uniformly thinner. The arthropod raised the frontal half of its body off the ground by almost a metre, its plethora of curved tipped legs flailing before it gripped the trunk of the lycopsid. It couldn't climb up it as it was way too large, but it had sufficient leverage to reach up and with a pair of large, formidable horizontally set pincers spread out from its mouth, it began to nip at the caps of parasitic fungus that had colonised the base. This colossal, menacing-looking arthropod it turned out had a benign diet. The jagged stumps of fallen lycopsids usually remained stood long after the expiration of the rest of the plant, many of them either moss or fungi ridden were present near or in the shallower parts of the swamps and were an exceedingly common sight, acting as proxies to hills and rises in more open parts of the globe, which remained unseen by most creatures.

Flying above the surface of the swamps nearby the arthropleura were *hailieanletheopterus*, members of the palaeodicyoptera order of insects, these smaller siblings of meganeura could be distinguished not merely by their shorter, fatter abdomens, but an inch wide pair of additional broad wings extending out the thorax above the first pair of limbs, giving them the illusion of having six wings. Hailieanletheopterus were *beautiful* organisms with golden brown carapaces and bright, orangey wings, their eyes reddish brown. One of them landed on a fallen lycopsid trunk, where it beat its wings, shaking off droplets of humidity from them.

In the water, the bed of the swamp seemed to move continuously from the congregation of life, and the fire heading its way of no concern for the moment being. One of the inhabitants was a *xenocanthus*, a cartilaginous fish related to the sharks, less than three feet long with a golden, khaki body mottled with small dark brown spots. But it was a fresh water species that didn't look too much like its marine relatives; it had a broad skull, a spike behind its head four broadened fins, plus some thin, trailing appendages behind the rear fins, and instead of having triangular fins on the dorsal it had a simple, elongated crest running down its entire spine, including the tail.

The xenocanthus cruised cautiously above the swamp beds, out of reach from the *uggligrs* crawling along the bed. They were eurypterids, aquatic arthropods with flat, elongated bodies, circular heads with large and dark motionless eyes, long, thin arms ending in slender, grasping pincers lined with long, asymmetrical teeth, three pairs of slim and short, outstretched legs between them and a pair of paddled rear limbs, and a fat segmented tail with a keratinous horizontal fluke, an elongated spine in the dividing notch. These hideous invertebrates were among the first apex predators to have evolved, but their heydays had passed. These carboniferous eurypterids thrived in fresh water, where once they had in the seas, where now sharks had outcompeted them. But like the land invertebrates the uggligrs were massive, at six feet they were very noticeable, the falsehood was them being apex predators. In this era, there existed new breeds of predators.

Slithering through the moist soil on the banks among the bright green moss and equisetopsia was the legless, metre long *nolagjaz*, a big-eyed, swampy green and soft-skinned feeder of small, soft-bodied prey that strongly resembled a worm. Though bizarrely it was in fact an amphibian. Swimming just below the surface of the swamp and heading towards a slanted lepidodenron trunk was the ultra-stupendous *ankercephalus*, a metre long amphibian with a flat and wide skull with elongated, foot long prongs on each side partly bending backwards. Floating plant matter stuck to its peculiar head as it breached the surface, its small, dark pupils encircled by yellow eyeballs peering upwards.

Some expired lycopsid trunks slanted against other standing specimens while submerged in the swamps. And with short, webbed limbs the amphibian slowly and cumbersomely made its way up one of these natural ramps, which was wide enough to accommodate the ankercephalus, sunlight flickering through the lycopsid canopy above it as it progressed. Out of water its fleshy yellow and grey/black, speckled skin folded and sagged downwards for inches along the flanks, its long, paddle crested tail flopping side to side and water spilling off it and raining down on the swamp surface, the bubbles attracting attention from below. Fallen lycopsid trunks acted as bridges for animals that didn't have flight and provided an alternative form of shelter from land. In the deeper end of the swamp, an uggligr crawling along the bed alternated its course and swam away, its segmented tail undulated up and down for propulsion. Behind it emerged a *lambtonophis*, a temnospondylid amphibian three times bigger than the eurypterid.

This imposing, predacious lurker measured six metres long and weighed nearly a ton, had a large, flat triangular-shaped head a metre long, an elongated yet bulky cylindrical body deep green with wide, vertically stretched black spots, a paddled tail and tiny limbs with webbed digits, which served little to no function on land. Unlike the majority of amphibian species, lambtonophis was fully aquatic and retained the external gills from its larval stage (instead of internal gill slits as seen with fish). These anatomical features were lined with odd dark grey stalks that branched out like plants, somewhat giving it the appearance of a water dwelling plant from the front.

The lambtonophis slid slowly through the murky water, its body bending and form visible from above the swamp, leaving ripples in its wake. Drawn to the bubbles from the dripping ankercephalus the lambtonophis rose to the surface, clouded eyes peering above with orange markings mottled with black spots trailing behind them, the branches of its upper gills flattening down against the surface. Upon seeing the bubbles exuding from its emergence, the hailieanletheopterus, with wingspans almost as wide as the amphibian's head dispersed. The ankercephalus resting on the lycopsid trunk remained still, the size comparison between it and the giant below was jarring! The lambtonophis was an ambush predator, one that preferred a stationary approach aided by its camouflage, and owning gills it could afford to wait lying motionless on the swamp beds for prey to come to it, rather than having to pursue it or go back up to the surface routinely for air. With the interest of an easy picking diminished the amphibian dipped its head and submerged.

On the banks of the swamp, reddish brown cockroaches almost a foot long scavenged for decayed flesh amongst the jumble of bones of a large, unidentifiable predator. Darkness from the storm clouds was sweeping in and intensified twofold by the miles of smokescreen from the fire which blanketed the sun, the glow of the encroaching fire appeared between the darkened trunks of lycopsids. Many a life here could and would perish from this local holocaust. The feeding arthropleura was trying not to be among the casualties and began moving away, its tiny black eyes had captured the glow and appeared orange.

Metres away a foot landed down against the moss ridden soil, belonging to a vertically tall figure towering above all life and walking on two limbs, unlike anything seen on land with a pair of forelimbs swinging in coordination as it moved, each ending in five long digits that weren't webbed or clawed. The thorax of the anomalous creature extended into a duel, identical set of broad peaks, its skin was smooth and relatively pale and with the exception of the face and hands it was covered in some ultra-fine, loose type of pelt and the feet seemed to be covered in brown leather just below the knees.

This figure was Alyona. Except for the irrefutable fact that she was taller… She was an adult. She was in her mid-thirties, her long black wavy hair was unstyled and trailed down her back, her figure elegant and voluptuous, she was wearing a grey/green jumpsuit with black epaulette sleeves, a brown waist belt with several brown utility pouches attached and brown leather riding boots, a fitting shell for an environment such as this. Several translucent orbs materialised, continuously alternating in their shape hovering statically a few short feet above her shoulders. These spherical aberrations scattered in all directions and moved as quick as the insects but produced no noise. The mature Alyona stood still, her head turning as she surveyed her surroundings, the glow of fire behind her had intensified, silhouetting her figure and a loud hum heard quickly approaching.

The meganeura below the canopy were flying above her like fighter jets over a warzone. Then the noise from their wing beats got much louder from a blizzard of them flying past Alyona in the thousands heading north, the accumulation of buzzes was quite intimidating while their wings reflected the orange glow of the approaching blaze.

Alyona raised her right hand and after executing that act a translucent bubble appeared around one meganeura, then several others, and remained in place even while they flew away out of sight. The arthropleura trying to outrun the blaze, which wasn't possible now, curved around a static Alyona as though she was the trunk of a lycopsid. The same aura that had engulfed the meganeuras did the same for the giant ground dwelling arthropod, which responded in confusion by rearing up, miniature crackles of purplish blue lightning encircled the bubbles encapsulating the arthropods. Then they were gone. Vanished they had.

In response to the blaze, the ankercephalus slowly turned around on the slanted lycopsid trunk, bending its body then slipped back into the water in less than half the time it took to ascend where it picked up speed and fluidity, its body and tail bending side to side with its peculiar head acting as a steer, its sagging skin spread out, giving the amphibian more body mass. Around the swamps lycopsids burned and all other moist foliage, dead and alive exploded into flames. Meganeura too close to the blaze had their wings singed and melted away in an instant, causing them to fall from the air onto the floor, their only means of escape burnt from their thoraxes they had to wait for the fire to put them out of their misery. All this destruction would fuel some other era eons away. That was of no concern right now. The secretions of intestinal tracts were best to describe the orientation of such an ambition.

A screen, similar to what a younger version of herself had viewed appeared in front of Alyona. She raised her left hand and extended her index finger which she flicked to the left, the gesture bringing about a still, three-dimensional image of a lambtonophis onscreen. Several different ones appeared around it with similarly formatted images of other fauna. Alyona looked left and spotted a very distant relative of hers at the base of a lycopsid. It was a vertebrate no bigger than her forearm with a broad, and fairly high skull and a slightly arched back from tall neural spines, four limbs, a long thin tail, body covered in smooth, scaly skin, coloration uncertain underneath the present lighting. The scaly vertebrate scurried away from the blaze while Alyona shut her eyes, contemplating while embers drifted from behind her along with a rapidly intensifying glow of orange that cast her silhouette in front of her. The blaze was close. Alyona didn't feel anything as she stepped back.

~

An uploaded screen from the void presented an above POV homing downwards on another immaculate street, though not as advanced as the previous urban setting there was still no smog about, the vehicles exuded no fumes and had electronic hums as they rode along. Then the image switched to a sideway view of a street, a road width away from a young woman in her early mid-twenties, white skinned, blue eyes, her hair was a little longer than neck length, dyed red and cut into an angled bob. She was a highly attractive individual, her figure desirable and athletic, her application of cosmetics were kept simple; mascara, champagne eye shadow, pink lip stick, her fingernails painted pink. She was dressed perfectly for a night out, wearing a black, sleeveless crew neck vest, golden leggings with brown leopard print patterning and tall, noir black suede heels with a triple-looped strap detail on the front, the heels were wedged which gave her height, the peep toe design showing off her pink painted toe tails.

She had a horizontal black tattoo on the inner right wrist of the numbers: **15|6|2012**. Passing her by in the opposite direction was another young woman, white skinned, blue eyes, desirable build, her hair was also cut into an angled bob and red, but of a more natural-looking shade and she had a more freckled complexion, and she was dressed the same way. The same look was adopted by the young woman across the street, the young woman also exiting the shop and the young woman crossing the road. Everyone looked the same—almost clone-like—these young women were the same build with only slightly superficial variations such as height, freckles, eye shape and breast size, different styles of tops, different shades of leggings, and notably different footwear, but all tops and footwear were black with heels and suited for nightlife.

There were two white, life-sized statues of this preferential profile, posed sitting on a bench with her legs folded, and another in a different pose, stood with her back turned, gripping a clutch. A yellow sign in bold black lettering, and there was one at every street corner that read: **Be modest. Be beautiful. Be inspiring. Be divine. It's the law!** The young lady entered a convenience store where she encountered more lookalikes, including the cashier, their appearance highly consistent as the women on the streets. The ATM was two aisles away from the counter and stood in front of it was this woman who had blonde roots showing on her crown, wore black slip-on stilettos and a sleeveless black turtle neck vest. Done with the machine she turned around revealing a pearl necklace around her turtleneck.

"Hi?" She greeted then asked, "You from the barracks?"

She had an English accent. The young lady shook her head with a closed mouth smile.

"You got muscles?" The customer pointed out her defined biceps, raised a fisted hand to her mouth and chuckled.

"Tennis," the young woman explained, she too had an English accent. She got her cash then went to the counter for some cigarettes. The cashier was wearing a black, sleeveless blouse with a sheered feature on the shoulders.

The young woman exited the store and walked down street no more than three blocks and entered this bar, that had a rundown exterior and an almost featureless yard with a rackety wooden fence. No one to kick it down due to pitiful insecurity whenever that maybe. The music playing was something called *starships* by Nikki Minaj, because that was what it said on the screen of the digital duke box. The interior had wood brown, tiled flooring, the spirit stock colourful with faint red lights glowing underneath and a red oriental style lantern saturating the right end of the bar in colour. Sat at the bar with her legs folded was yet another red bob, black top, leopard print legging uniformed lady, nursing what appeared to be a cocktail of some sort.

The young woman sat down, slowly on her stool at the bar right next to the other woman and folded her legs. The two patrons turned their heads and faced each other, smiling. The other customer ran a hand along the thigh of her raised left leg and flexed her ankle, her nose was longer, her eyes slightly lighter, her bob was feathery and she wore a backless, halter neck top which showed off a tribal tattoo on her back. The barmaid had conformed to the same status quo, though she was clearly wearing blue lenses and wore a low cut top with her breasts exposed and a gold necklace.

"*Why* did the boss want to see you?" The other customer asked, she had a Russian accent. The young woman shifted in her seat. "To see if I could be her…" She replied cryptically, "Whoever she is…"

Both ladies and the barmaid had the same tattoo on their wrists.

"*Why didn't you come back with me?*" They both said simultaneously and playfully with the woman on the right flexing her ankles.

"Writing a book or something?" The young woman enquired giggling.

"To be dry, broke, sleepless and bothered by the racket of enemies offspring…" She monologued then giggled dramatically.

"He could have done something…" She said. Then the visual abruptly terminated.

~

February 17th, year 2011. Being in good health, good shape and having steady work and money made Emily stand out among her mates; *our Nick's loaded!* and, *will you lend us money?* were things she was fed up of hearing. Jody had gotten bigger—shortening her lifespan—she needed a crutch to just walk now, and she felt posting videos of herself online doing simplistic stunts on her crutches was sorted, as though she was an aspiring athlete…*fuck off!* Stacey had only put on a few grams, Gemma had another bun in the oven. Emily still had yet to move house and apply for a driving course. She had had a merciless night's work and was well asleep. Emily had lost the mouth ring and had traded her nose stud for a thin, silver ring, which was a popular choice for lasses these days.

It was the earlier hours of a Thursday morning with a two day short full of a moon in the sky. Outside on her street, a barn owl was drawn to her house and perched itself on the limestone wall, it turned its head in the direction of a hedgehog that appeared on the scene from the east, its prickly mass shifting side to side as it went to the edge of the footpath and stalled. The spiky mammal was joined with several rats that sought the same position on the street. There were no hostile responses from each other as they unanimously stationed themselves in the exact same spot. Then mice joined the scene. Squirrels emerged from crevices in local trees and ran to the near end of branches.

All the cats on Carnian Street that weren't inside were converging on the source, a plump, ginger tabby cat among them, oblivious to the smaller critters they wouldn't normally hesitate to hunt down on detection. Then one of the local dogs, a renowned passive Russell terrier came trotting on site, aroused by the unrevealed occurrence it wheezed but didn't bark, nor did its presence cause a panic to the smaller animals, all of which remained static, their eyes drawn…hypnotised, facing the same direction: house 56. A young man, intoxicated and ready for bed turned the corner and unwittingly faced the house before he could register the gathering.

"The fuck…?" He mumbled then shambled forward, where he blindly ended up joining the static animals. A second barn owl swooped past him, without startling him and perched on the front wall of house 56 a few feet away from the other bird.

In the warmth of her bed Emily tossed and turned, grunting mutely. She was oblivious to parts of her body glowing a golden light. A sort of *holy* light, she might describe should she have been witness to, cosmic particles of it that had motion to them best compared to fireflies or iridescent plankton—a life to them—they alternated randomly. Then the accumulative glow dyed down as if switching off a light switch. In response, the animals on the street scattered and fled while the drunken bloke blinked, perplexed, and other than the ginger tabby he didn't notice the other animals clearing the scene behind his back as he moved on. Then every dog on the street was howling and barking with neighbours heard almost mutely calling out "*shut up*", "*piss off*" and "*fuck off*", from behind the walls of houses.

Emily hadn't awoken to it, locked in her dream where she was looking at a field, like those seen while jogging in outer Sancrott only with a darkened skyline, as though there was a lightning storm. Except there was no lightning, but these orangey flashes, as though the area was being bombed by fighter jets you saw in news footage of places at war. And Emily was experiencing that scare, as though she was local instead of observing it a thousand miles away. She gasped, her right leg jerked and her eyes opened. She partly attempted to sit up only to fall back against her bed. *The fuck…?* Emily felt guilt ridden, for some reason. She was thinking of what to do next. Get a glass of water? Look at herself in the mirror…? Then she experienced this high—a…*super feeling*—a proper sensation; sort of like losing your virginity. She rolled her neck around, took her left hand and massaged her right shoulder briefly before falling back to sleep without squandering.

~

In the cold, grey sky a mile off the coast of Iceland were a flock of lesser auks, dark brown to the point of black with pure white underbellies and white bands on their dark bills. Some of the birds folded their wings in and dived, plunging into the ice-cold water and sought out their small, herring prey. A shadow below them caused them to disperse.

Then the water exploded when a *humpback whale* breached the surface, its 40 feet, barnacle ridden oceanic blue/black body spinning and prominently ribbed grey/white underside exposed to the sun and long pectoral flippers spread out. Something else was attached to the right flipper: a human, a female, a pale one, with long blonde hair bright as sunrays and sporting a simple black single piece swimsuit. She continued to hold on, even as the humpback spun 180 degrees and fell on its back against the surface, causing an explosive splash under its 50 ton plus weight, followed by a fizzing, foaming ripple. The human vanished…

Only to reappear floating with her arms spread out, and drifting away on the loudly foaming surface with cod swimming beneath her. Outwardly she appeared fine, her body still in spite of the chill of the Arctic water. With both hands, the human female pulled her long, fair blonde hair apart from her face, the hair spread out widely like a bunch of kelp revealing a pair of big eyes, the left was icy blue while the neighbour was brown with *purple* specks, both reflecting the image of the auk flying overhead. The humpback surfaced, sprouting water from its blow hole, its small dark eye looking the way of the floating blonde woman who exhaled a puff of ice. There was *inorganic life* flying a mile overhead, leaving a pair of incredibly long cloud white trails. It was an airplane.

~

Emily woke up, and with no stirring or hesitation she peeled her blanket forward, stretched her limbs, got out of bed and plopped down on her bedroom floor, where she elegantly did fifty sit-ups with ease, followed by forty press-ups. Afterwards her breathing was steady as it was on a chilled out evening, and she didn't hear her heart beating. She wanted to have a pull-up bar fitted on her bedroom door, and was determined sevenfold to get that done ASAP. Emily showered, humming the Divinyls *I touch myself,* then with her right index fingertip she drew a cheesy swirl on the fog on the bathroom mirror and pranced about. She felt good, but it was a different sort of good, not like a good run followed by chocolate, two glasses of wine and a perfect orgasm good…*rapture* might be the word for it, which she needed as she had work for eleven. In her new position at work, Emily was obligated to dress smarter these days, her nose ring still permitted though. For today it was a pair of black flats, a black V-neck sweater Mum had got her, and took into consideration the length of the cut, which was an acceptable medium height, some white and black small chequered trousers, similar to what cooks wore, only form-fitting.

Feeling up for a gym session after work she took her gym bag with her then got the bus into town, nearing the foot of Furnivall Road this proper *thick* fog enveloped the area, and it had to be the thickest mist she had ever witnessed. The bus slowed down, people were commenting on the phenomenon, car horns heard and the lights and shadows of vehicles passing by the window. There were bound to be accidents! Getting off the bus and navigating to work was quite an experience, with Emily bumping into a few people who just appeared out of the fog like ghosts. She stopped in Lytham Arcade for a latte to go while she wandered upper Furnivall Road and took a few photos of buildings near completely shrouded in the mist.

Arriving at the bar 20 minutes before her shift a conveniently peckish Emily ordered a full English this time and she couldn't resist dressing it in that homemade hot sauce. And it was a lovely breakfast. That Black Eyed Peas *dirty bit* was playing and that newfound enthusiasm of hers was still burning away— she felt interested by everything; the lager pumps, the glasses, the shape of April's jaw, the curvature of Thorold's big belly, this big, grey-haired fella in a blue T-shirt who kept smiling, even while coughing into a white napkin was just weird but amusing, as was his Welsh accent! Serving customers felt euphoric, her smile and demeanour had rewarded her with tips. Emily felt she could handle owt now. On her evening break, while munching down on a pulled pork burrito she was watching a film clip on her phone, just for some inspiration, hoping she could laugh over it. And it was another Kashiwagi film.

There was a bloke in a black leather jacket lying on a beach, he had short brown hair with a receding hairline and had a large earring in his left ear. And there was a perfect rectangle arrangement of *sandcastles* around him. He opened his blue eyes and gasped, panicked with his limbs flailing about and destroying the sandcastles. Then he paused, frozen from fear before the next shot; an upward panning view of a big, muscular red-haired bloke with folded tattooed arms, a beard, black frame glasses and a tight topknot. There was a smoking volcano behind him and this tribal drum beating, which was overly dramatic!

"What are you doing here?" He asked softly, but in this menacing voice. Then the awoken bloke yelped, scrambled to his feet and fled.

"Sand castles!" the big fella called out like an angry customer that hadn't yet been served. Then it cut to a left side shot of the sandcastle destroyer running, panicked with this heavy metal track with all these garbled vocals that made no sense. For some reason, there was this included shot of someone's hands as they sliced up limes and some fella heard giggling in the background.

The sandcastle destroyer was running towards this rusty car that had been left on the beach without any tires for some reason. He dived in and shut the door, which didn't close and just bounced back open. Then he grabbed the steering wheel and pounded his feet on the accelerator.

"Come on, come on!" He panicked. He hadn't put any keys in so what on earth was he doing? Then the big ginger fella appeared into view and opened the door, not viciously, but slow and calmly. The fella in the car recoiled into the passenger seat, opened his mouth and screamed like a little girl.

"You must come with me!" the big fella insisted.

Then it suddenly went to a shot of this wooden barrel rolling and bouncing down a grassy hill.

"Robert Powell!" some childish voice shouted out and repeated, "Robert Powell!"

Without trying, Emily giggled and put the back of her right hand to her mouth.

It was dead inside and both raining and windy outside, and the orange glow of the streetlights had a depressive vibe. Then she looked towards the window, saw people walking past, some stopping and pacing about unsure if they wanted to come in or not. She blinked and all that over excitement came to an end like the dinosaurs. She felt boringly normal. After work, she went to the Hoperwood gym for an hour workout, in a casual black two piece this time. She was proud of all the work she had done on her body and experienced another explosion of confidence from the endorphin rush, topping up that sensation from earlier today. That's how she needed to be! Against the gym mirror she took a selfie.

Emily was famished. At home she showered, changed and put on an oversized white sweater, plain black velour trackie bottoms, her white socks she didn't bother adjusting, though she felt as though she would trip over because of them. She tied her hair up into a lazy topknot and committed the sin of wiping off her makeup. She wouldn't feel comfortable in public looking like this. She wanted pizza, not the frozen sort you put in the oven but the freshly made ones. Though she didn't want to be spending any more money, she thought fuck it and called up the local takeout and ordered the biggest pepperoni pizza they had available. Emily went downstairs to join her Mum in the living room. She was on her laptop and wearing a light, corn flour blue velour tracksuit with a thick white hair band and her hair tied up high.

"These lasses are *gorgeous*!" She said resentfully slouching down in front of her laptop's screen. Emily sat down next to her and saw that her mother was on this website with all these foreign lasses with perfect figures and long hair. "East Europe lasses!" Mum moped further, "They've all got lovely hair!"

"You're lovely, Mum!" Emily said comfortingly.

"You were born perfect!" Mum said enviously, sounding like she was gonna have a fit then pinched a lock of her hair, pulling it her daughter's way.

"I'm gonna go grey soon!"

Then there was a knock at the door.

"Who's that?" Mum enquired. "Meet a fella at the gym?"

Emily chuckled.

"That's us pizza!" She said, got out of her seat and opened the door, handed the delivery bloke a tenner, but regretted not having enough change to tip him.

"Why've you ordered a massive bleedin' pizza?" Mum complained as she came back into the living room, holding the box with both hands.

"Cuz I'm starvin'!" Emily replied then sat down, clearing some space on the coffee table. She opened the pizza box, delighted by the tasty, cheesy waft. Fearlessly she tore off a slice, the strings of cheese extending off the sloping piece.

"Want a slice, Mum?" Emily offered. Mum delicately took the slice while Emily picked up another, which she ate as though her life depended on it with Mum watching her critically.

"What?" Emily said.

"You're gonna put on weight!" Mum said back and giggled.

"I don't feel like I can!" Emily said, blinked then took another bite. She giggled while chewing—*God, why do I do that?* Might as well put it on her CV!

Chapter 14

Saturday. Emily was wearing that fit pink trackie Mum had got her for her birthday, though it was still winter it was a really nice day today, with the sun bright and no clouds she felt more than warm enough she could wear the trackie, but with a couple of under layers and a light blue/grey top over them, the top unzipped just short of halfway down, the bottoms were low rise and the flared ends were tucked into the Uggs Nan had bought her, their material matched the texture of the tracksuit even if their colour didn't. Emily loved this tracksuit so much that she didn't have words to describe it! She still had her bob cut, hadn't grown it or trimmed it, and she had dyed her hair last week, this time it was a fairly bright apple red.

It had just past afternoon, and today Emily was wearing foundation, mascara, eyeliner and blue eye shadow and had put on some pink lip-gloss. Also today: she was visiting Heather, the poor lass had had a melt down and made a complete cock of herself with plenty of witnesses (her family among them) at this pub in town. Apparently she had been eavesdropping on this couple where the bloke was apparently being abusive and had stepped in. She had assumed she was standing up for women's rights, but the lass didn't need defending, and she had started with Heather, who wasn't too good at reasoning with people. So naturally she had caused a scene. The police had been called, and for her own good; she had been sectioned and was in the Langbar Centre, a loony bin near Geldard Hospital in the east side of Oldmill Brig neighbouring Warritson, which was the dodgier part.

It was a horrible-looking area; no surprise it was the scruffiest district in Thewlington. While going back and forth to hospital appointments, Mum had always complained about how there was no development or improvements. The place was from the 1800's with withered red bricks exposed from the long crumbled plaster, rackety, broken fences, uncut grass and there was a stupid lack of sanitation about; litter every foot or so like it was perfectly acceptable. The streets were filthy, except for the way the locals dressed, especially the women in their colourful outfits, headdresses and all, and some people were driving around in fancy cars. Along with her brand-new red handbag, Emily had two big bags of shopping with her in white and red reusable bags she had picked up at a shopping centre with an Aldi just on the way after Mum had asked her to, though she really should have picked it up on the way back. But the extra weight was good exercise!

In her gorgeously pink trackie, Emily got plenty of attention from both sides of the road and motorists, even while listening to *I'm coming home* she could hear all the beeps, wolf whistles and cat calls from these Asian lads inside the cars. Emily didn't say owt, ready to have a bloke or twenty come up to her and chat her up. Two blocks past Geldard Hospital she turned right, headed up a steep road towards a barrier like one of them seen in car parks with **Langbar Centre** printed on a council sign. Emily walked past on the single pathway to the left, down a downward steep pavement into a perfectly flat car park.

She entered the Langbar Centre, there was an NHS blue seated waiting area to the left with two vending machines, a café to the right and a barrier with an atrium beyond. The receptionist was a lovely woman that looked to be near 50 with a black bob cut and had these bright, watery blue eyes.

"I'll let you in love!" The receptionist said kindly and pushed a button, the barrier opening up, a single housefly being witness to this event with organic compound eyes instead of artificial camera eyes placed about on the ceilings. The atrium had a concrete floor, some slabs of which were lose and wonky, there were dead flowers in heavy pots and boring stone decorations about, the sun shining directly above them, and there were a couple of wooden benches about which weren't damp.

Instead of going straight upstairs to see Heather Emily set down her bags and sat down on one of the benches, adjusted her Uggs as she stretched her legs then spread out her fingers, inspecting her nails which were painted white, she lit a cig while she checked her phone for messages. She had work later evening but Mum had sent her a text, letting her know she could have a lift into town.

"Aright?"

Emily was soon distracted by this big fella in his late-thirties with a shaved head striding up to her right. He wasn't decent looking, had unhealthy skin, wore a loose black T-shirt, black trackie bottoms tucked into his socks and football trainers, a proper chavy look to him.

"Like yah trackies!" He spoke slack and very immaturely as though he was 12 years old, and he had nearly no teeth left; what few could be seen were plaque yellow and rotted.

"Tah…!" Emily said, knowing it wasn't going to be a pleasant chat.

"You a patient?" He asked sounding really excited while his fingertips pinched a roll-up.

"No." Emily shook her head without making eye contact.

"What you doin'?" The unwanted company asked.

"Seeing me mate."

"Who's that then? I might know 'em!" The nosey twat's words got louder and had aggression to them. Emily didn't say owt after that.

"I'm Adam Q!" The toothless wanker said. Emily chuckled and shifted aside slightly.

"You got a boyfriend?" Adam Q grilled. Emily squinted and faced him.

"You what…?" She said without watching her tone.

"Yah got a fella?" Adam Q said then licked his roll-up. Emily shook her head then returned her focus to her phone's screen. "Yah an't got a fella?"

Emily didn't reply to the annoying twat.

"Where yah from?" Adam Q continued to be pushy.

"Hoperwood Beck."

"Posh place!" Adam Q said almost patronisingly then lit his roll-up.

"No, it in't!" Emily complained without having to shout.

"I'm from the *roughest* part of Thewlie: Kirkbrit Park!" Adam Q said like he was so proud of it. What was he in for anyway? Emily wasn't too sure if she wanted to know, but had a few ideas she could mull over later once she was out of here. She sighed.

"Alright, good for you! Leave us alone will yah?" She said passive aggressively.

"You what?" Adam Q said back. This cunt must be a handful for the staff here! Emily dared to make a stupid, throaty chav noise, not caring if she would get a slap.

"Fuck off!" She said—*I don't care who you are!* Adam Q giggled from his stomach and smiled, there was a pink blob of tongue in place of teeth.

"Fuck off…!" He said softly and inhaled his roll-up.

"Fuck off…! Fuck off…!" He repeated like some malfunctioning electronic dictionary or summat, smoke billowing out of his mouth, then he started pacing about for some reason. Schizophrenia perhaps?

"I'm fuckin' Adam Q…! I know them psychos up at Kirkbrit Garth!" He said, "Who the fuck are you?" His eyes were wide, and he looked pretty pissed off. This class A knobhead was every bit as ugly on the inside as he was outside.

"Ergh, excuse me? I'm *me!*" Emily practically belched her reply without making eye contact. "Watch your language!"

"You what?" Adam Q blabbered and took another drag on his roll-up.

"Who the fuck are you?" Emily said back, tossing her tolerance aside and stood up facing Adam Q. "You a gangster or summat? I don't fuckin' care who you are! Just fuckin' leave me alone, please!"

Adam Q didn't say owt to that. Was there any security here to protect visitors or staff? Emily didn't notice this golden streak of light that appeared almost like a spark across her forehead, and the rat running out from a crevice across the atrium to her left. Her heart beat increased, she expected more abuse. Adam Q mumbled summat, and Emily didn't care.

"Fuck off, you!" She snarled. "Fuckin' *silly* bastard!"

She didn't hear any further abuse and saw Adam Q walking away up this corridor in the reflection of the windows, his back to her and not looking back to have a pervy look at her. She had actually scared him off!

"Fuck sake…!" Emily breathed then sat back down, returned to her phone's screen, not even caring that her tactics had worked; most blokes like that always stayed and gobbed off until someone struck a punch. Less than a minute later she was calm again, her heart rate steady. She didn't notice the blue and black character to her right walking behind her with a cast on the left arm that could be seen a mile away. There was a ghostly suspicion to its moves in the way it slowed down and took its time as it ascended the stairs a floor above Emily. Halfway along the corridor it stopped and looked at her… Emily had a message from Abby, who was 17 and really unsure of where she was going in life, even though she was loaded and was going to Venice tomorrow. Envious, Emily didn't reply. The figure beckoning down on her a floor above moved away as though a time limit had been exceeded. Emily stubbed out her cigarette. It was time to see her dysfunctional mate.

~

Emily buzzed the female ward entrance and was let in through two sets of double doors, there was a depressive hospital smell about the place from the use of undesirably scented disinfectant. In the reception area, the patients either sat expectantly or just pacing about aimlessly, some of them muttering to themselves. Emily sat waiting for one of the nurses to fetch Heather, not wanting any of the lasses to come up to her and say owt dodgy. This skinny Asian lass in her forties came staggering her way as though drunk with an unlit cig in her hand, her long hair parted in the centre and she was dressed like she worked in the office in a pink blouse, a black, but wide mid length skirt, and shabby ankle-high boots that had no appeal.

"Love your tracksuit!" She said with a child-like blabber.

"Tah!" Emily said without making eye contact.

"*Love your tracksuit!*" The patient mumbled again then laughed for some reason.

"You been shoppin'? What'd yah get?" She asked and there was no way Emily was going to answer her. There was this other lass walking the patient's way, whom she went up to, staggering on her heels.

"I were sayin' I like her trackies! She's wearin' pink trackies!" The dodgy lass said to her and the other lass giggled. *What* was her problem?

Heather arrived, and instead of going someplace private she chose to sit here where all the nutters could see and hear. Heather was such a wreck, her eyes whipping around all over the place, her hair not straightened, no makeup on, her concealed freckles fully revealed and her breath stank; she probably hadn't brushed her teeth this morning, she was wearing a very lose fitting plain grey tracksuit, that didn't look right on her—it might as well be a prison uniform! She was miserable to put it short. Emily didn't want to tell her about Adam-bloody-Q. To make the air more breathable, she went into her handbag and sprayed some perfume onto Heather who tilted her head back.

"Is the food here alright?" Emily asked referring to hospital food, especially this horrid chicken pasta with sweet corn and bits of red pepper which she had no choice to eat after she had badly twisted her ankle at age 11, then had spent the night over at Geldard Hospital, having to listen to all the children and babies crying and complaining, and she couldn't play footie in school PE lessons for nearly a month afterwards.

"It's alright," Heather answered. Emily looked about, observing every lass, wondering how much of their chat they had heard, though none were looking their way.

"What are these lot like?" She asked.

"Everyone's fine!" Heather said though it was likely a white lie. She'd be fine here! There was no reason to see her again from here… She was a liability. Before saying a decent good bye, Emily needed to pay a visit to the loo first, she asked Heather who pointed down the corridor. Emily ventured down, relieved there was no one coming up to her, the doors for the patients rooms were yellow and similar to those seen in prisons with them sliding windows, except they weren't that solid, and half of them were partly open. There were two toilets next door to each other near the end of the corridor, Emily opened the door on the left, where the worst smell she had ever come across hit her like a punch to the face that she nearly fainted.

She shut her eyes tightly, held her breath and went to the other toilet, where she discovered a horror story; some loony bitch hadn't flushed! A deep, dark fucking turd as thick as a wrist and maybe a foot long was sitting there half submerged in the toilet bowl. Unhealthy! Unclean! Unethical! Rather than scream and cause a fuss, Emily held her breath, calmly turned around and closed the door, not too slow or too quick then walked away hoping no one saw her enter or exit. The dread of it compelled her bladder to be patient. Emily marched back down the corridor trying not to throw up, or think about food.

"I'm off!" Emily said to Heather, who was telling fibs to her about the people being *decent* here.

"Are you going?" Heather complained.

"Yeah…" Emily said lazily, no hugs or owt after that. That was it. Emily exited the ward, hoping she wouldn't run into Adam Q. Thankfully she didn't, she plugged in her earphones, *it's beautiful* by Spiderbait was playing. She exited the centre and walked down the same street she had come up through then crossed the road, the heads of more fellas turning.

~

There was a pub across the road which Emily entered and was met with the stares of blokes inside, all were old white blokes, which was odd considering the area. They all looked at her, but she didn't care or greet them in anyway. Emily answered her minute long call of nature, then bought herself a half pint of lager with lime cordial, sat in the corner which had no privacy, and she had difficulty enjoying her drink as the dodgy blokes in the pub were gawking at her and whispering stuff, some of them in the adjoining room behind the bar were laughing. *Just be charming…* She wished, *recite the bloody alphabet, just don't stare at us!* Emily blinked upon spotting this flickering flash, maybe a reflection from someone's watch or summat in the corner of her left eye.

"A…" One of the blokes sat at the bar to the left started, the first letter of the alphabet spoken loudly enough for Emily to turn her head and face him.

"B…" Her attention was redirected the other way by this other bloke sat by the window.

"C-D…" That fella continued.

"*E-F-G-H-I-J-K…*" Then everyone, including the barman joined in, looking at Emily with big, wide happy eyes! It was like a welcoming or birthday party! Emily had the longest pause from reality she had ever had. After the "Z", all the blokes went silent. They were all smirking, but not making eye contact with their gazes aimed a few degrees elsewhere. And it didn't make Emily feel any less comfortable. *Okay, time to leave!* She drank her half pint almost as quickly as a shot, grabbed her shopping then left without saying thanks.

"Fuckin' hell!" She cursed outside. Was this like a weirdoes-only pub for twats like Adam Q? It wouldn't be a surprise as it was across the road from the loony bin! Instead of getting the bus Emily decided to walk into town along the main road, her attention not buried on her phone's screen as her hands had fairly heavy bags to carry, Passion Pit *"To Kingdom Come"* playing. For a mile, she could spot all the stares from people in the corner of both eyes from both sides of the road, but there were no call outs, and the main road began to slope sharply. At the foot of town, she couldn't resist looking back at this sun drench view of Oldmill Brig, which was practically built on a hill like some witch's house, all them red bricks and black roofs visible nearly two miles away. Bad place to build such an ugly place where everyone could see it!

Emily was feeling peckish despite having stared into a literal shit hole recently. In fact she was famished, and couldn't care about any memory of owt disgusting. In town, she went into the Coverdale at the foot of Furnivall Road and a block away from the police station. The Coverdale was a decent pub, Emily and Mum usually went here after shopping trips before catching the 175 back home, and it wasn't one of them dodgy ones. The pub had these light green walls with some framed, vintage black and white photos of the city from the previous century, there were several wall mounted plasma screens and more fruit machines than usual. But it wasn't just an all blokes pub, there were people of various ages here, and it was mostly young people behind the bar.

Emily ordered a chicken burger with avocado, she skipped the chips and had a glass of ice water. The burger was decent and she demolished it in a few short minutes, wiped her mouth then went to the ladies room so she could sort out her makeup and clean her nails of the avocado stuck underneath them. Before she could wash her hands, she smelt summat. It wasn't bleach, it wasn't urine or crap some bitch hadn't bothered flushing, but a fresh, clean and inviting smell like in a fancy hotel, only much better. Emily brought both her palms to her face and sniffed instinctively. Her hands smelt of it, and she couldn't help but sniff several times. She washed her hands, soap and all and sniffed again. That lovely smell was still there.

Emily looked at her own reflection, paused briefly then leaned in. She didn't need to get out her makeup kit as there were no *imperfections* to her face, makeup smears or bits, she was very content with her appearance. A closer inspection and she noticed that her hair seemed a bit *brighter*. Was it the light? The lights in the toilets were quite bright, and…she did down a half pint proper quick and had been walking around with a bit of heavy luggage. There was summat dodgy going on with Emily's senses; particularly her thoughts—she felt like she was being attacked inside her head by some unknown force. It was proper scary, and not summat she could describe too well other than it being like a camera flash right in her face in pitch black, and there were outlines of summat. Emily recoiled seeing it and blinked, glad she wasn't out in public. No more booze for a few days!

She went back to her table, sat down and noticed this fella staring at her, the same way them old men had back at that other pub. *What are you looking at now?* Emily thought angrily. Then he looked away in a proper abnormal way; his eyes were partly squinted and his head was twitching, as though he was resisting the urge. Then more heads turned Emily's way, this was too much. Then these blokes just started laughing! Emily was feeling proper agitated—paranoid actually. She was about to get up and leave. But then everyone went silent. The only sound was from the traffic and people outside. Emily looked at everyone as far as she dared, all the patrons were sat still and expressionless like dolls, creepy fucking dolls no one would dare buy for their kids!

"Everyone gone quiet?" She commented then chuckled.

"*Yes,*" everyone mumbled. And at the same bloody time! Emily's heart stopped and her bowels felt weird, the need to go was strong and she moved without considering her shopping. The need subsided as quickly as it came, then she stopped, tickled by an additional panic. Hallucinations and tricks of the mind aside, Emily really needed to know if someone was following her. While this all may be a well-put-together prank, she didn't want to be in town. She was giving serious thought about stopping at the police station. But how would you explain all this to them? And the Chamberlain station didn't have the best reputation in town. She wished she had a gun in her handbag right now like them lasses in America.

Emily grabbed her shopping and left the pub. There was no hassle at the bus stop just gawks of passers-by, but thankfully the bus arrived in like two minutes or so. There was this middle-aged fella getting on in front of Emily, he looked like he was on summat and was waddling side to side like a penguin in slow motion, he asked for a ticket to Kirkbrit Park, paid then walked off without collecting his ticket.

"Ear? Your ticket!"

The driver, a bald, middle-aged fella whom was seen quite frequently, called out to the passenger holding his arm out of the till.

"No…it's just for…" The fella mumbled.

"Naah! Go on, you need yah ticket!" The driver said loudly and waved the ticket.

"I'm only going to—"

"Argh no, you need a ticket, love!" The driver protested, the passenger took it, people were laughing and the driver's expression was hilarious with his face all creased up and cheeks reddening. Emily would have laughed if she wasn't so weirded out by the recent events.

She was listening to Paramore's *crush crush crush* and wanted quiet all the way. And that's what happened… Never had there been such a peaceful ride back home. And she was grateful. Getting off the bus underneath the tree she saw this lad just stood smiling at her with these big eyes—*yah fuckin' kiddin' me?* Another fella with a boner for her look today and bad charisma! Emily strode by him without making eye contact and headed down Carnian Street. She looked back and saw that the dodgy lad wasn't gawking at her, but was still stood still. Thoughts went through Emily's mind, that same energy she had with her around Adam Q making her eager and ready. *Just be yah daft self then!* She heard a slamming noise followed by a car alarm go off. She looked back while walking and stopped for good reason; the creepy div was doing a *headstand* on the bonnet of the car going off and he was giggling with his legs kicking about.

"The fuck…?" Emily mouthed but didn't shout owt as this cunt was trouble. Cautiously she walked off.

"Fuckin' hell!" She remarked safe inside and checked the peephole to see if he had followed her. He hadn't. What a proper dodgy start to the day—it was like a bloody Kashiwagi film!

~

It was night, and Mum had dropped Emily off at work for her evening shift. April was Emily's partner for the evening, she was cutting up strawberries. Emily noticed that the chandelier by the stairway was missing. "Alright Nick?" April said.

"Where's the chandelier?" Emily asked. April cackled and showed off her teeth.

"Some div pissed out of his head thought he were bloody Tarzan! He were comin' downstairs and he jumped on the chandelier!"

What? Emily laughed in denial.

"He fell!" April said. "Ambulance came in and took him way—think he had a broken leg!"

"Seriously…?" Emily said and laughed pitifully, wishing she could have seen this Tarzan wannabe just throw himself at the chandelier! That would be an epic laugh on video! Then it started chucking it down outside, with thunder and lightning glowing. Wait…now that was proper odd for England this time of year!

April looked at Emily with a wide-eyed look and cussed while Emily went around back to hang up her coat. Her work outfit for tonight was nowt special; a thin black sweater with grey work trousers, she tied her hair back then went to the bar. Then all these lads came in, complaining about the downpour, swearing and everything, acting like apes and making similar howls as they pulled out chairs and made a racket. God, this was gonna be awkward… And there was no bouncer about to deal with them—this was just bad timing! Every time the boom of thunder was heard the lads cussed loudly and dramatically. Any customer stopping in was gonna be annoyed over this! There was this spiky, ginger-haired lad among the group, he was a midget and the gobbiest of the lot. Weren't they all? From life experience, whenever you came across a ginger midget you knew there was gonna be a problem; because they *always* started on people for no reason. Emily passed a word to April about him.

"Don't serve 'em!" She said then April marched over and confronted the lot.

"I'm not servin' yah lot!" She informed.

"What?" The ginger lad blasted. "Why not?"

Winner of the most predictable response. *Will you just get fucked?* A fed up Emily thought, wanting someone to just slap him across the head. Then that tension dropped like a real heavy barbell as she experienced this sensation— another surge of that rapture she had been experiencing recently. She sniffed, not at the smell of lager at the bar, but this sweet banana-esque smell, like them powdered custard packets you added water to that were popular when Emily was a child.

She noticed the loud ginner fella started acting weird; he was blinking and looking about as though he was watching a fly. Then he opened his mouth and said, "Do you do cunt?"

That, Emily heard as clearly as a burp in a silent library.

"Oi? Language!" April called out. Ginner ignored her by turning around, walking up to one of his mates who was stood up and giggling at his short mate's offense.

"You what?" Ginner said, his mate looked utterly confused.

"WHAT?" The lad shouted back unnecessarily and daft as shite. "*I'm here to give yah cunt!*"

Then Ginner ran at him and yelled, full of testosterone. His mate caught him by the shoulders. These knobheads were fighting amongst themselves, and there didn't seem to be any reason!

"YOU WHAT?" Ginner's mate roared instead of trying to calm him down or owt. The other lads just sat in their seats, with their heads…bobbing, instead of trying to break up the conflict.

"Okay, yous all have to leave now!" April retorted with the fighting lads muttering shite.

"Give over!" April looked ready to forcibly pull them apart. Then they stopped tussling, at around the same time.

"EH?" Ginner said casually while his opponent made this dodgy noise Emily had a hard time describing; the closest she could compare it to was an attempt at sounding like a dolphin and a revving up car engine at the same time. Ginner inhaled rapidly then puffed his cheeks up.

"*A riggy boom-boom foggy-fog!*" He blabbered then grabbed his mate by the shoulders and pulled him towards him as though he wanted to hug him. He didn't resist and ended up kneeling from the force of the jerk, he opened his mouth and made this groan, his lips slacked on the left side of his face, like he was having a stroke.

"Me sister's a *virgin!*" He almost shouted then made this pathetic, lazy giggle.

Then Ginner slapped him across the face! And it was a proper backhand, and the impact of it could be heard!

"OI?" Emily called out and was ignored while Ginner slapped his mate again, and he just let him! What on earth was going on? Emily reached underneath the counter, hit the panic button and confidently skirted around the counter to confront them. Ginner slapped his mate again.

"OI?" She shouted again. Then they stopped, swaying like plants in a wind. Now this, looked disturbingly familiar, that Emily couldn't deny.

"Okay-okay, pack it in!" April said then had herself a laugh, looking back at Emily without any commotion or abuse. The lads were mumbling, and the act could kind of be compared to a steam train on standby, only it was just ridiculous. These lot who thought they were the best of the best were just sad, piss-taking weirdoes that didn't move for more than a few inches. Both under pressure and mystified, Emily had forgotten the similarities to the events this afternoon… Quiet was what she had wished for. And she had done what she could to ensure that had happened. Emily felt like throwing summat at them for a laugh.

April was trying to talk to them, but they were saying fuck all. Were they pulling another extreme prank on Emily, or had they recently taken some new drug that really messed around with your senses? Customers came in, stopped and looked at them as though they were dodgy tourist attractions and laughed. And instead of spewing insults and threats their way, the lads remained still. And they continued to until two male coppers came in, one officer tilting his head as he walked towards the troublesome lot.

"*Hello* there mate?" He said with sarcasm while Emily resisted the urge to laugh. The lads didn't say owt. Emily and April pointed out the trouble starters, then Thorold—wherever he had been during all this—came out of hiding and took one of the coppers round back to view the footage while the other one took a statement from Emily and April, kept brief thankfully. Then the other copper returned and had his partner escort the troublemakers out, no handcuffs or owt, though the lot exploded into quarrel as they went.

Then the bar was quiet, the rain tapping against the windows was soothing, as some writers would say. There was a single boom of thunder but no lightning flash, so the storm was probably almost over. Emily hoped the coppers wouldn't ring her for a follow up statement up at an inconvenient time. She needed a vacation! It wasn't long before a pair of rowdy lads came in—*just brilliant!* Like the previous lot, they were college-aged, athletic, wore tracksuits and not that handsome, but they had two lasses accompanying them, whom were complaining about the rain, a lean black lass with her frizzy hair worn back into a severe bun almost the size of a melon, and this other lass with large, disk-shaped earrings and long blonde hair tied back into a high ponytail.

Both lasses were laughing, they took off their thick, fancy overcoats and shook rainwater off them. The black lass was wearing the same white beautician uniform Emily had worn last year while the blonde lass was wearing a fancy, fluffy black body warmer over a velvety cherry red tracksuit similar to the one Emily wore earlier today, but it was more expensive and she wore a slim, black waist belt, didn't wear Uggs and the ends of her tracksuit bottoms had tapered ends, allowing her to wear these black, platform heeled booties which suited her. Two of the lads came to the bar and ordered lagers without farting about, Emily ID'd both and they quickly presented them from their back pockets while chatting with the lasses.

"What you's avin'?" One of them called out.

"Long island ice tea," the blonde replied.

"Get it yah selves!" The lad said while his mate chuckled.

While pouring a pint, Emily had another look at the blonde lass. Her blonde hair was fake as she could see the darker roots exposed on her hairline, she was lean to the point of skinny, East European-looking with brown eyes big as an owl's and a small dark spot on her left cheek. Where did she remember her from…? Emily felt lager pour over her fingers but didn't react. After wiping her hand, she had another look at the lass in the red trackie, who was laughing out loud showing off her pearly white teeth. Now Emily remembered. The lass had taken the piss out of her in the corridor back when second year had started, that day she had had power over her with her mates and all.

But in this bar, Emily had more power over her—*go on and start then—give us a good reason to kick you out…!* She thought, not having a smile for any of them for when they next placed an order, right now she hated them all and wanted them to piss off. The lads took their pints and went back to the table, then the lass that had dissed her came up to the bar, laughing along the way. Emily didn't make eye contact with her.

"*Smile…!*" She said, which wasn't a good idea, even for lasses to say.

"What can I get yah?" Emily asked lifelessly.

"Two long island ice teas."

"Can I see your ID?"

"It's in us purse!" The fake blonde in red said cheekily then trotted back to her table, really taking the piss by taking her time and chatting to her mates before returning to an impatient Emily. She was one of them characters in horror films you just begged to have killed off by getting an axe through the head or summat… Emily wasn't creative with violence.

Then the fake blonde returned to the bar and showed her ID, Emily still not looking at her. The lass had parted dark brown hair on her photo instead of that hair dye, and she didn't look flattering; her brown eyes looked dead while her face appeared more blemished. Her name was: **Valerie Garner**, born: **25.10. 1991** in **Kiev Ukraine**. While Miss Garner here did look like she came from that part of Europe, she didn't have the accent and was just a boringly posh Thewlie bimbo with a big, obnoxious gob. Did the lasses in Ukraine behave like that? Probably not. Without thanking her, Emily handed Valerie her ID back, and she paid by card then went back to the table to join her mates. Emily took her drinks to her table, both lasses had the decency to say thank you without taking the piss! Without anything to do Emily hung back behind the bar, thinking of what to have on her break. She looked to the windows and noticed rain droplets sliding down the screen. The freak storm, which would likely be on the news tomorrow morning, appeared to have stopped.

Don't look back by She & Him was playing when this lass walked in with them rowdy lads turning their heads her way. The customer was fine skinned with a bone shaded complexion and square jaw line, she had a bulgy white woolly hat, as though she had a cloud on her head, these dark, oversized sunglasses concealed her eyes. Why was she wearing shades in this weather? She was wearing a black, zipped-up biker jacket with mustard *yellow* jeans, (who wore yellow jeans?) and dark brown, suede calf-high boots with laces. Her jeans were high-waist like a certain X Factor judge, except they actually looked right on her! She only had a few droplets of rain on her, so she must have gotten a lift here or summat.

She removed her hat and out fell this really nice hair, dyed a deep purple, like night sky when there weren't clouds about. She had a sophisticated fringe; it was a bowl cut, but with some saw-teeth-like texture to the bangs, which were a bit loose, so it didn't look severe, and there was a peak detail at the centre, but it actually worked for her. She had trailing locks of hair in front of her ears, like tentacles from a jellyfish and a neat head band braid in the centre of her crown and two smaller braids wrapped around the side of her head and joined a really long, mid-height ponytail down to her bum, which swung out left to right as she walked to the bar. Her right hand reached up and removed the shades from her face.

This lass was so youthful-looking with these proper big eyes. Her large, caricature-like eyes were blue like ice caps, the right was slightly brighter, and she didn't appear to be wearing any makeup. Emily sank with envy, she was compelled to admit that this lass was *prettier* than herself! In fact, she might just be the most gorgeous lass she had ever seen in person. And she was real tall— well over six feet with an amazing vase-shaped figure held up by these long legs. The customer sat down at the bar stool right in front of Emily, placed her hat down on the counter along with her elbows, the lads behind still gawking at her. She peeled her jacket apart and set it down on her seat. She was wearing a sleeveless, non-revealing, dark purple vest tucked into her jeans, had a B cup size bust, a perfectly flat stomach and muscles on her arms like an Olympic athlete. Her ears were pierced with basic silver studs, one in each earlobe, a pair in the tragus and another pair on the forward helix.

"I'll have twelve vodka shots," the tall lass requested and stylishly slotted her shades against the top rim of her vest like a celeb.

"Got any ID on yah love?" Emily needed to ask, and the lass promptly went into her jacket with one hand, no fumbling around, just a single, smooth dip where she handed out a leathery cardholder and opened it up with her thumb. This lass looked brilliant in her photo like a Da Vinci painting, despite not being able to smile and do any other quirks the arsehole government said you couldn't do. Her name was **Luna J. Premos**, she was 26 years of age as of the seventeenth of this month and was born in Leeds. She had such a lovely first name! Her surname sounded French.

"Cheers love!" Emily thanked as she handed Luna back her ID.

"Wish I looked as nice on me ID!" She complained. Luna stuffed her ID back into her jacket then reached over the counter and helped herself to a sliced strawberry.

"Go ahead, love…" Emily said initially stunned by the cheekiness, but wasn't complaining. Luna paid for her drinks by card and Emily got them sorted out arranging a dozen shot glasses into a horizontal holder, then poured vodka into them with a single, experienced sweep of her arm.

"You got mates joining you?" She questioned the customer.

"No," Luna said, "I'm here by myself."

Her voice was very distinctive; it was low and child-like, smooth but with an unknown accent. Emily presented her the shot rack. Luna picked up the first shot, downed it and placed it on the counter. Then she reached for a second. Emily grinned.

"You're gonna drink *all* of 'em?" she asked concerned. Luna then drank the second glass.

"Not just yet," she said and placed it neatly in row with the first shot glass.

"How you today? What's your plans?" Emily asked making conversation.

"Arrived here without any of that plane turbulence!" Luna answered. Had she got caught in this unusual storm? Emily had been on this flight back from Lisbon during some turbulence which had shook the plane about, it was as though a child had grabbed a rattle and shook it, people had been screaming, yelping and panicking—Mum had been one of them—and when the pilot had announced the successful flight back people were clapping.

"I know what you mean!" A smiling Emily said then asked, "You fly in from Leeds and Bradford?"

Luna shook her head.

"Manchester?" Emily suggested. Luna shook her head again.

"Just come back from the Arctic Circle." Luna said. Emily hadn't heard that from anyone before.

"Oh? *What* were you doing there?" She asked. What was there in the North Pole anyway other than ice caps, polar bears, reindeer and Santa Claus?

"Swimming with *humpback whales.*" Luna replied.

"Whales?" Emily said smiling with just the right side of her face. "I wouldn't dream of getting in the water with 'em!"

Luna flashed a smile of her own.

"Oh you can!" She said back, turning her head in the direction of the rowdy lads behind her. "As long as you know them…"

She picked up and downed her third shot.

"I love whales! And I'm a bit different from my Viking ancestors…" She said coolly.

"Oh, you're Scandinavian?" Emily said. Luna was way *too* tall for an English lass, and them eyes of hers were too bright, and it would also explain why she was so pretty. Luna didn't answer the question though.

"So…were you born here? Where you from, Norway or Sweden?" Emily asked.

"Iceland, mostly." Luna answered, and hearing that Emily could only think of pure, icy cold weather with no sunlight for half the year. It really wasn't some place Emily was keen on visiting. Luna stood up and turned around exposing her ponytail, which was the length of a child was tall! And it didn't look like she was wearing extensions. She walked off in the direction of the ladies room, shaking the most amazing bum ever! It was like Mum's, like it had had a very serious workout done on it. Emily wanted to ask Luna about her workout routine when she returned.

~

Emily poured herself a can of this strawberry pop exclusive to Zaks and Marias into a highball glass and went on her break, but did so stood behind the bar, not wanting any of them gobby lot to come up to her. A remix of *just be good to me* was playing when she checked her phone, Mum had sent her a text telling her she was going to order takeout for when she returned, which was nice. What should she have though? Another curry? Then Luna returned, distracting Emily from her phone's screen. She seemed to slide into view from the right side of the bar, her hat and jacket draped over her left forearm and carrying the rest of her shots in their tray with just her fingertips, and without asking for permission she set her jacket down on the seat in front of Emily and sat down, her tall figure obscuring all behind her.

Emily didn't say owt—to be honest she welcomed her company. Luna dropped the shot tray down an inch from the counter's edge without causing any racket, Emily counted eight swilling glasses remaining. The tall Scandinavian lass was so pretty, and Emily was probably going to have to apologies repeatedly for saying it to her. Her nose was beautifully pronounced with a bit of an upward curve, her eyebrows were tan shaded with no signs of plucking, her lips soft and pink, her cheeks high with a droop that accentuated her jaw line. She had these bags beneath her eyes, while not summat any lass would want, they didn't make her appear aged at all, they actually made her eyes appear bigger.

"How long'd it take you to grow your hair?" Emily needed to ask.

"Eight years," Luna answered. That was just too long! Most lasses would change their mind and go for a different hairstyle by then!

"I went to the salon last week for a modern look." Luna said then picked up and tossed back another shot.

"New look, aye?" Emily remarked. "How much did it cost you?"

"Over thirty thousand kroner." Luna replied.

"What's that?" Emily asked. Wasn't that Swedish currency?

"Near two hundred in sterling." Luna answered.

"Take us weeks to save up for that!" Emily said.

"Not with you…!" Luna said, a reply or what Emily was unsure of.

"What were that?" She said. Luna didn't answer her. She did another shot. She didn't appear tipsy, didn't show any of that rapid eye movement. And she didn't blink that much.

"Not drunk yet?" Emily challenged.

"I'd…be useless if I was!" Luna replied just before one of the lads in the background could drown out her words. They roared out F words and started drumming their hands on the table like arseholes, which had the lasses laughing. Obviously they had been drinking before they had come in here and it was turning out to be a repeat of earlier. One of the lads had a Scouse accent and one of them spiky flick fringes and a heavy brow that gave him a perpetual frown, even though he had a full, toothy smile. He got out of his seat, headed for the bar and approached Luna calling out, "Ear love?"

The tall lass didn't look back at him.

"Ear love?" He repeated with a raised voice, stubbing his foot against his other and almost tripping. Again, Luna didn't react.

"Love yah hair…!" The approaching lad said immaturely while his mate at the table giggled.

"It's like fuckin' *Rapunzel*—I could climb up it!" He said rudely, made a pulling motion with his hands then started calling back to his mates, that dodgy Valerie lass was laughing with her eyes shut tight. Still, Luna didn't react to him.

Then he looked at Emily and asked to be served. Still seated and partly grinning, she shook her head.

"I'm not serving yah!" She said.

"What? Why?" The unruly customer barked in protest.

"For fuck sake, why's everyone always pickin' on him?" The black lass shouted out, cutting him off before he could start further.

"Chill out!" Valerie added in, looking Emily's way. "We all love Ash!"

That wasn't helping, especially for someone so polished and full of them self. Emily wanted summat humiliating to happen to her; like if she shat herself at the table that would be enough at the least. She felt that lift of rapture again, though not as strong as earlier.

Then Luna started laughing, for what reason Emily didn't know. The tall lass had this addictive laugh; it was low, lazy but full of character. Before Emily could ask what the reason was, there was commotion from the other three at the table, they were squinting their eyes and making these disgusted expressions.

"Were that you?" The other lad said. The Valerie lass got out of her seat and quickly trotted away.

"Fuckin' hell!" The two at the table exclaimed, showing disgusted expressions with the other lass waving her hand and coughing. The Scouse fella was staggering back to the table, twitching with all this erratic and edgy body language and all, then he started kicking one of the chairs, though he didn't make any physical contact with it that was just daft and intimidating. Emily didn't say owt about it. But then summat smelt proper bad. It was like that trip to the loo in the ward earlier but not as bad, although still it was awful and likely from the Scouse fella as booze made people inconsiderate.

"Fuck sake!" Emily mouthed and covered her nose with the back of her right hand. Luna though was unresponsive to the stench and downed another shot. Emily didn't want to get out her seat, but with the smell of fart in the air she couldn't help and after an irritable sigh, she stood up.

"Fuckin' hell!"

She didn't keep her voice down. Did she have to press the panic button again? Luna reached over the bar, picked up Emily's empty strawberry pop can and got up out of her seat, striding towards the table of loudmouths and showing off a mesmerising roll to her hips.

"Think you better leave…!" Luna said boldly to the drunk Scouse lad, like some decent people rarely did.

"What…?" The fella said. Luna raised her can-carrying arm, her lift elegant as a swan raising its neck.

"Hold still," she was heard telling the lad who chuckled and said, "You what?"

Luna didn't repeat herself for the lad, and somehow she was able to place the can on top of his head without him reacting, because he was stood so still from his confusion.

"What yah doin'…?" He muttered, looking ready to laugh or say summat else rude. Luna turned around, gave the fella her back then walked back to the bar. Then she did summat amazing; she spun around with her long leg extended and swung it like a crane arm at lightning speed in some karate shite move. She kicked the can off the lad's head, it made that typical crack when crushed, and it was sent flying towards the bar. Before Emily could complain the flight of the can lowered and it landed in the bin behind the counter, as though that was where it wanted to be. Ignoring that she could have knocked the lad's head right off, Luna returned to the bar, with the fella just stood there blinking and them lot at the table not reacting the way some people would; they looked hesitant.

Emily suddenly felt like that YouTube worthy stunt was a normal, everyday thing, though her blinking eyes and twitching of her cheeks, readied for a laugh suggested otherwise. Luna sat back down, her fingers picking up another shot.

"You…do martial arts?" Emily asked Luna who looked at her with a frozen expression that made her big eyes appear hypnotic.

"I've been in a couple of conflicts," she replied. "Not worth speaking about."

She grunted, as though she had thought of summat interesting.

"It's in your hands now!" She said. Emily heard her clearly. Though she would ask her to explain she knew in her heart, precisely what she meant.

The lass at the table made this loud laugh, snapped out of her trance. Then one of the lads joined her in it. Emily looked their way and squinted. *You lot, leave…!* She thought strongly. The world felt like it was moving in slow motion, she remembered rewinding a video when she was a child from end to beginning and was entranced by the moment and Nan was there, asking what she was doing. The lads and lass at the table went silent like the people had earlier today and then headed for the door at the same time. The sound of Luna placing a shot glass down was the last sound heard before quiet returned to the bar, before David Bowie *it ain't easy* blasted over the speakers. With the smell of shite out of the air and calm about Emily, wobbly with excitement, was ready to have a stimulating conversation with Luna.

"I'd like a burger!" The tall lass requested, her voice sounded engaging—cinematic if not. The sort of thing for some reason you wanted to replay like a music track.

"They do really nice burgers here!" Emily informed her. Luna reached out to her left and plucked up the single page menu lying down on the counter, and without even looking pointed at one option as though she had already decided long in advance.

"The American burger," she asked. Even though she was on her break, Emily got up and processed her order at the till, though the tall lass had to sit at a table. But before she could ask, Luna got up out of her seat, carrying her garments the same way she had earlier and with her shot tray, sitting at the closest table from the bar.

While burying her attention on her phone's screen, which had plenty of texts, Emily went in back and fetched her compact mirror from her handbag. Luna's burger arrived, served by April and Emily leaned back against the liquor counter and put on another coating of lip gloss, looked the tall lass's way and noticed her pick up a bottle of that lovely house hot sauce with one hand and lift the top bun of her burger with the other. It was natural to put a splash of the hot sauce on summat here, but no, she doused it like it was ketchup! Nearly all the sauce was gone from the bottle and it had Emily stall in disbelief! She felt like saying summat. With just one hand, the giant lass ate her burger, and took another bite like it was nowt. And normally you'd get mess and juices dripping out, but she tilted her burger, took a mouthful and rotated it then bit off another mouthful and repeated. She was proper weird!

"Your burger alright?" Emily called out and made a smile on the right side of her face. Luna didn't answer and kept on eating in this cartoon-like manner. Emily put her phone away in her back pocket and stood up straighter.

"What your plans for the rest of the day? Meeting friends?" She asked her. Luna just looked at her like she was on pause.

"I have friends," she said after a delay. "They're your friends, too. But I like to say family."

What did that mean exactly? Luna ate her burger and made a grunt of satisfaction. Emily felt her phone buzz against her bum from a text and was halfway through investigating when that Valerie lass returned, heels echoing.

The fake blonde went to her table, discovered that her mates were gone, she whipped her head about searching, all puzzled and that. And she had been absent for quite a while! Emily didn't need to guess why… That had taught her a lesson! Instead of leaving to join her mates she slouched forward over the table. She looked unwell, paranoid even; in need of healing or summat, and she clutched her stomach. Emily wasn't concerned about her, and the duty of insisting she sit down and order another drink had vanished from her staff etiquette. The counter glowed gold as the bar's lights suddenly flickered blue, which had Emily look up and question herself if that was even part of the bar's colour display.

"You take charge!" Luna said, even though she hadn't moved her lips. Emily blinked, realising that she had heard her inside her head.

"Just *tell* them…" Luna said with her mouth this time.

Chapter 15

Stretched out along the Northern Hemisphere was an enormous, extended continental landmass, comprising of two continents known as *Eurasia*, its western edges fringing the expanse of a mighty Atlantic Ocean. This interconnecting land had descended from what had been a once long broken and divided Laurasia, through the ceaseless shifting of tectonic movement and its enduring impact on the region. Towering glaciers and ice caps dominated the north, the glaciers dripped with water, slowly releasing it into the salty seas and pieces of it regularly broke off, and fell into the seas from small as pebbles to large chunks, the size of rocks that fell from beyond the clouds. Mountains were prevalent in a region the centre south. The sea was cold and grey in the west territory that was the Atlantic Ocean. In the east were expanses of snow-covered tundra, stretching far across the planet, concealing most of its features.

Near the coastal fringe, hundreds of short miles south from the ice caps was an island surrounded by several smaller, sister ones, those on the east of which were interconnecting land bridges to the vastness of Eurasia. Depressive grey skies lingered above the coastlines of these regions, and congregating around them were large colonies of *pinguinus impennis*, or great auks. The coastline resonated with their honks, and the rocks were stained grey/white with their guano. These peculiar birds stood four feet tall with black beaks with slanted, grooved ridges, their bodies covered in sleek black plumage and oval, off-white bellies. While their smaller, aerial relatives flew above them these grand specimens stood in an upright posture instead of horizontal and had short wings with no feathers, the males were distinguished by white patches around their beaks.

The auks didn't move with that steady gait of normal birds, instead they shifted their weight side to side, *waddling* slowly on black webbed feet with their wings outstretched. Some members of the colony were heading for the sea, wading into the water, where they dived gracefully beneath the waves and exploded into bursts of speed that carried them away from the shore. The short wings of the great auks had been repurposed for swimming, the beats propelling them like flippers as they darted under the freezing waters, leaving a thin trail of white bubbles behind them.

Resting on another area of the shore were herds of *odobenus rosmarus*, or walruses. These bulky beasts, commonly weighing in around a ton, had pouted muzzles with long, yellowish whiskers, their hind limbs almost fused together, the joints concealed by a thick layer of brown blubber to give them a singular shape while their hands and feet had evolved into paddled flippers. Their blubber was incredibly thick and insulated them from the freezing temperatures and acted secondarily as armour from predators. And it took plenty of effort to make a healthy walrus bleed, never mind kill. Despite appearances, they were actually members of the carnivora order of mammals.

Though they had formidable metre long tusks in place of canine teeth which could end a predator, they were docile animals, their tusks were mainly used for probing shellfish from the seabed. The walruses emitted chesty grunts and bleats, and moved along the rocky shores on their bellies with their fore flippers, their blubber flubbed lively as if bubbling. While seemingly sluggish, they could accelerate in a charge whether that be at a rival or a predator. Washed up on shore were fossilised *megalodon* teeth, which were plentiful, but not as much as those of the countless species of long extinct ammonites they mingled with as well as the teeth of much smaller sharks.

~

There was a larger bridge of land connecting that archipelago to Eurasia, called *Doggerland*. Snow began to fall, it was light, slow and steady. The dreaded winter had arrived. Running packs of *canis lupis*, better known as: grey wolves were a common sight on the steppes. These swift, coordinated cainids were a constant, abundant threat to anything that bore flesh. The carnivora had exploded into a diversity of apex predators, many of which were hyper carnivorous. Some predators of this icy landscape though were less plentiful, but existing through their own unique lifestyle, such as *homotherium*, also known as: the scimitar-toothed cat.

This three plus feet high felid was a mile away from the wolves and moving out of their range, having picked up their scent downwind from them.

Homotherium was the fastest predator in the area, long legs with non-retractable claws allowed for short bursts of speed, its body compacted with a muscular neck, a sloping back and a pitifully short tail. Its skull was low and rectangular, long whiskers spread out around its muzzle, green/yellow eyes peered forward, ears had brown edges, nostrils dark brown with wide nasal passages, and the body covered in an elegant cool, light grey/khaki pelt with faint brown spots that were elongated horizontally along the neck and flanks.

Against the sun muted by the grey clouds the homotherium opened its mouth, yawning and exposing long, yellowed double-edged canine teeth with serrations on both sides. This predator had the fangs of a specialist. The scimitar-toothed cat's range was vast, inhabiting five continents including the northern sector of the interconnected New World, known as the *Americas* on the other side of the Atlantic. But homotherium's days were numbered. The wolves were one of many competitors pushing its existence to the edge, thus perpetuating a historic rivalry between cainid and felid. In this part of Western Eurasia there were lower sea levels on account of the big freeze, with fresh water locked in the glaciers north.

This prolonged chill was dissipating, as the planet naturally began to warm from its periodic fluctuation every couple of tens of millions of years. More fresh water being dispensed into the seas resulted in rising sea levels and incurred altered weather patterns. Land bridges and lower lands were slowly beginning to flood, a fading window of opportunity for anything that intended to journey to these areas on foot. *Something wasn't right*, hadn't been for several generations as far back as words could illustrate. A flock of honking geese flew over a leafless forest further inland, a depressive environment with the songs of the birds remedying such feelings to anything that could feel such emotion. Like the *Neanderthal man* walking through the woodland with a spear, a foot taller than he was in his right hand constructed from a tree branch with the twigs shaved off, ending in sharpened flint held in place by tightened animal hide, and carried over his left shoulder was the carcass of a boar he had slaughtered after chasing it into a pit he had covered with twigs and leaves.

Mammals had come incredibly far. The last four million years had been hyper charged in the variety, but in the last couple hundred thousand years the big global chill had produced a new species… This particular mammal stood upright on plantigrade feet, his hands free from the ground, his light, delicate and mostly hairless flesh protected from the cold by sewn together animal hide, intricately wrapped in layers to form a secondary skin, his feet were insulated from the cold wrapped in various layers of hide tied in place by strips of it. This Neanderthal male was called Hands of Rock, or HORs for short. He was a diligent hunter and a master tracker whom had killed many a beast during his 20 years of existence. The dirt and grime ridden fur of a lion he had trapped in a pit, intended for something bigger he had killed with his spear, he wore with pride as a cloak, draped around his shoulders over a tunic of brown and grey shaded pelt.

HORs was everything required of a male; at 5'5" he was taller than the average Neanderthal man with broad shoulders, a tubby chest and muscular arms. Not a centimetre on his body was without a smear, and his flesh bore plenty of scars and grazes, two ribs on his left had been broken with a lump formed beneath the flesh, his left middle finger had been dislocated and snapped back into place, and he had a knob of healed bone over his left collar bone, his most distinctive injury was a curved healed gash on his left jaw that looked like a second set of lips. HORs had a pasty, wind grazed face, his forehead was short and sloped backwards, his eyebrows ridged and big brown eyes bulgy. His nose was wide and bulbous, nostrils encrusted with mucus, his cracked lips had a pronounced pout, long reddish brown, unkempt hair was spread out in all directions. Balancing the boar on his left, he raised his shoulder as he raked the dirtied, grit and rotted meat-stained fingers of that arm though his scraggly facial hair.

HORs was heading back to his tribe's campsite. The site was concentrated mostly in a limestone cave on the foot of a cliff face carved out from glaciers that had retreated from the area thousands of years ago from the warming planet, which provided invaluable shelter, especially from rainfall. These formations were very common throughout Western Eurasia. The site had lit fires spaced out to keep the inhabitants warm, as well as to cook whatever meat the men brought back from their hunts. Meat over fire had become common practise with this tribe, since a couple of tribe's members from a previous generation had fallen ill and died, seemingly from the regular custom of eating raw meat. Cooked meat with all them burnt bits tasted *better*, was there a way of making it taste…much better?

Animal hides from this year's hunts were being processed, scraped of tissue and hung about to dry on racks made from tree branches, some were seen being sliced into strips for binding, the pelts stretched out with one hand while being held between teeth, while the other hand hacked through with sharpened flint.

Some of these pelts were *extremely* large and could clothe the entire tribe of twenty-nine. HORs acknowledged a fellow male tribe member Lascaux, a veteran of twenty-two winters and the most respected member of the tribe after himself and the chief, his face heavily pockmarked and with hair down to his back, crudely tied in place, his beard had been trimmed raggedly. Lascaux was carrying a rabbit by its ankles in one hand, HORs landed a large hand down heavily on his shoulder and was reciprocated with a laugh.

HORs kneeled down and smacked the boar down on the ground so the others could butcher and cook it over fire and went in search of his object of desire. Blood Stone, a Neanderthal woman, was sat down on a large stone by a fire draped with animal hide for comfort, several other stones were placed around the fire in a circle, her back turned to HORs as he approached her, the tribe's children hollering as they ran around her. She was the centre of attention and a surrogate mother to many of the children, some of whom had died giving birth to them. Blood Stone was an orphan herself, taken in by this tribe. She had been given a red rock upon birth by her long gone father, which had inspired her name. Blood Stone had been through seventeen winters and was the most desired female of the tribe's populace. She looked over her shoulder, spotted the approaching HORs and smiled.

Getting around her yellowed teeth, crusted, dry lips and heavily flaking skin on her face, she had wide, deep set eyes as grey as the winter sky with a slight squinted accent, her cheeks were high and sunken with a squared jaw. With the exception of her thick arms and head, her body was draped in a coarsely stitched dark bear hide, which HORs and the tribe's hunters had also trapped and killed. Blood Stone's dark, curled hair was swept back messily from her face and held back ingeniously with a bone that distinguished her from the rest of the tribe's women. She wanted to know other ways of making herself more…*presentable*, whether that be the feather of a bird, or strips of animal fur which were always appealing. Only the voice of others could tell her, as she couldn't assess her own appearance. She looked away, distracted by one of the children nagging for her attention.

HORs was looking at Blood Stone, contemplating his next move with her when the tribe's chief, Go'Bok appeared. The alpha had survived forty winters, his long hair greyed, eyebrows absurdly bushy and deep creases all over his heavily withered, orangey face, some folded over giving it a mashed, pulpy appearance, his eyes were so heavily wrinkled that he had a perpetual squint. He had a long beard, tied up below his chin while the hair on the sides of his face had been sheered away. Although Go'Bok was muscular he had been crippled from a hunt many years ago, where he had shattered his right leg from a blow by a mammoth which caused him to limp along uselessly. His duties as a hunter were long over, but his wisdom kept him useful to the tribe, and he was well looked after.

Behind Blood Stone's back HORs lowered his knees and stealthily crept towards her, his fellow tribes members discreetly observing as he kneeled down and buried his palm in a patch of some white ash from a previous fire on the ground. Directly behind her he took hold of her and jerked her back, she yelped as HORs smeared the white ash over Blood Stone's face, turning it white. She cringed, coughed and tussled with her stronger brethren who managed to pin her to the ground, her bear hide gown spread out all over the floor.

HORs kneeled over her, eyes beckoning down while witnesses exploded into laughter, teeth of varying shades of yellow and white exposed with the children jumping up and down. Approval of the enthusiastic two had been unanimous with the tribe for a while. Blood Stone coughed, jutted her tongue out then looked up at her subjugator, the two staring at each other for a prolonged moment. The distraction allowed Blood Stone to dig her fingers into the ground and grab a handful of dirt, which she slapped and smeared over HOR's right cheek. He allowed her to continue for a few more seconds before grabbing hold of that wrist. Blood Stone arm wrestled with him but was defeated, HORs tenderly reached for her hair and pinched a lock of it. Blood Stone laughed.

~

A Neanderthal girl was running playfully around the camp, when really, she had been tasked by her mother to collect firewood from the forest edge surrounding the site. She had bushy ochre brown hair, her nose not as broad as the adults, yet and donned a simple gown of tarpan hide. She jumped over a log, one of several laid down by the tribe's men as a barrier against any animals that might enter the camp and ventured further out. Time and time prior she had been warned about predators; a certain noise would prompt her to run back to the camp at full speed. After foraging the child had an armful of wood in both arms and was on her way back. She stopped upon spotting several small fiery orbs between the trees to her left, slowly moving her way. Torches of fire from another tribe were they? Other Neanderthal arrived at this camp every few weeks, or sometimes months. Always they were a source of fortune; men and women got together, left and returned with babies the following year or two.

Instead of informing the tribe the Neanderthal girl remained stood, in excitement. The other tribe appeared into view from the cover of the forest, torched branches and spears in hand. The Neanderthal child did not recognise any of them, simply because she couldn't identify what they were. They were different from her kind. They were slimmer and taller, their skin was darker, like lighter shades of wood, their heads were taller, their noses longer, thinner with pointed tips, their faces had smoother, more defined features. Their clothing was more sophisticated, woven tighter and more intricately and covered their bodies completely, some members had smears of coloured dirt on their faces in elaborate patterns and sophisticated styles of hair. This individualistic group of men were *Cro-Magnon*. The two species stared at each other. While the Neanderthal girl stood still, two members of the spooked Cro-Mag tribe said something alien to the child, who didn't know how to react. Especially when they shouted and came running forward remorselessly. The child dropped the wood.

~

The winter sun was setting. And away from the Neanderthal clan, a lone grey wolf ventured down the slope before a river system to drink, its muddy banks were littered with imprints of big, circular feet along with large piles of green dung. The wolf lapped up several tongues of ice-cold water, undisturbed before a beast emerged from the chilly waters stepping onto the sludgy banks to the left, causing small tidal waves in the process and emitting an airy snort. This was *hippopotamus antiquus*, or the European hippo. Three metres long and weighing in at two tons it was a large beast, with a broad, robust body covered in thick, brown hairless hide that shined from the water racing off its body, stubby multi-toed legs supported this bulk. The hippo had this massive head nearly a third of its body mass with a broad muzzle, tall eye sockets a pink patterning around the mouth and eyes, its oval-shaped ears fluttering and flicking off water.

In the grand, hot continent *Africa* a thousand miles south of Doggerland, cold-blooded crocodiles patrolled the waters. But up in the glacial-locked north the waters were far too cold for reptilian predators. And the European hippo thrived here, in a region where there were far more lethal, calculating predators. Even though herbivorous they were belligerent beasts, with jaws that could crush any apex predator. The lone wolf did not retreat and boldly continued to drink, even as the hippo yawned revealing its yellowed, tusked teeth. Its thirst satiated, the wolf ran back up the slope to join the rest of its pack on the clearing above, which were facing the way of a fire in a forested area further west that became more vivid as dusk transitioned into night. The pack became curious and began trotting in the direction.

~

Daylight. The entire camp had been ravaged, smoke still billowing from fires that had been set to every dwelling, not that there had been much to burn to begin with. Nervously, a trembling Blood Stone emerged from a pile of branches and dried moss kept towards the rear of the cave, a stash of firewood that had concealed her after she had run for her life upon seeing one of these Cro-Mags put a spear through the back of An'th, one of the tribe's women, her first friend since being adopted by the tribe. While hidden, Blood Stone had had to listen to the sounds of her community being slaughtered, and when the screams died down there were roars of triumph, the sound of beams being knocked over followed by the rapidly thickening smell of smoke. Blood Stone had sat as still as she could for hours, the slightest noise triggering her into panic. She hadn't slept a wink, and once dawn had come her eyes (adjusted to the extended darkness) had been momentarily blinded.

She ventured out anxiously from the cave, every mangled, motionless body on the floor her eyes set upon caused her to cringe and weep in silence. Every few feet were trails of blood leading to a body of what had once been a fellow Neanderthal Blood Stone had relied on for her survival. She passed by the roasting spit set up for what would have been last night's dinner, the boar HORs had brought for the tribe to eat was gone, only blood and the uncleared organs from the butchery were what remained. And to add to that, almost all of the precious, dried out animal hides had been raided. Blood Stone stopped upon spotting Go'Bok sprawled on the floor with several gaping holes in his torso. She wanted to approach him, though knew she couldn't do anything to help him. She turned her head to the left and discovered that not even the young ones had been spared. This was a remorseless massacre.

There were far too many bodies in sight for Blood Stone to accost, so many she couldn't hold in her arms. Without any concern for her own safety, she cried out aimlessly and dropped to her knees. Seconds and minutes passed by as she sobbed, no sounds of the killers were heard in response. Blood Stone got back on her feet and walked with the greatest indecision of her life; she really wanted to walk away from the camp, but at the same time she wanted to stay. Neither choice seemed good for her. During this slow and dazed walk forward she discovered HORs who was lying on his side, she noticed his prized lion pelt had been stripped from him. She kneeled over him and shook him desperately, hoping he hadn't perished. He was too strong for that. He stirred, his eyes opened, he groaned and rolled over onto his right side, he winced and clutched the back of his head, his palm covered with coagulated blood.

HORs recalled trying to fight off one of these murderous, alien invaders, had been close to putting a spear through its chest, when he had been struck over the head from behind and rendered unconscious. They probably thought that alone would have killed him, but he had been through worse, and it was going to take more than a petty blow to the head to bring down this experienced hunter. HORs was comforted momentarily by the sight of Blood Stone looking down on him, before the reality stabbed him like a stone knife through several layers of hide and fat of the thickest skinned game out there. He rolled his head left to see the eradication of his tribe from one angle, then another. Every turn yielded horrors not even his physical strength and endurance could prepare him for. At the sight of one of the dead children lying with his half opened eyes gazing permanently up at the sky, HORs ground his teeth and exploded into tears, stricken by his failure to defend his tribe. Blood Stone wrapped her arms around him and held him like she had held the tribe's children. Who better to console him right now?

Both wept for a lengthy period, exposed out in the open, their tears freezing their faces. They moved about the camp, searching for survivors with any hope of recovery no matter how badly injured they were. All the bodies were as cold as the winter chill—there was no one to save. HORs and Blood Stone were the only two left of the tribe. Both wanted to stay, hold their dear kin and express their grief before enduring the dreaded tradition of moving the bodies away from the camp, far into the deep of the forest. But it wasn't safe to do either task. The raiders may very well return to eliminate any survivors.

The sudden, piercing howl of a wolf ripped through the morning ambience, spooking the lonely pair who looked about in all directions. That howl was followed by another, then another in a threatening chain reaction, a pack of an unknown number cascading through the forest.

With no tribe to back them up the howls of the wolves heard were more threatening, and with the weight of the situation bearing down upon her, Blood Stone covered her ears and ground her teeth, stressed. HORs though landed a hand on her shoulder reassuringly and ran a short distance away, not to escape the situation, but acquire two spears from a communal rack, which surprisingly hadn't been raided. Without adequate clothing the pair were going to freeze in the winter, HORs reappeared with some rolled up auroch hides held underneath each armpit, which contained whatever essentials he could scrounge up.

He and Blood Stone desperately wanted to do something about the dead, but the necessity to leave was finally decided by the mega threatening groan of something that terrified both: a bear. The Neanderthal pair remained quiet, looked around and crept back. Then the bear appeared in sight onto the burned down camp from the left. It was an *ursus spelaeus*, or cave bear. It was a broad, bulky beast taller than a Neanderthal at the shoulder with dark brown fur, moving along on thick, muscular limbs that could break a human hunter with a single swipe.

The cave bear stopped, tilted its head back, loudly sniffing the air, head turning slightly with a bobbing motion. It snorted erratically before rocking back onto its hind legs where it stood at over three metres tall, some patches of lighter fur revealed on the chest region as it continued to sniff in that pose, its big head sweeping about, searching for something that might pose a threat to its presence. The cave bear groaned, thick icy breath steaming out from its mouth, before it fell back on its front paws. The bear was out to gorge itself and build a fat layer for the winter, and the site's now unoccupied cave was an ideal spot for it to wait out the winter. The Neanderthal couple held their breath and quietly backed away, not daring to take their eyes off the bear, even as it began to bite into the corpse of their former leader. Though HORs and Blood Stone were together, this was no time to embrace this much-yearned company, but rather exploit it for the sake of survival.

~

HORs and Blood Stone had to move on away from the familiar lands and head north westwards into the unknown, via Doggerland. The sky was bleak, and the land at the other end could be seen over the hazy horizon as an icy rise along with all the grey glaciers that occupied the visual of the northern horizon. The Neanderthal pair carried a spear in one hand and wrapped up hide underarm, which contained flint and carved stone blades, very basic essentials. Every few steps they looked back, checking for pursuers. There was no snowfall, but the steppes they journeyed across were damp from yesterday's light fall and their furry footwear was soaking up the moisture from the grass, they were going to have to dry it out over a fire. Other than birds flying overhead and the fleeting sight of hopping hares, the pair hadn't encountered any significantly sized fauna.

After nearly a half day on the move, they reached a forested area and sat down, stretching their feet. They hung up their footwear over a rack they had made from local branches. They had tinder, sun-dried grass from the summer safely secured within the hides HORs had retrieved. This spot wasn't too densely a foliaged forest and was too exposed, and there were no other woodlands as far as the eye could see. HORs lit a fire, and it was well over an hour before they felt warm enough to even speak to each other, though that wasn't lifting moods anyway. They were both hungry, and there was no game on the steppes or in the woods. The pair sat with their backs against a tree, snuggled against each other for warmth. The lack of activity and exchange of words HORs normally would have given Blood Stone before this situation was usurped by a sustained, fearful focus on the surrounding ambience. As of now, any odd sound or sight could mean the difference between life and death.

HORs stood up, looking out onto the steppes, as he had every half an hour or so for potential game.

He panicked upon spotting a glow of fire in the distance, and without hesitation he covered the fire with the hide meant to keep him warm for the night and gestured for Blood Stone to keep silent. Were these users of fire their own kind or that other savage species competing for dominance? With the recent, traumatic events it wasn't worth chancing it. Devoid of fire, HORs and Blood Stone sat in place as day turned into night, the only sound being missed meals in the backdrop. As the night came into full grip they snuggled against each other and blanketed themselves with the animal hides, which were too short for comfort. The night was sleepless.

~

Four more days on. A hundred miles more west, diverting northwards. A thousand grams less on the Neanderthal pair's bodies were from the lack of sustenance. The sun was up high in a cloudless sky and appeared ten times bigger than normal, encircled with rays of purple and blue and flocks of unidentifiable birds flying past its glare. The steppes were dominated by many a majestic fauna, such as the *tarpans* which were an equinid that stood on a single hoof. They were dark brown, almost grey with black mane, their hooves and ankles black, thin, bushy tails swishing about at their rears. Tarpans were a good source of meat for the Neanderthal. Mingling with the tarpans were another great source of food; the *aurochs*, another ungulate with muscular shoulders, cloven hooves, wide, long skulls and curving horns on the sides of their heads that pointed forward, their dark brown pelt was almost black.

These bovines weighing the best part of half a ton had a deadly, nimble charge; HOR's collarbone injury had been the result of such. The hides he and Blood Stone carried about came from them, and auroch provided great meat; in fact they were preferable over tarpan. Although there was plenty of game in sight, the conditions for a successful hunt were poor; the Neanderthal pair were completely exposed with no cover for an ambush. Walking further the pair encountered a crash of *coelodons*, or woolly rhinoceros, which were mostly loners with humped backs, their bodies covered in a brown shaggy fur with a band of grey wrapping around the mid flank from the upper side. The rhinos had two horns made not of bone, but fibrous keratin, the nose horn was flat, over a metre long and almost crescent-shaped with a banded patterning, the second horn behind it only a fifth of the size and conical.

The woolly rhinos were powerful herbivores not worth contending with, and that big nose horn would impale and end the life of a hunter, albeit usually not so swiftly. Should one not stand up and tend to his wounds the cold provided a cruel end to existence. Stepping into view of the rhino from the right was another horned beast, a large brown pelted ruminant with a whitish band around the abdomen, snout dark brown and hooves black; a *megaloceros*, or giant elk, even though it was more closely related to deer. This stag stood three metres high, his antlers were his most iconic feature, each one was nearly two metres long, a light bark brown and wide, curved and spiked, his head held up high with tall vertebrate and connective tendon on his back facilitating this posture. His great antlers, nearly 12 feet across from tip to tip, cast some mesmerising shadows and silhouettes as he moved and weren't ideal for moving within the confines of woodland, which seemed to be popping up against these open plains.

The stag paused, opened his mouth and raised his head, eyes bulging with the white of the eyeball visible even at a distance as he looked about. Aware of the Neanderthal presence he emitted a buzzing roar. Megaloceros were too risky a game, and there was too much of it on the steppes right now that could kill a hunter. HORs and Blood Stone sat away from the giant deer, as wolves or lions would out in the open. The absence of fellow man was…depressing on top of the grief, wounding both Neanderthal that didn't dare sob as it would draw attention. On the muddy patch to his side littered with imprints from hooves, HORs took his right index finger and unsurely began making patterns in the cold, wet soil.

~

Night. HORs and Blood Stone made camp within a skimpy thicket of naked trees near a slope leading down a shallow, rocky ravine. The cover provided was inadequate and there were no high spaces safe enough from predators. They were still exposed, so there would be no fire for tonight, just snuggling for warmth. HORs fell asleep quickly, whereas Blood Stone couldn't. She remained awake, gazing up at this most unusual sight high above her. Of all things her memory could register, there was a hazy *red* moon in the cloudless sky tonight, and a sleepless Blood Stone was captivated by it, but not in awe. In her perception of surrounding matters…this mysterious phenomenon was symptomatically ominous in ways she could not comprehend, but it had to be observed and taken in with caution.

Upon hearing a soft bleat in the distance, she sat up and looked about. She recognised the silhouettes of small deer on the plains and informed a sleeping HORs with a whisper. He awoke, acknowledged her but didn't plan on executing anything and irritably dozed back off. What would be the point blind in the dark anyway? Blood Stone remained sleepless, the red moon up high above her sole focus. She turned her head and her torso at an angle so that the sight of the branches of the winter stripped trees appeared against the odd moon, accentuating the ethereal intricacy of the sight.

~

Daybreak arrived torturously slow, the monotony and inaction of the new situation weighing down hard on Blood Stone, whom had eventually fallen asleep. HORs had awoken shortly after, the morning's sky was full of dark clouds with the promise of rain or snowfall to come. Awake but groggy from malnutrition and cold, he wrapped himself up as best he could in the hide on his body then lay on his chest and surveyed the landscape ahead of him. There were deer still about, though probably not the same Blood Stone had pointed out last night, but plenty nonetheless. HORs calculated a hunt strategy then quietly crawled back and surreptitiously shook Blood Stone awake. She was going to have to join in the hunt; one would chase a deer towards the other who would spear it. It was a hasty but necessary tactic. The light was still poor, but that aided with the tactic of ambush. The pair picked up their spears and inched in towards the open, a readied Blood Stone tense with the announcement of any instruction from HORs, as they awaited the perfect moment to branch out and execute their plan. The experienced hunter was to walk out innocuously, so as not to spook the game, looking like he was harmlessly heading out into the horizon.

But something was coming the herd's way from the left, and very fast, darting across the steppes.

HORs whipped his head in that direction and spotted a homotherium, running for that same herd of deer he sought. The startled Neanderthal pair froze and watched the deer springing away while the long toothed predator pounced on one individual with its arms outstretched. One clawed paw latched onto the rear of the fleeing prey, hooked into it with the momentum of the homotherium's dash knocking it off its hooves, causing it to tumble multiple times against the cold, muddy grass along with the predator, that coated its pelt in muck, yet managed to cling on while being flipped itself, roaring as it did. Both predator and prey scrambled to their feet, the deer's forelimbs flailing, but the homotherium with a muddied pelt managed to land its other paw down on the deer's hip and wrestle it towards its mouth, claws tearing through hide as it made its way towards its neck, the shock of the trauma causing it to lose its footing.

That's when the homotherium successfully pinned the helpless deer down with its chest, then slammed its right paw down against the side of its head, which was held down firmly. With wide-open jaws, the homotherium thrust its elongated teeth into the throat of the ungulate with the aid of its muscular neck, its back teeth clamping down on the windpipe, muffling its cries while it bled out, limbs jerking with spasms. The big felid inhaled from its exertions even while it had its mouth around its prey's throat, possible due to its wide nasal chambers. With the prey dead, the homotherium withdrew its pink stained canines, the two clean puncture wounds of its prey gushing out blood. The deadly toothed predator looked about, searching for any threat to its fresh kill—no such thing of which was seen—then opened its mouth and yawned.

Even though homotherium stood almost as tall as HORs, there was no way he was going to risk challenging it head on. The deer was sizeable enough, but the Neanderthal pair would have to wait for the felid to have its fill and salvage what was left and cook it over a flame. The homotherium consumed the deer's flesh using its incisors and molars, angling its head to the side to facilitate the sheering motion. Being able to open its mouth so wide, it didn't have such a strong bite and would waste so much of its kill in the process; its inability to crack open bone here was beneficial, leaving bountiful scraps. There was so much marrow in unbroken bone that could supplement a hungry creature, like the Neanderthal, of whom were regularly accustomed to breaking them open with rocks.

The sun eventually broke through the clouds and moved with the turn of the earth, the angle of shadows slanting and elongating with the passage of time. The two impatient Neanderthal sat with their backs against the small trunks of the trees in their thicket with caution, the sun's rays creeping into their peripheral vision.

Then they were distracted by these identifiable *laughs* that raised hairs and sent them into an instinctual panic. Carefully, the pair got into a kneeling crouch posture to investigate. Coming the way of the homotherium and its kill was a gang of *croucuta croucuta*, better known as cave hyenas. They were foul creatures shorter than the homotherium with a similar body plan with sloping backs and tiny tails, though far from as elegant; their bodies were stockier, their legs were shorter, they had a light grey pelt mapped with brown spots and a shaggy underbelly.

Snub, moist black snouts extended out from faces that appeared widened further and rounded by the presence of a surrounding, furry tuff, black, expressionless eyes peering forward, big, rounded ears spread out and a strip of fluffy dark brown mane stood up around the neck. As the hyenas cackled they exposed their teeth, which could be described easily as thick white nashers. They possessed a bite that could crush bone like it was nothing. The laughing beasts wore toothy grins and bobbed their heads about as they inspected the kill site, then lowered them as they approached, their unremitting giggles creating visible mini clouds of ice in front of them. Their dreaded looks and echoing laughs in the face of danger made this category of beast more unsettling than others.

The Neanderthal watched as a mob of them appeared and moved towards the homotherium's kill. Despite their appearance closer resembling wolves, aside from their circular black ears, they were actually in the same branch as felids. And the homotherium, as formidable as it was with its long teeth and larger size, didn't intimidate the snub-nosed hyenas which freely advanced towards it. The fanged cat growled and ran at them a few short metres and stalled in a mock dash. The hyenas fled and dispersed, making piercing laughs as they went... Then they turned back around and approached with a more guarded stance. The homotherium repeated its mock charge, with the same results. From there, each attempt became less effective at scaring away the bone-crushing gigglers, aware that they were exhausting the long-toothed predator. These specialists lacked the compact strength and stamina of the smaller, stockier predators.

The sun was setting, the steppes' grass appeared yellow, then orange as the ice age sun began to retreat from view. Worn out, the homotherium turned away and dashed off. Immediately the hyenas went in for the carcass and ripped it to pieces, the crunch of bones heard over the distance. There would be very little left on this carcass to salvage when they were done, so HORs and Blood Stone had to move. This had been a wasted day and if hunger and approaching darkness wasn't a concern, snow began to fall. It wasn't a blizzard but the flakes descending from above were thick and fluffy, and it wasn't long before the steppes turned white, the Neanderthal pair's footprints a mile back almost covered up, which a keen-nosed predator didn't require to track them.

The snowfall had ceased, yet nightfall had darkened the whitened steppes. Again, the pair had no ground to protect them from the reach of predators. In the dark, lit by the moon shining its usual soft blue/white, they walked miles more than they had to until they arrived at the edge of a coniferous forest, which was a world better than last night's thicket with the pair protected from exposure. Within the cover of the forest the pair stopped, cleared away a patch of snow on the floor, broke off snow-covered branches and began to assemble a shelter. HORs got out a handful of usable tinder, set it on the ground and produced a spark from a strike of flint, which he cautiously blew to start a fire that produced a glow of orange against the snow in front of them.

Fire was the most important resource out here, along with water, meat and shelter. The Neanderthal pair sat against each other for warmth, draping their cloaks over one another's shoulders as the fire began to do its bit. Warm enough, HORs picked up a stick, crushed up a handful of cooled down charcoal from the fire and tossed it into the exposed soil, the dampness turning it into a viscous substance. With the end of the stick he dug into the dirt, and began to creatively construct a pattern, that was somewhat recognisable. Was it a bear or hyena? Blood Stone couldn't distinguish given how crude the image was. HORs looked to her, she smiled, their moods lightening.

~

The Neanderthal pair slept decently through the night. A thick fog engulfed the steppes the next morning, that layer of snow from yesterday had disappeared, and HORs awoke to a world of grey with droplets of moisture on his face. He sat up ahead of Blood Stone, their visibility comprised, a predicament otherwise dangerous; they couldn't see anything coming at them. But they could hear these deep, beastly rumbles resonating around them, and this collective stench of dung. They weren't comfortable staying put, so they packed up post haste and ventured out onto the steppes. And every rumble heard prompted a readied spear thrust from the pair as they moved out in the misty grey open. Massive, wide shadows began to materialise from the fog, one of which appeared directly before the two, where a pair of long, smooth, white structures curving upwards, pierced through it. Bridged between them was this long, hairy appendage thicker than an arm, ending in a pair of nostrils surrounded by a fleshy, finger and thumb like grip, it was a proboscis that had to be at least three metres in length attached to a massive, hairy head.

The Neanderthal couple moved out of the way and were met with a loud, trumpeting bellow of caution, the beast turning its head their way, trunk swinging and the mouth opened with an icy blast from a roar coming out of it. Appearing onto the scene was a herd of some of the largest megafauna: *mammuthus primigenius*, or woolly mammoths. Like the hyenas and woolly rhinos, they had originated in the mighty continent south. These behemoths covered in brown, metre long hair stood nearly four metres high with peaked skulls with fluffy caps, sloping backs, their ears were short, as were their tree trunk legs, though their trailing, shaggy fur made them appear much shorter, the iconic tusks comprised of metres of glossy ivory extending from the mouth. Another individual appeared behind it to the right and raised its trunk, where it held it in its curved pose. More members of various sizes and tusk lengths appeared, the tusks of the larger males overlapped.

The Neanderthal pair tried to navigate away from them without spooking them. There were plenty of trunks and tusks swinging in agitation, rumbles, guttural growls and bellows that erratically shifted in tempo. The mammoths were alert to their presence. The range of the woolly mammoth was incredibly vast; they had thousands upon thousands of miles of plains to graze upon and even inhabited the coldest, northern most fringes of Eurasia—even the Northern Americas across the Atlantic which was connected at the further eastern ridges. They were the quintessential megafauna of this ice-cold age. To the Neanderthal, mammoths were the ultimate prey; they were a vital resource, their giant bodies provided fur, meat and their tusks and bones could be made into tools, weapons and support beams for shelter. The woolly mammoths were *everything*.

Though the Neanderthal pair were starving and confident, mammoth were not something to consider hunting. Even in perfect lighting, to hunt one down without a sizeable, vigorous tribe would be incredibly risky, never mind wasteful. HORs and Blood Stone stopped and spotted infant mammoth moving protectively near the legs of the adults, they lacked the tusks and domed crowns. There was no way they were going to attempt to kill one and risk the wrath of the herd. But Neanderthal weren't the only hunters of mammoth calves. Unseen to the pair, a pack of wolves appeared on scene, yellow and black eyes against a furry grey and white face and ears standing up straight. They could smell the couple but were too focused on the abundance of moving, sizable hairy flesh. One of them licked its lips.

Time to move clear. HORs and Blood Stone negotiated the fog, following the round footprints of the mammoths embedded in the moist grass while cautious of their moving silhouettes and the barks of wolves, they expected to jump out from the mist. Over the next few minutes the ground became slightly steeper, and there were uneven boulders of moss-ridden rock in sight. The Neanderthal pair climbed up onto a rise, which was safe enough from the reach of wolves and hunkered down, both sat together draped in the auroch hide they carried with them, but lit no fire. Slowly, the fog began to thin…the mammoths and the wolves stalking them were still in sight. This spot seemed safe, and as far as the eye could see the wolves hadn't made any kills and the mammoths were grazing the grass of the steppes. Then the fog lifted, the mammoths hadn't moved. Cold, HORs lit a fire, the pair stayed together on their rock, the mammoths aware of the flames in the distance, but not instigating any calls of panic. With no opportunities to hunt presented before them they sat in place, until the sun sank beneath the horizon and left a glowing wink seen by many eyes for hundreds upon thousands of miles.

~

Night. On the rise, the Neanderthal couple slept as well as the previous night. Until awoken. By what HORs was unsure, he sat up quickly then looked around down the rise, Blood Stone followed. There was moonlight above them, no snowfall had settled on the steppes. The knot in their starving stomachs, tightening with urgency restricted their postures. Heard were these bestial groans, and both Neanderthal nervously bent down and reached for their spears lying next to them. HORs was faster, and more agile as he lowered his posture, extending his spear forward in less than a second, then spun around in the opposite direction. With their back to each other and spear flints aimed at the steppes, the pair looked about the dark landscape from all angles, there wasn't a mammoth in sight.

Another groan was heard from somewhere to the right of the rise—*wolves?* Not wolves, it was a different noise; it was lower but more robust. It wasn't as heavy as a bear's either. Whatever it was, should it be spotted it shouldn't have an eye taken off it.

Blood Stone felt HORs grab hold of her arm from behind. Slowly, she turned around and saw what he saw just below the rise. There were these pair of glowing spheres reflecting the moonlight—all the land predators produced eye shine— but it wasn't clear what it was, other than that it was big. A puff of icy air came between the pair of eyes before they vanished as the unknown predator turned around and disappeared into the dark of the night. Several tense minutes passed before the Neanderthal pair were comfortable enough to sit down. HORs was tempted to light a fire, but refrained with Blood Stone snuggling against him, her eyes whipping warily about. Hours passed…dawn approaching painfully slow, fatigue rendering the pair dreary as they anxiously continued to watch the steppes.

Eventually daybreak came and with it, a pinkish light saturated the steppes, advancing towards the rise the Neanderthal pair sat on, the moss-ridden rocks appeared brown. Another one of them alarming groans was heard after so long, which prompted HORs and Blood Stone to spring up on their feet, searching the steppes with a single small bird flying past their view from the right. With the improved lighting, the pair could see a hint of the source of their prolonged terror; a pale, upward curving tail ending with a tuff of darker fur quickly disappearing out of view behind one of the rocks of the rise. Then a vigilant HORs spun around, cautiously stepped forward and investigated below, where he spotted the tail's owner galloping into view: *panthera spelaea*. A cave lion. They were bigger than their arid dwelling African ancestors and weighed over a quarter of a ton, the fur was pale, soaking up the sunrise light which gave it a soft reddish tint with faint, patchy outlines of spots and some shaggy fur at the belly, making it appear bigger.

This individual was a lioness, and it was clambering up one of the rocks onto the rise. Too front heavy, cave lions could not climb trees, though they were capable of scaling objects their height or more. And these rocks around the rise were no exception. HORs screamed and thrust his spear forward defensively in a repeated jabbing motion.

The lioness paused, both its paws still clinging onto the rock. How to engage it from there? HORs contemplated in a reserved panic. The lioness remained still, its eyes staring up at would-be prey, its head was massive; nearly as wide as HOR's chest. The lioness made this snorting noise and jerked its head right a few short inches, which promoted tension, the heart beats of the Neanderthal pair heard against everything else. The lioness tore itself away and landed back on the ground, curved itself back around, took two steps forward then stalled looking back up at HORs, its eyes reflecting glints of the pink sunrise light.

HORs yelled and boldly jumped off the rise onto a mossy rock, flouting his spear. The lioness flinched, turned and ran away, its muscles bulging under its fur. Under the adrenaline rush each step it took seemed to appear longer as though time had slowed down. Blood Stone crashed down to her knees, hyperventilated then looked towards the red skyline, blooming with other colours as the sun began to rise higher. That's when she discovered horror beneath the beauty; a pride of seven lions advancing towards the rise from the left! There was a larger individual lagging behind the lionesses, the alpha male, his larger size and the tuff around the neck area distinguished him. He opened his mouth, the resulting roar tore through the dawn with the utmost menace.

Two lionesses broke off from the pride and began trotting towards the rise with petrifying audacity, while the rest of the pride slowly moved in. Running away wasn't an option for the Neanderthal pair stranded on this rise. HORs was terrified, his nerves were beginning to rattle. The last and only time he had killed a lion, it was trapped in a pit, and he had had the support of his tribe while beckoning down on it before landing the killing blow with howls of mutual triumph from his kill. But that tribe was as dead as the lion he had skinned and worn over his shoulders.

There was a roar, a stone's throw away from behind, it was from a lioness trying to climb up and was about two rocks away from reaching the pair. HOR's charged, yelling with his spear pointed at it. The lioness didn't back down and was so close its odour could be smelt. HORs roared again and jabbed repeatedly. The lioness lunged forward and swiped the spear with her paw just in time.

It deflected it, a snap of the spear's pole heard as it flew free from HOR's grasp, landing two rocks down to the left. A panicked HORs scrambled for his spear, his right flank exposed. And on the uneven ground the lioness made a lunge for him, narrowly missed him, its claws though managed to strafe a piece of his tunic, leaving a long tear.

Blood Stone was heard screaming, but a distracted HORs managed to pick up his spear while the lioness, delayed by the rocks by a precious second came at him. He thrust his spear upwards, trying to get the flint's end into its neck, even as the predator continued to rush upwards and swipe at it. A panicked HORs struck the predator on the left shoulder multiple times, while the stab didn't make a smooth connection there were visible, bloodied bruises blooming, confirming injury flushed against the light fur. The lioness slid back against the rocks, claws scratching against it and tearing away moss while glaring at him, its posture tightly lowered and tail swishing. HORs screamed furiously, jumped down a rock while thrusting his spear forward. The lioness squinted, exposing its teeth and gums, its growls threateningly louder, agitated with ice clouds spilling out from its nostrils and the sides of its mouth. The beast lifted its right paw slowly and hesitantly, then sprang and broke into a brawl of swipes, so fast and frequented HORs failed to defend against, and consequently the spear was knocked out from his grasp, again.

Another lioness had found its way up onto the rise and leapt from the right side and knocked him off the rocks, he felt its muscular arms envelop him and the pressure of its teeth only beginning to sink into his left shoulder, just before they tumbled in mid fall. They hit the ground and separated, HORs rolling to the right, Blood Stone heard screaming. HORs got on his feet, ignoring the tremendous swelling pain on his entire right side, which included his arm that had cushioned his impact, his flaring elbow weakened as a result.

He had no weapon, but there was a rock to his left no bigger than his palm. The lioness that had jumped him was on its feet and running for him. With his survival at stake HORs ran for the rock, diving almost and scooped it up without any slippery grip. The lioness reared up on its back legs and flailed its paws, deadly claws extending. HORs ducked out the way, felt the beast's paw on his right shoulder as it ripped away a piece of his tunic, the ends of the claw only just grazing his flesh. He gripped the rock with both hands due to his weakened right arm, and with all his strength he smashed the rock against the feline's skull.

The impact had an affect; the lioness grunted, reared up slightly several times on the spot and staggered off, shaking its head, its steps were wobbly and cumbersome and it groaned from the trauma inflicted. HORs roared furiously then threw the rock at the lioness, hitting it on the flank and causing it to drop to its knees for a split second, then checked his wounds, from which fortunately just small trickles of blood exuded. The lioness could have effortlessly broken his shoulder and caused fatal blood loss should it have been a few inches closer. That bout of victory though was short-lived as that other lioness jumped down onto the ground, breaking into a dash, grunting as it went, and with no time to evade it let alone go for the spear, HORs braced himself as it pounced, its bulk obscuring view of all behind it. He caught both its arms by the wrist and screamed at the mighty beast that almost knocked him back to the floor from the momentum, his resistance at its peak. On its back legs the predator towered above HOR's, who was looking up at it.

With the smell of blood in the winter air, the predator was getting excited and roared in his face, its foul breath splattered against it, while its extended claws were inches from raking it. He jerked his head back, only just avoiding the teeth. The lioness grunted repeatedly and HORs avoided another bite, but felt the force from the attempt against his head just as though it was a deliberate blow. While he flinched, HOR's remained stood and focused. Then the towering lioness jumped, the momentum forcibly raising both his arms, its feet kicking.

Not only did the claws tear through HOR's abdomen, the predator's weight tore off his tunic, his bare, hairy chest exposed and the deep scratch marks running freely with blood. Yet the hunter still remained on his feet with the lioness in his grip, the adrenaline keeping him strong enough to contend with the predator he tussled with, hoping to get it on its back so he could make a run for his spear.

The moss and surrounding grass took on an orangey red with the sun's current elevation, and HORs roared, glaring at his adversary in the eye and pushing it back with all his strength, which only sent it a step back. Blood Stone was too preoccupied by several lionesses climbing up the rise on her side. Terrified, she kept looking back and forth at her companion below. She saw another lioness, running his way from behind. That's when she called out to him and abandoned her side of the rise to assist him.

But that lioness had succeeded in its ambush and sank its teeth into his right thigh. This caused him to cry out and fall on his side, where the lioness he wrestled with opened its mouth and bit into his shoulder. HORs yelled, his arms flailing with desperate, aimless blows as he fell. The moment he landed on the ground that lioness pinned him down with a paw on his face and chest, and transferred its jaws from his shoulder, to his throat. While his blows continued to make contact, that didn't stop the lionesses from doing what it did. The one with his thigh in its jaws reached forward and sank its claws into his already bloodied torso, drawing more blood, the rapid flows visible under the rising sun.

HOR's muffled screams continued, pitching as he was slowly strangled, his movements becoming slower with each second. Uncertain of what she could do, grossly outnumbered and outmatched, Blood Stone screamed at the predators and waved her spear, not daring to take a step forward. The lioness at HOR's thigh was glaring up at her, even while locked in that position. The helpless Neanderthal woman remained stood with her spear, not watching her back, frozen by the horror. Then in her peripheral vision below, more lions appeared on sight to the right, running in at the opportunity, each biting into a limb, one lioness biting into the same arm as another to kill HOR's resistance completely as their claws mauled his flesh. Blood Stone had heard many a story over a night campfire of Neanderthal men being killed by lions. Having been safe in the comfort of her tribe, never did she think she would witness such horror.

The male lion appeared, it was moving slower, its steps heavier, jaw opened and tongue hanging out, each breath of its producing ice puffs. It stopped, turned its head and looked up at Blood Stone, its eyes reflecting the orange of dawn she would not forget. The two locked gazes, Blood Stone evasively rolled her eyes left, the stood lion still partly in view, but her view of the pride unhindered as she saw them jerk their heads, growling with their mouths full. Amongst the mass of pale fur bodies, she spotted an arm of a lifeless HORs being raised and a lioness biting into his triceps, its mouth bloody from the mouthful of flesh, which it tore away. A lament wave of emotion engulfed Blood Stone as she looked away from the kill that was once her companion without making a sound, her gaze returned to the lion below. Challenged by her presence it roared, baring its teeth along with a gust of breath.

Instinctually Blood Stone backed away, the sun casting her shadow on the grass below, the lions distracted, their grunts and growls heard over the wet noises and cracks of what their teeth bit down on, until she couldn't see them. Pressured with the heaviest weight of primal fear she didn't collect the precious hide that had kept her warm, or the other essentials, though she managed to hold her spear. While listening to the beats of her over hyped heart inside her head, she clambered clumsily down the rise, gasping for breath, the grip on her spear weakening. With her feet on the ground she had the steppes ahead of her, the sun rising and the greens of the grass materialising with the new day. With a very distraught face Blood Stone looked back at the rise. Surely the lions would be after her... There were none in sight. Then she ran.

Chapter 16

With no trees or any other kind of cover, Blood Stone was completely exposed out in the open, she continued to run while sobbing, with memories of her deceased mother and tribe flashing by. She wanted them all with her, to teach and protect her from the dangers of this cold, harsh world. Minutes went by and the orb of the sun was prominent, the grass was lit up a fresh green and the details of the horizon and the land beyond Doggerland visible. Ahead of Blood Stone by less than a hundred metres was a drop of some sort, and she could hear animal rumbles, of what she didn't know under the adrenaline. She stopped, slouched forward and hyperventilated and let her grief spill out from her eyes and lungs. She dropped to her knees. *What* was she to do now? Acquiring meat, water and shelter were the least of her worries in her state of trauma and loneliness.

After minutes of sobbing and inaction, she stood back up weakly, aided by her spear and walked forward. Though she couldn't help but turn left and look back. As if things didn't get any worse than they already were, she saw a lioness, the pale whites and melded light browns of its fur visible against the grass, otherwise would have been perfectly camouflaged against snow cover. It was walking her way, its head twitching and jerking erratically, bloodstains on the left side of its head, none staining its mouth. It was the individual HORs had bashed with a rock, and while there were no other lions accompanying it, that was of no consolation. Blood Stone felt her heart go up her throat and ran, she wheezed in panic. In an activated predatory response, the lioness chased her. Blood Stone could hear it, the throaty grunts and steps as its paws slapped against the grass. She looked back and saw that it had covered two thirds of the distance between them, yet was slowing down. No other lions were seen gathering in the backdrop.

Blood Stone kept running, her spear still gripped firmly. Then she looked back to see that the lioness was maybe four strides away from reaching her, yet had stopped, its head twitching again. Blood Stone could hear water as she neared the edge of the drop. She reached the edge and looked down, realising that it wasn't a perilous fall, but merely a steep, muddy incline. She looked back and saw the predator block out half the view of the grass as it closed in on her. There wasn't enough time for her to step aside or thrust her spear as it pounced. In fear Blood Stone recoiled.

She lost her footing, screamed and tumbled down the slope, the spear fell free of her grip just before she could risk impaling herself and was sent rolling down. She managed to regain her footing and shifted so that she was sliding down to the bottom on her back, where she witnessed a racing stream about ten metres wide in front of her. At the bottom of the slope, she rolled for several feet, her bearskin gown coated in cold mud and any naked flesh grazed and smeared with dirt.

She looked up at the top of the rise several metres up, where she spotted the twitching lioness looking about aimlessly. It roared, lowered itself and inched towards the edge. Ignoring the many bruises and grazes on her limbs, Blood Stone shuffled back and scrambled to her feet, confident enough she raced to her right for her spear, which she gripped firmly with both hands and aimed up at the lioness that lingered in its crouched posture. After shaking its damaged head, it turned around out of sight. For now, Blood Stone was safe, albeit alone, a feeling completely new to her. The roar of the stream muted out her sobs as she moved along its rocky banks, far ahead of her the rise slowly dropped, and across the water were rises and peaks obscuring view of the land beyond. Urgent to get out of the area, she kept looking back up at the top of the rise.

Thirsty and with a chest hurting from grief, she kneeled down by the edge of the stream, put her hands together and scooped out the ice cold water she brought to her mouth and slurped, repeated several times until her thirst was quenched. The rays of the elevating sun caused the stream to sparkle and glisten, and as bright as the ambience appeared there was *nothing* to look forward to on this new day but a new era, one of despair. Blood Stone negotiated the uneven rocky floor of the stream's banks, she wouldn't risk hypothermia wading into the water to cross over. The further she walked the shallower the stream became with some rocks exposed, that were of manageable distance as stepping stones. Carefully, Blood Stone extended her leg, hopped and stepped onto the stones, her spear aiding her balance, her toes stinging with cold that shot through her veins and caused her to shiver tremulously. After minutes of careful negotiation, she leapt onto the other side and ventured forward, though had to look back across the stream. There was no lion coming her way.

Blood Stone was met by the sight of a woolly mammoth herd occupying the steppes ahead of her, which had their backs to her. It was probably the same herd from yesterday. Better to be around them, risking their mercy than that of a predator. Cautiously, Blood Stone kept to the right, keeping a wide birth between herself and the mammoths, trying to look invisible. Every time one of the grazing adults turned their heads it caused her to freeze with her heart skipping a beat. Blood Stone didn't make it more than a couple dozen metres away from the stream, when out of nowhere an infant mammoth came running her way, and even though it was a baby it stood up to her chest. Increasingly accustomed to having regularly been killed by Blood Stone's kind the adults would be protective of it. Hyper anxious she needed it to be distracted from her, otherwise it would draw the attention of the herd.

The infant announced its arrival with a squeal of excitement, yet no triggered rumbles from the adults were heard. Without making a noise Blood Stone tried to ward it away with her free hand. But this baby was curious, likely having not encountered a Neanderthal before, it raised its trunk and continued its way towards her without slowing down. Mere feet away from crashing into her and with no options to deter the ecstatic infant, an unprepared Blood Stone fell back on her rear, managing not to drop her spear, which she did not need for this sort of situation. No adults were alerted by her fall. The infant stopped, its yellow and brown eyes gazing down at her and its trunk, as flimsy as a coiling worm reaching out, the end constantly prodding Blood Stone's face gently, trying to make some contact which she didn't dare try and swipe away. In any ordinary circumstance, she would have tried to have taunted it for fun.

While undesirable, the infant's contact was gentle, it made these non-threatening rumbles, punctuated by these higher pitched shrills. Blood Stone just sat and let the infant do what it wanted, her eye trained on the herd. After a couple of seconds of humility, she held out her hand, quickly becoming fond of it. Instead of wanting to fend it off, her partly coiled hand cupped around the end of its trunk, it ceased any action and rumbled. Then it moved in closer, its trunk tip swung out from Blood Stone's hand and found its way to her plump nose, the moisture of its nostrils dampening it. She could laugh, she could mock the innocuous creature, as much as she wanted to weep and embrace it. Then she heard a superfluously memorable groan to her left.

Blood Stone turned her head and spotted a single lioness splashing her way across the stream. It was the same one that had chased her minutes ago, and just it alone. Its jaw was opened, dangling almost and left eye totally bloodshot, visible even at this distance. Then Blood Stone's nemesis erupted into a run, the streaming water exploding as it went. In response, the infant mammoth emitted a different sound, it was a deep, loud noise empathetically evoking its distress. And that call of the young one caused the entire herd behind it to cease all previous activity, heads turning and the collective rumbles raised in tempo with the promise of hundreds of tons of aggression to follow.

But Blood Stone ignored them all and grabbed her spear, but knew in her gut that would not repel the lioness. She looked about and saw a cluster of dirtied rocks to her left. She plopped down and with her other hand grabbed hold of the nearest rock she could find. The lioness was at the banks, water dripping off its pelt and altered its course towards the infant. Blood Stone shut her eyes and threw the rock in hand. The infant mammoth bellowed and instead of fleeing, it ran into Blood Stone instinctively for security, knocking her down while she screamed fumbled for another rock and threw it. She reached for another, and another, blindly throwing them while the baby mammoth obstructed her view as it huddled into her in its incoherent message of defence. Blood Stone got a peek of the lioness that was still running for her, no contact made from the missiles she had chucked at it.

She threw another rock, her sight again obstructed by the body of the needy infant before she could see if it had struck and was reaching down for another rock. She threw it but couldn't confirm a hit. When she could see again, she witnessed the lioness staggering, a stream of red trickling out of its right eye either from the trauma of HOR's blow or the rock Blood Stone had pelted at it. Even though the predator was grossly uncoordinated it still had speed on its side, which allowed it to trot up to Blood Stone and was a leap away from contact when she pushed the nagging infant mammoth aside, heard it squeal as she bent down and desperately snatched up another rock, one that wasn't so large this time, and threw it. It just struck the earth before the lioness and bounced about repeatedly to its right. Then with both hands she angrily presented her spear, the fretting infant mammoth didn't calm her trembling arms.

Blood Stone screamed as loud as she could, her throat aching and heart pounding in her chest. The lioness roared and came forward rearing up on its back legs while swiping the air with its clawed paws, no strikes of which touched the spear. And because of that lack of focus Blood Stone successfully managed to stab it, in the neck, the flint not going in deep as it needed to. She strained and pushed forward, the bulk of the lioness only moved back two steps from the shock of its injury. Blood Stone risked retracting her weapon and stabbed it again, this time the flint ended up in the predator's chest. There was a short, but vivid spurt of blood, but not satisfyingly enough. The lioness roared again, its head whipping about in all directions in confusion and left paw slowly raised.

Taking advantage of that precious moment of inattention, Blood Stone went for its neck a second time, the stab was smooth and more blood was drawn than the previous wound.

But then it reared up, the spear being raised with it and the bloodied flint tip slipped out from the cord and natural adhesive holding it in place. Blood Stone skipped back in a panic while simultaneously unknowingly thrusting her blunt spear into the lionesses' reddening underside to get them flailing claws away from her. She jabbed and jabbed hysterically, the infant mammoth's cries drowning out the injured groans of the lioness that fell back on its paws and made a short lunge at Blood Stone, the swipe it made connected with her precious spear and the force of the blow snapped the first third of it causing it to dangle on a slither of splintered wood.

The lioness ceased its prance, panting and snorting loudly as it shifted on the spot to a disconcerting rhythm with it springing and bucking up mere inches, bleeding from its head and chest wounds, its movements becoming increasingly slower and weaker. It exposed its fangs and staggered to the left to the point of collapse. It was completely disorientated. The frightened baby mammoth ran into Blood Stone's side, inadvertently shoving her aside, where while staggering she discovered another cluster of rocks, one of which was temptingly large. Instead of pushing the infant mammoth away, an exasperated Blood Stone reached for the largest of the rocks at the floor with her left hand and nervously raised her opposite arm and threw her blunt spear at the lioness, striking it on its right shoulder with the useless spear bouncing away on the ground as though it was dancing. The predator's response was almost non-existent; it turned its head away and groaned, its paws soaking with the blood dripping from its body.

Without a moment's hesitation, and charged up with hateful vigour, Blood Stone rushed at the lioness, which didn't react to her as she took both hands and raised the rock up to the sky just steps away from it, where she brought it down with all her strength on the killer beast's bloodied face. She felt the impact beneath the fur and muscle that covered its skull, then a ricochet. The once lethal predator toppled chin to the floor, its arms spread out. Blood Stone didn't even give it a chance, she screamed like an animal and brought the rock down on its skull a second time, causing it to tilt its head to the left side from the trauma.

Again and again, this brutally forlorn Neanderthal woman pounded that rock against its face, not deterred by these unnervingly vulnerable squeals it made or the blood splashing onto her face and gown as the skull cracked. The pale fur diluted red, them killer of Neanderthal jaws split into two, them fangs broke off and flew out of sight, the tongue hanging out and blood coughing up thickly onto the grass, the predator's musty odour collided with a fresh new waft of foul hotter gases released from within its ruptured skull. The body jerked in spasms, the once dangerous flailing limbs reduced to harmless twitches, then static. But that wasn't enough. As though any threat in existence was extinguished, Blood Stone screamed at only half the tempo as previous, yet with over twice the fury, rage, anger that had her strength intensify, the baby mammoth heard bellowing as she landed one final blow on the already decimated face of the lioness.

The red, blood stained stone stayed in place, it reflected the memory of when this newfound killer of a beast had put a tree branch in the earth as a child, although unlike then there was no marvel to this. She was alive, and that was that. Blood Stone fell back onto her buttocks, slouched forward and panted with a thunderous heartbeat, she heard the yelping squeals of the baby mammoth and felt its trunk land behind her right shoulder, tugging at her for attention. She didn't try to deter it as she caught her breath, contemplating her next course of action. There were shadows forming in front of her, like clouds blocking out the sun, although it was in her sights in the now blue sky high above... Slowly and nervously, Blood Stone turned around to see the herd of adult mammoths approaching her way, having witnessed her act of savagery.

As their eyes met, a mix of rumbles and bellows resonated across the occupied steppes, their dark, shaggy mass accumulating and blocking out the landscape behind them, the whiteness of their tusks brightened by the sun. The eyes of the mammoths were almost completely concealed by the hairs on their heads, making them appear more intimidating than they already were. One individual stood out from the rest of the herd; it was larger, its ears spread, tusks not as curved as other members of the herd, and not as smooth or glossy. Its approach towards Blood Stone was sure and devoid of the hesitation a life form smaller than itself would show. This was the matriarch of the herd. She raised her trunk and growled, her strides were steady but uncompromising, the rest of the herd came to a unanimous stop while the matriarch proceeded Blood Stone's way, her steps were neither slow or quick, and it didn't look like she or her herd was going to move.

Blood Stone's kind had hunted these behemoths to feed and warm her since birth, and now she was presented with two options for survival: the first was retreat into the freezing water, which was too shallow and perish from hypothermia afterwards, or the second of finding her way around the mammoths that would trample her within seconds. Neither option was feasible, and Blood Stone couldn't think clearly under all this additional life-or-death situational stress—unwittingly she shifted back in the direction of the stream. The approaching matriarch came to a stop before the lioness carcass, the distance between it and the Neanderthal woman was the length of her tusks. Blood Stone paused, breathing through her nose instead of her mouth and watched as the mammoth matriarch extended her trunk over the lioness corpse, it hovered over as she inspected then prodded it.

With no response from the dead predator, the matriarch aimed the end of her trunk Blood Stone's way. The Neanderthal woman remained still as her trembling limbs would allow her. The baby mammoth moved towards the feet of the matriarch and made a loud squeal, that had the rest of the herd make these low rumbles, while the first third of the matriarch's trunk coiled and recoiled in response. Her silence was mystifying as it was terrifying. The static matriarch made this most peculiar growl that transitioned into a rumble and raised her trunk, which swung about. Fear was not the way to describe this moment, even if the matriarch could just step forward and send Blood Stone flying tens of feet into the air with a jerk of her head. The other mammoths remained stationary, their breathing producing short bursts of ice clouds that corresponded with the chorus of their rumbles.

A third option for survival was made available as the matriarch passed judgement on the Neanderthal woman, her decision spread throughout the herd that turned around and headed off. This judgement was lenient. The infant lingered at the legs of the matriarch that slowly raised its trunk and made a call out with its widened eyes facing Blood Stone's way. She had no emotions to display as the superlative relief drowned all her other feelings like the floods that came each spring from the melting ice. Then the infant turned around and rejoined the herd, disappearing into the cover of the adults.

Blood Stone watched them for minutes, her view of the Doggerland morning horizon beyond returning with each step. As tempted as she felt, she couldn't stay here. Blood Stone eventually turned around and looked at the reason why lying on the floor. More predators would be drawn here and she was starving, her energy drained from all the action as well as her low emotions quickly returning to plague her like a prolonged illness. She didn't have any flint or tinder to start a fire, and there was no way she was going back to that rise to reacquire what little supplies were left, which stuck as a phobic image in her head.

Without thinking Blood Stone kneeled down and sank her fingers into the openings of the bloody pulpy mess that had once been the lionesses' head. She probed under the fur of the cheek area, her fingers sticky with blood, tissue and remnants of feline brain, she coiled her fingers, tugged and ripped at the muscle, her fingers getting grazed by the broken shards of skull bone. Blood Stone scooped out a shredded mass of pinkish red muscle, she stared at before bringing towards her lips with hesitation. Then she stuffed it into her mouth and chewed down fast and hard, the raw meat was tough, tender and slimy. She swallowed back, wiped her bloody mouth with her right forearm then dug her hands back into the remnants of the head for a second serving. While trying to chew down on the meat she ended up retching a mouthful of bloodied saliva. This was why her tribe cooked meat.

Blood Stone took another mouthful of lion meat and chewed slower, a lifetime of eating herbivorous, grass flavoured game made it stand out. It was foul yet bearable, but not as bad as the dark red meat of wolf, one of which had been killed by her tribe, skinned and its meat shared about over a fire at night. Blood Stone searched for and recovered the broken off spear flint and plunged it into the shoulder of her kill, hacking into the muscle then around the socket of the arm which took more effort than she could expend, weakened by the depression from her overly inflated grief. Eradicated was the communal encouragement from a tribe, the throaty laughter and chastisement when mistakes were made when butchering the hunt. If she wasn't so destroyed by the recent onslaught of trauma and loss she would have considered thoroughly processing the carcass for its pelt.

This kill while anything but pointless, was wasteful and without a tribe to share it with, she didn't care. Blood Stone ate as much lion meat as her stomach allowed and as quickly as she could, cleaned her hands and face in the stream and drank while looking out for any other lions. Then she walked, heading off towards the land north, whether walking to her doom by predator or the elements that had an easy chance in her loneliness. In one hand, she carried the broken remnant of her useless spear, and in the other a chunk of flesh from the arm of the lioness, nervous of it attracting predators. There was no plan other than walk, walk up where the sun shined at its brightest, hopefully in that spot there would be a space of sanctuary with a tribe that would welcome, protect and comfort her… If only life was that easy though.

The freezing steppes were so vast, and there was no cover from the next predator that would subject Blood Stone to a fate as bad as HOR's. The image of that rise flashed in her head, her tumultuous memory distorting it in many frightening ways. Blood Stone hadn't gotten that far from the stream, when she dropped what she was carrying and collapsed to her knees in another bout of grief and buried her face in the palms of both hands. She had lost everything. She yearned for the company of the mammoths, she wanted their protection, the curious affection of the infant. But they did not exist for that function. With her grief, a fruitless Blood Stone got back up and walked for miles, the view of the new land on the horizon appeared still as the rock that founded it, like no progress had been made.

Trailing far behind her, but not far enough out of sight should she turn around, was a lone Cro-Mag man with long, autumn red/brown hair tied back from a bearded face to resemble the tail of a tarpan, dressed in a finely stitched, almost tan shaded body suit of aged megaloceros hide that almost disguised him under the sunlit grass. In each hand he held a spear, the poles were sleek, and strapped across his back was a sack of dark, almost new-looking hide. His hands were covered in the same type of aged hide that covered his body, almost finely highlighting the outlines of his fingers and insulating them perfectly, as would the hood of hide draped down his back to better protect his head should a blizzard fall. The Cro-Mag man stopped, and set the foot of his spears into the grass and leaned forward slightly with the two spears supporting him. He remained stood for several minutes, took the time to survey his surroundings and waited until the Neanderthal woman, still oblivious to his presence, disappeared from his line of sight against the curve of the earth, then continued his trek…

~

Gentle snow fell against a moonlit steppe. Then as swift as the blink of an eye there appeared that rise, where tragedy had taken place on the other side, the moss covered in snow took on a delicate tint of purple from the moonlight.

After a lioness pounced in a full front view, it was frozen in posture mid-air instead of flying towards its unknown prey. It began to take on a wavy appearance and melt into the backdrop, which was saturated with sunrise colours, then it slowly began to sink into the grass as though it was water. Then a bare-chested, and very alive HORs was seen slicing a vertical cut on the belly of a deer strung up against the branch of a tree with a flint knife, its organs spilling and splattering out onto the ground.

HORs turned his head to the left, smiled and laughed. For some reason, it sounded unnaturally terrifying and had this echo that boomed like a thunderous crash through a valley. Then there was blood oozing from the fibres of hacked meat, tendon was being pulled away from the bone and the teeth of Neanderthal, betrayed by the pouted lips, gnawing at handfuls of meat. This common sight— a necessary chore of everyday existence had morphed into a frightful sight, the laughs of hyenas heard over it, which got louder over a view of the feet of a lion as it ran. A cave bear was rearing up on its back legs, the white gust from its roar clouded its face like a blizzard, a white out of which flurried around it before the image of the beast dropped out of sight like a fall.

Then a horribly nostalgic sight of a Cro-Mag man with a wooden club in hand, savagely charged at a screaming Neanderthal woman then smashed his weapon into her face, her corpse falling to the floor in a shaking visual, her eyes open, still and gazing emptily. That same Cro-Mag turned his head to the left and began to approach the viewer. His form shifted with each step, his outline looking like it was being plucked from sporadic places, and was turning a mud colour with the background darkening, a feminine scream of denial followed over the sound of a lion's roar, that sounded wetter, as though its throat was being obstructed—drowned to be specific. The Cro-Mag started swinging his club, with no indication of contact made and the viewer moving backward.

~

Blood Stone woke up feeling a sharp chill stabbing at her chest and gasped a cloud of icy breath in response, her body exploded in a shivering fit that rattled her limbs. She was lying on her side in a foetal position under a simple but unforgiving snow covered den of branches, her nose and upper lip crusted in a layer of flaky mucus and face red and sore having had another layer of skin grazed by the cold. The sting of the cold triggered a brief spell of reflexive tears as her eyes rolled about, the ground in front of her covered in snow, but nothing that could kill or harm her in sight, that she could see. That precious hunk of lion meat she had acquired was still there at her side, but had become frozen stiff. With nothing to keep Blood Stone warm other than her bear skin gown, some parts of it covered in snow, she thrust her hands inside, each hand grabbing a fistful of hide, desperately to insulate her freezing fingers. She stayed in that position until she felt strong enough to move from it, which took her over an hour.

Last night Blood Stone had come across a patch of forest that had some trees knocked down at its edge with their roots exposed; evidence of mammoth encroachment instead of man, that chopped them down laboriously at the trunk. Under the dark, cloudy and near moonless sky she had constructed a shelter from what she could scrounge together, the cover while sparse was sufficient enough, then had passed out from exhaustion instead of having to endure a painfully sleepless sight. Although a well awake Blood Stone had enough energy, her willingness to do anything was drained like the blood of a butchered hunt, but it didn't stop her from crawling out of her stick den looking up at a grey, featureless sky, a layer of snow had covered the top of her shelter with the gaps allowing snow inside.

Using a stick, instead of her bare hands, Blood Stone brushed away the snow a few feet from her den, seeking out some rocks which she used to carefully break off a piece from the tip of that precious spear tip. She gathered some local twigs, even though they were too damp to be used in starting a fire, that she solved by ripping off a handful of fur from drier parts of her bear skin gown as substitute tinder. Fortunately for Blood Stone there was no winter breeze blowing about, but the cold harshly impeded her ability to start a fire demonstrated by her trembling hands, as she struck that small flint piece against the broken spear end. A lifetime of living in natural shelters with fellow Neanderthal to aid her made her completely unequipped to deal with this solo situation. In desperation, Blood Stone continued to strike and produce sparks that didn't make contact due to her tremors, which brought her to the brink of crying as the recent events weighed upon her. Eventually a spark made contact with the fur, Blood Stone's eyes widened with anticipation.

Carefully she lowered her chin to the floor of her den and blew at the improvised tinder, as steady as her life-threatening shivers would allow her. Smoke billowed and a flame sprouted like a bud in spring, never before was a flame so small yet so comfortingly bright! Blood Stone tried hard not to breathe, she shifted around in her den to block the flame from the elements with her back side, then she added more bear fur to the flame until she had a fire going, she kept fed steadily with twigs. This tiny and fragile, semi exposed den had become incredibly comfortable. With her fingers warm enough and her self-made fire large enough, Blood Stone went back out to survey her surroundings under the grey daylight. There weren't that many trees in this woodland patch, the widely spaced gaps between the leafless trees revealing the expanse of the steppes as well as a view of the land beyond Doggerland that hadn't changed.

Blood Stone snapped off a tree branch as long as she was tall, with her feet she cleared a space in the snow outside her den and passed on a fire to that spot to keep her warm from the front. Seated, she delicately shaved away the branches twigs with her spear flint and stripped off the bark of the twigs into thin strips. She broke some more rocks, piece by piece until she had something sharp enough, which she chipped into shape. Blood Stone used the spare rocks to bash the frozen lion meat, a solid fist size block came off and she made a rack of small branches over the humble fire. As the meat melted it oozed sickly grey/brown fluids that sizzled as they dripped into the flames, and it took precious moments of living before there was any browning to the meat.

While it cooked Blood Stone kept herself occupied by slotting the newly crafted spear tip piece into the opening gaps of the branch she had broken off and tied it meticulously in place with the bark strips. She cupped her hand around the base of the spear end and tested the firmness of it, it was stiff enough to stab something maybe once or twice, but too wobbly for repeated jabs. Some of the surrounding snow melted from the fire, she collected handfuls of it in her hands and sipped at it carefully, not wanting the snow to blister the blisters that were already developing on her tongue. With a new spear in one hand and frozen lion meat in the other, Blood Stone headed towards the new land, trekking through the snow drenched steppes. High in the sky, the sun's rays broke through the clouds and multicolour orbs of light bounced blindingly off the snow, the sunlight spreading and brightening the previously muted terrain ahead, that began to undulate up and down into shallow slopes and hills extending the trek, the land ahead visible one moment appearing as a hill, blocking the lower half of the land beyond, then an hour later back to normal.

A half day (Blood Stone counted) on foot and she had had no eventful encounters with the fauna other than a herd of tarpans, revealed by their dark hide against the white in the far distance. She was near the top of a rise, reaching the top there was another downward incline that smoothened out into flatter land, and congregating below were a pack of wolves. Camouflaged immaculately against the snow they had spotted Blood Stone first, their legs stiffened and heads raised. Instinctively she dropped the lion meat, but knew it wasn't going to distract them from her. They growled then barked repeatedly on the spot. This was it, Blood Stone knew this was the end for her, in seconds they would be running up the hill and dragging her down. Even in her trembling state of shock and doom, she aimed her spear down at the wolves. She wasn't going down without putting up a fight.

The wolves relaxed their threat poses and looked around the landscape for a very brief moment then dispersed to the left, running into the horizon. Blood Stone watched them while cautiously manoeuvring to the right of the hill. Was this some form of deception? Were the grey pelted predators planning on ambushing her elsewhere? Time passed and Blood Stone picked up her frozen lion meat and boldly ventured downhill, where she spotted something sticking out from the snow below in the centre of the icy open with several rows of wolf tracks encircling it. The object of curiosity—and the deepest sort being that— were a pair of mammoth tusks stuck into the ground, positioned very specifically; both tusks were curved towards each other as opposed to outwards. Blood Stone investigated the strange foundation, alarmed as she was curious despite the threat of being attacked.

There were all these sophisticated decorations ornamenting the tusks; smears of charcoal and other earthy colours in elegant patterns painted on the ivory and lightly snow dusted bones of small animals, bound by organic thread dangling from them. While this structure was indisputably mesmerising and worth stopping for in the midst of the most hazardous moment in Blood Stone's life, she didn't see it holding any solutions to her grief or survival, the same way she didn't see the formless, translucent entity hovering behind her, lowering itself without making any noise that would trigger an instant response from the Neanderthal woman. But should she turn around and face it she would not be able to describe it. The unnoticed surveyor shifted its intangible form to a flattened, horizontal disk shape, then quickly slanted left to a 45-degree angle, and repeated that rapid shift from various angles so that it appeared to twinkle, like a star then altered to a more discernible cloud form and gained height, cruising above Blood Stone.

The Neanderthal woman stayed around the mammoth tusk monument until she noticed the sun beginning to drop, the shadow cast against the tusks pointed north, to the land beyond Doggerland. Blood Stone resumed her trek the same direction she had been headed, going up and down the hills while the sun set, her depression heightened with each phase of its descent. There was some forest over a mile ahead, blackened being cast under the shadow of the sun. Blood Stone came to a stop, a spillage of tears restrained from her eyes, the longer she waited, the more anxious she became.

She remained stationary, oblivious to the lone Cro-Mag man with two spears headed the same way. He didn't exercise any stealth this time, he had to be thirty metres away before the sound of him treading through the snow gave him away. Blood Stone turned around and froze spotting him. The Cro-Mag man did the same and hoisted the tips of his two spears up at the same time, his facial hair tinted with sunset shades and his outfit boldly saturated, his expression didn't convey bewilderment like Blood Stone who was paralysed by fear, having seen what his kind had done to her tribe. A small bird flew between them in the direction of the woodland, wolves howling in the background as the two species of human continued to stare at each other…

~

Fifteen years had gone by since the massacre of her tribe. Blood Stone stood on top of a hill overlooking the mountainous plains of the new land hundreds of miles beyond the coast of Doggerland. While the lower regions of this land were dominated with forest, the higher lands consisted of grass-covered moors of ancient limestone, which eroded after the seasonal blanket of snowfall of each winter. These highlands were great vantage points, anything dangerous could be seen in plenty of time; like wolves, which could venture just about anywhere. It was summer. Swarms of biting insects were the prime source of bother instead of frostbite, and the sight of an eagle always entertained the observant. Blood Stone had found another tribe, which she turned around from her view of the new land to face. In a state of irony as great as the sun giving life, the same way as it would destroy it, they were Cro-Magnon. The species that had eradicated her tribe were now her's. The Cro-Mag's did not require caves to shelter themselves from the elements, but erected structures made from branches, deer antlers, mammoth tusks and various animal hides. These huts were tall—over two metres high, and provided near infallible cover and insulation, fires could be made within them and their flames were not vulnerable to the winds and blizzards, and these structures were portable and could be relocated and assembled from place to place.

Having spent a copious amount of time invigorated by the summer sun, Blood Stone walked with the sun shining down on her, a slanted, trailing shadow to her left side. Each member of the tribe acknowledged her, either with a smile or gesture. In the summer, they dressed skimpier with frocks of hide around the waists, men and women with bare torsos displaying painted markings and decorative accessories, mainly necklaces of small animal bones. So physically different from Blood Stone they were, yet so hospitable. The dialect of the tribe she understood; she knew when they were blissful, angry, upset, terrified, needed something, but didn't know their past, only the history she witnessed being around them.

Blood Stone passed by the centre of the camp, where a deer was being cooked on a spit with a branch through the mouth and rectum and placed over two other branches at either end so that it could be rotated over a fire. All meat was cooked in this tribe. The scent of the blistered browned flesh was enticing and eliciting an impatient, famished youngster who ran in circles around the fire, taking a break to watch the cooking process. Sometimes tossing in certain leaves or pieces of bark would create a different smell, would make more smoke and an enticing aroma. Blood Stone was approached from the right by her spouse Tu'spee, his tarpan tail hair grey, his beard he had trimmed down for the summer, had scabby cuts from doing so days ago, he wore a tan shaded frock around his waist halfway down his hairy thighs and a necklace of teeth and the bones of smaller game he had hunted. Tu'spee swiped away a fly buzzing around his face as Blood Stone joined him along with several younger members of the tribe, which gathered around a certain hut, the entrance framed with megaloceros antlers.

These were their children, present were five girls and three boys, the latter of which were established hunters. They had Blood Stone's eyes, they had her lips, and as result of being interbred with a Cro-Mag, they had slender noses, smoother eye ridges, taller foreheads and leaner figures. They were strong, fit and healthy, unlike herself. A thirty two year old Blood Stone was frail, at the praecipes of her life expectancy. Her hair while still long and textured, was almost rock grey, her face mottled and wrinkled, eyes squinted from age, but retained their alluring blue shade. But this Neanderthal woman was at ease, having made the second half of her life fruitful. She will be fine, until her final days.

There was many a place in this new land to explore. Blood Stone's children and their descendants had every opportunity to be hunters, parents, tribe leaders, settle and dominate their environment as they had for hundreds of thousands of years prior, facilitating livelihood in their environment, advancing and passing down knowledge, technique and guidance through word of the parent or on stone, or a streak of charcoal left on a cave wall—all in the effort to be grander than their ancestors. Right now the shores of seas seemed to be the limit. The howls of wolves echoed in the background, the laughs of hyenas to challenge them were less frequent here. Inside that hut was Blood Stone's first born, Black Burn.

With his left hand he snatched up a spear, the pole finely trimmed despite the limitations of what a stone knife could achieve, the flint at the end had a near smooth double-edge finish to it. With his right Black Burn fetched a flint knife sheathed in boar hide with a strap, he slung over his left shoulder and flint axe and rolled it and other smaller tools up into a bag made from mammoth hide, which he slung over his back. This young hunter had been given his name having been smeared with a streak of charcoal on his right cheek upon birth by his father. Black Burn had a drooping jaw line, his lips were pronounced and unlike his siblings his eyes were brown, at fifteen he was as tall as his father, his face ridden with short stubble darkened by smears of dirt and grime, that wasn't long enough to be trimmed by sharpened flint. His long, dark brown hair was tied into a collection of braids, pulled back tightly from his face, his upper body muscled and hairy, stomach flat and body carried by the long legs of a runner.

In the summer, he did not require the furry tunics and boots of animal hide, but wore simple, stitched up covers of tan hide up to his ankles to protect his feet from dirt and grit. He walked out the hut into the open, unsurprisingly greeted by his family and tribe, the sunlight shining down on him illuminating the same confidence he had before any assisted hunt with his father he displayed. And this young mixed breed hunter had engaged in so many. Now he had to venture out into the world and explore solo, custom of the older males of this tribe. Mother Blood Stone hadn't told of what practices her kind had engaged in, though she seemed more than eager; it was the language barrier, father said. Black Burn looked at his father who lowered his head, his aged mother's smile curved against her creased face. She stepped forward and embraced him.

The young hunter looked to his siblings from left to right, all wearing smiles and lowering their heads. The last to meet Black Burn's sight was his youngest sister Holly, who was five years old, stood metres away from her older siblings, shadowed against the sun. She was wearing a soft brown gown of auroch hide from last month's hunt, her hair braided and tied together into a tarpan tail. As Black Burn walked towards her she demonstrated an endearing habit of hers, pouting her lips and making a buzz like a bee while she strummed her right index finger against her lip, creating a different sound completely. That was her unique way of communicating with her brother. Black Burn kneeled down and Holly treaded towards him with heavy steps on her bare feet, her eyes wide and watery, she wrapped her slender arms around him, and the young hunter returned the gesture.

Having looked up to her eldest brother all her life and aware of his imminent, prolonged absence Holly sulked like a wounded creature with her older sister Rain stepping forward to comfort her. The two had always been close. Rain had reddish hair worn up high, she was the middle of the half-breed siblings, and the most attractive, with a distinctly triangular jaw that accentuated the pout of her lower lip. Her tunic had the aged hide of a hyena stitched into the shoulders for style. Black Burn took one final look at his tribe and family before turning his back on them to face the landscape ahead of him, brightened by a high sun. He inhaled softly through his nostrils, raised his spear which caused his tribe to cheer loudly into a collective spell of hollers and claps immediately after. Then Black Burn ran.

~

On his own, he would explore and scout out new lands for his nomadic tribe to habitate. And everyone was depending on this freshly developed hunter, ready to take on the world. Black Burn headed downhill for the north lands, the cheers of his tribe instilling him with energy as he continued to run without stopping, the all green landscape changing with each mile; hills and mountains rising, edges of forest along parklands stretching and cutting off. Deer fed upon this infinite greenery, and seeing the young hunter running their way they fled. Black Burn laughed while running alongside them, continuously looking ahead and their way. The bucks could be distinguished by a moderate growth of antler, covered by a fuzzy, almost moss textured layer of flesh, the previous pair shed during the spring, usually collected by the tribe in the forest alongside tree branches.

Soon these new set of antlers were going to branch out and increase exponentially in size, and that fleshy covering was going to be shed off into bloodied shreds dangling off the new antlers, turning these placid-looking creatures into disconcerting blood soaked terrors for a few days. Better to run with the deer and not from the wolves. Normally Black Burn, father and his fellow hunters would have stalked them, with the most practiced of stealth, spread out then scared them, isolated an individual and chased them towards another hunter, who would have thrown his spear at one and pursued it for as many miles needed, until it tiered to deliver the finishing blow. But Black Burn would not be feasting on deer once hunger arose.

He stopped noticing all these *really* long brown hairs amongst the grass, they were woolly mammoth hairs; obvious by their metre length, he kneeled down, picked up a handful and wrapped them around his forearm. They had use, for a necklace or binding together something. He ran for the best part of a mile before sighting a herd of mammoths to his left. While they were far enough for him to outrun a charge from one, he kept his distance from the herd. They weren't as shaggy as they were in the winter, as they had shed their winter coats and for the season they appeared leaner and fuzzy, the summer sun made their pelt appear reddish, and instead of falling snow, insects swarmed around them causing them irritation they showed by their erratic twitches and grunts. Black Burn ground his teeth and looked away from the mammoths to the mountainous horizon ahead, turning his head, deciding which direction to take. He settled on a centre eastward path and ran.

While running he jabbed his spear front, left and right at an imaginary adversary, the thought of a beastly predator chasing him frequently came to mind since his earliest child years. He looked back without slowing down, saw that there was nothing coming after him. Black Burn felt ecstatic; he felt like he could fight a predatory beast with just his hands alone. An hour without rest, he stopped by the edge of a forest to his right, panting moderately, sweat dripping down his body ridden with grime and insects that had flown into him, the woods he wanted to investigate for resources. Black Burn ventured in, the pungent smell of wild garlic filled his nostrils, the songs of unseen birds perched elsewhere tuned his ears, the canopy shading him from the summer sun that had partly scolded his face and shoulders, the forest floor was mapped with a dense population of ferns with swarms of tiny insects buzzing above them which he swiped away. Black Burn need not be plagued like the mammoths. He jumped over a fallen tree and discovered a patch of damp soil he kneeled down, dipped his hands into the soil, rubbed his palms together and smeared the muck over his reddened face and body, the mud acting as a protective layer against the insects' bloodsucking mouthparts.

The young hunter found a spot to rest and unrolled his mammoth hide sack for his stone axe, where he chopped off branches and assembled the foundation of a shelter for the night, them mammoth hairs were useful tying the pillars and beams in place. He placed his mammoth pelt over the frame, should it rain during the night. Spear in hand, Black Burn went out in search of game, with the temperature and clear skies, summer was the easiest of seasons for that, rabbit or squirrel were an ideal meal for a single hunter. The spear was not the tool for dispatching game of such small size. Black Burn was heading in the direction of this noise he heard amongst the songs of the birds, the familiar sound of a stream.

He stepped back out into the open, onto a short, sloping meadow, its edge ridden with uneven, mossy rocks, the water source turned out to be a racing stream about three metres wide and beyond more grassland occupied by a grazing herd of aurochs in the distance beyond. Black Burn opened his mouth in peckish anticipation as he negotiated the rocks of the bank, while turning his head down to the right looking down at the water to see the broken image of another human looking up at him as he moved. Himself.

He had always wondered why water did this…showed faces of his own people. Fresh water, despite being tasteless was needed to sustain existence after food, and it was perhaps one of the greatest mysteries out in the world; it came down from the clouds of grey skies, sometimes in soft droplets or vicious torrents, flowed through streams, lakes and rivers, but happened to remain still as a rock at times. Water had no substance to it, yet it could shape land, it could turn dry earth into raging mud flows and engulf megafauna and drown them or sweep them away for many miles; bodies of bison and auroch from river banks had been salvaged by Black Burn's tribe after seasonal floods on several occasions, which saved hunters plenty of energy and the risk of injury.

Black Burn positioned himself on a rock and stood still, his spear tip aimed and lowering at the water's surface, his breathing steady and arms still in spite of the prolonged run and recent labour. He waited…eyes searching for anything edible. He spotted a fish swimming down. The water game were a seasonal delicacy and a favourite of Black Burn's, though this individual no bigger than one of his fingers—too small for a morsel—was swimming his way. He let it pass and awaited another opportunity, his ears allowing the grunts of the aurochs to peacefully meditate the passing of time, until another fish came his way, this one temptingly was over a foot long.

With momentous force, Black Burn drove his spear into the water, felt contact and raised the spear up to the sun, laughed at the sight of the successfully impaled, silvery green fish flapping its body scales glistening against the sun. A good catch! He put his foot down on the flopping fish's head as he removed his spear from it to prevent it falling back into the stream. Safely gripped in his hand, Black Burn unsheathed his stone knife and hacked through the gill of the fish, severing its neck vertebrate and rendering it permanently static, then sliced up the belly of his hunt, plunged his hand into the cavity and removed the organs, tossing them into the stream, then shaved off the scales and dunked it under the streaming water, cleaning it along with his hands. Black Burn returned to his camp space and lit a fire, jammed a branch through the mouth of his catch, set it on a rack to cook and let his nose be treated to the aroma of the fish's soft flesh being charred.

He sat cross-legged and fetched a smaller bag that he had stashed within his mammoth hide sack, revealing a cluster of mammoth ivory pieces. These were *figures* he had carved himself, basing them off the fauna he had encountered and had had a good look at whenever venturing out from the tribe's camp, each one the size of his palm, with short legs and very basic but with identifiable features, every attempt at detail made despite the limits of stone tools and memory. Black Burn assembled them in rows, as he always did with sunlight peeking through the canopy shining down on them. His sculpts were of: the deer without its antlers, the eagle, the auroch, the tarpan, the wolf, the lion, the bear, the hyena, the rhino, and the mammoth. Some were smeared in minerals, soils or charcoal to crudely match the skin of the animal; black for the tarpan and brown for the rhino.

Black Burn wore a grin of energetic optimism and picked up the sculpture of the cave lion, inspecting it while rolling it around between thumb and finger. How many more animals were there out in this world for him to sculpt? A memory of a megaloceros—the ultimate deer—came to mind. At the age of eight and not strong enough to be involved in the hunt, Black Burn and his younger brothers had watched from the edge of forest, where they had been witness to their father and fellow tribe's hunters running at this grand beast, shouting and flaunting their spears and had safely avoided its charges and being struck by its antlers, which while dangerous had the biggest downside to them. In winter, the antlers of megaloceros were at full size, which prevented them from fleeing into the forested parts of the land to escape like the smaller deer could.

Cornered against the edge of forest the antlers of the megaloceros had become entangled in the bushes, and no matter how hard it struggled or bucked it had remained stuck, safe enough for Black Burn and his brothers to come up close and watch as his father had put an end to the life of the great beast with his spear. The hunters had dragged the giant deer back to camp on a sled made from local branches for easier transport, where Black Burn had been given the task of hacking off the antlers with an axe and placing them in front of the entrance of the family hut to distinguish it. Those grand antlers were more than just a resource, but a source of inspiration begging the creative question: *what would it be like if man had such adornments on his head?*

His fish done, Black Burn picked it up by the stick he roasted it on and carefully bit into it and chewed, his tongue cherishing the light and earthy flesh flavoured by the char of the fire while having to regularly spit out unremoved scales and them small bones in the meat he had on one occasion swallowed and choked on, with his father aiding him coughing them up with heavy pats to the back. His hunger satiated, Black Burn began carving one of the raw ivory pieces with a harder oval-shaped stone that had a cornered edge end. Slowly, a shape emerged, the conventional stubby limbs of the collection were chiselled, the songs of the birds refined his focus, he stopped only when hearing the rattling of a bush or call of an animal, his spear on the floor to his right was an arm reach away…

Black Burn continued carving until night fell. It was warm enough that a fire wasn't required, but he lit one anyway, wanting to see his latest creation. With sore, hard-worked fingers he held it up and blew away the ivory dust.

The glow of fire against his face showed a content grin. The figure was an abominably plump attempt at a megaloceros, the antlers stubby and with only four prongs, while very inaccurate were still distinguishable from the other figures. The young hunter/sculpture took his finger to the outer edge of the fire, dipped the tip in the cooler charcoal and ash and smeared it over the antlers and the snout creating additional detail. Black Burn called it a night and slept well throughout.

~

Next day. The oranges, pinks and yellows of a fading dawn saturated the parklands before the sky turned blue, the few clouds around were puffy and white and Black Burn woke to the songs of birds. The young hunter sat up, his sun burnt face felt tight and the cracked and flaking mud mask covering it didn't help. He stashed away his supplies into his mammoth hide carrier, rolled it up and returned to that same stream he had sourced yesterday, this time to drink from it before washing away the cracked layer of mud from his face, the loose bits of hair from his braids he swept back. His morning thirst quenched, Black Burn ran and left the woods, where he headed for the higher ground.

Throughout the day Black Burn kept his runs to half hour intervals with the other half walking, the activity remained uninterrupted as he strived in his efforts to cover a vast distance over the hills. Green mosses, small, dry reddish shrubs and mingling growths of yellow buttercups and lavender flowers dotted the grass and a seemingly endless abundance of rabbits were seen hopping about, the grass littered with their droppings. As the hills got higher so did the regularity of slabs of exposed limestone, that came in all shapes and sizes, the taller rocks casting slanted shadows from the sun. Black Burn looked down at the shaded patches of grassland and forest below melding together and streams seen splitting and cutting through them.

Overdue on a rest from his venture and captivated by the rocks, he sat with his legs outstretched under the shadow of one and contemplated his next hunt, which might just be rabbit today from the abundance available to him. Resuming his trek he kept his head tilted west towards the lower lands, but his eyes were drawn to a spectacle in the sky; it was a flock of small birds, hundreds of them alternating their trajectory in a bending, wavy motion. Then this buzzing noise interrupted. It wasn't like that of a swarm of bees—it was louder, much, much louder and far more threatening. It was heard from the left, over the plains where Black Burn turned his head. It could be seen high up in the air and had to be hundreds of metres out. This had to be what was causing havoc amongst the birds. It was big, precisely how unknown, with an elongated, dark green cylindrical body with yellow markings, these long, flat rectangular appendages on its side like really stiff wings, and a smaller pair towards the rear end and a fin-like structure above. It was flying westwards, descending and turned Black Burn's way without flapping its wings.

The young hunter blinked following the instance of phenomenon, his heart pumping. Of what was that? Certainly it wasn't a bird. The buzzing aerial entity tilted to the right, revealing these dark blue spots on them wings and this spinning appendage at its front. Was it going to descend on Black Burn from above like eagles did to rodents? The anticipation was beginning to cause a fleeting ache in his chest, and before the question of whether spear be effective or not against it could be conjured up, it just vanished from sight. Nothing had ever disappeared so quickly. In the absence of the big, loud flying thing the flock of birds in the background immediately changed their flock formation into a slower, singular structure. A bewildered Black Burn looked about, remembering father warning the family of certain mushrooms and plants that could make one...*see things* whether they were consumed on purpose or accidentally contaminated with them. Was this one such instance?

Black Burn decided to head on, somehow hoping he might encounter the mysterious flying thing again. He began to descend back down to the lower lands, it took him over an hour and there was another peak ahead of him. Back on the lower plains he spotted a stream further out, congregated on by aurochs and deer, which he felt like investigating and not just to quench his thirst. His attention was ripped away by the laughs of cave hyenas, a gang of five of them snub-nosed menaces came running into view from the right on the plains. This wasn't some trick of the sense as they did not vanish into thin air, but remained in sight along with the source of their laughter that walked into view; a herd of *elephants*.

While they did look like mammoths with their huge size, trunks and tusks, they were in fact older relatives. Over five metres high they were bigger, had a grey/brown hide, lacked the shaggy fur, had longer legs, slightly larger ears, and their tusks were long and curved only slightly, giving them a near straight appearance, the tips almost high above the ground as Black Burn was tall, the folded, ribbed patterning along the front surface of their trunks was interspersed with sparse, bristly hairs.

As of now these giants were the biggest animals to walk the land. They were *palaeoloxodon*, or straight-tusked elephants. They were an endangered species not as vast in numbers as mammoth, which were also increasingly shorter in numbers with each passing year, migrating up north from warmer southlands beyond Doggerland for the summer. Several palaeoloxodon raised and curved their trunks, and stricken with awe Black Burn thrust the end of his spear into the soil, creating a support beam then leaned gently into it with both hands resting on top of the end. What must the experience of hunting one of these titans be like? How many a man would be injured, maimed or killed in this conquest? That wasn't Black Burn's desire. He wanted to get closer, interact…befriend them.

The way the straight-tusked elephants passed him by, rumbling with their ears flapping and a flock of migrating geese flying over them elicited a surge of inspirational excitement within him. Them incredible tusks, like mammoth's were acquisition worthy of a hunter. How many a hunter would it take to bring one of them down? That was a prospect for another time. One of the straight-tusked elephants turned its giant head Black Burn's way and stopped. He remained still and studied the elephant that made eye contact with him, the two continued their state of inaction until the beast moved on. Having to leave the majestic beasts behind, Black Burn cautiously headed for the water, the rears of the palaeoloxodons facing him and the threat of the hyenas at bay, the deer springing away as he neared by but the aurochs remained present but alert to his presence. The water source was another flowing stream, which Black Burn drank from before hiking back up the limestone mapped hills.

The next event was the sighting of a kite that circled at a speed observable against the sun, of which Black Burn managed to make out the reddishness of its plumage. The need to eat was still a priority, and there were plenty of rabbits grazing. Black Burn sat down and slouched back against one of the limestone slabs and clutched hold of a stone that his fingers could hardly conceal and sat still, cross-legged with a stick of grass in his mouth, the angle of the limestone shadows changed with the passing of the sun. Eventually a rabbit hopped into view from the left and had to be no more than six metres in front of Black Burn. Normally traps would be set to capture the small mammals, usually in bunches with a single rabbit feeding two people in the tribe, but there were so many about, and a solo hunter needed to be frugal. Black Burn raised the hand that held the rock.

The rabbit reacted to his move, but the rock had already been thrown, and struck it on the flank, stunning it with it lying on its side, flailing in alarm and confusion. Then Black Burn sprang up, snatched up his spear and ran the rabbit's way, where he swiftly ended its suffering with a clean jab of his spear. Black Burn had always been a great shot with his throw arm, it was paramount—a miss meant the difference between hunger and a meal to get one through the day. He picked the rabbit up by its legs and continued on.

The skies slowly blushed with colour as the sun began to retreat for the night and Black Burn decided to settle down. This spot looked ideal; there was forest and a stream down below in plain sight. It was the perfect place for a tribe to set up camp. Black Burn unrolled his mammoth hide bag, lit a fire, gutted the rabbit and roasted it, pelt on. While his meal cooked, he picked up an ivory piece, hands stained with dried rabbit blood and pride guiding him as he started work on a palaeoloxodon. Them magnificent tusks would require some delicate carving— a bigger piece of ivory was needed. As with the previous night, Black Burn carved with already bruised fingers until he was tiered. He slept well.

Black Burn woke to the earlier stages of sunrise. Three days away from family and tribe…now it was time to go back and inform them. After packing up his gear, Black Burn looked down at the plains and spotted a pack of wolves gorging on a deer kill. While they were beasts that brought death, there was something *affectionate* about them.

It would be nice if they were more docile and be able to live alongside. Actually, they would make ideal companions. The same fantasy was conjured jumping onto the back of a tarpan and riding one, that would be quite an experience, and it would allow a man to cover plenty of ground. With the area memorised, Black Burn ran back south towards his tribe's land with the bold orange rising sun shining against him the same way as it set. All these colours he wanted to depict in his craft works, yet didn't know how to.

Chapter 17

Yesterday Emily had fed more pigeons than she had seen in her entire life, at this square, which was at this *grand palace*. She had never felt so laidback in her life, nor had she experienced such heat or endless reasons to keep a smile on her face. There was no place for an ego here. Emily was on the train in Kanchanaburi, heading back to the bridge after paying a visit to a gorgeous waterfall, and then there was a stop at a cave with a giant, gold Buddha within where people prayed for fortune, several gorgeous photos of them places of which she was flicking through on her four hundred quid camera worn around her neck. Emily was wearing a plain black body vest, silky, baggy and low crotch bright pink and purple summer trousers with black elephant caricature patterning and some white, platform soled crocs with that Swiss cheese holes design in them, her fun red bob still styled the same, and her nose ring and crucifix pendant was absent. She had a brand new handbag at her side, a black one with some gorgeous etching on it, but at only ten quid in local currency it was nowt expensive.

With an opened bottle of water in hand, Emily bobbed her head out of the train's paneless window, her hair ruffled, and a black sign post ahead, which weren't as spaced out like back at home, ready to collide with her face.

So she had to quickly reel herself back in and was met with laughter from fellow passengers. It seemed to be every half kilometre or so you had to do this!

"Careful!" This bloke with an accent Emily didn't see called out while his partner was heard laughing. The train carriage had a cocktail of foreigners, mostly European blokes with Thai partners.

And the carriage, which was rocking as though it could tip over, was ancient with these yellow walls that needed a new paintjob, worn-down dark brown leather benches that needed replacing. After noticing a sign pass by, Emily leaned out again and stuck half her body out the window, seeing the same scenery she had seen a few hours ago but in the opposite direction. Seeing another sign she reeled back in, then almost immediately leaned back out the window, water bottle hand extended out and the bottle whistling from the speed. Her Capricorn tattoo was gone, just bare skin in its place as it had been before she had had it impulsively inked into her.

The train was passing by a bright green rice paddy, under the blinding sun the surface of the brown water looked as smooth and glossy as a brand new coffee table. Emily took several pictures of it.

"*Ba mee haeng?*"

Hearing a bloke call that out she pulled herself back in, and saw this fella with a black fisherman's hat walking down the carriage her way, carrying a bamboo woven basket in each hand. Emily had already eaten some delicious marinated pork on skewers on the ride to the waterfall, but here you could not turn down the opportunity to eat. Emily held up her hand.

"Can I get one, please?" She said, searched her handbag for local currency and was handed a parcel of grey paper with a pair of skinny bamboo chopsticks.

"Twenty baht." The seller asked with Emily handing him a hundred baht.

"Keep the change," Emily said then put her hands together and thanked the local way, "Khrap khun kaa!"

Curious to what was in the parcel she opened it up and got a very pleasant surprise: thin, glossy, yellow egg noodles, white meatballs, slices of some white meat sausage/fish cake, some green veg that looked like spinach and plenty of chilli flakes. Despite her love for oriental food, Emily still hadn't gotten used to chopsticks yet, but it didn't stop her from digging in, where she carefully mixed all the ingredients in and had a bite. Them egg noodles were delicious, and them meatballs were spongy with a very light meaty flavour, there was the salty, acquired taste of fish sauce and the sweet, delicate crunch of some sugar. The ba mee noodle parcel was amazing and that handy way it had been served was impressive; perfect for a picnic or pick-me-up.

The train had arrived back at the River Kwai Bridge, which wasn't that big; about a hundred metres long with these old-looking, semi-circle bends of girdled black steel, and below it the River Kwai, a brown, snaking river which Emily had heard of in that film her granddad had gone on about when she was a child. The tourists seen walking along the tracks had to move onto the platform spaces out the way, some people leaning out, waving or clashing palms like sound people. The police officer walking back and forth along the carriages was a proper moody fella. The copper didn't have all the equipment on him like you'd see back at home, just handcuffs, a radio and he had one of them old six bullet guns in a holster and some silvery extra bullets around his belt. His uniform was smart, milky brown trousers and a short-sleeved shirt with all these emblems, a red braid looped through the left epaulette sleeve and a hat with a black visor and emblem.

Emily stepped off the train (which scarily enough had no doors!) and onto a platform lined with souvenir shops, which she explored and filled up a small blue carrier bag with stuff while under the glare of the merciless sun rays. She waited for the train to leave then walked over the tracks along with the other tourists, who went up along the bridge while she went into an open market area, then beyond into a maze of streets. Emily reached for her handbag and took out not a pack of cigs but her phone to check her texts. There was a bushy clearing with a stunning view of the mountains covered in arid yellow and green jungle, which Emily had to stop and take a photo of with her camera. While passing by one of the bushes on her right, she was startled when a bird just came running out without making a sound. And funnily it was a *rooster*—it had that thingy on its head—was a lovely blue/black, coppery orange colour, but unlike the chickens back home it was taller and skinnier. Emily wasn't quick enough to photograph it as it disappeared behind a tree across the road. Suppose she should just ask it to repeat it?

Further up the street, past all these restaurants and these mobile stalls selling fruit, barbecued meats on skewers, noodle soups etcetera, there was this clearing the size of a football field with some goal posts, except there was no grass but dusty sun-dried dirt, and the focus of the clearing was a big tree, it was like a sycamore tree but weirder; the leaves were smaller like those seen on hedges and the branches were longer and more widely spread out, even the roots were more spread out and curved like a bunch of snakes. It looked like summat out of a fantasy tale! Emily took a photo of it. There was this bird heard singing, and it had a repetitive, very distinctive, high-pitch call; it was like a whistle, repetitive then broke into this weird chocking cackle. But it was the whistle the bird made that was so memorable.

There was this tubby bloke sat bare-chested at the foot of the tree on a stool smoking a roll-up, he had a black tattoo with these inscriptions on his right pec and wore shorts and sandals.

"*Por leow!*" The bloke said trying to call the bird in a whistling tone to match its song, "Por leow! Por leow! Por leow!"

"What's that mean?" Emily asked. The fella smiled without eye contact and tipped his cig ash.

"Is mean: *enough*!" The fella answered. Yes…it was bound to get irritating!

"You smoke?" The fella asked holding up a white pouch of loose tobacco which had the simplest labelling on it in the local language.

"I quit." Emily said proudly then looked up at the tree, searching for the singing bird.

"What sort of bird is it?" Emily asked without moving her mouth, her words echoing as they had with one particular stranger back at work.

"*Cuckoo?*" The bloke said. Emily giggled.

"It's…a cuckoo bird, eh…?" She said then laughed in the most ridiculous way.

~

There was a restaurant not too far from the unknown cuckoo bird, which could still be heard singing in the background. Bless it! The place was exposed with no doors or windows, just pillars because it was so hot obviously, and it was a bit fancy with white tiled floors and fish tanks with what Emily guessed to be local species of fish swimming in them, they weren't colourful or owt and the water within had that muddy, greenish river tint. She sat next to one that didn't have owt in it…just dark roots and water plants sat in a bed with bits of plants drifting about. The tables in this restaurant were simple plastic ones—the sort you'd put in your backyard for when the sun was out, and the condiments did not include salt, pepper, vinegar, ketchup or mayonnaise, but four metal jars in a pink plastic rack with small, metal ladle-like spoons in them. And Emily had become quite well acquainted with them, it was the new normal for her now. There were laminated menus in Thai, English and Chinese with plenty of choices; there were even hamburger and hot dogs available, though whole, deep-fried fish appeared to be popular.

Glockenpop by Spiderbait was playing, which Emily hadn't heard in ages. As it was so hot, Emily ordered a bottle of Singha beer and a *kuey tieow*, it was a noodle soup, and this was like the twentieth time she had had it since arriving in Thailand. And there was a good reason for that. The noodle soup came in a large light blue bowl filled with a light, brownish soup and some rice noodles, garnished with fried garlic, shiny white bean sprouts, some green veg which included coriander, spring onions and another local leafy green veg and minced pork and them same sort of meatballs she had had with the ba mee on the train and some crispy, bubbly textured wonton triangles. It was colourful, extravagant and the smell of garlic was just so tempting, Emily had to take a photo of it before digging in.

First thing, she took the plastic pink soupspoon, which was also provided with chopsticks and had a taste.

The soup was lightly flavoured, a bit meaty a bit citrusy and garlicky, but that's what them four condiment jars were for… So Emily went spicy with them chilli flakes, put on a bit of saltiness with that fish sauce, sour with that clear chilli vinegar, and a bit of sugar for sweetness. And Emily went madder with the chillies than one night back in her college days without fear of consequences, mixed it all in and took in a mouthful of noodles from what was now a perfect bowl of noodle soup. She hummed and titled her head to the right and put the back of her hand over her mouth to cover it as she giggled, content with the results. A bowl of kuey tieow brought comfort with each customised mouthful, and they just seemed to taste better with each place Emily visited, soon she was gonna have to pursue how to cook it!

There was a small racket to her left from this fella opening up a small, portable flight of stairs and climbing up the edge of the fish tank, where he dropped a bunch of small, live fish into it from a bowl, the fish swimming about and descending to the bottom. The bloke noticed Emily looking and pointed at the tank.

"You see?" he said. There was summat in it, of which Emily initially thought was just a root, but it had more features to it; such as shiny scales with these dark grey and black bands and this familiar flickering tongue at the end of the supposed root.

"*Ngu kra saen,*" the bloke said.

"Snaayk."

"Yeah?" Emily said not pretending to sound interested. It was a snake, and that was obvious after a second.

The fella spoke a full sentence in Thai, pointing at the snake.

Emily stood up and rolled her eyes further down, noticed that the well-camouflaged serpent's tail was wrapped around one of the surrounding roots in a hook shape. The snake had these two short antennae-like thingies on its snout that wiggled about like a pair of maggots fishermen used. One of the fish that had been released into the tank swam in the direction of the snake, mistaking them wiggly thingies.

The snake lunged and caught the fish, instead of wrapping its body around it, it began swallowing it whole. Emily chuckled with amazement. It was summat you'd expect from a sea creature than a familiar animal! Emily raised her camera and took a photo. Then she hesitated and cupped her left hand, the bright light of her surroundings concealing this light coming from within her palm.

Then the snake unwrapped its tail from the root and began bending its body, swimming right towards the glass. The snake reached its head and upper body upwards and pressed its belly against the pane, them ribbed scales fully exposed with a suction cup like effect as it swayed tightly left to right with its tongue flickering and them antennae wiggling about. Emily took a photo, then sat back down and checked on the freaky picture she had taken. The fella feeding it laughed and attracted attention.

"*Mai key hen kao tam yang nan!*" He said loudly, whatever he meant though his words were praiseworthy of comedy. He tapped on the glass, clearly trying to entice the snake's attention but didn't succeed.

"*Hooh!*" He added, sounding elated. Emily chuckled, the strange light from her cupped hand still glowing discreetly. The weird snake peeled itself away from the glass, its body bending as it swam further back towards the tank and took refuge among the roots.

Emily finished off her noodle soup, paid the amazingly affordable bill of just a hundred and fifty baht, which was less than five quid back home! Time really flew by quickly here, and the sun was beginning to set. Emily was going around in a circle, heading back towards the bridge, there were so many people on motorbikes and there were these pickup vans with roofs over the back. The inspiring sight of the nearby green and orangey tinted mountains were making her think things: like what she would be like ten to twenty years from now. She felt like having another lager, as cider and wine didn't seem to be sold here.

There was a bloke sat at a stall, selling a rainbow medley of exotic fruit wrapped up in cling film with white Styrofoam trays and clear bags with local pork scratching, which she had had plenty of times already as a guilty pleasure. The stall next to it had these fabrics and summer dresses, pinned up on white racks with washing pegs. Emily approached the clothing stand. And with an extended finger, she touched this piece of fabric that caught her interest, which was a silky floral pink over white, similar to her sarong trousers.

She stepped aside to the other stand with the bloke selling fruit and decided to purchase some from him, which she took and sat down on this stone table that had a marble patterning near a ginnel wide enough for a single car, between a hairdressers and this shop selling these altar/shrines which seemed to be everywhere here, adorned with decoration, joss sticks and fruit and water. The alley led to some garden full of banana trees within white stone walls with these petal-shaped gaps and a large, silver SUV with black windows parked there.

As she ripped her fingernails through the packaging of the fruit, Emily passively watched a bird perch itself on the leaf of a banana tree, it was sparrow-sized and dark brown with a dandelion yellow belly. Was this the por leow bird? Emily wanted to photograph it. In her head she urged it to keep still, which it did like a wish granted allowing her to successfully snap it. This lass wearing shorts came out of the hairdressers, leaned down and chucked a bucket of water onto the floor, clearing off some grime and stuff which spilled out over the edge of the raised footpath. She looked Emily's way and said hello with a heavy accent, which Emily returned by putting her hands together.

"Swasdee kha!"

Her reciprocation was met with a short laugh and a smile.

The fruit at Emily's fingers was proper interesting; there were slices of some green mango or papaya and this yellow peach like thingy and a purple version of it, a red passion fruit thingy and the star: summat with fleshy pink skin these leafy parts to it and a grey/white interior with all these black bits, she had seen on travel shows. Emily tried the pink fruit first, it wasn't so much as sweet, but rather bitter...an "acquired taste" was the word. Like with watermelon (Emily rarely got the chance to eat back home) she didn't eat the skin. She looked across the road and spotted several scrawny, but scary looking dogs trotting about, some loud and fighting with each other like them dangerous wild ones in Africa, summat which would be concerning to tourists, but Emily didn't feel an inch of anxiety.

Despite the barking of the dogs, she gave the green mango thingy slices a try, they were choky and sour and, there was a packet of what looked like pink salt that came with the package, which Emily prickled on. That pink salt was a little bit spicy, gave it flavour and was refreshing after the density of the noodle soup. Ignoring the dogs, Emily turned her head and looked about the setting.

This massive black/brown wasp thing flew past her, making an unsettling buzz about as loud as a dentist's drill. And she didn't want it near her! That bloody thing was after her fruit like wasps were after picnic food. Then that scary bugger flew off. Because she wanted it to.

After finishing more than half of the exotic fruits, Emily abandoned her seat and walked on for a couple hundred metres and passed by this well-kept cemetery, with flowers and small headstones. It was for British soldiers in the Second World War fighting against the Japanese, a sign posted explained. Emily wondered if she was related to any of the fallen. She crossed the road and got out the way of this modified red pickup truck, which had a megaphone on top of its roof. She was heading past this building on her right with marble white stairs, she turned her head and looked down to see this cat walking towards her without looking up at her. It stopped just centimetres from her ankle and lay down to rest, its tail curled into a J shape and eyes squeezed shut.

Taken back by the cuteness of the action, a giddy Emily blushed and had a good look at it. It had the most beautiful fur; surely it had to be a mixed breed or summat. It resembled a tabby cat, had them markings similar to a tiger on the forehead and face, its underside was pure white while the upper body was a soft grey with these U-shaped spots on the body, these tiger-like rings on the tail, a collar of grey patterning around the neck, and that same grey shade on the back of the legs. It opened its eyes, showing off a pale blue pair then meowed, giving Emily no choice but to kneel down and pet it. It continued to meow, getting louder and more frequent. Gosh, it was a proper whiny thing!

"You want him?" Some bloke called out. Emily looked about and saw this fella with a cap, wearing a loose red vest with a graphic print.

"He no home!" The bloke said pointing at the cat. The poor cat was homeless! And the por leow bird was singing again.

Emily smiled and confidently picked the cat up by the back of his neck and held him in her arms without him flailing his paws about.

"I'd love him!" She said. She had always wanted a pet, now she had one, whether Mum approved or not! Next she was walking the streets with the cat carried in her arms, and it was so cute the way he was still while turning his head, looking at people and Emily got her fair share of attention from locals and tourists alike. She was passing by another shop selling them altar shrines, many of these were golden, had sparkling details to them and more colourful than the previous. Emily thought of getting summat for her furry new mate to eat when her phone rang, and she had to use one hand to hold the cat, which managed by putting its paws on her shoulder. It was Mum.

"Where are yah?" she asked sounding concerned.

"I'm out."

Emily hadn't told her where.

"When yah comin' back?"

"Soon, I hope—"

"Say cheese!" A lass in a distinctively accented voice called out to the left. Emily turned that way, cat still held in her arms. There was a tall white lass stood in front of one of the altars, her face obscured by her phone aimed her way. Her fingers tapped down on the snap button, without her asking.

"Erh, I'll call you in a sec Mum," Emily said without hanging up.

"I'm worried about yah!" Mum stressed.

The tall lass lowered her phone, revealing a gorgeous, sun irradiated face. It was Luna. She was dressed for the weather in a bright yellow body vest tucked into some fluttery yellow summer trousers with a rainbow print of tropical leaves, they were high-waist with the strings tied symmetrically into a perfect bow, the bottoms tucked into black combat boots instead of sandals. It was a bit odd but it suited her, and she seemed to meld into her surroundings. She had a folded, foot long topknot on top of her head that gave her already sorted fringe some extra sophistication, and she wasn't wearing makeup or owt and didn't have a handbag or clutch in sight. Luna stepped forward and tucked her phone into her back pocket. With the cat still in her arm, Emily carefully held out her bag of fruit and scratching.

"Want some fruit?" She offered.

"Just had jungle curry."

Whatever Luna had had, it sounded interesting. She had this look to her, like a teacher telling a child summat important. Maybe that was because she was taller?

"Be careful!" She told Emily with unflinching eyes reflecting the sun like ten pence coins.

"Emily?"

Though she could hear her mother calling out to her over the phone, Emily ignored her.

"What'd you mean…?"

An answer to Luna's caution was more important.

"I can't see it," the tall lass said, her big eyes calmly scanning the area behind Emily. "*Just* when you get hurt by it." Then any and all concern was destroyed when a small, sparrow-sized bird just flew into view from the left, and landed on Luna's head. She didn't react. Emily though would be screaming! She gasped with laughter and looked around to see other people doing the same then softly cleared her throat.

"Luna? There's a bird on your head…?" She started without raising her voice.

"Of course!" Luna said, emitting a squeak to that Scandinavian accent of hers and adjusted the waistband of her trousers. The bird pecked into a strand of her hair then flew off, and again there was no reaction from the lass, while a few laughs were heard in the background, she tilted her head back and rolled it around her shoulders while Emily chuckled over how random she was.

"Got any nice photos?" Luna asked raising her left hand to her shoulder and giving it a massage.

"Loads!" Emily replied, then with both hands she held up her cat, which didn't flay about. With a static face Luna grunted.

"Should have got a tiger!" She said and walked past her. "You're ready for it!"

~

It was late evening. The hotel Emily was staying at was tranquil, the white stone walls brightened up by the local sun during the day, and saturated partly by the bluish hue of these local streetlights at night. Like every place here the hotel had cooling air conditioning and had a view of the blackened River Kwai, which reflected multi-coloured lights from surrounding businesses. There were these odd chirping sounds about, combined with the sounds of crickets, a night chorus playing over the background traffic. Lo-Fi-Fink *this is the end*, another favourite from a long while back, Emily was listening to on her phone while doing sit-ups on her bed, dressed in a white two piece swimsuit with a pink floral print. And it was the same fabric she had touched earlier at the stalls. The hotel had a pool she wanted to have a swim in. Done with her workout, Emily stood up with a smile on her face. She felt unstoppable, her optimism was like a drug and her workout only amplified the effects of it. She slipped on some sandals, picked up a white towel and draped it around her neck and wrapped a glittery cream coloured sarong around her waist.

The cat she had adopted was at her feet looking up at her, meowing for attention. She had already fed him some barbecued pork when she had checked into the hotel, along with some water served in a fancy bowl she had bought from this shop around the corner from here.

"Alright Millie, yah whiny thing!" Emily fretted. Though the cat was a male, she couldn't resist naming him after this tiny and proper adorable black and white she dog she had seen in a park as a teenager, being walked by a muscular bloke and couldn't resist the urge to go up and ask him her name. Millie, unable to tell the difference for namesake, remained static, waving his tail about. The adorable meow he made forced Emily to kneel down and pet him.

She left the room with Millie running out, the hotel staff hadn't complained or owt about him. The lights in the corridor were out, leaving it near pitch black, the lights of the hotel foyer to her right and the swimming pool to her left were both visible in a sharp, bold rectangular frame that was cinematic almost. Emily could see the white floor tiles and some framed pictures on the walls, the artwork which she couldn't make out. She didn't freak out seeing this tiny lizard on the wall to her left; she had seen plenty during her trips to the Mediterranean and they had never bothered her. The further she walked the smells of freshly grilled stuff wafting from the streets intensified, over this already present scent which, to be honest wasn't pleasant though it wasn't a bad one, it was sweet yet overpowering with some overwhelming pungency. Then some bloke called out summat on a megaphone—it was probably from one of them pickup trucks she saw earlier.

Emily was gonna head out into town and eat out tonight. But all that food from earlier on today needed some calories burning off whether you felt like it or not! And Emily was eager for a swim. Though she wasn't sure what she was going to wear out, she was sure she'd make her mind up after the swim. The hotel's swimming pool wasn't that big and glowed green/blue under the lights shining underneath and there were a couple of leaves drifting in the pool, but that was fine. It had a diving board and a separate shallow pool for the kids, tall, decorative palm trees surrounded it and there were these pink flowers with giant thorns that put those on roses to shame. There was no one about the area, and no one seen on the balconies and there was a closed bar shack by the pool. Emily sat down on one of the white plastic poolside benches, set her towel down and peeled off her sarong. She massaged her shoulders, interlocked her fingers, stretched her arms over her head then stepped into the pool, the water was warm and a relief from the heat. Emily hadn't had a swim for a while.

She lowered herself down, kicked her legs and flailed her arms, got adjusted to her body being in water. She inhaled and submerged, feeling the sting of chlorine in her eyes which wasn't so bad after so long. Underwater she contemplated the adjustment, life had never been better. Then the feeling was vanquished, as if there was no such contaminant in the water to begin with. Emily surfaced, kicked her legs to stay afloat and with both hands, swept her hair back and breast stroked forward then rolled back and backstroked towards the end of the pool. She threw her feet forward and pushed herself away nearly halfway across the pool, getting the knack of moving about in the water.

"Careful!" She heard Luna caution her, the tall lass's voice echoing as though she was shouting out in a valley…even though the tall lass was nowhere to be seen. Emily didn't react to her and rolled back onto her front and breast stroked, thinking about what fancied her appetite for tonight, a spicy curry with pork as the protein came to mind.

Then everything went dark. Were the surrounding lights dimming down from a local power cut?

No, it was darker in a different way; everything else was obscure. Emily looked down at her arms, her flesh stood out against the blackened water which continued to ripple, even though the ambient blue glow had suspiciously vanished as though edited out like some cinema effect. She held up her hands to her face and experienced this distortion of reality that had her see things in slow motion. She looked to her right, where the pool bench with her sarong and towel should have been, now replaced with an image of *herself.* Her whole body for some reason. From what her mind's eye was showing her, Emily wasn't in water, though she could still feel it around her, her doppelganger was stood up still and expressionlessly as a statue and was dressed in that white beautician outfit she had worn during college last year that stood out against the void, her hair was that reddish purplish colour she had dyed it and she could see her old piercings.

This proper horrid smell was shooting its way up Emily's nostrils, and her kicking to stay afloat ceased from the distraction, nearly resulting in her going underwater consequently. This, was by far, the most dreadful bloody smell to have crept up her nose, someone having eaten summat rancid then doing a shit inches from her face didn't qualify as a decent enough description for it. Emily turned her head left, the view still black, and saw this thing… It was a centre view image against the void, an ugly thing, the mystery of it was more troubling. It was brown, and not like furniture or wood, but the worst possible shade of brown; like rust, dried blood and crap. This entity was set low to the floor with this wide dark hole at its top that made it look like a toilet, but with long arms and boxing-glove-shaped hands outstretched in front of it.

And this repulsive thing was moving Emily's way as unsurely as one of them flat, sole fishes on the seafloor. Panicked, she looked away frightfully unsure of how to react to this new, featureless world. Then her menace's shit brown skin flooded her sight.

Some unseen force clutched her by the waist. Emily jolted helplessly as this force dragged her down. Without opening her mouth, she screamed as loud as she ever had, but didn't hear it. Then that horrid brown contaminating her vision looked like a sight seen by one of them medical cameras going down someone's throat. Emily saw another copy of herself, this one was dressed differently; she was wearing that same pink tracksuit she had a few days ago when she had had all them other weird episodes, though she was bare-footed. This pink version of Emily was squatted down with both knees bent evenly and her arms tucked in against her thighs, foetal almost, her makeup-coated eyes were shut tight and it really didn't look like she was asleep or passed out.

All over her body were these small, weird lights that had a stretched worm-like motion to them, they looked like proper old video games where you were just simply moving a very simple character about the screen. A partly blurred view of her face appeared in a slowed down shaky, up and downward view of her with this noise that sounded like the beat of a dance track, the sort Emily felt embarrassed to say sounded like farts. Her eyes were open but with no motion to them, the implications just as scary as the bog brown menace that reappeared, and it was closer to her—these tumours seen bulging on the surface of its flesh like a beating heart.

Before Emily could decide on her reaction, the menace moved and threw its limbs forward, lobster-like and grabbed her, pinning her arms against her side just above her waist. In the quickest moment imaginable, this pale, fleshy sack encased her from above and tightened, the outline of her trapped figure visible and swung around viciously in all directions, as though within the grasp of some overpowered serial killer, parts of it seen bulging from her resistance within. The action reminded Emily of these sea slugs from documentaries that could expand a part of their mouth to catch prey. And that sack thingy around her was slowly shrinking, squeezing from whatever was going on inside. Emily felt her mouth being partly smothered, while shortly after she felt a soft, blunt force between her crotch, while it wasn't painful this invisible violation expounded her panic. But she could only scream in her head. Then the stinking nightmare submerged below the black void, taking her with him to wherever it was going.

A blink of life's existence went by and that menace reappeared. It was changing rapidly like one of them time lapsed cameras on nature documentaries that showed plants growing. It rose, getting taller with its arms falling to its sides as this pair of stumps formed below it then thinned out halfway, it had legs now and they took on texture, the thighs baggy. Though the gobbler menace was now the size of a big man, it had no head, just this stump where that toilet hole was leaning upwards that way, shrinking and taking the place of where a face should be, these ragged creases forming around it. This football-sized sphere-shaped thing bulged between its legs and these pair of tumours ballooned on its torso in a swishing manner until they were the size of children, each of which moulded themselves into some very distinctive shapes. They looked like the backs of headless, nude women in a foetal pose. Though it was lighter and had more reddish tones to its flesh, it still had the same shit colour to it.

It sounded awfully strange, but Emily recognised the gobbler menace. It was the subject of this drawing done by this one fella… So, that's what all this was about then? Emily questioned desperately while remembering this advert on the telly when she was really young of these chocolate men walking down a street made of chocolate, which made her want to nag Mum to buy her a bar of chocolate. As a child you felt bad eating one of them chocolate men. Chocolate was one of the best things ever in existence, but this thing Emily was seeing made it seem convincingly the opposite.

She saw her pink self again against the void, where the gobbler menace held her in its big hands. But she had shrunk to the size and shape of a football, that was made up of her head, and pink velour to appear perfectly round. There was glossiness to some parts of the surface of this ball she had been turned into, that of a white slime running down. Her eyes were shut, mouth partly open and lopsided, her nose looked broken, and a hungry sounding groan roared over while the view of her ball-shaped remains shook in a shudder, the noise was almost identical to this burp she had shamelessly let rip one time with some old mates, having been starving from a day out shopping, after she had wolfed down a burger, but her gob had been so full it came out weird.

Under the water of the pool Emily's eyes opened with these pin prick blue lights flashing about in every part of her vision…that grinding, farting noise heard as she felt that lively, optimistic soul sucked out of her body as rapidly as the vacuum of space, while a crushing depression filled that empty shell that was her body. She felt this pressurised warmth between her legs that enveloped her, fear of the unknown trumping humility when she realised that she had pissed herself!

Emily splashed about in a hysterical panic, on the verge of drowning, she yelped, partly swallowing half a mouthful of pool water and swam to the edge with what felt like her last bit of energy. She looked around left and right maybe four times in a second, her focus distorted as she witnessed the skin of her flailing arms being enveloped in a turquoise sleeve in a smooth, brush-like motion, the same thing happening with her torso and lower body. In her dizzied view, she noticed Luna sat squat by the edge. The lass was wearing a plain pomegranate velour tracksuit that went well with her hair, the back of which was styled up high into a beehive with two metal chopsticks slotted through it in an X-shape.

The tall lass looked indifferent to Emily's trauma, just staring at her like she was a fish in a pond. Before Emily could beg her for assistance, Luna helpfully reached out and grabbed hold of her left wrist and pulled her out the water as if she weighed only a kilo. Emily felt the strain in the socket of her arm as she dangled, water dripping from her new clothes into the pool. This lass was really strong! But Emily was too shaken up to react, even while dangling, she gasped searching the poolside for what had been devouring her while Luna swung her to the edge of the pool with a slow motion like a crane, dangling from her wrist as though she was a fish caught on a line. Emily didn't even ask what she was doing.

"Turquoise…suits you!" Luna said lightly, her pronunciation of words as sharp as a pencil tip pressing down hard against paper. She dared to chuckle.

"*Blonde*…no!" Luna added. Covering Emily's body was in fact a turquoise tracksuit, the fibres of velour material she recognised despite it being soaked, her eyes rolled down to see that white gladiator sandals with silver rhinestone studs covered her feet. Her new outfit had soaked up the water and she was dripping like mad onto the pool edge. Emily looked about for the nearest thing she could see her reflection in, which was the darkened window of one of the hotel rooms, no lights on hence unoccupied.

Immediately she gasped seeing her reflection, slouched and went up to the window for a better look. Her face was darkened as though she had just carelessly smothered on fake tan, and her hair, which was a bright blonde, was tied up into a high ponytail that was stuck dripping to her back, these locks tucked back against her ears behind these big gold earrings with overlapping plates that looked like them eye ring bone thingies you saw on a bird's eye sockets. She had a small, dark spot on her left cheek, her lips glossy with a bright strawberry pink lipstick. *What?* Forgetting the triple trauma of being gobbled up, pissing herself and her sudden makeover, Emily had what you might call the cognition to realise just how *fake* she looked. Luna gently dropped her to her feet and stopped her from falling over as her legs gave way. Emily fell to her knees, noticed Luna was wearing these wooden flip-flops with simple black thongs, they were them Japanese sorts.

"Too much makeup!" Luna said, her sarcasm remarkable if it wasn't for the situation. Not looking up at the tall lass, Emily took a breather like she hadn't before and looked around the poolside, panicked like an animal that had just lost a predator after an adrenaline charged chase. This lass appeared out onto the pool area. She was dressed *exactly* the same as Emily; earrings, hair, makeup and all, though her tracksuit was brighter and the flared ends of the bottoms apparent with the lack of water soaking them. It was Valerie, the lass who had dissed her back at college and had done so again at her place of work a few days ago. She looked different—in fact she looked incredible; she wasn't as bulimic and had about an inch of curve in the right areas, her bright blonde hair had no dark roots showing, her makeup refined and her face naturally tanned, the broad shape of her forehead was far more suited to the high ponytail. Despite her panic, Emily wasn't surprised by her arrival.

"What's up with her?" An approaching Valerie said relaxed as though it was a night in the pub where you spotted a patron acting dodgy after too many.

"Why you *copying* me?" Her tone changed, she sounded more surprised by it and her eyes did show alarm. They weren't dark, they were blue as gems.

"She wasn't!" Luna said and Emily knew what she meant, she would argue with the blue-eyed Valerie, if she wasn't so drained. She was really starving, that she wouldn't resist running across an open field with some dangerous wild animals about for a burger someone had just left randomly on the floor. If she didn't eat within minutes, Emily reckoned she would fall into a coma.

"We'll meet you downstairs." Luna told Valerie, who shrugged bobbing her head.

"I knew this would happen!" Luna said emotionlessly with Emily too weak to question what she was on about.

"Better not be all the time!" Valerie called out as she walked off.

Her voice was different. There was an accent to it, Emily didn't know and hadn't asked about it, but it wasn't posh Thewlie.

"Got you some *food*!" Luna said, pouted her lips and heavily emphasised the middle two letters then jerked her head towards the bench where Emily's sarong and towel rested. Emily staggered towards the bench, noticing these firefly-like shimmers on her sleeves. Luna presented her with a Styrofoam box with these mini hot dogs, each one wrapped up in a thin crêpe like pancake that tasted of coconut, while a weird combination they were irresistible. Emily didn't need owt else, though at this moment she would prefer it if Luna had hand-fed her them cute hot dogs.

The tall lass sat next to her right, her left arm reaching out to pat her on the shoulder, which wasn't exactly gentle but it wasn't cause for concern, unlike her unflinching stare off into the night. What was it with her hyper quirky expressions, normal people would ask? Emily liked to believe as of now she had half the answers.

"Careful what you think of," Luna said. "A high *positive* thought keeps it away."

The tall lass's words while cryptic, weren't one of them annoying types in films where you would just ask for a simple explanation and never get it until summat bad happens. Yet it was easily compared to not looking a dog right in the eyes when it was pissed off sort of advice.

Emily gasped without conveying any confirmation, and having a peek at Luna's tracksuit she quickly felt dry naked at the tanning beds, because she wanted to for one, the unknown, soft golden video game lights glowing against her face as she looked down at her turquoise tracksuit covering her legs, it was lighter both in shade and weight having lost all the water it had absorbed.

"Speedy recovery!" Luna remarked over the songs of insects in the background and pinched one of the pancake wrapped hot dogs for herself. The tall lass had lady in red vibes to her, which she could complete with some makeup.

Emily contemplated putting on summat comfy and similar to what her two mates tonight were wearing, she didn't like this colour covering her body though. She looked to her reflection and watched as her hair glowed with them same lights that had appeared in the pool, but brighter. The unwanted ponytail retracted into her scalp, the bangs of her hair peeled back down against the side of her face and fell like flower petals, taking on the form of her usual bob, though the bright blonde converted to a bright, neon pink—a rather erotic, fantasy look, but not so severe cut in the fringe you saw in wigs that strippers wore, these beads of light ran down from crown to bang, leaving these natural brown highlights in a chameleon-like way.

That bright light that had caused her hair to turn pink reappeared around her eyes and left behind thick, black winged eyeliner surrounding her eyes that stretched nearly to her ears, a theatre makeup sort of look. The bright lights then shrouded her tracksuit shoulder to ankle in a thick, glowing sheet, and changed into a raspberry purple colour, melding in with these black leopard spot outlines appearing along with some blue versions, which clustered randomly in some parts so that they looked like clusters of skulls without looking creepy.

Emily's shifted trackie had a mixed ice cream look to it and reminded her strongly of this one flavour she had had on a holiday in Lisbon when she was fourteen, it had been vanilla blended with some sort of berry and grape—it was so addictive that she had kept coming back for extra servings each day, and she would have put on some weight if her holiday hadn't ended! While not quite what Emily had in mind, this was a very luscious look. Having pissed herself, Emily naturally wanted a shower. Weeing yourself in water was more discreet than wetting yourself in public, that growing wet spot visible between your legs being pointed out like some of her classmates did to other pupils back in primary had and had the piss taken out of them for weeks afterward!

Chapter 18

The Farang trio went out on to the streets of town, while it was more than hot enough to be dressed skimpily, it wasn't too hot to wear a velour trackie with a tank top underneath. Emily had always wanted to be out with two other lasses as gorgeous and dressed the same way as her. Well, that was a reality now. But there were no kicking of legs or shouting out or singing, just smiles and enjoyment of the exotic location. Emily was carrying a black clutch, Valerie had a white one with decorative studs that matched her slippers, Luna didn't have one, and was walking in the middle, as she was so tall. And while she seemed aloof and disconnected, she went along with the act, locking arms with the shorter lasses, though looked more like a mother holding two toddlers by the hand.

The three were coming onto this street, the stall to the right selling these bright green, pink and purple foods of some sort in a creamy greyish white soup had Valerie interested.

"What's that?" She said releasing her arm and went over to investigate, the woman behind the stall stirring the gloopy substances and putting them into clear plastic bags for a female customer. Valerie cringed without overdoing it while Luna released her arm from Emily.

"They're too sweet for her…" The tall lass said taking her phone out from the right pocket of her trackie top. She wasn't texting, in actual fact she hadn't once been seen doing that, she was taking pictures and that phone she had was proper smart and had some words engraved on the back too small to make out. Luna didn't stop to take any of her photos, it was like in them action films where the hero just walked in and shot a gun and never missed and repeated without stopping.

On the street, the three lasses had heads turning—guess it wasn't common to see lasses behave like this here! Good thing they weren't going to a holy site; *dress modestly* would be the words on a sign of such a place, respectfully cautioning visitors, the cave visited earlier today being one of them. Emily was looking about nervously amongst the sea of smiles from the people around her, which she returned, a good lot of other Farang were about dressed for the night. The three lasses found a restaurant with polished white tiles and pillars, similar to the place Emily had had noodle soup in, but bigger and fancier; there was a pond with colourful fish swimming about and a water fountain in front, Thai karaoke music playing from the floor above with a glow of red light, which Emily was tempted to pay a visit to after dinner.

The lasses went up a short flight of white stairs wide as a car and had exotic plants in big clay pots laid about on the steps. Inside a waitress with long hair dyed auburn in a green/blue silky blouse and black skirt uniform greeted them and guided them towards a table with a balcony that overlooked the night activity of the streets, their presence turning the heads of other diners. There was this big floating fish made of wood hanging from the ceiling that looked like a skeleton, the white walls had framed, very complicatedly crafted wood works, elephants and trees were seen in most of them, and there were these bold paintings of sceneries, their style so different from western artwork with thinner, more delicate streaks. Emily wanted to buy some similar works. These ceiling tall stalks of bamboo and their long green leaves decoratively divided some parts of the restaurant, one of the pillars had a shrine on it with a gold framed portrait of the country's king displayed.

The three sat down, brown leather bound, multi-language menus were handed out, Emily was eager but uncertain, while Valerie was confused and almost nervous with her glossy lips jutting out, expressing her indecision and looked about, presumably to see what other people were eating.

"I dunno know what to order!" She remarked. "I'm okay with noodles…"

"I'll order you *pad see ew.*" Luna said.

"What's that?" Valerie asked. Luna didn't answer and aimed her phone upwards at the night sky, the flash from its camera people reacted to. There was summat in the air, these silvery glints of small wings were lit up briefly by the flash. Emily was certain it wasn't a bird.

"Fruit bat," Luna said as casually as dismissing herself from the table to go to the loo while Valerie shuddered.

"I can't stand bats! Their ugly and creep me out!" She complained looking around the place as uneasily as Emily, though had nowhere near as much reason to be fearful. Luna turned her phone around, onscreen was a perfect photo of the bat, wildlife photographer quality.

"Nice!" Emily said. "Looks professional!"

Valerie was indifferent, she reached up with her left hand and adjusted her ponytail.

"I'm famished anyway—let's just ask what's good!" Emily insisted, her optimism so deadly that she hoped it would murder the next thing that scared her.

"Ready to order?"

The waitress with the auburn hair came to the table and without asking the other two, Luna ordered automatically, and in Thai.

The tall lass actually sounded like a local lass with the high-pitch and the nasal pronunciations, her voice nowt short of musical! The waitress curved this smile on the right side of her mouth while Emily and Valerie looked at each other and coughed with laughter. It would be safe guessing Luna was a proper good singer as well...?

"*Phoot Thai?*" The waitress said looking impressed.

"*Nit noi khaa!*" Luna said with a smile Emily missed as she looked around the place, Valerie erupting into banter with Luna just sat there turning her head only slightly.

A waiter with a short, spiky quiff came around with a tray with a bottle of whisky, tumblers, a bucket of ice and coke in perspiring glass bottles. "Do they do wine here...?" Valerie asked him.

"No wine here. Sorry!" He answered.

"But you can bring your own." Luna said. Valerie's blue eyes fluttered.

"Sound—next time I shall!" She remarked happily.

"Yeah, brilliant!" Emily included, filled a tumbler with hollow, cylindrical ice cubes and poured herself some whisky and had a sip of the stuff straight. It was awful, but mixing it with coke was just so right.

"Not a fan of whisky!" Valerie expressed before pouring herself a glass and mixing it with some coke. Luna just drank the whisky on the rocks like some hardcore pro.

"Neua pad see eew?" The waitress with the auburn hair announced. She presented these flat noodles, brown from what looked like soy sauce and had some green veg, sliced carrots and burnt bits of egg and strips of beef and smelt gorgeously of garlic. Valerie peered over to investigate the dish, sniffed gently and nodded her head in approval. Then another waitress and the waiter with the quiff came with bowls of boiled rice, some soup that was in this steel, doughnut-shaped bowl with a funnel in the centre with a lit candle at the bottom to keep it warm, which was just fancy. Then came a plate of what the waitress announced as "catfish", which looked like the loose batter at a chippie back home accompanied with an interesting mango, chilli, shallot and fish sauce salad in a small bowl. Emily helped herself to some rice and catfish, mixing in that colourful salad, her tongue pleasantly surprised by the sweet and spicy combination.

Luna handed Valerie the noodles, the blonde lass of which stuck her fork in them and winded them up like spaghetti and had a taste.

"Their nice!"

A bowl of a greenish brown curry smelling soup was laid down in front of Emily.

"Pork green curry, Thai version." Luna informed her as she took a spoon, elegantly leaned over the table and nicked some curry, which she dumped on her plate of rice.

"It spicier?" Emily asked.

"Much *more!*" Luna said mixing the spoonful with her rice and ate a mouthful without blowing on it. Emily took a half spoon full of curry sauce and delicately slurped it, there was nowt mild about it, it was spicier than a vindaloo back home and herbier! She coughed in reflex, her tongue swelling from the rough rush of Thai chilli.

"You alright? It too hot for you?" Valerie teased as normal as anyone would while Luna continued on eating with zero empathy.

Underneath the table, Emily flipped her left hand over her knee and cupped her fingers, that inexplicable glow of gold she was becoming even more acquainted with shinned softly under the table, and while that happened the burn in her mouth subsided about as quickly as she could say "no" to going on a date with a registered sex offender, while the more mellow effects of the chillies remained. The glow dyed down and Emily helped herself to more curry, each mouthful tasting better than the previous.

"Never had so much food, only time is Christmas!" Valerie, a complete stranger to this cuisine stated, the catfish she was fine with minus the gorgeous dressing. From there the lasses drank, ate summat, drank, tried summat else—all the food Luna recommended brilliant—while enduring a compliment and question from a local passing by. A proper girl's night out had commenced.

"So, what were you doin' today?" Emily asked Valerie who was alright that she didn't deserve an axe through the head.

"Laying in the sun all day! Had a Thai massage," she answered. "The lass nearly pulled my toes off!"

"Gonna have me self one!" Emily said, her left hand reaching over to her right shoulder and dug her fingers into the flesh, trying to imagine such a massage.

"Love this place!" She said without looking at all the lights and friendly faces beckoning her way. "Gotta make it home!"

"I prefer the city!" Valerie said, her eyes rolling upwards.

"Not a fan of the city!" Emily said then looked left, wondering if anyone had overheard her and taken offense. She didn't see any signs of that, just men and women looking her way and back.

Then she looked further right, towards the entrance of the restaurant and saw the gobbler menace again. It felt like the idealness of the night was on the verge of being destroyed, it stood at the top of the stairway, only the left half of its form was visible from the angle and people were walking past it, oblivious to its existence like a ghost. This time it was more animated, holding something that swung like the pendulum of a grandfather clock partly in view back and forth, but it was more than close enough. It was Emily's head, with the same pink hair and makeup she currently donned, the menace swung it gripping the hair from her crown. She looked away, the deep fear and disgust she did a brilliant job of not letting it show on her face then took a drink. Then more food came with the waiter with the quiff laying down two plates.

"Oh my God, *what* is that?" Valerie said almost in a panic, which was enough to snap Emily out of her horrified trance. There was a plate of clearly recognisable, steamed chicken feet and what looked like deep-fried cockroaches! A second after the plates were laid down Luna reached out and picked up one of the cockroaches with her fingers.

"You're not gonna eat it?" Valerie said squirming, looking like she was about to pitch a girly fit. Luna's expression in response was otherwise priceless; she squinted partly, smacked her lips sulkily down to the right and without any hesitation, popped the insect into her mouth and started chewing, this crispiness heard. Valerie covered her mouth and complained while Emily, pokerfaced from her fear of the gobbler menace, poured herself another whisky.

Valerie turned her head towards Emily who inhaled a wisp of air to her right while Luna reached for one of the chicken feet, her thumb spreading the toes, which she began gnawing on, much to Valerie's disgust. She looked away and leaned across the table Emily's way, both hands grasped around her tumbler, her gorgeously manicured fingernails were shining with these suspicious, silvery pixels that jumped like popcorn kernels hitting the pan. Nowt seemed surprising to Emily anymore given recent events, and before she could ask her blonde pal them shinny particles clustered together around the tumbler in an instance and in a spiral shape manner as though they were a circling school of silvery fish. Not only did the mass expand to twice its width and height, it was being raised as a stem formed below it about a foot high, while a second mass spread out below it into a perfectly circular base. The tableside spectacle while easily labelled as magic, had some identifiable natural world actions seen all at once on its accumulated surface: the movement of a swarm of ants, grains of sand blown by the wind, and there was some rolling storm cloud motions.

The clustering activity of the pixels ceased, then appeared to have been flattened and smoothened out at light speed that a bright, silver shine radiated in place.

"Gotcha!" A smirking Valerie said as though she was prepared to laugh it out in victory and ran the tips of her thumb and index up and down the stem. The modest tumbler had turned into a *chalice*, a silver one that glistened with clear gems of various sizes with some of the smaller ones forming this visible, yet unrecognisable patterning.

"Now that's royalty!" Valerie said excitedly without sounding too smug and reached up with both hands to mess around with her ponytail. Barely surprised Emily gazed at the chalice, not saying anything as she gripped it and pulled it slowly towards her, then looked about for witnesses. There didn't seem to be any. Emily looked at Luna, who hadn't reacted and it wasn't because she was gorging on chicken feet.

"So, how…" Emily started, "*big* can you make them…?"

"Me? I wanna do up a house or summat!" Valerie said without hesitation and rather snootily took the chalice back from Emily, which she began filling up with the last bit of whisky from the bottle. Emily blinked more than she had in a while as thoughts began to bubble in her head.

"Do us a mansion!" She insisted. Valerie's higher-class sassiness here was not doing her head in.

"Emily's fit!" She said, peering at said person without moving her mouth.

"You're hot!" Valerie said the same way, aiming her right finger at Luna, the pixels buzzing around her fingernails trailing like dust from a moth. Emily wasn't paying attention, her eyes focused on this swarm of mosquitoes around this light dangling down the restaurant's ceiling to the left, which Luna was facing with her phone and taking a photo of.

"You can sleep in the same bed with us, anytime!" The blonde lass said with her mouth so the world could hear. Emily lowered her eyebrows only slightly and turned her head her way.

"Eh?" She expressed her confusion so casually with her lips. After a few more drinks she wouldn't even be bothered. And they needed another bottle of whisky.

Valerie got up out her seat and fetched her clutch.

"Off to the loo, anyone coming?" She invited. Argh, that female trend back at college and bars that baffled blokes—*not missing it!*

"No thanks…" Luna said while Emily shook her head not wanting to know what Valerie would get up to if they were alone together.

"Fine! I'll go on my own!" She said disappointedly and turned around, her ponytail swishing, allowing anyone to see this impressively large, golden rhinestone print on the back of her trackie top of what looked like a roaring leopard on the prowl in a simple but jagged tribal design.

Emily's eyes then drifted passively towards Luna's wide shoulders, which she wouldn't mind massaging if she asked her to, before looking to the left again. Stood with its abominable figure in full view was her shit coloured menace, about a jump away from grabbing hold of her again. This time she tightened her lips almost angrily and looked away, but not so quickly.

"Don't look!" Luna cautioned with still lips while just sat there, calmly filling up a bowl with that soup from the steel doughnut candle contraption. That lass was one tall bag of calm! The steadily progressive insobriety was beginning to numb Emily's response to the gobbler, and life was good again! She thought of herself all bubbly after a half-day's shift, sat at a table with a big juicy burger to satisfy her hunger. Then for some reason she was thinking of this bloke with a very big hat just walking by and stealing it from her, and she would cry like a baby. Weird, but somehow hilarious!

Emily looked at the cockroaches Luna was snacking on and reached in for one, awkwardly slipping it into her mouth head first and chewed. Actually, it wasn't too bad to be honest; crispy like a chip, but way more flaky and with a stale, meaty texture that could be improved with some sort of seasoning. Luna didn't ask her how it was, the same way Emily didn't answer to the familiar golden glow in the lower part of her vision. Still chewing on the bug Emily looked down to see that her tracksuit had turned black—*again?* She didn't even get the chance to begin correcting it.

"OW?" Someone exclaimed as though injured which had Emily half jump, still chewing. The waitress with the auburn hair appeared.

"You change?" She commented. Emily didn't say owt.

"You okay?" The waitress asked. "You want more drink?"

That'd be lovely! Emily nodded, pointed at the empty bottle of whisky and put her hands together. She looked around making sure there was no one catching on. The waitress returned shortly with a new bottle of whisky.

"What you name?" She asked. Emily thought about this one fella a while back, who had called her summat… She thought of him for as long as she dared and hesitantly replied, *"Venus."*

Epilogue

What was the opposite of blue? Red. Sapphire and ruby, two rival gems, both stunning and originating from the far depths of the earth. It was dawn, the rays of sunrise were slowly creeping where the immaculately dressed Gangster person sat on a bench behind Geldard Hospital, the hills of Oldmill Brig in sight. His hair was recently trimmed but slicked back still with a loose piece trailing down his forehead, he hadn't bothered shaving his stubble. He was dressed in the same three colours, though every piece of clothing was brand new, his ocean blue shirt still had the folding creases from being out of its packet, his cosmic purple tie was plain but had a silky gloss, his black trousers crisp, his footwear were a pair of black wranglers with a polished sheen to them, plain but hardly boring, though the black leather jacket he wore was heavily worn.

Gangster person raised his right hand, which held a near finished cigarette between two fingers and inhaled. He hadn't slept well, as the dark bags around his eyes indicated. Stepping outside was a form of consolation, like the bottle of Irish whiskey stood on the bench to his left as though another person was sat next to him. Gangster person took a quaff from the bottle then chased it with a pull of nicotine, sunlight beaming down on him. Outwardly he appeared pleased, content with the sight, eyelids fluttering. He turned his head to the left, revealing a purple/pink scar on his right eyebrow, shaped like a correction mark.

A bird came swooping down before him, slender, butcher red three-toed feet landing down on the floor. It was an everyday urban pigeon, *columba livia domestica*, that fearlessly made its way towards Gangster person's feet while hooting, the downward tilting of his head conveyed a very welcoming look. Regrettably he didn't have anything edible on him to toss its way. Gangster person exhaled smoke, making an effort to keep it away from the columbiform and grinned, tilting his head a few short degrees to the right, conveying comparable affection as if one wished to pet a dog or cat. Though he didn't reach out to touch the bird he did say, "The far future…It'll be far past."

Gangster person spoke as though reciting important, functional words. For a meeting or lecture maybe? Well, people were inclined to listen now instead of going about the opposite direction of what he inferred.

Gangster person exhaled, looked up beyond the sky and the pigeon flew off. He put his cigarette in his mouth then slapped at his head with both hands somewhat irritably.

"I'm right! I'm right!" He declared to the air and looked in the direction of the flying pigeon which disappeared behind a building.

"They're wrong!" He said harshly, gripped his near finished cigarette and slouched forward.

"Need company…!" Gangster person breathed, the pinkie finger of his right hand wiggling, then stood up, tucked the whisky bottle into his jacket and walked off, but not before courteously disposing of his cigarette butt in a bin conveniently placed two feet from where he sat.

Despite his jagged appearance, Gangster person walked along with a sense of peace to him, even if his striding steps were very hurried almost as though in a perpetuated state of rush. As he moved the inner city transitioned into the suburbs of Dilke-Sutton, patches of woodland to the left, birds singing with Gangster person trying to spot and identify some species amongst all the thick green foliage. It was him and nature, and the essence of peacefulness showed on his scarred face, only to be disrupted by two teenage, tracksuit-wearing boys riding his way on bikes. They were of the chav variety, they indicated by their senseless stares, heads turning as they neared Gangster person. They were both ugly; one had a slack, goofy expression and a severe blonde crew cut while the other looked like a girl, one with a spoon-shaped nose and short, spiky brown hair.

"Me mate wants to *bum* yah!" The goofy one heckled, causing the one with the spiky hair to giggle at the perverted insult just before they were both far enough to ensure a safe getaway on their bikes. At least, that's what they were deluded to believe… Gangster person squinted, felt his chest swell up in fury and spun around.

"SHUT UP!" He yelled thunderously, hoping to hurt more than just their feelings.

"Shut up-shut up!" Parroted back the girly one with spiky hair.

"Piece of shit!" Gangster person fired back.

"Piece of shit! Piece of shit!" The perverted goofy one said. They were bioorganic dictation machines, and they weren't amusing. So Gangster person took a liberty himself and ran at them.

"Fuckin' hell!" They both laughed and began pedalling furiously. Normally they would escape, laughing and flipping the middle finger and telling their friends about it. But that was an old, undesirable era.

What actually happened was that they fell off their bikes, as though they had been struck by a strong gust of wind, which wasn't about, and tumbled multiple times over the road, no oncoming traffic to run them over. While they cried out in pain, Gangster person broke left, where he grabbed the one with spiky hair with both hands by the waist off the road and flung him off to the right, he felt no lighter than a pillow and went as far as twelve feet, where he hit the floor hard, face first and didn't move afterwards. Gangster person approached the goofy one and stomped down on his left knee, breaking it with a crack heard over his resulting cry, his arms and other leg flailing and slapping pointlessly against the floor. Then he put his foot down, hard on his crotch as though it was some dangerous bug that needed exterminating, his screams were worse than his partner.

"I don't need that again!" The Gangster person said very lightly then turned around, walking away. He interlocked his fingers and stretched his arms forward. It was very apparent that these boys had something to disagree about; obviously they were one of these kinds that would "agree to disagree". Gangster person never understood that term, as it was used by people that just liked to argue for the sake of it. That thus provided certain people with the right to do bad. Either you win or you don't, either it is or it isn't. Those were categorical and *not* opinions. To his right, across the road was this thing coiled around one of the trees, translucent as a jellyfish with a foot wide width and moving like a snake.

Ignoring the near invisible entity wrapped around the tree, Gangster person walked until he couldn't hear the pathetic, regretful sobs of the offensive pair. *I'm walking forward. No one will stop me from walking forward. I'm doing nothing wrong.* He contemplated. It was that simple, and the bar was not invented for no reason. He checked his phone held in a black leather pouch attached to his belt, which still wasn't an updated model after all these years. While some places were open, alcoholic beverage was not served at this time. The skies above him turned a dark grey, with the promise of releasing a torrent, which failed to unleash.

Gangster person was coming into another district: Giberford, rows upon rows of council housing, from the 1980's lined the streets, slanderous graffiti was a common sight. He was walking by this shop, the shutters for the takeout adjacent so heavily graffiti ridden that no words could be made out, this rough young man with cropped light brown hair was heading his way, he was wearing a grey sports jacket with black stripes, his pants were a quarter foot too short, showed his red and black striped socks, and he was talking loudly and aggressively to people that passed him by, so instantly Gangster person knew there was a problem. In fact, there was double trouble; he peeked left and spotted a homeless guy in a green coat slouched by the entrance of the shop with his legs concealed in a sleeping bag, strategically placed so everyone could see, and felt inclined to spare a fund. The bum looked up at him expectantly with bright blue eyes that glowed like an evil entity and a silvery white beard, that was suspiciously well kempt.

Then he thought it was ok to make a "connection" with Gangster person by saying "hello" to him with a stupidly low, gargly voice, as though he thought it was time for comedy. Gangster person had yet to walk free past him, when the mouthy guy came marching his way. He was ugly with a freckled, unhealthy looking pockmarked face with these big grey eyes and a nasty expression.

"Your livin' on the streets, aren't yah?" He asked the homeless guy with a stupid, thick, chavy accent which instantly betrayed him as a bad character, then instantly diverted his attention to Gangster person.

"Ear boss?" He dared to intrude with a loud, unnecessarily aggressive tone of voice. Gangster person didn't look at him.

"*Boss?*" The chav repeated. If Gangster person was the boss, he would not be speaking to him in that manner. He would be fired at the very least. Also, he didn't want him for company!

"Can you help him out for forty pence?" The ugly character asked the Gangster person. Yet why didn't this stupid character give the forty pence himself? It was one of them pitiful opportunities for a bad person to appear noble and redeem themselves, like these sudden religious converts. *I said: I'm walking forward, no one will stop me or obstruct my passage! Must I fear or feel inclined to surrender to you?* The Gangster person walked past both pathetic creatures without a care in the world, because he could.

"Fuckin' ignorant bastard!" Cursed the privileged do-gooder—whatever it was meant to be—when he could have just walked on by.

"Fuckin' ignorant cunt!" He added prompting the Gangster person to turn around and face the fucking ignorant bastard cunt guy.

"Fuck off, hobophile!" He rasped causing the…thing to spin around—*I am walking forward now…*

"YOU WHAT?" The FIBGC dared to fire more useless ammo, his grey eyes widening. Gangster person walked towards him and pointed toward the homeless guy.

"He was sat there…waiting for you!" He laughed. The hobo just looked at him.

"WHAT?" The FIBCG shouted.

"You…What…?" Gangster person parodied in a toddler's tone and let his tongue slide out from his mouth to further insult the FIBCG.

"Who the fuck are you…?" Gangster person continued, unheard despite owning the power of being able to talk without being interrupted. That was a contemporary privilege!

"And I don't believe in coincidences anymore!" He calmly added—*inferiors must stay inferior!* Nothing was to stop reality from being silenced for the sake of comfort—*junk evolution extinguished!* Walk away, do not engage…do not taunt them in reflex as they have taunted you, let this deadly vermin continue to be a threat, blah-blah-blah, stop them in their tracks and be met with resilience as hostile as them, act like there's a reason for it, worship the enforcers of this privilege. Respect them, fear them even more…let them take everything from one. All this logic and deep reality check blaring out to Gangster person at a comfortingly high volume as he tilted his head to the left. *The problem is: like some rapist, he* chose *me. He chose me!* Really, he didn't need to listen to or fear the FIBCG!

"Give him it yourself!" Gangster person suggested sensibly, blinked and watched the vulgar creature's cheeks bulge out, as though he had puffed them up. He then clutched his throat and coughed out a stream of blood onto the floor, that didn't touch Gangster person, who was already stepping back and noticed some tiny white objects bouncing about the concrete. They were the FIBCG's teeth, and he did not require them as they served no purpose other than to chew any food he ate to exist, which he was no longer entitled to.

"You wanna kill it?" The Gangster person said, asked rather.

"I shall!" Another speaker responded immediately in this creepily distorted voice followed by these clicks similar to whales and dolphins. And he sounded close by. This red coloured jolt of electricity zapped on Gangster person's left shoulder. ***"You just watch!"*** The voice added.

Gangster person and the world watched as the FIBCG's eyes suddenly swelled up, bloodshot and bulging to make him appear uglier than he already was. He said something incoherently before his eyes exploded in their sockets and sprayed out the gelatinous contents, the owner toppling to the side with his tongue sticking out of his bloodied, partly toothless mouth. Gangster person did not blink, nor did he lend a helping hand. The skies above turned darker, and suddenly there was snowfall which conveniently seemed to distract any potential witnesses from the violence… A real *correction*, compared to other forms that had to be viewed as acceptable and correct by incorrect minds. Hit it again, the opposition would impose a penalty. Hit it harder, the opposition would increase the penalty. Hit it harder than last time, they would sentence one to more years than one could serve; a thousand years… Get real! How about the opposition get penalties themselves, just for existing?

But in fairness all this drama wouldn't have happened had it not been for that hobo, sat where he was at this time. Oh no! Gangster person turned and approached him, seeing fear in his eyes.

The advantage of luck has become extinct!

Those words heard inside his head were forcibly engrained into a sense. Deaf, it shall be signalled. Blind, it shall be messaged in flesh. Both deaf and blind…plenty of room for experimentation. Gangster person stopped in front of the degenerate, who looked up at him.

"Is he ok?" It said, referring the FIBCG who was no longer part of the equation and able to skip the reality of events.

"You started it!" Gangster person said with utmost honesty, fingers of his left hand reaching up to adjust his tie. Did he think he could just be friendly now? Gangster person shook his head tightly two times.

What next…? A hot sandwich and a pint of fine alcoholic beverage! They weren't so-called illegal or regulated substances! Why would they be? They were going to be acquired, consumed in peace with no interference! And like nothing had ever happened, Gangster person was walking along Sancrott, smoking a cigarette with the snow still coming down, but only settling on the ground in a thin layer.

"Steal from lions, they kill you!" He said as if singing. *"There's no law to stop them!"*

He emphasised the liberties of nature. The more the law imposed on harming a criminal, the more necessary it was to defy it—the more the need to oppose this regime that empowered vermin.

It had stopped snowing, and Gangster person came to the edge of some woods, the trees of which were displaying green buds for the spring. He stopped and slouched back against a tree, pulled out the whisky bottle from his jacket, looking to the grey, snowy sky and fearlessly took a gulp. Anyone that disturbed him for antisocial reasons was going to experience a repeat of the previous two incidences in the two districts. From behind him, within the seclusion of the woods, approached this enormous figure, as tall as the two storey council houses across from him.

"Don't make a sound, you'll alert everyone!" The Gangster person urged it without turning around. The figure within the woods stopped.

About an hour later the Gangster person had done a loop around Thewlington and had walked five miles back into town, the skies were still grey but with nothing falling from them. Right now he was in town square in front of a fancy bar called Altheas. Gangster person looked up at the grey sky, just as hailstorm fell from above, the sight and sound of it was beautiful with them white pea-sized pieces bouncing off the darkening concrete. He entered Altheas, the bar was fancy and was the sort of place to take a lady to for date night. The bar had a vast, colourful stock of liquor, the lights of the draught beer pumps were shining, the furniture immaculate, the tables and bar counters a polished varnish shade, music playing at a soft, bearable volume.

Gangster person had been here before, but back then his mother had paid for everything. Now the experience was to be as ideal as could be; no assholes spewing profanity unnecessarily, no unrestrained kids running about crawling under one's table, no need for some unnecessary individual to just sit next to him and start uttering obnoxious comments. None of which were present, so far. Then again, it was a shame that no one decent was about, apart from the barmaid complaining about the hail and snow to an unseen staff member behind the bar. She was in her early-thirties short, had a pear-shaped curve at the hips and wore an all-black work uniform, her long, dirty blonde hair tied back in a bun, **Carol** her name was—it said on her nametag. The Gangster person sat at the bar, the barmaid greeted him.

"What can I get yah love?" She asked and the hail outside came to a stop.

An Avenged Sevenfold song was playing, *the beast and the harlot*, which seemed out of place in this lavish set up.

A ten mile walk out on the morning with a hot sandwich and pints at the end was the life, sandwich here being a BLT, the bread toasted and for beverage a pint of Guinness. Gangster person finished his sandwich off quickly and was on the last quarter of his pint of the black stuff.

"Your sandwich alright love?" Carol asked.

"Lovely!" Gangster person said wiping his mouth with the serviette.

"Got any music that's crap?" He asked without hesitation.

"Ermm…" Carol mumbled without acting offended. "Don't know if we have any on our playlist!"

Nearly finished with his drink Gangster person checked his phone, it was minutes away from noon and he accessed his photos section and gazed, entranced by a portrait of a young lady his age with blonde hair tied back from her face and big brown eyes. He sighed in despair, his hand laid over a tempting stack of pound notes that caught the attention of Carol. Gangster person knew money could not buy him love or affection, but it could grant him pleasures a life of honesty could not.

"You wanna hang out with me?" He asked, hesitantly but firm. "We can go anywhere."

Carol looked at him sceptically.

"I'm married, with kids!" She said, smiling weakly. At least, she wasn't rude. "Sorry…!"

Gangster person grunted and held up a hand apologetically, the frustration and anger seethed within him, but subsided. Still, no more would it be a case of annoying ugly women asking for his seat in a crowded bar and cock-blocking as he tried to accosted the perfect woman. He peeled off a note from the stack and set it on the counter.

"You wantin' another?" Carol asked. Gangster person smiled and raised his near empty pint glass.

"Drink more and see how interesting today gets…!" He said then looked around back at the windows of the bar, where two blurred figures stood outside, one dressed in all black with a red tie and black hair, and one in white with white hair and a long white coat.

"Sure!" Gangster person said lowering his pint. "Think I'll get to know the world better."

The End

To whoever she is, I really want to thank you for birthing the inspiration behind all of this!

AKWAS

As we live now a mentality, whether good or bad, can be classed as a separate species, as it continuously procreates and defends itself from disassociation with others of identical physical form.

March 7th 2017. It was a late Tuesday evening in Leeds, and Abigail Hartley was on her phone, scrolling through photos she had taken of all the meals her taste buds had had the delight of experiencing throughout the start of the year. At a Japanese restaurant in London, she had been given a chance at *cooking* some noodle dish on a table-sized skillet with a pair of spatulas, where she had failed in that she had forgotten to include the egg in it, but that wasn't like noticeable as it was just lovely.

Officially, Sriracha sauce was Abby's go-to condiment, and she had plenty of it dressed on different kinds of food this year. A freshly made chicken shawarma wrap from one of them new Turkish takeouts that were about the city. Sushi, from every popular shopping centre around Leeds. A jerk chicken wrap with salad at a temporary Jamaican food stall. A dinner last Sunday at her aunt's that included roast lamb with trimmings purchased from some pricey place.

A pad thai at a really posh Thai restaurant by the city wharf, presented fancily in a dome shape, though Abby was mad for Thai food, the *ridiculously* spicy som-som—whatever it was called—a papaya salad that had been recommended was really pungent, too spicy that it couldn't be enjoyed. A holiday to Miami last month had been a very pleasant getaway, South Beach was a massive break from the cold, crappy English weather and while there, Abby had had the chance to try *real* Mexican food, that involved this mild chilli broth with slowly stewed chicken that included dark chocolate of all things.

A work night out, before meeting up with her family for a weekend in Edinburgh had resulted in a regrettably bad hangover for most of the first day, but it was the amazing chicken balti she had for tea at a curry house that sorted her out. And she had a photo of a near burnt beef top rump—**the star** [Abby had remarked] of a homemade Sunday roast she had cooked for mates—and had almost ruined!

There was a grey/light blue entry card displaying bold letters of a club venue, held as if cherished, by the frustrated-looking, yet smartly dressed drinker of a big green bottle of lager sat a table away, which an oblivious Abby would not be drinking—she wasn't a fan of lager. Abby was twenty three years old with big brown eyes, foundation and mascara applied meticulously, eyebrows drawn on and her luscious lips coated with coffee bean brown lipstick, her long brown hair straightened with a centre parting, her relatively dark features and complexion attributed from her half-English, half-Cypriot descent and not the tanning beds.

For tonight, she wore a plain black choker around her neck, a thin black sweater with a revealing lacy patterning shoulder to sleeve tucked into her plain white jeans, some right fit black suede boots, thigh-high with three inch heels, her waist small and thighs big and rightly proportionate, kept fitly in shape from a dedicated gym membership and diet. Tonight's outfit was the latest in lasses fashion and really complimented her physical attraction. She was five years into adulthood; she could buy alcohol and enter a nightclub to drink more booze, after presenting ID, when she would not be hassled about that any further was not a question to dwell on.

The crime of youth. That wasn't something she would say or conjure up, but would have a say in the matter if someone said it to her.

Abby had taken a selfie before coming down along with a photo of her legs folded while sat down on her bed, then had posted it online, and with positive reviews! She was sat upstairs in the pub with her mate, and scrolling on her phone, she accidentally came to another selfie, one that had depicted her wearing her hair in a severe sock bun on top of her crown, a thick and light creamy brown sweater sat with a mate she was no longer seeing.

The photo was from over three years ago, she recognised the background and it had been taken just around the corner on the second floor here in this same venue. Abby came across another selfie from nearly a year ago, where she had her hair dyed blonde with a centre parting but didn't do too good a job straightening it, and were wearing one of them green, grey and black camouflage print tracksuits with the roll over collars, popular at the time. Her hair though…it was too bright, her complexion didn't suit, though didn't quite look as wrong as the smirk she wore.

Abby was sharing a bottle of white wine with her mate Gabby, who fairly enough could be described as being equally attractive, she wore fake eyelashes, had blue eyes, long blonde hair in corkscrew curls and wore a short grey/blue dress with a glittery patterning. Paired together the two of them were called "Ab's and Gab's" by mates. Abby gripped her wine glass and took a drink, her eyes rolling to the left at nothing but the pub's ceiling, her nails, glossy with brown nail polish shimmering from the light, two fingers of each hand baring rings of decorative pure metal.

Abby had work for 10 in the morning, she worked at a cosmetics shop on lower Briggate, but was bent on having a good night. She dipped her hand into her black designer clutch, which had this engraving of a horse she had bought in Phuket, checking her tickets for the concert then chaffed her thighs and looked the lager drinker's way, betraying the slightest of grins. He did not return it.

This you shan't have! Abby's dishonest thoughts sounded like song lyrics.

Ab's and Gab's got up carrying their glasses and clutches with them and passed by the lager drinker, who wore a plain, navy blue jacket over a plain white shirt, their eyes not meeting his even though his were trained on them, Abby most noticeably. Was there a reason he was sat alone? Was he waiting for someone? Or was he drowning his sorrows for being stood up, hence his moodiness? Abby made eye contact with him, she didn't manage so much as a grin, let alone a greeting, her mind focused on other things.

The time was 20:00, and stepping cautiously in their high heels, they went downstairs, it was packed and there were so many lasses about that looked similar to Abby; in that they had long parted hair, wore chokers and slight variations of her outfit. The fashion was the same with the lads with their army style haircuts, muscly builds and T-shirts! *Plenty of them fish in the sea…* Abby thought, having had two serious relationships over the past three years and preferred to stay single, for the time being. Ab's and Gab's finished their wine and courteously placed the glasses on the pub's counter then headed outside. They talked about going to the cinema, particularly to see that new film about the giant gorilla on an island.

There was a lass stood in the doorway on the phone and she was literally a copy of Abby; she appeared the same age, had the same physique, wore a black choker, white jeans and an identical brand of boots, though her hair was dyed black and had chunky, bright red streaks like that lass from The Addam's Family and wore this fit black top with a silver sequin patterning on the front, which Abby felt like asking where she got it from.

"You heard about fuckin' Trump?" Abby heard her say. *Interminable* was the word for this unfunny joke that the American president was. It was just shit having to look at that hair, them lips…and hear all that crap that came out of his mouth! And who in America were letting him rise to bloody power?

"*Where are's yah? We're just on us way.*" Abby's preoccupied raven-headed double said as she and Gab's stepped outside into the night, struck with the chills of a winter that refused to leave with haste, the beer garden overlooking the Millennium Square faced with the cinema-sized TV screen, flashing various images and saturating the square with coloured light.

Then some middle-aged woman nearly bumped into Abby, spilling half of her drink onto the floor, with a couple of splashes hitting her boot, not that it mattered.

"Sorry love!" She said then laughed, quickly looking at everyone in the beer garden, as though they would be interested in what just happened. Abby though was adequately inebriated enough not to care, though Gab's had to cheer, like half the people on the beer garden. Abby exhaled and saw a gust of icy breath, like everyone else around her.

The concert was at the Leeds O2 academy only a half block away, and there wasn't just one gig on but two, the other at the arena further up road which was like a mega attraction, the glow of the flashing and alternating multi-coloured lights visible. The O2 academy had the basic design of a church—had a flower-shaped stain glass window feature high above and spires—for all Abby knew it might have been one a long while back or summat.

If that was the case it now had a different flock, one that didn't appear so welcome; the barriers herding the queue of concertgoers that went around the corner of the building, like cows going to the slaughter and the searches by the obnoxious men and women in yellow and black event security uniforms. It made you grateful as to how a couple of drinks in your system numbed out just how dodgy and aggravating it all was! And the claustrophobia you were waiting for inside just belied all the fun! Abby did not notice the lager drinker pass her by as she checked the time on her phone. It was 20:12.

Bathed under purple lights spilling out from the academy, which transitioned to red and pink, an underdressed Ab's and Gab's rubbed their poorly warmed arms, shivering, there were three more paired rows of people to go until they could get in the warm. Before stepping forward to get herself searched, Abby paused in midstride. She turned around to her right, in the direction of the lager drinker. Her name had not been called out to her, or within her forgivably intoxicated mind. She did see him smile though. A memory of childhood crept into her mind, and Abby had had a good upbringing; primary, secondary and college had been joyous, though Uni was gonna have to wait a couple more years, while her relaxed job at the beauty product shop financed that.

But it wasn't Uni on her mind as the one big thing she could not fulfil in her life. It was something that shouldn't even matter as an adult. Right now Abby couldn't imagine singing *happy birthday* for someone at the top of her voice in a crowded pub with 20 mates, nor did she want to dance with hundreds of other bodies rubbing and bumping against her. And with a very clear and abrupt change of heart she started back through the queue, slipping past everyone.

"Where you off?" Gab's asked. Abby shamelessly ignored her.

"*Just being normal...!*" She called out over her shoulder without looking back at her mate. That what Abby had said, she wasn't doing perceived by the minds of those around her, as she went around the other side of the academy so no one could see her. She pitilessly ignored the ugly, smiling, expectant beggar in the wheelchair rolling her way, whom she and many others had seen so many times around the square before looking back at the sheeple (she dared say) in queue, and didn't see Gab's following her. Abby looked up to the sky and saw no stars. She couldn't remember the last time she had seen them. She took out her phone and plugged her wireless earphones into her ears and played *I need your heart.*

~

While walking on a sort of *autopilot* mode (Abby could proudly say to anyone enquiring to her activity, as if she had thought of it up herself), she made it priority to get inside some place away from the winter cold as soon as she could. And she was feeling quite peckish from the wine. There was a lot of development and scaffolding around this part of the square, that included a hotel that had work stopped on it for about a year with a towering crane stood out in the open, almost like a temporary landmark.

Abby headed up hill in the direction of the university, the soles of her hundred quid boots working their way around the broken glass, dropped food, vomit and dog crap on the pavements that needed some redoing. Coming up ahead to the left was another church that had been converted into a nightclub, black as coal and darker than the night, very gothic looking and had a taller, sharper roof with pointier spires.

Past the church and nearing the corner where the road turned left into the university car park, Abby reached back and chaffed the back of her left thigh just below her buttock, sure she still had a destination, while nervously checking to see if anyone had witnessed her unintentionally provocative act, though she was sure a pair of eyes were focused on her, and guided her way. That quickly became a reality—*shit!*

Abby panicked as an imposing silhouette emerged out from the corner and blocked out the view of the car park entrance, and assuming it to be a stalker she stalled and gasped mutely. No, it wasn't some weirdo, though she was still greeted with an explosion of fear that had her jump on the spot without her dropping her clutch. The memory that had her ditch Gab's and the concert she had wasted her money on returned, flaring like a nightclub laser light in pitch black. Then she was relaxed, blanketed with a heavy sensation of awe that didn't make her appear silly. She paused her music and removed her earphones.

"Hello…?" She said looking up, her reaction almost child-like. "Sorry…you just scared us!"

The stranger said nothing.

"Sorry to bother you!" Abby started with an unintentional sulk to her voice and brushed hair out of her face. She didn't know how her squeaky, middle class Durham accent sounded to the locals, though hoped it wasn't embarrassing or anything. But she instinctively knew the stranger didn't care. Abby stashed her phone back into her clutch.

"I know you don't want someone like us bothering you!" She said then heard a growling noise, that of some nearby vehicle—one that had likely malfunctioned, mixed with a cow's mooing. At the same time, there was this unpleasant smell in the air, it was common to smell summat bad when walking down the city streets; sewage, nasty habits of some people etcetera. This though smelt like rotten vegetables and had a sort of farm-like smell to it, with a warm blasted wind of it in her face that blew strands of Abby's hair, as though…farting in her face.

She wrinkled her nose, her expressions not betraying her disgust and the stench of the crude perfume against her designer perfume still lingering strong. Abby held up her right hand and wagged her finger at the stranger.

"You're American right?" She awkwardly enquired while trying not to gag over the smell. "I remember looking at the book…"

Abby gasped and held back a belch, covering her mouth with the back of her right hand.

"Yes! I remember you now!" She cheered and bounced about giddily despite the restriction of her heels. The stranger remained silent. Then Abby had her destination spelt out for her.

"Can you wait for us? I'm just gonna get us summat to eat." She asked of the stranger and started up road while looking about so she could cross over. She heard the stranger follow her.

~

How and why some things happened and continued to go on were not for Abby to answer, and not for lack of trying. Abby arrived at a takeout across the road a block up, called **AKWAS**, its red, blue and white commercial light lettering shinning against a black banner. The takeout was one of them cheap places, and it wasn't busy. Lasses didn't normally come here by themselves, but Abby was a bit too pissed to be bothered with all that. Before entering her jeans took on a purple hue, cast upon by the mixing of blue and red lights.

During the short relief from the cold inside she ordered a doner kebab with salad, chilli sauce and yoghurt mint sauce wrapped in a naan bread—summat quick, though not something she would normally eat as that stuff were messy to eat. She got plenty of attention from the mainly lads crowd inside, though she couldn't hear any audible words she knew they were commenting about her figure over anything else.

Abby wasn't given a carrier bag to carry the foil wrapped takeout, which was as thick as a clenched fist! Her newfound company was stood there waiting on the other side of the road, other people would surely be put off with, not especially concerning how tall he was. And Abby wasn't like talking lanky or anything like that. They were minding their own business. That same peculiar rotten veg odour was still there. Should she ask her company if it were him as though it were a fart joke?

"Come on up then *you*!" Abby said jerking her head up street where she proceeded to walk up, her companion following her at a speed of her own pace, the heels of her boots taxing on the balls of her feet and ankles, straining against the long incline of the hill. And everyone looking their way looked as though Abby was mental as she chatted away to her mate, who remained quiet, though what sounded like grumbles were heard. What must it be like for him though? Was it easier as he wasn't wearing heels? He didn't seem to like the smell of her takeout, indicated by this deterred grunt as though it would make him sick.

"I like chattin' away, me!" Abby said a bit loudly. She and the stranger passed by the university, then up past a pub Abby felt disgraced not entering. The further up road they went, the fewer people there were seen about and beyond that pub was nearly a mile of main road with open green space on both sides blackened in the night, spots of orange from the streetlights lining the curbs sort of like safe spots from demonic creatures that dwelled in the dark.

Abby and co were only a few steps away from the pub, which had groups of loud patrons storm in and out. There was a division at play, that didn't concern the alternative character welcoming crowd of the pub and her strictly mainstreamed pop cultured preference, but the line between the city and nature; urban lights on one side and the void of night on the other, with Abby and the stranger in the middle…another thing that sounded like song lyrics! The other side, as dark as it was, was ideal with trees, grass and bushes as far as the eye can see on both sides of the road, but she knew she'd be safe with her new mate.

"Ah…! I need to sit down!" Abby complained girlishly without drawing too much attention to herself. She trod on the dampened grass, her heels sinking partly into the cold, damp soil and journeyed out of the supposed safety of the lights further into the field and found a smooth stony stump, which she sat down on. The stranger stood and sort of walked off to the right, comfortably enough in plain sight with him blocking out the view of what little traffic came by.

Abby flexed her ankles, checked the soles and heels of her boots, not just for muck but scuffs and grit and glass from walking up that may be stuck beneath them, then delicately scraped both her heels against the sides of the stump simultaneously. She stretched out her legs then folded the right over her left knee, and peeled off the foil and kitchen paper around her kebab. Not date night food but…*oh well.* First bite: meaty with a crunch of typical salad, the chilli sauce stinging the sides of her mouth and lower cheeks, nothing too special, it was just nice, and…necessary under the circumstances to be clear.

Abby wiped her mouth with the back of her left hand and grunted. After two more bites, the kebab was beginning to fall apart, the meat, spicy sauce and bits of salad stuck under her nails, but no stains on her white jeans, just yet anyways. She looked the stranger's way and saw him pacing about, just minding his own business. Abby could just sit back on her home settee and watch summat classic. But this occasion involving a kebab with a stranger would be branded a neo classic. Except for the bad veggie smell accompanying them though…How and why she could eat was her own business.

~

Abby wasn't feeling as cold as she should, but was nonetheless getting full, and there were these crunchy bits in the kebab meat, pieces of bones or gristle that hadn't been removed during the process, which could break the teeth. Abby lazily let a leaf of spicy sauce soaked lettuce slide out from the corner of her mouth to the ground, then elegantly tried to suck in a tomato coming out without getting anymore stains around her mouth. The tomato dropped to the floor, instead of on her boots. She cursed, sighed and looked at the stranger.

"You're not gonna diss me, are you?" Abby asked her companion who stood staring at her, waving his thing in the air. And he had plenty of things to wave at her, the streetlights revealed in partial glints. Abby playfully swung her right leg back and forth.

"You're lovely, you!" She said. The stranger's response was that same weird vehicle growl she had heard before she had gone into AKWAS, and that pungent stench intensified threefold. Though Abby didn't react to it.

"Can I touch you?" She said, stood up then stepped forward with an outstretched free left hand and touched the stranger's face. His touch was rough, dry and bumpy like a handbag, one of her many—unlike them.

"You were my favourite!" Abby said softly, rudely enough with a full mouth.

"You look a bit *different* though…"

Them books were so easy to read, and everything featured looked different in each one depending on the artist, for better or worse. It went with the ages.

A car with a silver paintjob passed by on the road, which Abby paid no attention to as she finished off the remainder of her kebab, scrunched up the wrapping and searched for a litter bin. Luckily there was one about she could actually walk to straight across from her, though the distance of summat like twelve to eighteen metres was a little bit inconvenient. She tossed in her rubbish and looked back at the stranger, yawning loudly as she walked back his way.

"I was a kid once, you know!" Abby shouted out hearing the vroom of a vehicle behind her. "I had one of them little toys!"

The stranger made another growl. Abby stopped and looked towards the field across the road, there was a row of dilapidated buildings, essentially slums she and anyone passing through here would become ever so familiar with, their unsightliness concealed by the night.

"But you gotta *grow up*…!" Abby tagged, almost sadly.

I still love you… Her thoughts were so aloud in her head, they might as well have been spoken out over a concert microphone. Her phone buzzed from a text she dared not answer.

"Now I *really* love yah!" She said, actually using her mouth to communicate. In her Mum's days, there were like only five or six types to categorise the stranger… But in Abby's day and age there seemed to be thousands.

The innocence of this all! She wanted to orate.

~

Abby reckoned it had taken herself something between five to ten minutes to demolish that kebab. She turned her head the stranger's way, wondering if she would see a fox somewhere on the green space. There was nothing wrong with seeing a fox, but her current company exceeded a fox a galaxy apart.

"Do you run?" She asked him as though she was flirtatiously asking a fit-looking fella at the bar, implying if he could charge like a football or rugby player. She did not get the answer she wanted, though her admiration and affection for him remained strong. Abby sighed.

"I gotta head off now," she said, and just as her words began to terminate she dipped her fingers into her clutch for her phone, so she could take a photo of the stranger. Though it was dark, his highly recognisable shadow remained distractingly visible. Abby held up and focused her phone's camera and took a picture. With very little surrounding light, the flash was totally maximised and spooked the stranger, causing him to recoil dramatically and take a step back, and grunt (understandably enough) as he shuffled about, lowering himself into a partial squat.

The flash revealed his eyes being dark and beady, almost bird-like. His complexion couldn't be certain, and appeared to have effectively soaked up the orange of the streetlights, though there was this dark banded patterning along his sides along with several other colours Abby couldn't discern, yet looked just as appealing as the annual switching on of the city's Christmas lights at the Millennium Square. But to Abby, and everyone living and dead, it was all about them cardboard thin triangular things on his back. They had a hinged motion to them, swaying like hands raised side to side at a concert and had an orangey look to them which stood out against the black, wood detail-like framing. There were these four partly downward curving sharp thingies swaying behind like some dangerous medieval weapon shadowed against the ground. It didn't drag. It was *high*. And it bent downwards and had this broad motion to it. It "whacked" about, like that song sung in primary school inferred.

But the truth was he looked very *different* from them books. Them books that were meant for children, and children alone, so easy to read and with all them drawings… His neck though was longer and his throat looked…baggy and had a crocodile skin bag texture to it and them things on his back were shaped differently; some like leaves, some like pentagons, they weren't in a straight line but deranged. He swept his head back and forth, he looked keen on eating summat but didn't appear to have anything available to him. What exactly did he eat again…? He was a vegetarian. That Abby remembered. Why wasn't he having a nibble at the grass, which was plentiful? Abby held up a hand and waved.

"It were lovely to see yah!"

The stranger produced this call, even though he didn't open his mouth it was louder than the sounds he had made before, and had a different character to it Abby couldn't describe. The stranger would never know that she didn't know. And he didn't care. How long ago had he like been…*still about?* The dare of thoughts as deep as the bottom of the ocean, that had all them nightmarish fish lurking about Abby could not access. These were thoughts restricted not by society, but by her own lack of clarification.

But now she felt like giving in, as though doubting the appeal of some ridiculous religion. Her new mate here was remarkable. And he didn't even try to be. How could you *not* love him? Abby rang up a taxi. The winter chills returned to her as she left the scene. *No one could judge until they actually see.*

True from all manners of thought. Abby would have loved to have seen them flying ones, them underwater ones. And what was the one with horns…?

~

A taxi pulled up at the side of the road. It wasn't a standard one, it was one of them black cabs you got in London. Funny, as Abby was pretty sure she had dialled a regular taxi. Regardless she climbed in back and clipped on her seatbelt. The light in the front was on, Abby could see that the driver had short grey hair and wore a dark fleece.

"Alright love?" the driver greeted.

"Chapel Allerton please," Abby requested. The driver turned the light off and drove. *Something just like this* was playing on the radio, which had been really growing on Abby for the past week. She nodded her head to it.

"Were you wantin' the radio off?" The driver asked.

"Sorry…?" Abby didn't hear properly.

"The music ok?" The driver rephrased. He had a builder's voice that sounded local and while harsh was at the same time very pleasant.

"I love this song!" Abby replied looking to the driver's mirror and saw the driver's lovely dark eyes focused on the road ahead. Abby's phone buzzed repeatedly from an incoming call. And without checking who it was, she turned it off.

The driver didn't chat her up, or talk to her and she was happy with that. She was already tiered. If he had asked her how her night had been, he wouldn't believe her. She could have fallen asleep at the concert. It was way passed a child's bedtime. The cab was coming into her street.

"Just there." Abby directed the driver aiming her left hand in that direction. Without asking where to stop the driver parked directly outside her maisonette flat and switched on the light in front. Not finding that suspicious Abby opened up her clutch and assembled some change.

"You're alright, love!" The driver said.

"Whaa…?" Exclaimed Abby, who didn't follow.

"Have a good night me love!" The driver said and switched off the light in front.

"Whaaat…?" Abby exclaimed again without really thinking about it.

"Come on love!" The driver urged pleasantly. "Me boss needs us!"

He laughed and delicately waved her off. That was all Abby needed to get herself moving.

"Thank you…!" She responded with an unbalanced gratitude then got out of the cab, looked back and spotted the driver smiling without looking her way. As she trotted towards her flat she thought about turning around to thank the driver more properly. But the cab had sped off.

~

I know air; I breathe it. I know water; I drink it. I know meat; I eat it. I know fire. Sometimes I use it to cook the meat I eat. I know sleep. I sleep well. I know shelter. I have one all the time. I know safety. I have it constantly.

I know death. I see it all the time. I know what a hunt is. I see it all the time. But I do not hunt. I know what an amniote is. I know what an ornithischian is. I know what a thagomizer is. I know what a thyreophoran is.

I know what a monsoon is. I know what an earthquake is. I know what lava is. I know what a glacier is.

I don't know what a conversation is. I know how to talk. I don't know what murder is. I don't know what an angel is. I don't know what a gun is. I just know it's bad. I know what politics are. They are very bad. I know what religion is. It's even worse. But I've never had to deal with both of them.

I know what evolution is. I know the difference between convergence and parallel. I don't know what a baby is. I don't know what a father is. I don't know what a mother is. I don't know what a sister is. I don't know what sex is. I know I'm taught. I know what education is. I don't know why. I don't know what. I know I live. I know existence. I know what a human is. Up until now, I've never seen one. Except for me… My mind sometimes speaks faster than my mouth can enunciate words. A force drives me. I want to see it all. Comprende?

~

Morning. Abby was lying on her bed, rolled up in her double duvet covering her and fully clothed in last night's garments, the morning sunlight irradiating her as though blessed, or instilled. With what though would the latter be? She stirred and woke, and instead of her usual routine of lying in for half an hour she sat up straight, and though she was still wearing her boots she crossed her legs and sat and looked up to the ceiling with a contemplative look to her. Theories and perceptions that may yield answers were being grabbed out from the air like an ugly squid armed thingy in a coral reef, ideas that made books, from having a drink too many or doing the naughty stuff. Abby had never been the creative type, but now felt she had a fighting chance.

In less than a million or so years she would be deep in the ground—and she couldn't imagine a week of being static—would she ever be on display in a million years and loved? No hangover this morning—thank goodness for certain types of food! And on this morning, babies and children didn't seem so adorable any more. A view point just as blasphemous as the thought of violin music playing towards a dodgy, abstract image of her upside down and falling, and with her name being mentioned in a squeaky, childish voice…

Abby got off her bed, and looked out of the window with a superficially blank expression to her face at her home district of Chapel Allerton, a lovely place that just felt even lovelier after tonight's experience. Before her was a new day, and she couldn't count the amount of days she had been alive. And the look of her just being at the window…the directorial of one part of a generic music video? No. This was life. To tell some eager male in search of sex that there was "no charisma" in his knob (for whatever *reason* that maybe). Well…there was a charisma to the cock. It was one half of a process that gave life, in all forms from the thick as pig crap to the genius, and the poorest to the royal. The reality was too harsh for many.

Truth was: this wasn't the same world anymore, hadn't been since Abby had turned eighteen, her education for awareness denied, if not ignored through the word of the many who *magicianed* invisibility on the implicit sparks glistening on the horizon. She needed a coffee, but after a shower and change of clothes though. She turned her phone on, saw that the time was 8:12 against her desktop image of her riding a lovely, mud brown warmblood stallion and dressed in designer riding gear, her screen was bombarded with several missed calls, the jiggles becoming irritating.

Within seconds, she got a call from Gab's which she promptly answered.

*"**The bloody hell were you?**"* Her mate enquired.

"I'm…at home…!" Abby replied almost merrily.

*"**You alright?**"* Gab's asked rather angrily.

"Ergh…Just seeing stuff…" Abby bluntly replied. A scoff from Gab's followed.

*"**You…what…?**"* She exclaimed while Abby absently faced the window.

~

Abby showered, felt no funny bowels, and with the weather pleasant enough dressed into a chocolate brown velour tracksuit with black work pumps, her makeup simplified and reduced to just mascara and foundation with her long hair pulled up into a topknot on her crown. The rest of her work outfit she kept in a locker at the shop for convenience. Abby thought about the weekend rather than the rest of the work weekday, she would spend extra time with Bluey, her horse (the same one on her phone's desktop) during the weekend down in Pudsey.

Abby's living room was white: polished white tiles, spotless white wallpaper with subtle silver patterning, she had a black marbled coffee table, a black couch and a 60-inch plasma screen. Hung up on her wall was a glass pane that had several smaller divisions spread outwards at random angles, a shrine with an overabundance of photos of various sizes stuck on by Blu Tack from her many holidays and nights out during adulthood.

Abby had had the privilege of sharing the company of celebrities; football players and soap opera stars at private parties all over the country, something people her age would die for. Her destinations included: Dublin, Ibiza, Tenerife, New York City, Florida, Barbados, Amsterdam, Germany—Abby spoke good German—Istanbul, Dubai, Thailand and Hong Kong—the latter of which was the farthest she had travelled. Her favourite holiday destination for certain was Phuket, a college graduation holiday with her parents.

Getting up each morning to a white sand beach, with clear blue seas and 30 plus degrees sun and a breakfast of *jok* she never got bored of, one dish she had had an unrequited crush on; it involved rice soup, eggs with minced pork and garlic, some sorta sweet, chorizo-like sausage. The people in Thailand were so lovely, she felt like royalty sat at the beach, eating the sweetest, most delicious fruits ever and getting massaged and having her nails and hair done for a fraction of the price back home. It was technically paradise. A return there was on her priorities along with Cambodia and South Korea.

With a full handbag slung over her shoulder, Abby exited her flat, the keys to her car in hand and a place where she could pick up a coffee, once she got into town in mind. The streets were clean, and lined with much desirable homes either brown or white in colour, the songs of unseen birds were heard without any other disruption, and there was no one about. Abby's newish black Vauxhall Mokka was parked underneath the shadow of this tree no corrosive bird poop on the paint as far as she could see. There was a limo parked on the opposite side, and partly blocking the view of the Vauxhall were these three lasses stood below the tree, who turned their heads Abby's way.

These three were super fit—in actual fact they were perfect, in their early-twenties, with physical attraction identical to Abby's, wore subtle makeup limited to mascara but had bright, glossy pink lips. All three had long and perfectly straight hair, worn back in high, bushy wrap-around ponytails as Abby usually did for the gym, and were dressed formally; black turtle neck sweaters, expensive-looking snug, peplum jackets with black, leathery-looking waist belts and looped brass buckles, black jeans over tall black riding boots. Aside from being very pretty they weren't afraid of standing out, as they were each wearing a different coloured version of the same jacket.

Abby's focus rolled far right, on the lass who was wearing a black jacket. She was a brunette, had slim dark blonde highlights and Abby's complexion and contour to precision, blue eyes, a straight, wedge-shaped nose with a button tip and triangular jaw, a cute look to her, despite her voluptuous figure. The lass opposite her on the left wore a blue jacket, she was a darker brunette without highlights, her ponytail slung over her left shoulder, a near half size leaner in the thighs giving her a more ballerina-like build, had a more delicate, olive complexion, her nose was slim and pointed, with a bit of an upward curve, her eyes brown and glassy, which emphasised her serious expression.

The one closest to Abby wore a red jacket, and would probably get the most attention from men; she had custard blonde hair, her otherwise pallid skin was the lightest shade of tan, she had a European look to her—as in Dutch or German—was a size bustier than the other two, had an athletic build, her nose was more pronounced with a bit of a downward curve, her big, icy blue eyes had dark grey/blue eye shadow. And as if to make her stand out more, her slender fingers with plain, polished nails were coiled around a medium-sized takeout coffee cup.

All three stood firm, no smiles and with a very focused gaze, like bodyguards—nothing at all nervous about them. Abby was ready to compliment them, ask where they got their jackets from, how much they cost and why they were dressed the way they were; a work due or some occasion—hence the limo? The one wearing red stepped aside, letting Abby see this bloke stood leaning back against the tree.

She froze, nearly dropping her car and flat keys that dangled, swinging gently on their ring. *Have I still been spiked? What drugs have they put in me last night?* Abby had good reason to be concerned; it was that same fella drinking the lager sat across from them back at the pub last night. And he stared at her with intent.

Abby got a better look at him this time; he was dressed well in a short-sleeved blue shirt, plain black dress slacks with a black belt that had a rectangular silver emblem over the buckle with an engraving of a ridiculously stretched, reared up snake, with a stylish *K* extension behind its back and black combat-looking boots that didn't have the ends of his trousers tucked into them. He was taller than average, tanned with flawless skin, short dark hair, styled into a non-severe and textured undercut, his hair three quarter parted on the left and swept messily to the right. His dark eyebrows resembled curved, thick felt tip marker streaks above his beach blue eyes, his jaw line drooped into a square point, his cheeks were high and had a chiselled effect with fashionable, dark stubble covering.

While he was more than good-looking enough, Abby didn't think she could make it through a dinner date with him, and lowered her gaze towards his folded arms that were sleek, with wiry muscle definition and no imperfections.

"You…?" Abby asked not sounding as concerned as needed, the three lasses didn't react, and it was them who divided her focus. Who did this bloke think he was having them about anyway? Some sorta playboy? Or was he one of them sleazy bosses that only hired women?

The songs of the birds on the street changed. Abby remembered walking through a tropical bird garden here in Leeds a couple of times, recalling the insane variety of songs they made. But right now, here on her street, they sounded so weird, so erratic; more like something composed on a computer, electronic, like pushing them telephone buttons of old models and older typewriter sounds.

"Fancy a *real* change of thought somewhere?" The bloke from last night said, his voice a bit intense but smooth, quite cinematic actually and had two accents married with it, English and American, but mostly English.

"No babies allowed though!"

What did that mean? Abby accidently looked in the direction of the lass in red, who stepped forward, the end of her ponytail seen swinging behind her, the lightly visible steam from the coffee trailing with her every step, which were muted, but Abby wasn't paying attention.

She looked dodgy; there was no life in her eyes, which were like glass with no moisture or motion to them. She held out the coffee cup to Abby.

"It's safe, I promise!" The bloke from last night assured her in the least assuring voice. The one in red smiled without showing any teeth, her smile was sharp, V-shaped and doll-like.

The sky brightened in an instant as if hitting a light switch, and the outfits of the trio seemed to shimmer every couple of millimetres as though they were covered in glitter, and a light breeze from out of nowhere struck Abby's distraught face. She didn't blink from the contact. Nor did she as the jeans of the three turned into exact coloured versions of their jackets in a smooth downward motion, as if done with a brush! The earlobes of all three winked with light reflected off the sudden presence of ear studs.

The bloke from last night grunted in a pleasing way, as if some wish had been granted, then took an unnerving step towards Abby with a straight back, his wide shoulders spread and arms swinging perfectly and with confidence.

"Don't mind them!" He said, looking in the way of the red outfit member of his female entourage and pouting his already pouty lower lip. "They're quick with anything!"

There were white blossom petals carried by the wind right behind him, swirling in a vortex pattern. Why were there petals flying about? There shouldn't be any right now. Too distracted Abby couldn't pursue that question.

"Haven't been able to get them to have a good conversation or interact with regulars yet," the bloke from last night said then paused, looking at the one in red from toe to head as he passed her by. "Still, from basic tetrapod to these…beauties!"

Not even trying to comprehend what that meant Abby asked him, "Last night, were that you?"

The petals settled to the ground. Abby braced herself for a reality of confusion. The bloke from last night didn't answer. He continued forward, Abby not hearing him say: "I like that you care!"

His lips bended up into a half smile. After last night, women changing the colours of their clothes seemed pretty normal.

"Who are you?" Abby had the nerve to ask the bloke from last night.

"Now we've time to chat…" He quickly cut in, ignoring her urgent question. "I'm Jean K."

A French name, with an alphabet attached. He stopped, he wasn't too close for comfort; a car length away.

"*Be my girlfriend for one second!*" Jean K said, eyebrows raised and smiling with perfect teeth. "No time for misunderstandings anymore…"

"W-what?" A baffled Abby blurted, unlikely was the thought of reaching in for Jean K's lips in mind. The bloke himself exhaled in a growling manner.

"Not what I meant…!" He said, not apologetically or in any sort of haste, then ran a hand through his hair.

"Why would I have to give up a seat for an inferior, so I can't sit near you…? So I have no chance to speak? Not even see you?"

The lass in black moved all of a sudden, though it was a simple right angle tilt of her head, not looking Abby's way.

"Imagine another six years?" Jean K stressed without having to raise his voice.

"What?" Abby herself stressed.

"Argh…*faux pas!*" Jean K said casually, drifting away from the subject. "See, I can't see the future!"

There was a car beep in the distance and a fella walking down the street her way, whom Abby didn't address as she wasn't certain if she needed help right now.

"I too like a wrap, when designing things." Jean K digressed, looked up to the sky without tilting back his head and turning in the direction of the noise, looking towards the lass in blue, a couple of degrees short of making eye contact with her. He smiled on the left side of his face.

"There's always a place open for me," he said, Abby unsure if he was referring to a kebab shop.

"My sister can cook up one, if you can wait an hour." Jean K said, inhaled gently through his nose then looked down. "Never tried a kebab 'til I was twenty two, believe it or not!" He detailed and looked about with his eyes only, as though he could see something others could not. And he might not be the first.

"I found it to be creativity fuel!" He said and yawned for a short while without closing his eyes or making a sound. "In this day n' age, having knowledge's bad as not having any!" He poetically quoted then turned his attention back to Abby, that grin of his lowered into a more sombre expression.

The one in red again advanced towards Abby, until she was an arm reach away. The bombshell looked into her eyes, which still didn't show any motion. But that didn't stop Abby from taking the coffee from the blonde in red who showed no impatience, her arm stiff as a pole. Her fingers uncoiled from the cup and she stepped back smoothly, where she mechanically ended up back exactly where she had stood previous.

"You wanna see *him* again?" Jean K asked Abby in a softer tone, the memory of them remarkable things that stranger's back silhouetted against the orange streetlights last night flashing in her mind.

"No one gets bullied for it."

Without hesitation, Abby nodded, certain she knew what he was on about and was absolutely positive that no one else, other than herself, would ever have the privilege of having a kebab with a Steg.

~

Evolution and the species it unfolds have plots—beginnings, transitions, and ultimately destructions, sequels, prequels and midquels.